I0552907

Man in the Crescent Moon

A Pirates of the Narrow Seas Adventure

M. Kei

KEIBOOKS
PERRYVILLE, MARYLAND, USA
2013

ISBN 978-0615829234
Also available for Kindle.

Printed in the United States of America, 2013.

KEIBOOKS
P O Box 516
Perryville, MD 21903
Email: Keibooks@gmail.com

TABLE OF CONTENTS

CHAPTER 1: THE SPANISH INTRUDER

Thunder and lightning were the only company for Isam Agha Hamet. His uncle and the rest of the crew had gone ashore. In spite of the rain, he climbed to the quarterdeck and rubbed his toe at the dark stain that had never entirely left the wood in spite of years of scrubbing and caulking. It was his father's blood. Seven years ago Hamet Rais al-Tangueli had died with his guts beside him on the deck while his son wept over him. Twelve-year-old Isam bin Hamet had become an orphan, and both he and the ship were placed under the guardianship of his uncle, Halim, who became master of the *Seahawk*.

Cold rain soaked through his short wool jacket and long pantaloons as he knelt and pressed his hands against the bloodstain. He was sure his father had been the greatest corsair to ever sail from the port of Tanguel. With a father like that, he could not fail to become a great corsair himself. With the surety of youth, he was certain that he would never catch cold, never be wounded, and never lose a battle. He would be famous around the world. So thought every young man who went to sea, but who could argue with them? Maybe one of them would be right.

Thunder cracked close at hand, but no lightning accompanied it. For a moment he was puzzled, then he heard the answering roar. Artillery! The fortress on the hill had opened fire, and since all the guns faced the Atlantic Ocean, it had to be a ship. He swore then: the *Seahawk* was bow first on the beach and nowhere near ready for sea. The sound brought a riffraff of wiry men with big shoulders tumbling out of a nearby brothel to scramble aboard the ship.

"What is happening, Isam Agha?" they asked him. "Who is the fort firing on? Is it the Spanish?" The Spanish were a recurring menace, although occasionally they were shelled by the Dutch or the Danes for the sake of variety.

"I don't know, but we must make ready!" he shouted at them.

"And do what?" they asked.

"We must get her off the beach and turned around! We should have beached her stern first. Then we could use our bow guns."

The men didn't move. He was the agha of soldiers, not the lieutenant nor captain of the ship. Besides, they were only twelve in number. They needed ten times that number to move the galley.

"Muskets!" he shouted at them. "We must make a defense!"

"Look!" one of the men cried. He pointed into the stormy darkness that was the mouth of the harbor.

A dark bulk with grey sails made the turn into the basin. "The enemy has found the entrance! A traitor must have led her!" The shoals and channels outside the mouth of Tanguel were a maze that only the locals knew how to navigate.

"May his father burn in Hell!" another sailor swore.

Isam Agha Hamet stared in despair at the alien ship. Then slowly he made out her lines in the darkness. "Hold your tongues! She's lateen-rigged."

They could barely make out the triangular sails in the darkness, but it was so. She was not square-rigged; she was not Spanish. The fortress continued firing into the darkness. Whatever was out there fired back.

The strange vessel put out her oars and turned broadside to the harbor mouth to bring her guns to bear. She brayled up the triangular sails and set her anchors with springs so that she could rotate far enough to present the other broadside.

"A xebec!" Isam said enviously. His father's galley had a bow battery. Stout as those guns were, there were only five of them. He had no time for comparisons. "Muskets!" he barked.

The corsairs broke out of their awe and ran for the armory. He went with them and unlocked the weapon lockers. Muskets, powder horns, and shot cartouches were handed out to all.

"Aloft!" he snarled. From that height they would have a better chance of picking off Spanish officers—if they could see them in the darkness and could keep their powder dry in the rain.

He slung his musket strap over his shoulder and grabbed the foot of the slanting lateen spar. He hauled himself up, wrapped his legs around it, and with the benefit of the wooldings that lashed the doubled spars together, shinnied up the wet wood. They followed him to the peak of the main antenna and kept their legs wrapped tight around it like camel jockeys determined not to be thrown. With the ship on the beach there was no movement and that made it easy enough in spite of the rain.

Suddenly the noise of ten guns from the stranger's broadside reverberated against the town and rolled back like thunder. The western breeze carried the whiff of brimstone to them. They were on the wrong side to see her shooting, but the lurid orange flash lighted up the harbor for just a moment. A square-rigged infidel was making the turn into the entrance. She was bigger than the stranger, bigger than the beached galleys, bigger than any of the vessels in the harbor. She was a frigate. Isam's heart sank for a moment, then he peered at her, determined to shoot her captain if he got the chance.

The gunnery had roused the town. The corsairs ran pell mell to the waterfront to launch their galleys and load their guns. They were ill-provisioned; winter was barely over and they had just started the process of making the galleys ready for sea. Halim Rais arrived, but he didn't have enough crew to launch his own galley. Instead he bellowed, "Isam Agha! Where are you?"

Isam shouted, "Aloft!"

"Come down! All of you! We're going to help Alman Rais launch his galley!"

Isam and the other men skimmed swiftly down the great spar to the deck. They hauled the lines to lift their own boat off the deck and into the water, then Isam climbed down into it. The sailors jumped down lightly and took their seats on the benches.

"Oars!" he called to them. "Out oars!" Rope grommets were put in place to hold the oars against the thole pins. "Oars, give way together!"

Twelve sturdy backs bent to the oars and the boat shot forward in the dark. He had no lantern, but it didn't matter. He had excellent eyes; he could see in the dark like a cat. He turned the tiller and joined the swarm of small boats abaft the rudder of the beached galley. They were the last boat. A thick cable was passed down to them. He bent it swiftly into a bowline and looped it around the sternpost. He had been at sea since he was seven; he could have tied the knot blindfolded.

He called out loud and clear, "Ready!"

From the deck above came the orders, "Take up slack!"

Every back in every boat bent to the oars. Slowly the lines grew taut and rose up above the surface of the water. As they worked, the thunder of gunnery increased. Some of the beached galleys had opened fire with their bow batteries. Fiery flashes lit the harbor like lightning. Heavy metal roared and rumbled.

"Boats! Give way together!" was shouted from the galley.

"Oars give way," Isam repeated.

They set the blades of the oars into the water and pulled. They strained until their sinews crackled and ached, then pulled again. Every boat was pulling as hard as they could. At first nothing happened. "Pull your guts out!" Isam shouted at them.

They redoubled their efforts. A few feet away, men in another boat groaned. Muscles bulged and swelled with the effort. Veins stood up in their temples as if they would burst.

"Pull!" the cockswains shouted at them.

Slowly, with majestic languor, the galley began to scrape across the sand.

"Pull!" Isam urged them on. He kept his hand to the tiller and minded the cable. Inch by inch, the galley slid down the beach and into the water. Sweat soaked the men's shirts from the inside so they hardly felt the rain; they were drenched from their own exertions. With ponderous grace, the galley slid into deeper water and floated on her own bottom.

At last the command came, "Boat oars!" Exhausted, the rowers braced their oars athwart the gunwales.

"Cast off cables!"

Isam flipped the loop off the sternpost and tossed it overboard. The men aboard the galley hauled it in. Around him the other boats did the same. His own men were spent, so he slid onto the aftmost bench, took up a pair of oars, and rowed them back to their own vessel.

Arriving on the *Seahawk*'s quarterdeck, Isam stood to attention. "Isam Agha reporting, sir. We helped launch Alman Rais' galley. Shall we make ready to launch too?" He was only nineteen, but he loomed over his uncle. Eventually his breadth would catch up to his height, but for the moment he was a gangly youth with long arms and a skinny butt.

Halim shook his head. "There's no point. We're nowhere near ready to put to sea. We have neither powder nor shot."

"We must do something! We can't just sit here and wait for her to attack!"

Halim shook his head. "I think the infidel is aground. She's not making progress. Frigates draft deep and there's that sandbar in the entrance. She can't get over it."

"Then she is an easy target! We should board her." Isam itched to fire a gun and make his mark against the infidel who dared invade his home port.

The lanterns glowed on the strange corsair who had taken refuge in their harbor. Figures were limned in the lantern light as they worked their guns. The Spaniard—it must be a Spaniard, who else would dare beard the sea leopards in their den?—fired on them. A continuous din of thunder reverberated from the heights, and the calm waters of the harbor shimmered with the furious blazes that leaped from the muzzles of the guns.

When Halim didn't answer, Isam begged, "Let me take our boat and participate in the boarding party."

"No, habibi," the older man replied. "I have no sons and you are my heir. There's no need to risk your life. There's no prize money for us tonight."

The galley Isam had helped tow off the beach was rowing up on the stranded stranger. She was not alone; three other vessels clustered around the frigate. They would carry her by sheer numbers. Surrounded, the Spaniard brayed defiance. There was nothing the young agha could do except watch. He smote his hand upon the top of the tafferel and swore, "May the pork-eating infidels choke on their grandmother's bile!" He wanted to say something equally strong to his uncle but confined himself to excoriating the enemy.

Halim placed a hand on his shoulder and pressed it firmly. "Not tonight, Isam."

Isam tore away from the shorter man's hand and stormed down the companionway to the main deck. He paced down the bridge between the rowing benches. Men got out his way when they saw the thundercloud brewing in his face. He sat on a cannon, a big bronze thirty-two pounder, and brooded. With her bow on the beach, her guns pointed at the city.

A sailor with the hood of his haik pulled over his head sidled up to him. "The boat is tied up alongside, agha," he remarked.

Isam lifted his head. He glanced over the side of the vessel, then glanced at the knot of idle men who were pretending not to eavesdrop as the ghost-like man initiated conversation.

"So it is, Aaban. It will easily hold a dozen men." There were just about that many gathered near by.

Aaban turned to look. "We helped to get Alman's galley off the beach. Surely some of the loot is due to us as well."

"By Allah, in justice, it is so," Isam replied. He slid off the wet gun and his feet thudded onto the deck. He approached the knot of sodden corsairs. "Who wants to fight the infidel?" he demanded.

All heads turned to him with fierce flashes of white teeth in the darkness.

"I do!"

"So do I!"

"Let's show these curs how real men fight!"

Isam bared his teeth like a leopard. "Get your weapons. Meet me at the side."

The young agha went below to get his Moorish scimitar: a short, curved blade about two feet long. It was better suited for shipboard combat than the longer blades of the Turks and Berbers. The wooden hilt was decorated with silver stars while two short quillons led forward along the blade and a third much longer quillon curved back to protect the hand. It was an old but sturdy sword he had bought secondhand. He thought an agha ought to have a fine sword. Not that it was best in

Tanguel, but it was the finest he had ever owned, and that made it the best to him.

He gripped it with his left hand and called up, "Uncle! I am taking the boat to support the attack on the Spaniard!" He was defying his uncle's orders, but he was doing it openly and boldly like a man, not a skulking cur. He turned swiftly and walked away, calling to the men, "Into the boat!"

Halim turned around. Seeing what he was up to, he called, "Nephew! Stop that!"

Isam walked to the gunwale, and putting his hand on top of the railing, easily swung himself over the side.

Halim called, "Isam Agha!" but his voice lacked conviction.

His nephew wouldn't even look at him. Down he went into the boat. The disobedient men followed him.

Halim ran down to the deck and leaned over the side. "There's no need! You'll get yourself killed for nothing! Isam, come back!" he pleaded.

The men in the boat paused in getting out the oars to see what the youth would do. Isam hesitated. He was disobeying his captain, his uncle, his guardian, the man who had taken him in when his own father died. He was wrong to rebel. He knew it. He should do what he was told. The roar of Spanish cannons made him turn his head. The gathered galleys encircled the intruder, but she was fighting them to the last. She would not surrender.

He settled in the sternsheets of the boat. "Cast off," he said. "Out oars."

The young agha had a boatload of willing men and they put their backs into it. The boat skimmed across the black waters of the night, racing for the cannon fire like a moth darting to the flame. He was a grown man. He would not be kept in a box like a kitten when he had the strength to run and hunt on his own.

Halim raised his hand to touch his heart, then kissed his fingertips in benediction, murmuring softly so that only the night heard, "Allah defend you. You are your father's son. You're going to die with your guts on the deck like your father before you. Fortunate am I to be a man with only daughters. I will never see my son die like that."

Isam felt no fear, only a wild exultation. He had stout-hearted men to accompany him as he raced to battle. He was only nineteen, but he had come of age. His fate was his own, and no one but Allah could gainsay him.

CHAPTER 2: THE BOARDING PARTY

The small boat shot across the waters with Isam at the tiller. Something dark and deadly skimmed above their heads as they approached, struck the water beyond them, ricocheted like a child's ball, and disappeared into the darkness. Isam's heart thundered in his chest. "Row faster!" The stroke oar increased his tempo. There was a momentary clash of wood and loss of speed, then the other oars followed the stroke. The boat hastened across the lustrous black waters of the harbor.

The orange-red light of the muzzle flashes guided them to the Spanish ship. The broadside had broken up into a series of single shots with each gun crew taking their aim at whatever they thought good. Gunners shoved the quoins in to depress them as far as possible, but a multitude of small boats was gathering around her. On deck, a Spaniard with a red kerchief tied over his head raised up a cannonball and let it plunge into the first boat. The eighteen pound shot smashed through the bottom and the small boat started leaking. More shot was heaved over the side, but the corsairs swarmed up the chains and accommodation ladder. The Spanish frigate was a high-sided vessel with her railing at least eight feet above the water, but her gun ports were much lower and accessible. Scimitars were thrust in to clear the way, then a corsair thrust his head and shoulders in, only to be shot in the face. His dead body fell and slithered backwards into the boat.

Isam shouted, "Up oars! Bowman, tie on! Wherever you can find." With the first boats swarming the easier accesses to the vessel, he was searching the side for some method of making the assault. A gun fired directly above them. A tongue of fire six feet long leaped from the mouth of the bronze barrel and two of his men fell shrieking beneath it, their hair, turbans, and fezzes alight. Their comrades doused them with salt water, but the men were badly burnt about the face and shoulders. Isam stared at them. He had felt the hot blast of the gun but had escaped unharmed. The difference between safety and a horrible maiming had been only three feet.

The Spanish gun was run in by the sweating, desperate crew. Footsteps pattered on the deck over their heads and the wild ululation of the corsairs broke out. It was a cry that raised the hair on the back of their necks and made them work faster. To load the gun the sponger had to send the butt end of his swab out the gun port, so Isam drew his sword and slashed that arm. The man fell back with a scream. Blood splattered and sizzled on the gun barrel. Inside a man roared in Spanish, but the young agha didn't know the language and couldn't make out the orders. Suddenly the worm-end of a gun tool thrust straight at his face. He ducked, but the iron spiral knocked the fez from his head. He slashed with his scimitar but struck wood instead of flesh. A chip of wood pulled out of the gun port sill when he freed his blade. The rain continued to fall and everything was cold and slippery except for the barrels of the steaming guns.

Without a hand on the tiller the boat drifted out of arm's reach. Another Spaniard, a young man with a brown pigtail, leaned out the gun port to ram the sponge home. Isam drew his pistol and took aim right at his back, but the pistol missed fire. He swore and tossed it into the bottom of the boat. It was impossible to keep the powder dry.

"Back oars!" he bellowed. He stood in the sternsheets with his scimitar in his left hand and his right upon the tiller. The rowers strove to come along side. It was a race between them and the gun crew that was frantically trying to load.

A burly Spaniard with his sleeves rolled up to the elbows took the canvas cartridge in his left hand and shoved it into the mouth of the muzzle. Isam swore at him in Turkish, but he was too far away to reach him with his sword. As soon as the loader disappeared, the rammer appeared, leaning into the gun port as he frantically shoved the rammer down the barrel. One of the rowers, seeing what was happening, lashed out with his oar and struck the Spaniard in the shoulder. He grunted in pain and dropped the rammer into the water below.

The bowman tossed the grappling hook into the gun port and it caught on the corner. He rapidly took a turn around a cleat to pull the bow up close.

"In oars!" Isam shouted. He let go the tiller and clambered over thwarts and wounded men to the middle of the boat. He stabbed the hand trying to pry the grappling hook loose. A pike thrust out the gun port and sliced through the sleeve of his jacket, tearing a line of blood across the fabric. Someone was shouting, "Board them! Board the dogs! Kill the infidels!" He didn't recognize his own voice.

The pike thrust again, supplemented by the wormer from the other side. Scimitars flashed, and the wormer was cut off a foot behind the iron spiral. Isam hacked at the pike and steel clashed with steel as he caught the pike on its blade. Metal scraped against metal, then the two weapons parted. In the pause, one of his men, a small wiry fellow, lunged, caught the sill of the gun port, and hauled himself through.

"After him!" Isam roared as the Spanish defenders kicked the corsair and brought their remaining gun tools down on his head.

The next man clambered through the gun port, took a flutter of blows to the head and shoulders, but slithered aboard. A blow knocked him against the gun and he cried out in agony as the heat of the gun scorched him even through his pantaloons. Isam lunged with his scimitar and received a blow to the head that made his ears ring. He clawed his way through the opening, feet scrambling at the slippery wet side of the Spanish frigate, then the corsair in front of him accidentally stepped on his hand. While he was pinned by that, somebody used a gun tool like a club to smash him in the face. The tang of his own blood in his mouth and the violent pain right between the eyes gave him strength. He yanked his hand out from under the foot, flung himself through the gun port, clawed his way to his feet, and shoved his blade at the heaving chest of a white-shirted Spaniard. He ululated like a madman, and his powerful voice rang through the crowded confines of the gun deck. The sight of a bloody-faced corsair looming large in the confined space, his sword dripping with gore, was more than the Spanish gunner could withstand. He dropped the broken haft of the gun tool and ran.

Isam paused to catch his breath, count heads, and look around. He had eight men with him who were fit for duty. Suddenly a pike thrust at him and he parried by reflex. The point went hurtling past his ribs, but it didn't touch him.

"*Seahawk*! Aft!" he bellowed.

The disorder below decks became general as the Spanish seamen fled their posts to barricade themselves in the forecastle or wardroom, or hid in the hold below. Isam darted his blade this way and that, but he was no longer being pressed by enemies. His own blood covered his hand and hilt as the saturated jacket sleeve could no longer absorb the blood.

One of his men, seeing the crimson gore in the light of the lantern, said, "Agha, you're wounded!" He pulled off his turban, and tearing off a piece of it, wrapped it around Isam's forearm, shirt, coat sleeve, and all. He bound it up tight, then tore off another piece and gave it to Isam who used it to wipe his hand and hilt. The young warrior did not clean or sheathe his blade—not yet.

Suddenly a short corsair appeared before him with a yataghan in hand. He was splattered with blood, but none of it appeared to be his own. He wore a white turban wrapped around a red fez, a curly black beard, a short black jacket, and black and grey striped pantaloons.

"Who are you?" the stranger barked in Turkish. He repeated his demand in Arabic.

"Isam Agha Hamet of the *Seahawk*. Who are you?" Isam barked back at him in Turkish.

"Rajet Rais of the *Grey Wolf*. That's Demirkan, my agha," he said, gesturing to a muscular black man. He had a squad of men to back him up, and they had the hardbitten look of veterans.

"Never heard of you," Isam replied.

"That's my ship the infidel dog was chasing." He used his chin to point in the general direction of the xebec, then he used a cloth to wipe his blade and sheathe it. A bit grudgingly, he said, "You have my thanks for helping to capture the ship."

Stooping awkwardly on account of his height crammed under the low deckhead, Isam shrugged and said, "The dog invaded my hometown. Of course I fought."

"Where's your captain?"

"Still on the *Seahawk*. She's on the beach, nowhere near ready to sail."

That news caused Rajet Rais to smile. "That's well then. One less ship to share the prize money. Don't worry, you'll get your share, agha."

Isam eyed the stranger dubiously. "I'm sure the division of spoils will be fair. Because I'll ring your hairy Turkish neck if it's not."

"Feh. What a kitten you are, showing me your claws." Rajet Rais rolled his eyes. He was so short he only had to stoop a little under the deckhead. He had sloping eyes, a pug nose, and a weak chin that was not entirely hidden by the curly beard. His lips held a sensuous sneer, if such a combination were even possible. All in all he was not a comely specimen; the most that could be said of him was that he was a masculine man.

Reddening, Isam snarled, "Let's flush these infidels out of the forecastle."

"After you, agha," Rajet replied. Then he gave orders to his men. "Follow Isam Agha. We're going to clear out the fo'c'sle."

Isam's men formed up behind him. They gave wary looks to the more numerous brutes that followed Rajet Rais, but all men are brothers in Islam, so they consented to fight alongside each other.

CHAPTER 3: THE MARRIAGE PROPOSAL

Isam Agha Hamet sat on a canvas rug in the great cabin of the *Seahawk*. Since she was still being overhauled, the cabin had no furniture to speak of, just a low table that served as a desk and a few other odds and ends, including a canvas tarp that served as drop cloth and rug. Lanterns hanging from the beams provided enough light for Halim to stitch up Isam's arm while the young agha held a cold compress to his broken nose with the other.

Halim gave him a rueful smile. "Both of your eyes are turning black. You're going to have a double-shiner. Ah well. The girls won't mind. In fact, I expect they'll fuss over you all the more. You're their darling corsair."

The thought of being fussed over by his female cousins filled Isam with more dread than any thought of the enemy could. "Ah, I think I'll stay with the ship. You know, just in case the Spanish prisoners cause any problems."

Halim snorted. "We don't have any Spanish prisoners. If I didn't know better, I'd think you didn't like girls!"

Isam didn't answer that, but the stricken look on his face (as much as could be seen around the compress) didn't fail to catch Halim's attention. He glanced up, but put his needle through the edge of the wound and drew the silk thread through. Isam's breath hissed through his teeth.

"You should think about getting married. You're old enough. You're not my son, but I've raised you since you were twelve, so I take a paternal interest in your welfare, above and beyond my duty as your guardian. You're old enough to claim your patrimony. Claim a wife while you're at it. I have nineteen daughters and only five of them are married. Anyone of them would make you a good wife. Except Rabiyah. That girl is mule-headed and will come to a bad end."

"I'm not ready to get married."

"Nonsense! I made you an agha because you're a fine strapping lad and a good fighter to boot. You keep your wits about you in a battle. The men respect you." The needle pierced the wounded flesh again and Isam gritted his teeth. Halim fell silent as he pulled the thread through, made certain it was snug, and tied the stitch. He cut it with his knife, then glanced at Isam's face again. He said quietly, "I can't hold you, Isam. You're headstrong, just like your father. A wife and family will temper your courage. Your father took foolhardy risks after Miriam died."

The needle stabbed again, and Isam felt it all the way to his heart. "I haven't thought about marriage," he mumbled.

The two threads tied together. "What do you think about then? Dancing boys?"

Isam's face colored a bright red. He hedged, "Why would I think about dancing boys? I know better than to visit the taverns."

Halim laughed. "Knowing better isn't the same as doing better! Besides, you have a bevy of beautiful female cousins, all young and supple and forever painting themselves with henna and making eyes at you, and you don't even notice."

Isam flushed and mumbled, "They're my cousins. Of course I respect their modesty."

"Umar and Samir are their cousins, too, but I have to beat them off with a stick, the impious rogues." There was no venom in his voice. Father of nineteen daughters, he had gotten used to defending his household from suitors of all stripes.

Isam extemporized hastily. "You're my guardian. I benefit from your moral guidance. I would never offend against you or your household."

"Feh. You're nineteen years old and as far as I can tell, still a virgin. That's not natural. Boys will be boys. There's always a scullery maid or a fishmonger's daughter who can be seduced. You've never even tried."

Isam chewed his lip and felt the sweat accumulating under his fez. He cast his uncle an anguished look. "I haven't met a girl I thought was worth chasing after. Umar and Samir are foolish."

Halim paid great attention to the stitch he was making. The firm muscular flesh of his nephew's arm rested on the low table. Black hair was thick on the young man's arm and even sprinkled his knuckles.

Finally Halim spoke. "I have treated you like you were my own son. Even if Hamet weren't my brother, I like you, and I pray Allah showers His blessings upon you. I hope that you will do me the courtesy of being honest with me. Are you a virgin?"

Isam flushed. "No."

"Who was it?"

Isam didn't answer.

"If it's a girl I need to know in case she makes a paternity claim."

"Not a girl. I've never touched a woman. I don't want to. They don't interest me."

"Was it the goat?" Halim asked seriously.

Isam nearly choked. "No!" The thought of being known as Isam the Goatfucker was too much to bear. Bright red he said, "It was your steward, Wadid. I commanded him and he obeyed. If you're angry about it, be angry with me. He's a slave. He didn't have a choice." He glared defiance.

Halim exhaled noisily and tied up the next stitch. "Ah well. If it's a slave, that's all right. Nobody cares what happens to a slave."

"I like him," Isam said truculently.

Halim peered thoughtfully at him. "Not too much, I hope."

Isam was taken aback. How much was too much? This was a new calculation for him. "I like sex," he replied, willing to fight his uncle about it.

Halim laughed at that. "Of course you do! You wouldn't be a man if you didn't." He slapped his nephew's shoulder.

The younger man rubbed his shoulder and frowned. He did not care to be questioned about such a personal matter, but he liked being laughed at even less. "It's my own business."

"So it is. Be discreet, lad. Be discreet. It takes four witnesses to prove anything, so never let there be four witnesses to anything you don't want proved. The penalty is a good flogging."

"I can stand a flogging."

"It isn't the flogging that hurts. It's the shame of public humiliation and the marks that scar your back forever."

"I won't get caught," Isam promised.

Halim sighed. "You are my heir, seeing as how I have no sons of my own, but if you are addicted to sodomy, you won't give me any grandsons. Think about your future. Any fame and wealth a man may earn are nothing if he has no sons to inherit. Do as you please with the slaves, but you need a wife."

"I don't want a wife," Isam said stubbornly.

Halim stuck the needle in him again. "Yes, you do. Who else will keep your house and give you children? A man's harem is his paradise on earth. His children are his comfort in his old age. If you pick one of my daughters, you will have my approval and my property. I'm not a rich man, but I'm not poor, either."

The burden of his uncle's advice weighed upon him. He knew it was good, but he couldn't accept it. He gave his uncle an agonized look. "I'll never marry, Uncle. I know myself. I've tried to think about women, but I can't."

The older man brooded as he tied off the last stitch. For a moment the silk thread led from his nephew's arm to his hand, then with a slow, sad motion, he cut it. "Allah will provide. He made a mate for every creature on earth. Even you. You'll see."

Isam didn't argue any further. It was useless to try and make the man understand. Halim was not well-versed in religion, but he was a devout believer. He had to be. Allah had given him four wives, nineteen daughters, and no sons. He had to believe a higher power ordained everything, even if he didn't understand it.

CHAPTER 4 : THE TURKISH CAPTAIN

A few days later, Isam was walking along the waterfront when he saw a slate propped against a piling.

WANTED
True brothers in Islam
to wage war against the infidels
GENEROUS PRIZE MONEY
and ENDURING FAME to those HEROES
who take up arms
in Defense of their Country
in pursuit of Righteousness
Inquire at the Grey Wolf,
Captor of the Santa María de Cervellon

He looked down the length of weathered wood, and there, at the end, was the xebec. She was about a hundred feet long, beamier than a galley, with her guns in broadside. She had a quarterdeck and lazyboard and three masts supporting lateen antennas. Her foremast looked down upon her prow while her mizzen mast looked down upon her boomkin. In between her mainmast stood straight and tall. She had the low slung, rakish look of a fast ship. In a trance, his sandaled feet carried him along the dock.

Arriving at the end of the vessel, he stopped and stared. The gun ports were open and the bronze guns run out. They were ornamented around the muzzle with a band of stylized leaves and vines, but among the leaves were thorns. He walked over and took a look at her figurehead: a fierce grey wolf with upraised paw and bared teeth. The xebec was in good condition; her holes were patched with new wood, and she was neat and clean. He walked slowly to her other end to study her stern quarters. Her lines were fine and formed a graceful curve. At the very stern was the latticed platform of the lazyboard. Two gun ports lurked under the lazyboard to house the stern chasers. She was bigger and better armed than the *Seahawk*, and he was embarrassed that his father's vessel was inferior to this stranger.

Yet he was drawn to it. He needed the opportunity to serve with a more daring man than his uncle, to take the chances of war in hopes of making himself a name and fortune, serving Allah by smiting the infidels, and defending his homeland. He wanted to earn enough money to build his own ship and become a captain in his own right; a bigger, better ship than even the *Grey Wolf*, a ship with which he would be the terror of the seas. The Nazarenes would piss in their boots when they saw him coming. Oh yes, he would be a great corsair some day! Let his uncle keep the small and aging *Seahawk*. He was a young man, and he would win his own fame and wealth and build the biggest and best ship any corsair had ever had.

His mind made up, he mounted the gangplank. "Ahoy the ship."

The watchman replied, "Ahoy yourself. What'd'ya want?"

"Is the captain aboard? I saw your notice."

The man unfolded, rose from the hatch where he had been sitting, and said, "Come aboard. I'll see if he'll receive you."

"Tell him Isam Agha is asking for him."

Isam stepped onto the rail. No accommodation ladder was set up inside the bulwark, so he stepped down onto a cannon and from there to the deck. He took note of the lines neatly coiled and hung on their belaying pins. The *Grey Wolf* was a taut ship. He stayed put until the watchman returned and said, "The captain will see you."

He ducked and followed. Even on the *Grey Wolf* the deckhead was too low for his great height. When he built his own ship, she would have enough headroom for his head and turban together. Some day. The man-at-arms guarding the captain's door opened it and let him into the great cabin. Isam stepped inside and the door shut behind him.

The great cabin was a cool, dim room, lit by the open gun ports. An unlit lamp hung on a chain from the ceiling. Rajet Rais was sitting cross-legged on a black divan located between the two guns. He wore a black short-sleeved shirt that revealed hairy, muscular arms, and matching pantaloons. A red and black checked sash was around his waist. A snowy white turban surmounted his homely face. Short hair and a curly short beard framed almond eyes, a pug nose, and a weak chin, but the brown eyes were penetrating. To the captain's right was a clerk in a white cloth cap sitting on a cushion. He was working on a long scroll that hung over both ends of the coffee table before him. Isam assumed it was a muster roll or pay roll due to its length.

The younger man bowed deeply with his hand to his forehead. "Peace be upon you."

"And also upon you. Please, sit," Rajet Rais replied.

Isam slipped off his dirty sandals and stepped onto the rug. He settled cross-legged on the opposite side of the coffee table.

"I see you are looking for men," he began without preamble.

Rajet's almond eyes narrowed. "I am." He contemplated the younger man thoughtfully. "Are you looking for a ship?"

"I am."

"I thought you had a ship."

"I do. But I want a better ship."

Rajet Rais' mouth quirked within his beard. "You flatter me," he said dryly, but he took one of the teacups from the tray and filled it from the copper teapot. He put the blue-green cup in front of the younger man.

Isam shook his head as he took the cup. "You're bigger and better armed."

"Why should I trust a man who readily deserts his own master?"

Isam folded his arms over his chest and made his biceps bulge. "Because I am my own master and cannot desert myself. The *Seahawk* belongs to me, but my uncle is her captain. I am an orphan. I am of age so I could demand my patrimony, but I won't. I want more than that."

Rajet sipped his tea thoughtfully as he studied the young man before him. "You're ambitious. I like that. You've been to sea before?"

"I have. I know how to hand, reef, and steer. My uncle made me agha of the men-at-arms this year. I can fight."

"I already have an agha. What I need are sailors."

"Then I'll take a sailor's position and prove myself to you."

"Can you navigate by the stars? Use a sextant? Do trigonometry?"

"A little," Isam replied.

"The height of the fortress at the mouth of the harbor is a hundred and fifty feet. With your sextant, you observe the angle of its height is 30 degrees. How far away are you?"

Isam wilted. "I . . . don't know."

"Let the angle be called 'alpha.' The formula is 'the tangent of alpha equals height divided by distance.'"

"What is 'tangent'?"

"Trigonometry."

"Will you teach me?" Isam fixed eager eyes on the smaller man.

"Do you know what a hypotenuse is?"

"The long side of a triangle."

"What is the Pythagorean theorem?"

"A squared equals b squared plus c squared."

"What do you do with it?"

"You can calculate the area of a sail and the length of its luff. Or you can go backwards. Knowing the length of your antenna, you can calculate the size of the sail you will need to fit it," he replied with assurance.

Rajet suppressed a smile. "A practical application. But what if you only know one of the sides?"

"The problem can't be solved." Isam was on certain ground now.

"Oh, but it can. You take out your trusty sextant, measure the angle, and by taking the tangent, solve the rest."

Isam ground his teeth together in frustration. "Teach me."

Rajet Rais folded his arms over his chest and stared at him with his inscrutable Asian eyes. "You ask a lot of me."

"I'll learn it. You won't be disappointed."

The man snorted. "That remains to be seen. But before I agree to such an arrangement, I have to know if you're worth the effort. I expect loyalty from a man to whom I have shown such favor."

"Of course, rais."

Isam's heart thudded. He understood what the man was hinting at; if Rajet would train him, it would take many cruises for him to learn. He was obligating himself to the man for at least a year if he accepted. Other corsairs would sign on for a cruise or two or three—whenever they wanted money or were feeling restless or needed to dodge the law for a bit. Recruiting crews was easy, but it was an endless business. If the crews were successful, they wouldn't be interested in another cruise until they'd spent their prize money and were broke again. A core of reliable men was needed to stay with the vessel, to repair her and keep her supplied, and to recruit sailors and men-at-arms for her next cruise.

Rajet spoke, "Do you have anyone that can vouch for you?"

"My uncle, Halim of the Many Daughters. Any of the officers of the *Seahawk*. What about you? Do you have any references?" There was a deliberate challenge in his voice. He was not going to commit himself to a fool or tyrant. Although he was eager for the post, he pretended he wasn't.

"Come back in a week. You'd better speak to your uncle before I do."

Isam fidgeted. If the man wouldn't take him, he didn't really want to tell Halim he was thinking about leaving, but all the same, he couldn't blame the man for wanting to make certain he wasn't bespoken. Mustering up his dignity, he feigned nonchalance. "That will satisfy me."

Rajet's eyes narrowed. "The question is, will it satisfy me?"

"I'll earn my keep, but I'm not going to commit myself to a captain unless I can respect him. No offense intended, but I don't know you."

"You will," Rajet replied. "You will."

CHAPTER 5 : THE TWINS

The yard of the mud brick teashop was very small and covered with a pergola of weathered wood that supported Moorish ivy. The vine's narrow pointy leaves were bright green beneath the veneer of dust. Isam was enjoying his tea when his cousins Rabiyah and Raidah passed by, water jars balancing on their heads, and slim arms reaching up to steady them. In this position their sleeves could not help falling back to reveal their slender arms. Their faces were unveiled. Only noble ladies went veiled, and those ladies only went out when carried in a curtained sedan chair. Allah had blessed Halim with daughters and not gold, so the twins walked to the well like the daughters of shopkeepers and butchers. They were dressed in blue and white with scarfs over their heads long enough to cover their hair, but the loose clothes could not conceal the curves of their figures.

Most men stepped aside to let the two comely maidens pass. It was forbidden to look an unrelated woman in the face, so pious men averted their eyes and let themselves stare at the feet painted with henna designs, naked within the thin straps of the sandals. All but one. He was a dark-skinned Moor with a hook nose and short beard. He wore a creamy white wool haik over his clothes, clothes which were good white linen for his shirt and tan camel wool for his pantaloons. His feet were encased in crimson boots. His scimitar was thrust into a red sash that could be glimpsed beneath the haik as he turned to stare after the sisters. He watched them pass, then immediately fell in behind them, melding with the crowd of donkeys, porters, and shoppers. Isam leaped to his feet and hurried after them. Being even taller than the Moor, he was able to pick out his turban and fez amid the throng and followed him. The Moor was as unaware of his tail as the sisters were of theirs.

The fountain was shaped like a great scallop shell supported on a base. Made of white sandstone, the interior was lined with turquoise, blue, and white tile work. A pair of thirsty donkeys drank from the basin while women waited in line for their turn to put their jars into the water and fill them up. As Raidah stepped forward and lowered the heavy ceramic jug, the stranger who had been following them stepped forward. Hovering at a distance so as not to be spotted, Isam couldn't hear what was said, but he saw Raidah shake her head. The stranger continued speaking to her, but she pulled her head scarf across her face and turned her back to him. She lowered the jug into the water, filled it up, and still keeping her back to him, heaved it onto her head. Rabiyah was not so delicate in her sensibilities. She smiled at the stranger and let him take the jug from her hands. The Moor bent to immerse the jug into the water, then lifted it onto his shoulder with a smile. Rabiyah pressed her hands to her face and shook her head, then held out her arms for the jug, but the man wouldn't give it to her. He smiled at her again and she turned back and forth between the man and her sister. Raidah remonstrated with the man, but he wouldn't let Rabiyah have the second water jug.

"What's this?" Isam demanded as he pushed his way forward.

"Cousin!" Raidah exclaimed in relief. "He wants to carry the water jug all the way to the house. I keep telling him it wouldn't be proper, but he won't give it back!"

The Moor's eyes flicked to Isam at the word 'cousin.' He gave a self-deprecating smile and shrugged the shoulder that wasn't weighed down with the jug. "Such pretty maidens shouldn't do such hard work. I'll carry both jugs if they let me."

"Who are you?" Isam demanded.

"Maureo, a man of the Glawa. I have many camels, sheep and donkeys. I am no corsair with nothing to call his own but a sword. I am a man of property," he boasted.

Isam had been more amused than annoyed, but Maureo's slighting of the corsairs altered his mood. "I'm a corsair," he snapped. "I'm Isam Agha Hamet of the *Seahawk*, and these women are my cousins. Hand over the jug and leave them alone. I don't care how many camels you have."

Maureo's eyes narrowed. His gaze swiftly raked the young agha's physique and scimitar. He concluded that although he might have the advantage in age and experience, there was no good that could come of quarreling with a young and able-bodied man. He surrendered the jug to Rabiyah and said to her, "Dear maiden, I wish I knew your name. I'm sure it's as lovely as your eyes."

Rabiyah hugged the jug to her chest and looked immensely flattered. Raidah slapped her shoulder and said crossly, "Go home. Cousin Isam, will you walk with us?"

"Of course," he replied. He fell in behind the twins. He glanced over his shoulder at Maureo, but the man remained by the well.

They were not even out of earshot when the Moor asked the people at the well, "Who were those girls?"

Isam whirled around with his left hand upon his scimitar. "Don't answer that question. He doesn't need to know. If he wants a wife, he can go to the matchmaker like a proper bridegroom."

Maureo's eyes narrowed once again and crow's feet appeared at the corners. A left-handed swordsman was no easy foe. "Peace be upon you, young agha. I speak out of admiration for what Allah has made." He touched his fingers to his chest and lips and swirled them in the air with a bow, but his smile didn't reach his eyes.

"Peace be upon you as well, and may Allah keep your camels safe," Isam replied, but there was anger in his voice.

Turning back to his cousins he said, "Go home. I'll watch over you. That oaf won't follow us." He looked back over his shoulder as he said it, and he kept checking the rear as they went along the street.

Raidah chided her sister. "You shouldn't have spoken to him. You shouldn't have let him have your jug."

"He was handsome and courteous," Rabiyah replied. "Besides, he has many camels and sheep! I want a husband and children of my own. I'm tired of being a servant in my father's house."

"You're not a servant. You're a sister. It's wrong to complain about what Allah hath wrought."

"I'm twenty-one and so are you! We're old maids! If we don't get married soon, we'll lose our looks! We'll have to settle for some scrawny old scribe whose pen is thicker than his dick!"

"Rabiyah!" Raidah wailed.

Rabiyah cast a sly eye over her shapely shoulder and let her hips sway as she walked. "Unless our cousin is ready to take a wife. I'm sure he could satisfy the most demanding woman." She let her eye fall below Isam's waist.

"Rabiyah!" Isam rebuked her. "That is an immodest remark! Stop swaying your hips. You'll ruin your reputation."

"Feh. What reputation? I go back and forth between the house and the well and nothing more. Men don't dare speak to me. Maureo is the first. I hope he follows us."

Isam took another glance over his shoulder, but there was no sign of the Moor. "If he does, I'll run him through for daring to molest my cousins."

Raidah turned and looked back in fear. "Is he there?"

"No sign of him," Isam replied.

They reached Halim's house without further incident. Isam smiled at them and said, "You're home safe. He won't bother you again. If he does, tell me, and I'll beat him."

Raideh smiled gratefully at him. "Thank you, cousin." She raised the lion's head knocker and let it fall on the door.

Rabiyah pouted at him. "You think we're pretty, don't you? You should marry one of us. Father has said he'll give you an inheritance if you do."

Isam drew himself up to his full height and glared at her. "That's an improper remark. No man will want to marry such a forward girl. Besides, you're too old for me." She was all of two years older than him.

She scowled at him and gave him tit for tat. "You're just a boy. I wouldn't want to marry someone as young as you, anyhow. I want a real man, a man with property. Maureo's right. All you own is the clothes on your back."

Just then the front door opened and the eunuch admitted the women to the house, thereby ending what would have grown into a quarrel.

Feeling that his manly dignity required him to have the last word, Isam drew himself up haughtily and told Rabiyah's back, "I am the agha of men-at-arms and the *Seahawk* is my property!"

She waggled her butt provocatively at him. "You're a boy who wouldn't know what to do with this even if you had it." She disappeared into the house.

His face turned red and he shouted, "I wouldn't marry you if you were the last woman in Tanguel!"

The eunuch held the door for him, but he shook his head and scowled. The door shut, leaving him cross and dissatisfied in the street.

CHAPTER 6 : SERENADE

Halim Many Daughters' house would have been just right for a much smaller family. Two stories tall, it was built around a central courtyard open to the sky. An orange tree stood in the middle where four walking paths met. Originally there had been a small lawn in the courtyard, but that had been dug up and turned into gardens yielding garlic, mint, and watermelons, among other delicacies. This was his wife Tanay's realm, the one aspect of the household that was entirely under her control, and she ruled it like a tyrant. Nobody trespassed there, not even the cat, who was thrown into the alley whenever it was caught digging in the garden.

The females of the household were domiciled upstairs, along with a nurse for the youngest daughters and a pair of maids for the rest. The lower floor contained the kitchen, storerooms, sewing room, antechamber, reception room, and the master's room. The cook slept in the kitchen and the eunuch slept in the storeroom and considered himself blessed. His previous master had beat him and made him sleep in the barn, so he held Halim in high regard.

When the twelve-year-old orphan boy Isam had arrived, he was already circumcised and therefore too old to sleep with his female cousins. There was no place to put him, so he slept on a divan in the reception room. Every night he had to wait up until Halim's guests were gone, then he would fetch his sheet and blanket from the cedar chest, make a bed on a divan, and settle down for the night. Each morning he rose and put the bedclothes away, dressed, and when he was old enough, shaved. He threw a kilim over the washstand to hide it from the day's visitors. For seven years Isam had done this and not much had changed, although now when he prepared for bed he propped his scimitar on a pair of dowels driven into the wall over his usual resting place. Stripping down to his drawers and shirt, he crawled into bed. Since he had become an agha he couldn't help feeling he was entitled to grander lodging, but that would require leaving his uncle's house and paying rent somewhere. He sighed and resigned himself to another night of sleeping on the divan. "Some day," he promised himself.

The house was dark and the street was quiet. Nobody stirred in the middle of the night; it was a respectable neighborhood. The young agha was sleeping soundly when something niggled at his brain. He yawned and burrowed more deeply into his pillow, but the sound continued. The thick adobe walls muffled it, but the wooden shutters that covered the small windows were not impervious. The plaintive tone insinuated itself through the cracks in the shutters and drifted through the room. Slowly he woke to the sound of a wooden flute. He lay there listening. The player was good; the sound was a haunting, lonely, alluring melody. The breathy notes quavered and failed, only to begin again more earnestly than before. Sleepily he wondered who was receiving the serenade.

He sat bolt upright as suspicion entered his brain. He dressed in haste in a pair of long pantaloons, shirt, fez, jacket and sandals. He wrapped his sash around his waist and thrust his scimitar into it. All the while the flute continued to play its haunting melody.

Going to the window, he peered through a crack in the shutters. The cedar wood pressed against his sore nose so he shifted to try and spy who was in the street, but he couldn't quite see. Something white fluttered down from above, and the music stopped. A young man dressed in a haik and pantaloons ran forward, bent down to scoop up the bit of paper, and carried it out of Isam's sight. He craned his ear and heard a soft voice say, "Here it is, master."

Isam withdrew from the window and debated with himself. Should he wake the house? It would panic the women, he was sure of it. Should he wake Halim? Perhaps he ought. But what then? It had to be Maureo, pursuing Rabiyah. And she was encouraging him! Maureo was not the first man to court a maid with music. Although Isam had no desire to serenade a woman, he had heard that such things were generally approved in the female parts of the neighborhood. He chewed his lip. Should he confront Rabiyah and demand to know what note she had sent? That wasn't his place. If anyone confronted her, it must be Halim. What if she denied it all? He had no proof. Maureo had come and played his flute. What was wrong with that? Yet as Isam had told him, if he wanted a wife, he should hire a matchmaker. Still, why hire a matchmaker unless you were certain your suit would be received, and what better way to assure the suit than to enlist the support of the woman herself? Isam was in a torment of indecision and it made him irate. He was a man of action. In battle he knew just what to do and did it. He didn't need to think.

Although it soured his disposition, he thought very hard about the situation. He finally decided that he ought to follow Maureo and find out where he was staying. Come morning he could ask questions to find out more about the Moor. Then he could present a full report to Halim and let his uncle decide what to do.

His decision made, he went to the front door, opened the speaking aperture a crack, and peered into the street. He didn't see anyone. Unlocking the door, he let himself out. Far down the street he saw a pair of white forms moving through the darkness under the starry night. Shutting the door quietly, he followed swiftly in their rear. He kept close to the building so he could press himself into a doorway if needed, but the pair never looked back. Whatever was in the note, it had satisfied Maureo for the evening.

The amorous Moor and his servant went briskly along the dirt street, reached the plaza where the well was, then turned down a side street. The Moor knocked at a door. Golden lamplight spilled into the street as it was opened, and Maureo disappeared inside. The servant continued past the front of the house and turned into the narrow side yard. Isam sprinted to overtake him.

The servant yelped as he was tackled and thrown against the wall of the building. Isam clamped a hand over his mouth and hissed, "Be quiet, or I'll gut you."

The lad nodded slightly beneath the hairy-knuckled hand that covered his mouth. His eyes were wide and black in the darkness, glossy like jet in the pale oval of his face. He had short black hair beneath a fez that was probably red, but the night made it difficult to tell. He was clean-shaven and young, a beardless youth. The face beneath Isam's hand was warm and soft.

The corsair slowly removed his hand from the servant's mouth. The man didn't scream, but he stared in fear at the stranger who had attacked him. His back pressed hard against the wall.

"Whose house is this?" Isam demanded.

"It's an inn, the Golden Lamp," the servant replied.

"Why is Maureo in Tanguel?"

"He has business with the Bey. He's waiting for an appointment to see him."

The servant straightened up now that it appeared he wasn't going to be robbed, or knifed, or worse. He kept watching Isam's face as he searched for a clue as to his assailant's intentions.

Isam was starting to feel a little foolish. He could have just marked the location in his mind and come back at a civilized hour to ask his questions rather than jumping a stranger in an alley. Yet his blood was up and he was loathe to let the young man leave.

He stepped up very close and the lad retreated, his back pressing against the mud brick wall. His eyes grew alarmed as Isam stepped up so close their clothes were brushing each other.

"Don't tell your master I was asking about him," Isam warned in a guttural baritone.

The young man shook his head.

"If you tell him, I'll tell him you did this!" He caught the shorter man in his arms, and using the strength of his body, pinned him against the wall and kissed him full on the mouth. It was wicked of him, horribly wicked, but he was laughing inside. The servant wouldn't dare tell anyone what had happened now.

The lad whimpered and squirmed, but Isam kept him trapped against the wall. The smaller man was panting in desperation as he jerked his head aside. That only revealed the white curve of his ear to the audacious agha. Isam found himself aroused by the situation. He was bold at sea, and now he was finding out that boldness could reward him ashore, too. He chuffed with laughter, then pressed his lips against that white throat, let his tongue draw a line along it, sucked the earlobe into his mouth, and nibbled it.

Claw-like hands grabbed his shoulders and pushed, but the smaller man wasn't strong enough to force the corsair away. He gave a despairing cry low in his throat, but Isam didn't stop. He was drunk on the sweet nectar of domination. There was nothing the youth could do about it. He was smaller and weaker. He wouldn't dare tell anyone for fear of ruining his own reputation. His master would beat him if he knew.

"Mercy, my lord," the servant begged him. "Don't molest your humble servant. He is only the slave of the Moor from Ain Joira. Whatever your feud, it is with the master, not the slave."

Isam lifted his head to consider the man's pleading face. They could both feel his erection pressed against the younger man. It was dark there in the alley. No one was about. He could do whatever he wanted and no one would gainsay him. He could get away with rape. He shook his head to clear it, then straightened up, adjusting the front of his pantaloons to conceal the effect the encounter had had on him.

"What is your name, slave?" he demanded in a stern baritone.

"Gregorio." The man replied in his soft, boyish voice.

"Are you a Nazarene?"

"Yes, lord. My master won't allow me to convert because he'd have to free me, and he doesn't want to do that."

Isam made a note of the information. He was sure it would come in handy. "Where did your master go tonight?"

Gregorio bit his lip, but Isam stepped up very close to him again. Panicked, the slave answered, "To a woman's house!"

"What woman?" Isam growled.

"I don't know her name."

"Why did your master go there?"

"To court her with his flute!"

"Did he have any luck?"

"She gave him a note, but I don't know what it said."

"Get me that note. Bring it to Hosaam's coffee shop. Leave it with him. He'll send me a message that you brought it."

Gregorio's face fell. "I can't do that!"

Isam thrust his body hard against the slave. Once again the smaller man was pinned by the hot, hard flesh of the corsair. Gregorio turned his face aside and shut his eyes. Long black lashes lay against his cheeks.

"You will. You know the penalty if you don't. I'll ruin your reputation, infidel. Nobody will believe a slave against the word of a true believer."

Without any volition on his part Isam's hands were feeling up the slender body of the slave. The power he had over this helpless, tender, enticing creature made him giddy. Why not do as he pleased? It was as he said; the youth would never dare inform against him. He liked the feel of the body trembling against his and could imagine it naked beneath him. He forced himself to step back.

Gregorio was frantic. "I can't! How can I get it? He'll keep it with him, or hide it."

"You will," said Isam confidently. He turned and sauntered away with the arrogant strut of a conquering corsair. He wasn't a boy any more. He was a man: a man who could win whatever he wanted through the strength of his body and the nerve to try it.

CHAPTER 7 : THE AMOROUS AGHA

At an hour when respectable men were in bed, Isam found himself wandering the streets of Tanguel. He was restless, aroused, bored with his life, and unwilling to betake himself to his couch and settle down for the night. How could he? He had enjoyed his adventure and didn't want it to end. He kept replaying the scene with the slave in his mind—the feel of warm flesh beneath the clothes, the trembling of his body, the quick, anguished pants, the sweetly masculine scent of his flesh, the sight of those large black eyes pleading with him—Yes. That was what he wanted, not some simpering, giggling, jiggling, henna-painted female. He was old enough to do as he pleased, an agha in charge of the fighting men aboard his uncle's galley, a tall and handsome man of nineteen years. He was old enough to have a lover. Some men his age were married. His mind was made up. The question was, what to do about it? Isam's feet led him to the waterfront while his mind was lost in reverie.

"Peace be upon you, agha," a male voice greeted him.

Isam turned and was blinded by the lantern held aloft by the stranger. "And peace be upon you also." He could make out the staff in the man's other hand: a nightwatchman.

"What are you doing out at this hour?" the watchman asked him politely.

Isam couldn't see the man's face beyond the glare of the lantern, but he could see the whiteness of his garments and the blue haik over them that was as much of a uniform as the watchmen had. He touched his fingers to his chest and lips and swirled them in the air. "To the waterfront. I can't sleep, so I'm looking for company."

The watchman's voice was amused. "The brothels are the only places open at this hour, agha."

Isam's face darkened with embarrassment, but he didn't want to admit to wandering aimlessly while daydreaming about a slave boy either, so he said boldly, "And that is where I am going, since you've made it your business. A courteous man would not have pressed the point."

The lantern dipped as the man bowed gracefully, "Forgive your humble servant for a foolish mistake, effendi. I thought you were someone else."

Dignity mollified, Isam replied, "It's dark. You can't be expected to recognize someone at night," even though the light was shining full on his face and they both knew perfectly well who he was. "I'll be on my way now."

Having said he was going to a brothel, it was now incumbent upon him to do so. He doubted his nocturnal wanderings would be kept secret. If he was going to have the reputation of a man who visited brothels, then he might as well visit a brothel. And why not? He wasn't married. He wanted company. Sexual company. The more he thought about it, the more it sounded like a good idea.

Isam put his hand into his sash and made certain of his purse. It was very light. He had no idea how much it would cost to hire a whore. Now that he was no longer under the guard's inspection, he had a fit of nerves. Would he actually do it? What about the diseases that were said to be rampant among the whores? The thought of infecting his noble portions with a disease cooled the ardor in his veins, but he was too stubborn to change his path. He had said he was going to a brothel, and by Allah, he would go. He was not a sheep-hearted man to bleat and turn aside at the first difficulty. After all, he had merely said he was going, not what he would do when he got there. Yes. That was the solution. Go, have a cup of tea, look at the merchandise, pretend to be dissatisfied with the wares, and leave. They would think him a snob, but that suited him fine.

He turned in at the first house of ill repute he came to. It had no sign or other symbol of its employment, but all the sailors knew it. A pair of lanterns mounted on either side lit a deeply recessed carved door. Light spilled out from small windows in the upper story. The strumming of music came faintly through the walls. There was no mistaking the establishment when all the other buildings in the neighborhood were dark and silent.

He lifted the brass door knocker and struck it once. It knelled through the house and made him tremble. He waited in dread curiosity and wondered just what he would find inside those walls. Nobody answered the door. He raised the bronze knocker and banged it down hard three more times.

After a minute the speaking aperture opened and a black face appeared. "What do you want?" a surly African voice queried him.

"A whore," Isam replied, annoyed by the tone with which he was greeted. His temper, always lively, was on a hair trigger tonight.

With a sigh the black face withdrew and the aperture shut, then the door opened. As the door swung inward, Isam stepped forward. A bronze lamp hung on a long chain from the ceiling two stories above.

An open staircase to the right zigzagged up. The entrance way was tiled in blue, green, black, and white tiles.

The black guard shut the door firmly. He was a large, fat, muscular, burly man with a short nap of kinky hair tight against his skull beneath a red fez. Heavy gold ornaments hung from his ears. "You're late," he told Isam.

"I had business to attend," the agha replied.

"Hrmph. Come this way." The guard—he must be a guard considering his bulk—led him into the courtyard.

A woman was dancing on a small round stage in the center of the courtyard. A drummer and an oud player stood on the pavement near her. The dancer herself was a short, plump woman wearing a bodice decorated with spangles to encase her breasts, but no chemise at all. More spangles decorated the gauzy pantaloons that did nothing to conceal the limbs within. Her arms and belly were entirely bare, and her curvaceous figure writhed and dimpled as she cocked her hips through an insinuating series of twists as her upraised arms formed a long white line to lead the eye upward.

Isam had seen boy dancers in the coffee houses where women were forbidden, but that had not prepared him for the sight of a half-naked woman wriggling lasciviously on stage. Men were sitting cross-legged on the cushions and rugs spread over the bricks of the patio, smoking their hookahs or drinking the forbidden wine as they watched. The young agha stopped dead in his tracks and gawked. The black man left him and went wherever it was that he went. Isam was entirely unaware of his leaving.

A woman dressed in a gauzy pink tunic and pantaloons came up to him with a smile. She was short and plump with generous breasts and full hips. Her long black hair was hardly covered by a gauze veil held in place with a cap of gold coins. She smiled warmly to him and bowed deeply. "Welcome to Paradise, effendi. May I get you something? Hashish, wine, tobacco?"

Isam swallowed hard. "A place to sit and watch the show," he replied. "And some cool water to drink. I came for company, not wine or hashish." He was having difficulty pretending to be a man of worldly accomplishments. He found it unnerving to notice the way her nipples poked against the thin fabric.

Her smile grew warmer. "Of course, effendi. Come this way."

She led him around the edge of the courtyard to an empty carpet and its cushions. He settled down on one of the cushions and couldn't help looking around with big eyes. The house was no bigger than his uncle's house, but how different the interior! The sound of feminine laughter and a door shutting made him look up. A man was leaving one of the rooms upstairs and making his way down the stairs at a languid pace.

The hostess disappeared to be replaced a few minutes later by a rather fat woman in the same sort of see-through clothing. She was old enough to have lines at the corners of her eyes and her breasts were heavy and full within the thin blue garment. She knelt and smiled at him carefully keeping her lips closed over the broken yellow teeth. She placed the tray on the rug beside him, bowed, and poured water from the ceramic pitcher to the cup. "I am Zaytoonah," she murmured in a throaty voice.

Isam nearly bolted. This old hag was being sent to keep him company? "You can call me Ali," he said quickly, absolutely not wanting his name linked with this creature's company.

"Ali Effendi," she said warmly and bowed deeply to him again.

He looked everywhere but at the woman. Now that he was over his initial shock, the place did not seem so inviting. The men in the audience were a rough lot, and the women who waited on them were not especially pretty, although they were all curvaceous. The carpet on which he sat was well worn, and its colors were darkened with age and dirt. The cushion on which he sat had been compressed to little more than a flat square by years of butts seated upon it. The walls of the house were whitewashed stucco, but the whitewash had been applied long ago and was now a grimy tan color. He deeply regretted coming.

Zaytoonah edged closer to him and breathed, "You're a handsome man, Ali."

He ought to have been flattered to be called 'handsome,' but he wasn't. He recoiled. He was afraid the woman might touch him and he didn't think he could stand it if she did. "Don't you have any pretty boys in this place?" he croaked. It was the first thing he could think of that might deter her from moving closer.

Zaytoonah's lip curled in a sneer, then she slapped him. She got up without further words and stalked away. Her heavy flesh jiggled with each stomping footstep and she spoke very harshly to the hostess. The hostess responded by cuffing her across the head. After a few more hot words, Zaytoonah bowed in mock submission and stomped out. Meanwhile the oud continued to strum and the drum to beat. Some of the men turned their heads to watch in amusement. The acrid whiff of hashish floated to his nostrils. Somewhere a dog howled.

Isam had had all he could take. He rose. The hostess was immediately at his side, taking his arm, and pressing her considerably more attractive body against his. She gave him a winning smile and said, "Forgive the old woman, effendi. She is merely a servant, not at all suited to providing company to a man of discernment like you. She was indiscreet. I will keep you company tonight."

Big dark eyes lined with kohl gazed up at him. Long lashes batted. Plump breasts were pressed against his arm and when his fingers wiggled in an attempt to free him, they brushed the crotch of her gauzy pantaloons. She responded by pressing her mound against his hand.

Another man would have been well pleased with developments and happy to let the comely hostess mollify him. Isam was not another man. Ripping free from her embrace, he took two quick steps to the side. "You're too forward, woman!" A few hours earlier he had been suffocating in the cloying femininity of his uncle's house, but now he was desperate to flee back to the embrace of respectable women who knew their place and kept it.

Her eyes hardened, but she forced a smile. "Some wine, effendi? It will soften the night."

"I don't want wine," he replied stubbornly. "I want a boy. Didn't the old hag tell you that?"

Her mouth formed a moue of displeasure. "We don't have any boys. We don't cater to that sort of customer."

Isam drew himself up to his full height, and mustering as much dignity as he could, he said, "Then I'll take my leave." Haughtily he stalked to the door.

"Don't come back!" she snarled after him.

The black guard opened the door for him, and as he passed through, kicked him in the butt and sent him sprawling. Male laughter rang out, abruptly cut off by the slamming of the door.

CHAPTER 8 : SHAKING OFF THE DUST

It was all Maureo's fault, Isam told himself. If it weren't for him and his damn flute, he'd still be asleep on the divan in his uncle house, not humiliated in the street outside a cheap whorehouse. He rubbed his butt and threw angry scowls at the house. Music continued to sound and golden light continued to stream from the upper windows. "Yes, yes!" a feminine voice shrieked, "Oh, Allah, I'm coming!"

"I'm going!" he snarled in the general direction of the open windows, but nobody heard him except for a stray cat who paid him no attention at all.

Unbidden, Gregorio's image rose before him. If it hadn't been for Maureo, he wouldn't have met the lissome male slave, either. How very different from the plump, soft, womanly bodies of the whorehouse! His cousins were forever eating sweets to try and gain the curvy figure so admired by Moorish men, but Halim's money was not unlimited, and it showed in the slender forms of his daughters. Isam had never thought much about his cousins' appearances before, but now that he had something to contrast them with, he thought they came off rather well. No wonder Maureo was after Rabiyah. He would have much rather had Rabiyah sitting down next to him than Zaytoonah. Although he knew he ought not approve, he couldn't help sympathizing with the Moor's suit.

Rabiyah was slim, but she still had female curves, soft flesh, and long lashes to bat against her cheeks. Even so, Isam's memory was filled with the angular cheekbones and thin, firm body of the slave.

He didn't want to go home, but he couldn't stay on the street, either. Still burning with humiliation, he turned his face towards the harbor and set off with swift steps to find the *Seahawk*. He'd sling a hammock and spend the rest of the night on board. Ships he understood. He'd been at sea since his mother died when he was seven years old.

Climbing up the side of the *Seahawk*, he encountered the night watch: just two men, gazing sleepily out at the night. "Hey, wake up!" he told the first man he encountered.

The man startled out of his dozing and looked chagrined. "Isam Agha!" he exclaimed.

"Good thing it was me and not a Spanish raid. Your throat would have been slit."

The man blanched, going white beneath his tan. "Your pardon, agha. I was merely daydreaming."

"Daydream when you're awake tomorrow," Isam snapped at him.

"Peace be upon you, effendi," the man replied in a placating voice.

"Peace be upon you as well, Kamal," the young agha replied, accepting the peace offering. "I'll be in the great cabin if I'm needed."

"Aye aye, sir."

Moonlight gave a soft silver luster to the inside of the empty cabin. Once his father had sat on his divan there, his only child nestled by his side, telling tales of the great corsairs of old. Admiral Khair-ed-din, whom the infidels called 'the pirate Barbarossa' because they wouldn't admit the greatness of his accomplishments. Torgut Rais, who escaped being trapped at Djerba by dragging his galleys over land to the sea. Murad Rais, the Dutch renegade, who had made Sallee great with his bold raids upon Iceland and Ireland. Sometimes, when the little boy begged for them, his father told him tales of the mighty corsair, Hamet Rais Fawad al-Tangueli, the greatest corsair of them all in the eyes of his adoring son.

Isam sighed and bent his head under the beams. He was too tall to stand up straight in his father's cabin, and from that vantage point he could see that his father had not been the giant his boyish heart imagined. Hamet and his brother, Halim, were typical of their kind: petty raiders who made their living preying upon the smaller traffic that wended through the Strait of Gibraltar. When they saw a Spanish frigate, they ran. Their sleek, lateen-rigged craft could escape the larger frigates by beating hard to windward where square-riggers couldn't go.

He leaned his forearms against the beam and bowed his head against them. How could he hope to accomplish what his father never had? What no man of Tanguel had done, no, not since those heady days of yore when all of Christendom trembled to see their golden galleys charging from the blue mist. Once upon a time it had happened that twenty galleys pulled up on an English beach, or so his father had told him. Now there weren't twenty galleys in the whole of Tanguel. Maybe he should go to Zokhara on the Middle Sea. Their eastern relatives could range the whole of the Mediterranean for their prizes even when the Spanish blockaded the strait.

Although he had been loathe to broach the subject with his uncle, Isam's mind was made up. He must shake the dust of Tanguel off his feet. Rajet Rais would teach him navigation. He would humble himself to the man's authority because the *Grey Wolf* was his only hope of getting out of Tanguel. If he wanted to be a bold corsair and raid the infidels from the Canary Islands to Iceland, he must learn to find his way across the trackless ocean. Rajet Rais could teach him. Whatever the man required of him, for good or ill, he would do it.

Taking one last look at the cabin that had belonged to his father, he committed it to memory: small, dim, and dusty. That would be his future unless he took the chance that Rajet Rais offered. He went out on deck and surveyed the *Seahawk* as she sat upon the beach. She was a fine galley, but there, moored to the end of the wharf, was the *Grey Wolf*, bigger, with more sails, and a bristling set of good bronze guns, ready to smite the Nazarenes. He went below, collected up the personal items he had aboard ship, and without any further hesitation, climbed over the side, never to return.

At dawn the sound of the muezzin rang through the streets and Isam presented himself to the *Grey Wolf*, all that he owned bundled into a canvas bag propped on his shoulder. To the bleary-eyed watchman he announced, "Isam bin Hamet, reporting for duty."

CHAPTER 9 : THE CAPTAIN'S TEST

The crew of the *Grey Wolf* came on deck at the sound of the watch crying out, "Come to prayer, come to success! Prayer is better than sleep!" Isam, very full of himself and the bigness of his decision, found himself jostled to the side. Feeling awkward to be caught standing when everyone around him was washing up to pray, he put down his canvas bag, and approaching the nearest bucket of water diffidently asked, "Do you mind if I pray with you?"

The man, small and wizened like a little black monkey, looked up at the tall stranger in surprise. He looked around for the watch, but guessing his query, Isam explained, "I've just signed with the ship. I'm new."

"All right then. Peace be upon you. What's your name?"

"Peace be upon you as well. I'm Isam bin Hamet. You?" He wasn't an agha any more. Losing the title hurt, but he swallowed his pride. He had told Rajet Rais he would serve as an ordinary sailor if that's what it took, and he meant it. The two washed in the bucket of sea water as they chatted.

"Jusepe," his new friend replied. "You're a strapping young man. Ever been to sea before?"

"I've been at sea since I was seven years old," Isam replied proudly. "I'm Hamet Rais' son."

Jusepe had never heard of Hamet Rais. "Why aren't you sailing with your father?"

"He's dead. Maybe I'll sail with him in Paradise, but not in this world."

Jusepe gave him a sympathetic look. "Orphan."

Isam nodded. The two finished their ablutions without further conversation and joined the crew on deck. Isam prayed aloud in a clear baritone and stumbled only twice in the recitations of his prayers. He bowed down, turned, prostrated himself, and raised up again in concert with the rest of the crew. His crew, he realized. He had cast his fate with theirs.

When the prayer was over, a man sang out, "Pass the word for Isam Agha! Captain wants to see him in the cabin."

The message was passed from man to man, and Isam held up his hand, "That's me." He grabbed his canvas bag and made his way aft.

Once again he was admitted to the great cabin of the *Grey Wolf*. Rajet Rais was breaking his fast with two other men. His eyes narrowed as he studied the young man. Isam put his duffel down and bowed deeply with his hand to his forehead. "Peace be upon you and all within this ship."

The two men murmured their replies, "Peace be upon you as well."

"This is the young whippersnapper I was telling you about," Rajet Rais told the other two. "Isam Agha Hamet, son of Hamet Rais, nephew to Halim Rais Many Daughters. This is Haris, my first lieutenant, and Demirkan, my agha." He indicated the Arab and African respectively.

Isam bowed to the men. He hoped it boded well that they were present.

Rajet Rais used his flatbread to scoop up couscous and vegetables from the tray before him. "He wants me to teach him how to navigate," he explained to the others.

The man to Isam's left, Haris, asked, "Do you even know how to read?" He was a compact, wiry, muscular man with a curly, light brown beard. He wore a yellow jacket with short sleeves over a linen shirt with long sleeves.

"I do," Isam replied.

"Make him prove it," the man advised the captain.

"How do you know the captain is even considering him?" the other officer asked. He was burly, thick-necked, and dark-skinned. He had the full lips and flat nose of a man who as at least half African. He wore a red vest over a white shirt.

The man in the yellow jacket waved his flatbread at Isam. "He wouldn't be here if the captain wasn't willing to entertain the proposition."

The black man grunted noncommittally. Both of the subordinates looked to Rajet Rais for further guidance. Rajet took a drink of sweet tea to wash down the couscous before he replied, "I'm considering it. Haris' suggestion is good." Calling out loud, he said, "Bring the Qu'ran." His steward rose from his place in the corner and went to the captain's sea chest. Opening it up, he had to dig to find the requested book; it was apparently not used much.

Isam bowed deeply and received the holy book with both hands. Not a pious man, he still regarded the Qu'ran as a holy thing, even if its mysteries were largely unknown to him. He had his favorite passages; what man didn't? They were passages that served his needs and he had no desire to explore further.

He settled cross-legged on the carpet, opened the book to page one, and peering at the calligraphy, intoned, "In the name of Allah, the Gracious, the Merciful. All praise belongs to Allah, Lord of all the worlds, The Gracious, the Merciful, Master of the Day of Judgment, Thee alone do we worship and Thee alone do we implore for help. Guide us in the right path, The path of those on whom Thou has bestowed Thy blessings, those who have not incurred Thy displeasure, and those who have not gone astray." The sonorous words of the holy text rolled off his tongue and the three men fell silent and stopped eating as they bowed their heads to listen. Suddenly self-conscious, Isam stopped reading and looked up.

After a moment of silence, Rajet Rais said, "You have a good voice. Are you a faithful man, Isam?"

Isam shut the holy book nervously. "As faithful as the next man, I suppose."

"I'm a pragmatic man. I won't have any pious fools telling me how to run my ship or my life," Rajet replied. Glances were exchanged with his officers. "If you want to join my ship, you need to know that."

Isam nodded, "Of course, rais. You are the master of the ship. I will do anything you command."

A ghost of a smile tugged at Rajet's lips. Amused looks were exchanged by the older men. "Will you? Maybe we'd better find out if you really mean that."

The younger man gritted his teeth and wondered if he had let himself in for some sort of humiliating test. "Very well. Command me as you wish. I shall do it."

Rajet grinned sardonically at him. "Very well. Come over here and give me a kiss."

Startled, Isam looked at him, then the other two. Haris smirked at him as he scooped up more couscous. Demirkan just shook his dark head with a bemused look. Neither of them protested the captain's peculiar order.

Rajet Rais sat erect with his hands upon his thighs. "It's a little enough thing. If you can't do it, I have no use for you."

Isam wondered if somehow Rajet had discovered his penchant for the male sex. Had he gotten the truth out of Wadid? Why would he even speak to him? Or was it the opposite, a test to see if he would do the manly thing and scorn such an effeminate order? What was the right response? He was starting to sweat as he stared at Rajet Rais. The man stared back at him. The young man could not read the correct answer in the captain's face.

Isam had been an obedient son to his father and a mostly obedient nephew to his guardian. Although he had high spirits and often got into mischief, he had accepted correction and striven to please the adults who had charge of him. Any boy wished to please his father, and if an orphan, an uncle in his place. He wasn't a boy any longer. He must stand and fall on his own merits and to hell with anyone that didn't like him.

Rising to his feet, he slipped off his sandals, and advancing further onto the rug, circled behind Haris' yellow vest, and coming to the captain's side, knelt down again. Steeling himself to do it, he leaned forward and lightly pressed his lips to Rajet's bearded cheek. Rajet watched him from the corner of his eye. Haris looked away. Demirkan watched thoughtfully. Nobody spoke.

Isam sat back on his heels. Schooling himself to nonchalance, he asked, "Do you have any further orders, rais?"

Rajet Rais shook his head. "That will be all." Shaking off the mood, he gestured to the spot opposite. "Join us for breakfast."

Isam rose and walked slowly back to his spot. All three men and the steward watched him as he settled down as a member of the group. He picked up a piece of flatbread with his right hand, scooped up couscous, and forcing himself to eat, joined the meal. His stomach was in a knot as he waited to see what would happen next.

"Bring the ensign a cup," Rajet ordered. The steward hastily went to a china chest, and opening it, lifted out the top section so that he could reach the cups below. He brought one, knelt beside Isam, and poured tea from the copper kettle.

A smile broke out on Isam's face as he heard himself referred to as 'ensign.' Haris and Demirkan both stirred at that, but it was Haris who asked, "Your pardon, rais, but what are we to do with an extra ensign?"

"We'll train him. He can help wherever he's needed. He won't have a watch of his own. He's an able-bodied man. Put him to work. Haris, take him into your watch."

"Aye aye, sir," Haris replied. He did not look entirely pleased to be appointed as Isam's keeper. His green eyes narrowed as he studied his new acquisition. Isam gave him an equally calculating look in return.

"Do you have your uncle's permission to join my ship?" Rajet asked.

"I don't need his permission. I'm an adult. I make up my own mind. Now that I know I've been accepted aboard, I'll send him a letter."

"Don't burn any bridges you might need later," Rajet warned him.

Isam shrugged. "I'm leaving Tanguel and not coming back. The world is much wider than this little town."

"So it is, young man. Much wider than you can imagine. But you'll see."

Isam grunted in acknowledgment. He was getting tired of being referred to as 'young man.' He was taller than everyone of them. He was certain that in a wrestling match he could beat both Rajet and Haris. Demirkan would be harder, given his greater bulk and strength, but Isam was an excellent wrestler. He was pretty sure he could take him. He would watch for an opportunity to show off his physical prowess. They would learn to respect him.

"We leave with the tide tomorrow morning," Rajet Rais announced.

Surprised, his subordinates looked up at him. "We haven't got all the water aboard," Haris objected.

"We've got enough to cruise through the Pinch. We'll pick up more at Tettiwan."

"As you wish, rais."

"Do you know anything about gunnery, ensign?"

"I do. I'm a good shot," Isam replied.

"That's something at least," muttered Demirkan.

"Ever fired a broadside?" Haris asked.

"No. But I'll learn."

"Train him on the guns first," Rajet told Haris.

"Gunnery training it is." The first lieutenant gave Isam a calculating look. "You'll accompany me after breakfast when I inspect the guns."

The news put the new ensign in a good humor. "Aye aye, sir. I look forward to it."

He was eager to learn something so useful to a corsair. He had served on gun crews aboard the *Seahawk*, so he was sure he would excel and show them his mettle. That it might be triply difficult to coordinate double the number of guns never crossed his mind. Gunnery aboard the *Seahawk* had been a simple affair: point and shoot. If the enemy didn't surrender, run her down and board. If she put up a stiff defense, sheer off and go find something easier.

Pretty soon he would learn that was not how Rajet Rais did things.

CHAPTER 10 : THE DEEP GREEN SEA

Isam was assigned to cry the town along with several other strong voices that were unlikely to get drunk and desert. They called out in the streets and went into the souks, shops, coffeehouses, inns, and brothels to announce the recall of the crew. They scrawled it in chalk at establishments that had slates. Here and there they found a man or two or six, some of whom started immediately back to the ship, but others of whom said they'd be back when they finished whatever entertainment was detaining them.

This mission gave Isam the opportunity to stop by Hosaam's coffee shop to see if Gregorio had left a note for him. He hadn't. He told the shopkeeper to send it to Halim Many Daughters if it came. He wondered if Gregorio would be able to steal the note from his master, but it didn't matter. The *Grey Wolf* was going to sea and he with it. Events on shore were no longer his problem.

The newly minted ensign scarcely looked around him as he hurried back to the ship. Although he was conscious that he might never return to the town that gave him birth, he didn't think he would miss it. Tanguel was tan and dusty and old. Not one of the galleys in her harbor was as large and fine and heavily gunned as the *Grey Wolf*. Although he was not a pious man, embarking on such a large adventure seemed to require due homage to the Lord of the World, so he stopped in the Great Mosque to pray. He couldn't remember the verse he wanted to recite during his prayers. That seemed a bad omen, so he went into the library attached to the mosque, and finding a greybeard there, approached him diffidently.

The man was elderly and thin with a long hooked nose and skin the color of old leather. A long wispy beard lay on his breast. He was well-wrinkled and his eyes were a clouded brown. He wore a pale green turban on his head to denote that he was a descendant of the Prophet, and his robes were white with green trim. He was reading a book, mouthing the words silently to himself. He paid no attention to Isam, but since the young man continued standing there, when he came to the end of his page, he looked up. "Yes?"

"Peace be upon you, sharif," Isam replied with a bow. "I'm sorry to interrupt, but you look like a learned man. I have a question that I am sure will be simple for one such as you to answer."

"What is your name, young man?"

"Isam bin Hamet. Halim of the Many Daughters is my guardian."

The old man nodded his head sagely. "I know him. I am Abdulhamid bin Azim bin Ulfat. I will be pleased to answer a question for your uncle's sake."

"I don't know the Qu'ran very well. I was praying just now and I couldn't remember a verse. Something about a ship plowing the bounty of the waves. Do you know it?"

The old man closed his eyes. In a low nasal voice, he chanted, "And the two seas are not alike: this one palatable, sweet, and pleasant to drink, and the other, salt and bitter. And from each you eat fresh meat, and take forth ornaments which you wear. And thou seest the ships therein plowing the waves that you may seek of His bounty, and that you may be grateful." He opened his eyes. "Is this the verse you mean?"

Isam bowed deeply, "It is, noble father. I wonder if I could trouble you to write it down so that I may learn it by heart."

"It is Sura 35, Al-Fatir, Verse 13, young man. Don't you have a Qu'ran?"

"I do, but I didn't remember where it was."

"Then memorize 35:13, and you will always be able to find it."

Chagrined, Isam bowed. "I will, Father."

"You are going to sea, then?"

"I am. I have signed on as an ensign with the *Grey Wolf.*"

The old man regarded him soberly. "Read the Qur'ran every day, young man. Even if you can't pray, Allah will keep you safe."

Isam bowed again. "I will, Father," he replied in perfect insincerity. "I thank you for your good advice." He backed away and made his exit. Softly reciting, "thirty-five thirteen" to himself so he wouldn't forget it, made his way back to the ship. Going below to his berth, he got out his Qu'ran, turned the corner down, and put it back without reading. Thus did he satisfy himself on matters of piety.

The day of departure dawned cool and fair with an easy breeze blowing on shore from the ocean. Rajet Rais called the crew on deck to address them. Standing at the rail of the quarterdeck, he looked down at them. He was flanked by his officers, all of whom were taller than he was, yet there was no doubt which one was the captain. He folded his arms over his chest as he regarded them. Isam stood on the main deck with Lieutenant Haris' watch.

"We are going to sea today. It's a fair wind and will carry us to the Strait of Gibraltar. We'll run through by night and hope we don't meet a Spanish patrol. We've done it before. Once night falls we'll be running dark and silent. Any man who shows a light or makes a sound will be caned once we're safe on the other side." This was not news to anyone but Isam, but he thought it fair enough.

Rajet Rais continued, "We have a new ensign, a supernumerary ensign, Isam bin Hamet."

He pointed out Isam where he stood. Isam straightened up and folded his arms over his chest to look imposing. He had a dark blue jacket over a white linen shirt and light blue wool pantaloons, a red fez over his short-cropped hair, and a scimitar through a dark red sash. The crew turned their heads to take him in.

"Obey him as you obey your regular officers, but teach him whatever he needs to know."

Isam scowled. He was positive they would not have anything to teach him, aside from navigation.

"That is all. Dismissed." Turning to Haris, the captain said, "Make ready to weigh anchor."

"Aye aye, sir." Turning to the deck Haris shouted, "All hands make ready to weigh anchor!"

Isam had no assigned duty, so he was put on the capstan with fifteen other men. He didn't protest, but put his chest to the capstan bar, cradled it in his arms, and braced his legs. When the command came, he put his back into it. The capstan creaked as the line drew taut and the wood began to take the strain. It felt good to exert himself. He raised his sandaled feet up high to step over the anchor cable as he came around and kept marching. The man tending the pawl crouched under the bars and used a mallet to beat the line on the capstan when it attempted to crawl over itself. After a few minutes, "Pawl the capstan!" was heard, and the sailor used his mallet to knock the pawl into the notch. "Capstan is pawled!" he bawled back.

The men on the capstan waited as the foredeck crew did their part to secure the anchor. After a few minutes came the command, "Stand down the capstan!" Isam straightened up and stretched his back. The harbor of Tanguel was not deep; it had not taken long to get the anchor up. The ship was drifting on the tide. Looking to shore, he picked a landmark and saw it slowly, very slowly, recede. Rajet Rais had timed it perfectly; the tide was ebbing. As it ran out it would take the ship with it, still on the flood, and over the sandbar in the mouth of the harbor.

Having no particular duty to attend, he went to the foredeck and stood at the rembate. Swivel guns were mounted there to clear the way when the prow was used as a boarding bridge. He petted one because it was so much smaller than the guns mounted at the rembate on the *Seahawk*. It felt like a toy, but the *Grey Wolf* had twenty guns mounted in broadside that more than doubled the weight of his old vessel's ordinance. The soft breeze blew against his face and the water murmured as the cutwater split it and sent it flowing along the sides. He looked down into the deep green waters and wondered what new port would become his home. For a moment he was homesick, and he hadn't even left.

"Out oars," came the next command. The crew passed out the sweeps, then put them out through the oar ports, and standing between the guns, awaited the next command.

"Oars, make way together!" The drum beat a long slow cadence and the oars rose, dipped, and caught water. A thrill ran through Isam's heart. He was going to sea! His great adventure was beginning!

The xebec rowed between the headlands with a stately, gliding grace. Outside, they turned north. A few feet in front of him the pilot called out his commands; the shoals outside Tanguel were tricky. After two miles they cleared the obstacles. A boat that had followed them came alongside and received the pilot. The boat dropped away and sailed back into the harbor. They were on their own.

A little before noon he was called to the quarterdeck. Rajet Rais was there, dressed as usual in black with a short coat, turban, and maroon fez. He had a brass sextant in his hand, and he asked, "Do you know how to shoot the sun?"

Isam shook his head. "No, I don't." He eyed the instrument in anticipation of a mystery being revealed.

Rajet held up the instrument. "You look through the spyglass here and line it up with the horizon. Then you adjust the index, this movable arm, until the image of the sun reflected through the glass lines up with it." He demonstrated. "Since the ship is bobbing on the sea, you must be careful in your choice of making the reading, and you must make a habit of choosing the same spot in the ship's motion every day. If you have a heavy swell, the distance the ship is above or below your usual sighting will introduce an error into your calculation. You must also be certain of your noon. If you shoot too soon or too late, that introduces more errors. We have a few minutes before noon, so practice lining up the horizon. You must keep the sextant steady."

Rajet undid the adjustment he had made with the index arm and handed the instrument to Isam. The ensign took it, and lining it up, discovered that keeping it trained on the horizon was difficult. The swell was mild, only three or four feet. He moved the index arm, but overshot his intended position.

Rajet watched with a smile on his lips. "Some men never get the knack of it," he remarked.

Isam gritted his teeth and muttered, "I will get it." Again he fiddled with the index arm, but failed to capture his intended reading.

Rajet reached over and tapped a small knob. "This is the micrometer. Use it to make fine adjustments."

"You could have told me before," Isam glowered. He tried again to capture the horizon. This time he used the micrometer to adjust. Watching the horizon, he chose a position he thought represented the ship at rest on a placid sea. He watched through several bobs of the ship, then lowered it and showed it to Rajet.

Rajet bent his head to examine the reading on the scale at the bottom. "Yes, very good. Close enough for a beginner. Now read the angle on the scale."

Isam bent his head to peer at the markings. "Fifty-seven," he said.

Rajet Rais paused to look up at the sun overhead, then looked down at the deck to note the shadow at his feet. "I call noon," he said.

The captain raised up the instrument and took his own reading. He required only one pass to make his adjustment. Satisfied that he had captured it, lowered the instrument. His reading differed only by a degree from Isam's. "If the sun were directly above the equator, this would be our latitude. Do you know why?"

Isam tried to imagine the geometry. "It has something to do with the angle?" he hazarded.

"Yes. Latitude is how many degrees north or south of the equator something is. If the sun were at the equator, this angle would correspond to latitude. However, the sun is only directly over the equator on the equinoxes. The difference between the sun and the equator is the declination. We must use a book containing angles of declination for every minute of the year to correct our reading."

"What sort of book?"

"I'll show you. Come to the cabin with me and I'll teach you how to work the calculations."

Entering the cabin, the two left their footwear on the floor and settled on the divan. Rajet used a slate, chalk, and book to show Isam how to reckon their latitude. The younger man leaned in close so he could peer at the slate as the captain was writing. Unseen by the youth, a smile flitted across Rajet's face. Isam was intent on the mathematics and didn't notice.

"Oh, so you must subtract the angle you shot from ninety?" the ensign asked.

"Yes. Then apply the declination adjustment. Since it's March, we are very near to the equinox. Little adjustment is needed. Since we are navigating by seamarks, we don't need to bother shooting the sun, but it will be good practice because you can check yourself against the coast. You'll shoot the sun every day. You may borrow my sextant until you purchase one of your own."

Isam sat up straight and beamed. "Thank you, sir!"

"Now make your own calculations from the number you shot."

Taking the chalk in his left hand, Isam worked it out. Their answers differed slightly. He frowned.

"Accuracy matters, but there are always discrepancies," Rajet explained. "The captain must decide which reading to trust." He took the sextant and changed the position of the index arm. "It is July 14. What is our latitude?" He handed the instrument to the younger man.

Isam used his handkerchief to wipe the slate clean, scribbled his calculations for the latitude, looked up the declination, and made his calculation.

Rajet checked his work. "Very good." He adjusted the angle again. "It is December 31. Where are we?" Isam settled into the problem with a happy smile. After several more problems, Rajet said, "That's well. You've caught on quickly. You have a head for mathematics."

"Thank you, sir!" He was proud of his accomplishment and beamed.

"You can also use the North Star." Rajet adjusted the index arm again. "It's September 15 and you have just shot the North Star. Where are we?"

Isam subtracted the angle of the scale from ninety degrees, and Rajet laughed through his teeth. "Caught you."

"What?" the younger man asked in bewilderment.

"We subtract when shooting the sun. We are not shooting the sun. The North Star is at the opposite end of the scale."

Chagrined, Isam erased his work and calculated again. He had white chalk dust all over his blue jacket and tan hands. "The mathematics are simple enough," Isam commented.

"For this, yes. Learning to detect noon and take a consistent shot is the hard part. You must practice every day," the captain replied.

"I will, sir." Isam smiled, feeling pleased with himself and his instructor.

Rajet Rais patted him on the back. "Enough for today." He moved away.

Isam laid down his slate and rose. "Thank you, rais. You won't regret taking me on. I promise."

The captain waved him away. "You've started well," he replied in a neutral tone, but there was a faint smile on his lips.

CHAPTER 11 : THE RACE FOR CAPE SPARTEL

A warm, strong breeze rose out of the south-southwest and the *Grey Wolf* took it on the beam, sailing northwest to claw off the coast of Africa, putting miles of lee between herself and the shore. The day was bright and chilly and the *Grey Wolf* rocked and rolled over the long swells. They had gained twenty miles off the shore and were half way to Cape Spartel when the lookout sang out, "Deck ho! A sail!"

"Where away?" Rajet Rais called up.

"Fine on the port bow. I can see her tops'ls. Square."

Rajet swore a vile oath in Turkish. "Helm, due north."

"Due north, aye," the helmsman replied and brought the tiller around to the new position. Now the *Grey Wolf* was running parallel to the coast of Africa hidden below the eastern horizon.

In a mood to be instructive, Rajet asked, "Do you know why I did that?"

Isam promptly replied, "To avoid an infidel ship."

"Any idiot can see that. Why this course?"

Isam had to work it out. "With the wind out of the southwest, you're running on your best point of sail."

Rajet said to the other ensign, "Toss the log."

"Toss the log, aye," the young man replied. He had the red hair and long nose of a Greek beneath his turban. The chip log went over and the seconds were counted out. "Nine knots, rais."

Rajet grunted. "Shake out the reefs."

Hands shinnied up the antennas to loose the knittles. The folds of the large sails fell out and they caught even more wind.

While they were doing that, Rajet Rais replied, "Just so. The infidel will have the wind on her beam, which is not the best point of sail for a square-rigger. Why didn't I run south to take shelter in Tanguel?"

"Because you're going to Tettiwan."

"All destinations are optional, ensign. Survival is always the first requirement. Think again."

The *Grey Wolf* gained speed as the full extent of her massive canvas was loosed. She heeled gently and threw spray all the way to the quarterdeck. The rolling swells rocked her more than rolling her, and the pitching motion grew more intense. The sailors automatically bent their knees to flex with the movements of the deck beneath them.

Isam furrowed his brow.

"Not seasick, are you?" Rajet asked.

"Hmm? No. Not at all. I'm thinking."

"You look a little green."

"I'm not seasick!" Isam insisted. He frowned in concentration, then held up his hands in front of him to represent wind and ship positions as he tried to work out Rajet's reasoning. "I don't know. If you ran south, the square-rigger would be pressing close to the wind, if she could make it at all. You can point sharper into the wind than she can; you'd have the advantage. You could make it to Tanguel."

"No. Because I have been watching the wind all morning and I have noticed it is backing south. I assume it will continue backing south, which means I will have to sail straight into it before I reach Tanguel. Therefore, it appears I'd have to beat my way against the wind to make Tanguel, if I can reach it at all. Meanwhile, the infidel will be closing with me. He'll have to beat too, but he has the weather gauge of me. I maneuver better, but he has more room, and I am in danger of a lee shore. If I give up and try running north at that point, he is on his best point of sail."

Isam listened carefully to this reasoning. "Are you sure it will keep backing to the south?" he asked.

Rajet gave him an amused look. "Yes. Experience tells me so. Therefore, I run north while I have the room and my best point of sail, stretching myself as hard and fast as I can. That means I'm committed to running the Strait of Gibraltar, but the current will aid me. The wind may be due south or even a little east at that point, but that is to my advantage. I can point higher into the wind than he can. I expect a tight race around Cape Spartel, then to lose him in the Pinch."

"What if the wind backs all the way east?" Isam asked, feeling dubious about this plan.

"I beat my way through. I point higher, so I make fewer tacks than he does. He falls behind. If the wind holds, we make the Pinch after dark and have the cover of darkness to help us through. What phase is the moon?"

Isam had recently been running around during the night, but the moon had been the least of his concerns. He squinted in an effort to remember. "Dark?"

Rajet said, "Correct. He'll be close by nightfall, but we'll lose him in the dark. He'll probably guess we're making for the Pinch, follow us, and hope he gets lucky. We'll run silently and be through by dawn. Let this be a lesson to you. You must always be aware of the wind, the sea, and the sky. You must plan ahead. You must know well in advance what you're going to do, otherwise you will be at the mercy of men who think more than you do. A thinking man commands other men, including his enemies."

"What if you're wrong? What if the wind veers westerly?"

"It'll be a tighter race. That is also something I give my attention to. If my plan fails, what is my second choice? What is my escape route? Always have three plans, then you will not be at a loss when fate turns against you."

Isam gave the wind anxious attention. He fancied the wind was fluttering a bit to the west, but maybe it was his own imagination.

Rajet remained placid. He shook his head as he watched the young ensign fretting. "Whatever it is, worrying never helps. You make your best choice, then you live with it. Don't second guess yourself, or you'll never make a decision. Whatever you decide, stick with it until you have good reason to do otherwise. A bad plan has a better chance of success than dithering."

Isam nodded. He understood the advice, but it was hard not to fret all the same. He paced to the larboard side of the quarterdeck and stared out at the horizon. A crisp white pyramid was now visible above the swells. That made her about twenty miles distant. "Here she comes," he said.

Rajet walked over and watched. He nodded. "Toss the log."

Twenty-eight seconds after the splash, the red-haired ensign replied, "Ten knots and a quarter, sir."

"Lace on the bonnets."

Halim Rais was not a man who had ever bothered with the bonnets. But then, Halim was not the sort of man who would pit himself in a race against a square-rigger. He would have turned tail and run for Tanguel. If Allah was with him, the wind would hold and he'd make his harbor. Rajet Rais was made of different metal. It frightened and excited Isam. Mostly, it exhilarated him. At her very best the *Seahawk* could make twelve knots, but Halim Rais never pushed her so hard. They were already making as much speed as Halim Rais ever had. Meanwhile, the sailors laced the bonnets to the bottom of the sails, and with the greater expanse of canvas, the ship heeled further. She sent up mighty sprays of spume as she slammed through the waters.

Rajet Rais commented, "More sail does not always equal more speed. She's pressing her head down too much. I'll have the bonnet off the foresail."

The men had just finished putting the bonnet on. With a grumble, they gave the lacing a pull, and it unraveled like a bit of Tunisian lace when a grandmother has made a mistake and must undo the work.

Rajet grunted. "Better. Toss the log."

Again the log went over. "Eleven knots."

Rajet considered. "If that's a frigate, she can probably better eleven knots. Jettison the food."

Ordinarily the great antennas would serve double duty as winches, but not now. Instead lines were rigged to the gallows on deck that were used to store the antennas, and the jury rig was used to haul the casks on deck. The barrels were tipped on their sides and rolled over to the gunwale. Men straddled the rail like horsemen and used a parbuckle to pull the barrels up a ramp made of boards. They sent the first cask overboard with a mighty splash, then let down their lines to receive the next barrel heaved out of the darkness of the hold.

"Halim Rais would never sacrifice his foodstuffs," Isam commented.

"We can get more in Tettiwan. We might be hungry by the time we get there, but we won't be chained to a Spanish oar. The time to jettison is early, not late. A quarter knot in speed multiplied over a hundred miles will matter. A quarter knot multiplied over one mile won't mean much."

Isam did the calculation in his head. "I see," he said thoughtfully.

Rajet waved a hand. "This is what will decide the race, not what happens eight hours from now. Victory doesn't go to the man with the longest gun. It goes to the man with the longest head."

Halim had not been a thinking captain and Isam had not been a thinking sailor. He stared out at the pyramid of canvas, then held up his left thumb to gauge its size. It did not appear any larger in comparison to his thumb, so he said, "She's not gaining on us."

Rajet nodded. "She's not. But it's close. Start the water. Keep one ton."

Down below the sailors' faces were woeful as they broke open the casks and the water poured into the bilge. They manned the pumps and sent it splashing over the side. They could tighten their belts and go hungry a day or two, but to go without water was to court a painful death.

"Tell the boatswain to shift weight aft," Rajet said.

Haris passed the word, but his voice was drowned out by a sudden thunder of sail as she luffed. A moment later the gust settled and she continued as she was.

Rajet swore. "That was a westerly gust. Damned untrustworthy wind." His previously placid expression grew grim. "Helm, give me a point west."

"One point west, aye," the tiller replied.

Clawing further off the coast would bring him closer to the stranger, but if the wind shifted west, he was going to want sea room between him and the rocky shore of Africa.

Rajet explained, "The real enemy is not the infidel, but the shore. If we fight him, we might win. The shore we cannot fight."

Isam kept his ears perked, but Rajet said nothing further. The grim set of his mouth was message enough. Isam stared out at the strange vessel, but Rajet paid as much attention to the eastern horizon as to the stranger. He checked the sky and sea, then studied his vessel and his crew. Isam had mixed feelings about signing on with Rajet Rais. He had grown tired of Halim's cautious ways, but now that he had left, he was afraid he might have made a mistake. He didn't know Rajet Rais well enough to have confidence in him. All he could do was wait, worry, and wonder.

Chapter 12 : Embayed

The stranger was trying to intercept them. Their two courses formed the long sides of an acute triangle. The wind shifted a little east, then back west, then settled in to blow from the southwest. When the wind shifted to the west, the stranger gained on them. The gain was barely perceptible, but it was a gain. When the wind shifted back east, she lost. Once again the wind shifted west, and the stranger gained on them.

Isam mused over events. If Halim Rais had been captain, he would have run back to Tanguel and that would have been the right thing to do, but it would have been pure luck. Nine times out of ten, Rajet would have been right: the wind would have continued to back, growing more and more easterly. Nine times out of ten, Halim would have been wrong. It was only in the current circumstance when the wind did something strange that Rajet was wrong. For that matter, Rajet had been right to jettison cargo sooner rather than later. As modest as the speed gain was, it might be the difference between escape and capture. Halim would not have abandoned his supplies until the last minute, and by then it would have been too late. Isam was none too happy to be aboard when Rajet was proved wrong, but he would have been even less happy to be aboard when Halim was proved wrong. Rajet Rais was a short man, but he was head and shoulders above Halim Rais in seamanship.

The helmsman leaned his hip against the tiller to use his body weight to steady it against the increasing breeze.

"You were wrong about the wind," Isam said.

Rajet Rais glowered at him. "Yes. I was wrong. Allah has ways of keeping a man humble," he snapped.

"We should have run for Tanguel."

"It's too late now. We're committed to Cape Spartel. Shut up about it."

"Sorry."

"I said shut up about it!" Rajet snarled.

Isam scowled and shut up. Rajet might be the better seaman, but he preferred Halim's avuncular style of leadership.

"Toss the log," Rajet snapped.

Again the log went over. "Eleven knots." The ship was heeling further, but the shifting of weight below had eased the pounding. She was still throwing up great shining arcs of water that sparkled in the sunlight, but she wasn't thumping the sea as hard as she had been. A gust heeled her over and they all grabbed for handholds and braced their legs.

"String life lines," Rajet said.

Haris said, "Don't you think we should reduce sail, rais? It's starting to get rough."

"Not yet. String life lines."

"Life lines, aye," Haris replied reluctantly.

The men strung lines up and down the length of the deck so that they had something to hang onto as the ship heeled and the deck became wet and slippery. Men donned foul weather gear: oiled haiks with the hoods up over their heads. "You should get your foul weather gear," Rajet told him. "Tell Ilidio to bring me mine."

"Foul weather gear, aye," Isam replied.

He trudged below, passed the word for the captain's steward, then rooted in his duffel and came up with an oiled brown haik. He doffed his fez for fear of losing it in the wind and wrapped a turban around his head with a long tail dangling to his shoulder. The turban was effectively tied to his head and would stay put even if he were knocked heels over teakettle. When he returned, Rajet Rais was wearing a long white oiled burnoose with the hood up over his turban. Another spray of water flew the length of the ship to splatter the quarterdeck. The ship bucked beneath their feet, then the wind shifted a bit east and stayed that way for an hour. They gained perceptibly on the stranger. She was too far away to make out her form, but the fact that she was pacing them so well suggested a frigate.

The afternoon wore on. Again the wind shifted west. At first it was a fitful shift, then it was stronger and steadier. The line of the coast of Africa appeared on their lee. Rajet swore in Turkish. "Helm two points west."

He must claw off, or he would be trapped against the coast of Africa before making Cape Spartel. The vicinity of the cape was lined with rocks and crags with the hills of Spartel rising above them, and beyond that, the smoky blue peaks of the Atlas Mountains. It was an inhospitable country until they turned the corner into the Strait of Gibraltar, but the only harbors in the Strait belonged to Spain. She held both Tanger and Sebta. If they were wrecked, no help would come for them. Only their enemies.

The frigate—there could be no doubt she was a frigate now—was gaining on them again. She had fallen behind during the backing of the wind, but as the wind shifted more and more towards her stern, she sailed stronger and faster. She was determined to catch them.

Rajet stared through his glass at her. "She has her stuns'ls out," he remarked. "She can't make any more speed." Neither could the *Grey Wolf.* "It's a contest of nerves now. Who will reduce sail first in the rising wind?"

The distance between the vessels decreased. They passed several small towns on the African coast near enough to see the plumes of smoke that rose from their dinner fires. Although they had harbors, they were too shallow to accommodate the *Grey Wolf.* They possessed neither fortress nor militia to defend her even if they did take shelter. Tanguel was the first substantial friendly harbor on the Sallee coast, and they had left it far behind.

The thunder of breakers sounded in the distance. Borrowing the spyglass, Isam could see the white gleam of foam made brilliant by the long rays of the westering sun. Halim liked to cruise the Western Sea outside the Strait of Gibraltar, so he was careful to avoid them. In fact, Halim liked to make his course a hundred miles offshore to be sure of it. That had been Rajet's intention too, before he was intercepted by the frigate.

"Any colors yet?" Haris asked.

"Not yet. She'll keep us in suspense until the end."

"Should we fly Spanish colors?" the lieutenant asked

"Not yet. Isam, how's your Spanish?"

"Not good. I speak a few words of the morisco dialect, that's all."

Rajet grunted an acknowledgment, then swung his glass to study the rocks looming ever larger on the shore. He swung his glass back to the frigate a few miles distant. "We're close."

Again the *Grey Wolf* heeled, harder and deeper. The wind roared in the rigging and whipped the tail of Isam's turban so that it lashed his cheeks. That hurt his injured nose, so he pulled it across his face and secured it on the other side, turning the tail into a veil. The cloth was soon damp with sea spray.

"So close," murmured Haris.

The crew was tense and silent. They all knew the danger. The *Grey Wolf* was fast. "She'll make it, you'll see. She'll squirt right between the rocks and the frigate. They'll cross our wake," one of the sailors on the quarterdeck said.

"And give us a hearty kick in the butt when she does," somebody muttered in response. "She's a two-decker."

The breakers roared louder. Still the wind pressed them to the lee. Individual plumes of spray could be seen as the waves crashed on the rocks in a foamy thunder. The bulk of Cape Spartel loomed above them. Its normally dark sides were lit up by the setting sun, but the glorious sight didn't gladden their hearts. Not when the rocks at the base were equally well illuminated. Hissing white foam swirled in the sea a hundred yards away from the visible rocks in warning of reefs beneath the surface.

The wind shifted further west.

The helmsman leaned his whole body weight against the tiller, but it wasn't enough. "I need help, rais! She has a bone in her teeth!"

Isam had spent hour upon hour watching and waiting; now there was something useful he could do. He flung his own weight against the tiller, and the two of them wrestled it.

Rajet snarled, "We're not going to clear the rocks."

The western wind was driving them ever closer to the shore. The momentary delay in making the helm mind had cost them. Both the tillerman and Isam braced hard to keep it in position.

"Helm, hard left!" Rajet snarled.

Isam and the helmsman strained their bodies. "Need more help!" the helmsman panted. Haris threw himself onto the tiller and the three of them labored to press her over.

Suddenly a loud snap sounded and all three plunged to the deck. The broken stump of the tiller swung over them. Rajet tackled it, but he had scant leverage. It dragged him across the deck. "Tiller replacement!" he roared. The stump beat him off and he stumbled away.

Without the guidance of her tiller, the *Grey Wolf* swung headfirst into the wind. Unlike infidel vessels, it was the nature of Arab vessels to turn into the wind when unattended. Leeway shoved her stern backwards towards the rocks.

"Let sheets and tacks fly! Out both bowers!" Rajet roared.

All hands scrambled. Isam leaped for the mizzen sheet. The sails were loosed and spilled their wind. They flapped loudly and their lines danced across the deck. The violent rearward career slowed, but the wind and tide were still carrying her towards the rocks. Both bower anchors splashed into the sea. She rode out her scope but still drifted shoreward. Both anchors scraped across the hard bottom without finding purchase.

The replacement tiller arrived. The pins were drawn out of the old one and the new one put in place. Rajet looked back over the stern towards the looming rocks. "Helm hard to larboard!"

The helmsman scrambled to his place. With the ship facing into the wind, his task was not as difficult as it had been. He put his body into it and the tiller answered. The ship's sternway began to curve towards the north and away from the nearest rocks, but she was well inside the foamy, swirling, white waters. They all held their breaths, but the swirls were eddies reacting to the rocks on either side, not shoals beneath their keel. Allah knew it was shallow enough even so.

"Hands to the sweeps!" Rajet howled. "Isam, tell the carpenter to get the lead out!"

The crew ignored the lines slapping across the deck to run out the oars and lean on them. Isam ran belowdecks to the carpenter supervising the pumps, delivered the message, then ran back up two flights of ladders. He hardly noticed the exertion thanks to the agitation he was experiencing. Meanwhile, the carpenter and his mates brought up the heavy leads and sent them over the side.

"Four fathoms less a quarter with this line! Sandy bottom!" came the cry of the first leadsman.

"Helm amidships," Rajet snapped.

"Midships, aye," the helmsman replied.

Suddenly a jerk transmitted itself through one of the anchor cables as the line came taut. Rajet swiftly checked his bearings. "She's holding!" he crowed.

A cheer went up. The *Grey Wolf* was between two files of rocks that were about a hundred yards apart. The rocks gradually came together at the eastern end of a small cove. The southern file of rocks was separated from the shore by only a few yards of water, but with the wind-driven sea boiling around them, it was impossible to reach the shore. They were trapped in Cape Spartel's stony jaws. The slightest change in their situation would chew them up.

"Three fathoms, sand and mud with this line," called the starboard leadsman.

The thunder of the Spanish frigate drowned out the call. She fired her bow guns as she ran right at them, then dropped her anchor and brought her broadside to bear, her stern swinging north. She pummeled them at a distance of less than a hundred yards. Her fire was accurate. Splinters flew and men screamed.

"In oars! Load and fire when ready! Rig preventers! Marksmen aloft!" Rajet shouted.

The Spanish ship with her red and gold ensign streaming in the wind was a majestic sight. She heeled hard to the larboard. Water sloshed in her lower gun ports and they were swiftly shut and dogged tight. Only twelve of her guns were able to fire. Even so, she still threw double their weight of metal. Had she been able to open both decks, she would have quadrupled them.

"Trapped like eels in a basket," Haris moaned.

"Shut up! I'm thinking!" Rajet snapped back. "Isam! How good a swimmer are you?"

Surprised, the ensign replied. "I'm a very good swimmer. Why?"

"Do you think you could swim to that frigate and cut her cables?"

Isam contemplated the Spaniards loading another broadside in a malicious fury. "If they don't shoot me, yes. But they'll definitely shoot me."

"No, they won't. I have a plan." When they heard it, they looked at him in amazement. "Can you do it?" Rajet asked the younger man.

Isam chewed his lip, saw the Spanish running out the next broadside, and said, "Do we have a choice? Yes, I'll do it."

He hurried below to find what he would need. The sheep's bladders were found in the kitchen offal, and when he explained what was wanted, the cook went to work to provide the stoppers he required. While that was happening, he got some sacks and put cannonballs in each. He stripped to his drawers, tied a sturdy piece of rope tight around his middle and hung the sacks from his waist with slippery knots. Two more broadsides pummeled the *Grey Wolf* before he was fully equipped.

CHAPTER 13 : CUTTING THE ANCHOR

Isam clambered over the side, took a deep breath of air, and let himself go under. The coldness of the water was a shock as painful as a blow. He shivered, but there was no choice. He must stand it, or the *Grey Wolf* would be destroyed. He blew out his breath, removed the wooden pin from the cork in the sheep's bladder, lost some air before he got his mouth over it, and took a small breath. Yes. It would work. He kept his tongue over the hole while he maneuvered the plug back into place, then shoved it in tight. Bubbles surged past the plug, then stopped.

The water was very shallow as he swam and walked along the bottom. The bulk of the *Grey Wolf* was sometimes overhead, and sometimes about knee level, depending on the action of the waves. He moved away from her as fast as he could; he didn't want to be smashed. The bottom was uneven with rocks, patches of sand, and holes. He took sips of air as he needed them. The cannonballs kept him under the water in spite of the buoyancy of the air bladders. The bladders floated up around his face, but they held. He couldn't see much because the water was a frothy mix of sediment and foam, but the declining sun sent a golden streak of light across the surface above him. He followed the golden path towards a dark splotch.

How long did it take him? A minute? Twenty? Sixty? He had no idea. It was incredibly difficult to move against the cold sea. He began to fear he wouldn't be able to breast the tide after all. When he fell into an underwater ravine he discovered that the waves descended as low below the surface as they did above it, so if he kept below that level, the water was a good deal less agitated. With that knowledge, he crawled and stumbled along the bottom, but his second bladder ran out. He had to switch to the third. He despaired of ever reaching his target, but if he failed, the *Grey Wolf* would be blown to smithereens.

Suddenly, a dark bulk loomed in the water before him. The frigate! Long strands of seaweed trailed from its bottom. He was pleased that he had never belonged to a vessel with such a foul bottom. That made her race against the *Grey Wolf* even more impressive. There was enough growth on her bottom to have cost her a full knot in speed. She was a large, fast, deep-breasted frigate with an aggressive captain. The *Grey Wolf* was at a distinct disadvantage.

Immensely cheered by the sight of his target, he jettisoned the cannonballs and came up right under her stern. His head broached water, but nobody could see him; the ship's own bulk hid him. He sucked in fresh air in gratitude and said, "Allah! I will be more faithful in my prayers if I survive this."

A cannonball went whizzing past not ten feet away. The *Grey Wolf* was still fighting back. How horrible would it be if his mission was cut short by a shot from his own ship! He studied the scene carefully. The cable for the stern anchor entered the water about thirty feet away. At that point he would be seen from the quarterdeck if anybody was watching. He took a deep gulp of air, dove down, and swam hard. The waves pushed him sideways, so he swam below their level. Once below the turbulence, he swam towards where he guessed the anchor to be. He had to use more air from his third bladder before he found it. When he did, he wrapped an arm and a leg around the cable. His knife hung from a lanyard around his neck. He swiftly unsheathed it and sawed at the thick cable.

He needed more air. He sawed harder. He was making progress; he just had to hold out a little longer. He sawed and sawed and another strand of cable parted. No good. He had to breathe. He paused to help himself to more air, then resumed sawing at the cable. Suddenly it parted and the severed end went swishing past his face. The ship immediately began to drift downstream of her bow anchor. That meant her guns couldn't bear on the *Grey Wolf*. A cheer went up from the corsairs, but he couldn't hear it. On the frigate somebody was shouting, "The hawse has parted!" but he couldn't hear that either.

He used the rest of the air in the third bladder and discarded it. Looking up, he swam toward the shadow of the ship in the water. The *Grey Wolf* pummeled her viciously. Shots plunged into the water and formed columns of wild ripples followed by clouds of mud as they struck the sea bottom. He swam over until he found the frigate's red hull, but the tide was pushing him along her side. He grabbed the weeds trailing from her bottom and used them to haul himself forward. He gained her bow, came up for air, and caught hold of her cutwater. Once again the ship herself hid him from the watch. The figurehead of a monk in brown robes held a chalice above his head, but the saint's wooden eyes were tilted up to Heaven, so he didn't see the young corsair either. Isam puzzled over the Latin script but he couldn't make out that her name was *San Juan de Sahagún*.

He tried to think what to do next while hanging onto the slippery wet wood of the cutwater. Having lost one anchor, they must be very alert to watch the remaining anchor. About eighty feet of line as taut as a virgin's hymen ran between the ship and where the cable disappeared into the water. Taking a deep breath, he let go of the cutwater and dove down below the waves.

Looking up, he could see the cable limned against the golden light. He turned onto his back and slogged hard through the water. It wasn't far, but he had to fight the rising tide. Arriving, he took a breath from the last sheep's bladder. Then, hanging onto the line, he sawed at it.

He was only half way through when the line parted. The severed end slapped him in the face like a hemp cannonball. He opened his mouth in surprise. He lost his air, tasted salt water and blood, and shut his mouth. He jerked the bladder up and gave himself more air, but the blow to his face hurt so much he could hardly breathe. Bubbles frothed out of the bladder and blood dribbled down the back of his throat. He felt like a mule had kicked him right between the eyes. He was so dizzy he didn't know where he was or which way was up.

His air was gone and the bladder empty. He had to surface. He twisted around frantically in search of the golden light. When he found it, he swam for it. He came up, treaded water and gasped for breath. He coughed up blood and was afraid he'd lost teeth, but running his tongue over them, found them all intact. The same could not be said of his nose.

Meanwhile, the frigate was drifting stern first towards the *Grey Wolf*—collision was imminent. Unable to do anything more than he had done, he watched as the *Grey Wolf* slipped her stern cable. She had rigged it so that she could bring her broadside to bear. Bereft of the second anchor, she streamed away from her bower. The Spanish frigate drifted past her and the *Grey Wolf* peppered her with shot. Three of her guns replied, but most of her hands were too busy trying to save her from the rocks to reload.

The frigate dropped her second best bower, but it dragged across the bottom before catching. Something thumped and Isam felt a faint shock through the water. The waves lifted the frigate, then thumped her down again, harder and louder. A crack like lightning sounded loud in the cove in spite of the hissing thunder of the breakers. A wave lifted her once more, there was a long scraping noise, and she drifted further astern. Then she came to rest on rocks, canted over, and lay with her bowsprit parallel to the water with her stern cocked up high.

The *Grey Wolf* fired on her. The frigate's list was too severe to be able to respond; her lower gun ports were underwater. So were a few of her upper gun ports. The unflooded guns pointed down into the sea due to her cockeyed position. The Spanish attempted to launch their boats, but the first one was seized by the sea, driven backwards, and smashed against the rocks. Men tumbled into the foamy maelstrom and were lost to view.

The *Grey Wolf* was only half a cable's length away from the Spanish frigate and very aware of the doom she would share if her anchor didn't hold. She set her last anchor while her marksmen sniped at the men exposed on the deck of the Spanish frigate. The flag of Spain came down and a white one went up in its place.

Isam had been so mesmerized by the sight that he had forgotten his own danger. Although he was treading water, the current had taken him into the narrow cove and he was drawing near the *Grey Wolf*. Swimming across the current, he reached the bow, was scraped along the hull by a wave, and grabbed for the accommodation ladder. His hand clawed a slimy wet rung but slid off.

The next wave lifted him up and he grabbed for the mizzen chains. He hooked an arm through and slid down to the bottom of the chain as the wave passed by. He was left hanging by the crook of his elbow. The chain chewed up his arm and he bled.

"Help!" he shouted in Arabic. "HELP!"

The rest of the crew had been fascinated by the wrecking of the Spanish ship, and nobody, not even the men on watch who were supposed to look out for strange things in the water, had seen him.

The next wave lifted him up and smacked his head against the under side of the channel. He saw stars and tasted blood again. "Ow!" he complained. It struck him as immensely unfair that he had come through this whole adventure only be to beaten up by his own ship. He was hanging by his elbow and hurting even more when two men scrambled over the rail and into the mizzen channel.

They held tight to the shrouds and leaned over to fish him up. He lifted his free hand and one of them grabbed it and pulled. The next wave lifted him again and he was able to get a foot into the chains. The other man leaned over, grabbed his waistband, and heaved. That helped, and he let go of the chains with his elbow and squirmed onto the narrow wooden platform. The shrouds were a black jungle around him and he grabbed on to keep from being thrown over as the ship pitched on the waves. More hands came to the rail to reach out for him, but now that he had escaped the cold clutches of the sea, he was able to crawl over the rail by himself. He thudded down onto the quarterdeck in a cold, wet, bloody heap.

Rajet Rais glanced over. "Take him to my cabin. Get him dry clothes and something hot to drink."

Two men led him into the captain's cabin and took care of him. His teeth chattered as sensation returned to his benumbed body. They toweled him off, and put dry clothes on him, then hot, black, sweet coffee appeared. He drank it down and it warmed his belly. He was suddenly ravenous and extremely tired. "Soup," he begged. Word was passed. A few minutes later he was gulping down hot vegetable soup with a slab of brown bread on top. That warmed him and satisfied his hunger, so there was nothing he needed but sleep. He curled up on the rug with a blanket around him.

He would have liked to have slept on the divan, but the ship was rocking too much. She would have pitched him off the moment he relaxed. Accustomed to the antics of a ship, he wedged his back against the side of the divan, folded in the middle, and flung out one long leg to prevent himself from rolling in that direction. The divan against his back prevented him from rolling in the other direction. He fell asleep like that.

Some time later Rajet Rais checked on him. The young ensign was dead asleep and didn't stir at the sound of the door opening, or the captain asking, "How are you, Isam?" Rajet contemplated him for a bit, then knelt down, arranged the blanket to cover him better, and left him sleeping. Rajet kissed his brow, but he didn't know it.

CHAPTER 14 : THE HERO'S REWARD

The next morning the buzz of masculine voices woke Isam. He sat up blearily and stared stupidly at Demirkan and Haris. The two officers were sitting cross-legged on the rug on either side of him as they ate porridge for breakfast. The wind was roaring through the rigging and the sound was loud even in the great cabin.

"Good morning," the two said to him.

"What are you doing here?" he asked them.

"Breaking our fast with the captain like we always do," Haris replied.

"What happened to you? You look like you got kicked in the face by a camel," Demirkan asked.

Isam put hands to his aching face and groaned. "The anchor cable hit me in the nose when it parted."

Rajet Rais slid off the divan and settled on the rug next to the ensign. Setting aside his bowl of porridge, he took Isam's chin in his hand and turned his face to study it. Both of the young corsair's orbits were black. Isam could see out of two narrow slits in his swollen eyes. Bruises and scratches marred his right cheek, nose, and the middle of his forehead.

"I think my nose is broken," the young man moaned.

Rajet gently felt the bridge of his nose. "Yes, it is."

"Ow!" Isam complained. "I broke my nose a week ago boarding the Spaniard, but it didn't hurt this much!"

"That's why. You weren't healed from that," Rajet told him matter-of-factly. "Ilidio, bring our hero some breakfast." Turning back to Isam, he asked, "Are you hungry?"

"Famished," Isam replied.

The steward handed Isam a wooden bowl with a spoon in it. There was even a pat of butter and some brown sugar floating on top of the porridge. He lifted the spoon and dug in. Hot food made his stomach growl. Coffee sweetened with honey appeared next. He ate and drank.

Rajet finished his porridge and put an arm companionably around the younger man's shoulders. "Thanks to you, we're still afloat and most of us are alive. You deserve a reward. Name it, and it's yours."

Isam's face was hurting too much for gems or coins to seem desirable. What he really wanted was to crawl into his hammock and sleep it off. He also wanted some more porridge, but that seemed like a waste of a perfectly good reward. Various thoughts tumbled around in his head, but the one that fell out of his mouth was, "I want to get laid."

The three men laughed. They grinned at him, but Rajet said, "Done. Anything else?"

Isam thought he was jesting with him. "More porridge," he said, holding his bowl up.

"Ilidio, more food for our fine and manly hero." Rajet's tone was bantering.

Isam wished they wouldn't tease him. "What happened to the Spaniard?" he asked.

"They wrecked on the rocks and surrendered. Unfortunately, I can't do anything with them. The *Grey Wolf* is shot to hell. I'm afraid when they realize how bad off we are, they'll hoist their colors and try to board us. They have no choice. Their ship is breaking up beneath them. They can't get over the rocks to the shore; it's too rough. Their only hope is to capture us and take our ship."

Isam grimaced. "We should shoot them."

"We can't. They've hoisted a white flag and are our prisoners. Unfortunately, we can't parley with them because the wind is blowing a gale and the waves are too rough to send a boat. The good news is, as long as it's blowing so hard, they can't make an attempt on us. We're repairing as fast as we can. As soon as the wind drops, we're going to try rowing out of here."

Isam ate his second bowl of porridge and felt better. The gnawing in his belly quieted, but his face still hurt.

Demirkan and Haris rose to take their leave. Rajet said, "However, if the Spanish do hoist their colors, blow them to bits."

"Aye aye, captain," his officers replied.

The two left and Ilidio cleaned up the breakfast dishes and withdrew as well. When they were alone, Rajet took Isam's chin in a gentle hand and kissed him on the lips.

Isam looked at him in surprise.

"I keep my word," Rajet explained.

Isam didn't understand, not until Rajet reached to untie his drawers. The younger man was wearing nothing but the undershirt and drawers he had slept in the night before. When the drawstring came undone, he squawked indignantly.

Rajet smirked at him. "Have you really not noticed I find you attractive?"

Isam's jaw dropped and hung open. The older man's hand dipped into his pants and he jumped. His breath quickened, "You don't really mean it, do you?"

"Of course I mean it." Then he shifted position and bent his head.

Isam suddenly felt a lot better. The pleasurable sensations emanating from his loins blotted out everything else. He forgot his aching face, forgot the Spanish a hundred yards away, forgot the *Grey Wolf* was damaged and embayed, forgot there was a fifteen year age difference between himself and the captain, but most of all, forgot that he had any objections to the proceedings.

He lay down on his back and rasped out, "When I said I wanted to get laid, I meant real sex."

Rajet looked up in amusement. "You don't look like you're fit for a romp. Let's try it the French way and see how you fare."

He fared very well indeed. His nether parts were entirely whole and hale and full of the vigor lacking in his extremities. He was still tired after his exertions of the day before, but it didn't matter. Rajet was keenly aware that he owed the survival of his ship to Isam and readily forgave any lack of skill on the part of his partner. In fact, he thoroughly enjoyed the opportunity to pleasure the handsome young corsair. A little while later he threw a leg over the supine youth and eased himself down.

Isam let out a groan as he experienced a tight muscular sheath wrapping around his virile member. The sensation was so extraordinarily vivid he knew he would remember it for the rest of his life. As for Rajet, it had been a while since he'd had a lover, but he was determined to give the hero what he deserved. They both enjoyed the results.

Afterwards Rajet ran his fingers through the younger man's chest hair. Almost shy, Isam stared at the man. Previously he had sneaked peeks of other men at the bathhouse, or while watching his mates change clothes, but he didn't dare get caught looking. Now he stared openly. Rajet was a small man, but he was definitely a man. His muscles were powerful and well-defined and his chest and belly were furred with dark hair. His genitalia were in proportion to the rest of him, so they were not large (especially not when compared to the well-endowed youth), but that didn't inhibit his libido. He was just as potent as a bigger man, and more so than most. Isam rolled onto his side so that he could stroke the other man's body. He caressed his flanks, squeezed the bulging pectorals, and trailed a hand down to cup the furry balls. Unlike most Muslim men, Rajet didn't shave down there. He was such a hairy man there didn't seem to be any point.

Isam couldn't help comparing him to the very limited sample of other men with whom he'd had any kind of intimacy. He was sure Gregorio must have a smooth body; he didn't know why he thought so, but he did. Wadid had had a little bit of body hair in the usual places and was rather soft in the middle. Isam ran his fingers over the captain's washboard belly and liked the feeling very much. The captain's masculinity aroused him.

Rajet pulled him close and kissed his mouth. Isam kissed him back hotly. They had had enough of a rest that they were ready for another round. Isam was not content to lie back this time. When his prick was hard he felt no pain, so pretty soon he was on top of the older man. What he lacked in technique, he made up for in vigor. By the time he was done, Rajet was a sweating bundle of orgasm face down on the rug.

Rajet said, "Nobody has to know about this."

"It's none of their affair anyhow," Isam replied. He was well pleased with himself. He had a cocky grin that wouldn't stop. He had saved the *Grey Wolf* and had been initiated into the brotherhood of men. "I'm never going back to Tanguel," he said with great feeling.

Rajet laughed, then pushed him off, and rolled over. Sitting up he sobered. "We may not be going anywhere it we can't get the ship together." He rose. "Get dressed, Isam. If you're in good enough shape to fuck, you're in good enough shape to work."

Isam gave a groan but joined his captain in washing up.

CHAPTER 15 : STORM IN THE HOLE

All through the day the wind increased. Clouds piled up, then it rained. The men worked to repair rigging and plug holes in the side of the ship. They spliced lines and mended canvas. The sound of hammers and saws replacing lumber and fixing dismounted guns was incessant. The watch kept a sharp eye on the anchors. They also kept an eye on the Spaniards, but the rising waves prevented them from attempting to board her. She was less than a hundred yards away, and they could sometimes hear the creaking of her timbers. Late in the afternoon, a mighty CRACK followed by the noise of rending wood made all heads turn. She had broken in half, and only a few timbers remained to hold her stern to her midships. The Spanish officers scrambled across the gap to join the crowd forward. Envious eyes gazed towards the *Grey Wolf*. The corsair was battered but still afloat. If only they could get to her, she would be their salvation.

The wind roaring out of the west channeled between the two lines of rocks so that their anchorage was the worst place to be. The shore was not far, but there was no way to get ashore through the vicious rocks and violent sea. The line of southern rocks were needle-like teeth or ragged crags as high as thirty feet washed by foam until they shone as black as evil. Spumes of spray flew as high as the mastheads. There was no room to squeeze a boat between them, and any man attempting to make the swim must necessarily be dashed against the rocks. If he could have made it to the other side, he would have found a jumble of boulders and water, and maybe, had the sea been calm, been able to pick his way across the boulders to shore, but no such feat could be attempted with the agitated sea boiling over them.

The southern line of rocks ran from the southwest to northeast, and the northern line followed the same path, but not so acutely. The result was a long, narrow triangle that concentrated the force of the waves at its eastern end where the Spanish frigate was breaking up. The formation was not unlike a set of crocodile jaws. The Spanish ship was stuck in the crocodile's throat, but the *Grey Wolf*, located nearer the lips, still clung to hope of escape, although that seemed less and less likely all the time.

Having jettisoned her food, the men were hungry as well as cold and wet. They had water to drink, but Rajet cut the ration. They were not going to make it through the Pinch and reach Tettiwan tonight. The one ton of water they still had would have to be made to stretch through at least two days, probably more. They rigged an old sail to form a funnel and lashed it firmly to the mast, quarterdeck rail, and gunwales, and secured a barrel to the foot of the mainmast to receive the rainwater that poured down the canvas. In this way they replenished some of their drinking water.

They had one bit of luck. As the wild sea broke over their bows, a great lump of something came crashing down onto the foredeck. When the water receded, there lay a marlin fish gasping on the planks. It was swiftly dispatched with an axe and the meat divided. A two hundred pound fish was made to serve two hundred hungry men. Half the fish was inedible bones and eyeballs and other tripe, but each man got a meal. They considered it a gift from Allah even if they did have to eat it raw.

Rajet ordered the remaining anchor shifted forward and slung off the larboard bow. With all three anchors holding, he had done as much as he could to secure the ship. The cables were well served with pudding to keep them from chafing themselves to pieces as they rubbed against the hawseholes, and an anchor watch was stationed to tend them. Within an hour the pudding had been worn to pieces and had to be replaced. Isam was put in charge of a team of men who were kept busy weaving junk lines into mats of pudding. Another man was sent over with the cable from the lost stern anchor. He dove down, followed the cable to the bottom, and secured it to the best bower. He resurfaced to tell them that the anchor had dug in hard in a crevice of rock. The stock was doing its job to keep the head of the anchor propped above the rock and the cable away from the stone. With the cable thus doubled and a strong anchor point, Rajet thought he would be able to ride out the storm, Allah willing.

The gale roared through the afternoon and into the night. Rain came down in torrents. Rajet forbid lanterns; he didn't want to give the Spanish the slightest bit of help. They couldn't see the rocks even though the roaring of the surf nearly deafened them.

When Isam was relieved at last, he was pleased to switch into dry clothes, and fully dressed, crawled into his hammock. His face hurt, but he didn't mention it. A broken nose was a small thing compared to the possibility of the ship breaking up. He fretted about sleeping below decks. Should the ship sink it would be hard to fight his way to the surface. He was bone tired though, and he slept in spite of himself.

Some time in the night he was awakened by a hand shaking him. "Huh?" he asked.

"Sh. All hands on deck. Silently and without lights."

Isam blinked into the darkness, then tumbled out of his hammock. He put on his sandals and coat in the dark, then joined the throng of men quietly climbing the ladders to the weather deck. The silence was eerie, then he realized the gale had dropped.

He made his way to the quarterdeck where Rajet, Haris, and Demirkan were already at their posts. The sea was still wild; the storm in the Atlantic was sending deep swells to hammer at them. He glanced over the stern, but he couldn't make out the Spanish ship in the darkness.

"What is it?" he whispered.

"The tide is ebbing. We're going to try rowing out."

Isam shivered. "Shouldn't we wait for daylight?" He stared at the phosphorescent water tumbling and hissing all around.

Rajet replied, "The wind has shifted northwest and eased. If we can shoot out the mouth of the cove and get the sails up, we can run for Tanguel. Now be quiet. I'm busy."

Isam kept silent.

Rajet gave orders in a low voice; he didn't want to alert the Spaniards. They might be tempted to do something desperate if they thought the corsair was going to escape. "Weigh the jury anchor. Let it hang. We won't bother getting it aboard right now." Rajet didn't mention they might need to drop it again fast if their escape attempt went awry. Isam ran the message forward, then returned to the quarterdeck.

The capstan went to work and the first anchor came up with a minimum of noise. The men worked in the dark. They were used to that. Rajet was a sailor of the night as well as the day, and he expected his crew to know their jobs well enough to do them blind. Isam began to hope. The northern line of rocks was now sheltering them from the northern shift of the wind. The breakers were still rolling in, but their force was partially counteracted by the tide running out.

"Weigh the second best bower," Rajet said softly.

Isam carried the message forward to the chief. He glanced back at the Spanish ship, but her single lantern was forlorn in the night. If it weren't for the golden pinpoint of light, he would have thought she had gone to pieces entirely.

The xebec swung when the second bower lost its grip. Her bow pointed to the northwest as if she intended to bull her way through the line of rocks they couldn't see. Yet the glow of the hissing white foam told them exactly where they were. Spatters of rain spit down and Isam pulled the tail of his turban over his face again. No stars could be seen.

A gust blew over the rocks, grabbed the upper reaches of the mast, gave the ship a rock, then passed on.

Rajet Rais spoke quietly. "Out oars. Silent running."

With a soft rustle and a few wooden thumps, the long sweeps were run out and secured. Men wrapped the oars with handkerchiefs or turbans to muffle the oar ports, then took their positions between the guns and waited for the signal.

Rajet Rais whispered, "Oars, out oars." They shot from the sides. "Oars, make way together. Slowly."

They rowed up on their anchor, and Rajet sent the message, "Weigh the best bower!" His voice rose in spite of himself; this was the moment. The control of the ship must pass smoothly from her anchor to her oars, or the leeway would drive her south and onto the crocodile's lower jaw.

Nothing happened. The anchor cable remained taut. Rajet swore softly. "Again!"

The oars swept the foamy sea and brought the ship to her anchor buoy, but once again, the anchor would not break loose. The oars rested, and the ship drifted backwards the length of her scope.

"Again," Rajet ordered grimly.

They rowed up over their anchor point and again the capstan strained and failed.

"Isam, you're a strong man. Go to the capstan. Get as many men onto the capstan as possible, all the big ones, the strong ones. Demirkan, you go too."

"Aye aye, rais."

Isam descended to the deck, set his scimitar under the quarterdeck ladder out of the way, then wedged in beside two men on a bar. More men joined until twenty-four bodies were crammed around the capstan. There wasn't enough room. The bar came about to the middle of Isam's chest, so he twisted himself to lean his side against it to better concentrate his weight against it.

"Oars, make way together."

Once more they rowed up onto the anchor point, and the capstan creaked and groaned as the men labored in vain. Rajet let them row over the anchor point, or more correctly, beside it, since leeway was blowing them aside, even under oar power. He watched the amount of leeway made, calculated his speed and distance, and concluded that with enough speed, they could clear the southern rocks before the wind blew them onto them.

"When the anchor comes free, row like hell, dash speed," he told the cockswain in charge of the rowers.

The anchor did not come free. The men pressed their bodies against the capstan bars with all their might, strained until the veins stood out on their temples, strained until they thought their guts would burst. Isam gritted his teeth and shifted his position; no matter how he put himself into it, it made not one jot of difference.

"Pawl the capstan."

The man with the mallet knocked the pawl into the place. Isam and the others rested. The oars rested, too, and once again the ship ran out her scope as she drifted to the end of her rope.

Rajet rubbed his face. He wanted to sneak out of the cove without alerting the Spaniards, but most of all, he wanted out. "Stand by to fire the starboard guns."

The cannons had been kept loaded and ready to fire at a moment's notice in case the Spanish got frisky. Fire was fetched, and the slow matches glowed in their tubs. The gun captains lit their linstocks and sheltered them with their bodies. Their crews opened the ports, and with a rumble of iron wheels, ran out the guns.

"Main chief, as soon as we break free and the capstan is pawled, raise the main antenna. Don't wait for my order, just do it."

"Aye aye, captain," the main chief replied.

Not all the men on the capstan were mainsail hands, but it didn't matter. Every hand was needed. They waited tensely.

"Capstan, take a strain."

They bent their bodies to the bars again.

"Oars, give way together."

The oars dipped and flashed in the silvery foam. The men marched around the capstan to take up all the slack. When the buoy was abreast the xebec, Rajet called loud and clear, "Fire!"

The guns thundered in a throaty roar, plunging back against their tackles, and sending a shock through the vessel. Suddenly the capstan spun free and half the hands tumbled to the deck, Isam among them. The rest charged around the capstan at a run until with a sudden thump, the anchor struck the bow.

"Oars make way! Pawl the capstan!" Rajet bawled, but they were already doing it.

Isam and the other men rolled out from under the capstan bars and ran to the halyards. More hands came to join them. With no need for silence any longer, Isam sang out in a chantey,

"Oh, Allah! Help us with our work; fill this great sail with wind, Allah helper, Allah helper! Give strength to our arms and all of us! Allah helper, Allah helper!"

The men sang along. The great sail went aloft with the strong pulls of two dozen stout backs. When the yard reached the accustomed spot, Isam belayed the halyard.

Meanwhile, the ship ran forward as fast as the oars could stroke. The black line of rocks loomed suddenly in the darkness directly before them.

"Port oars, back water!" Rajet shouted.

The ship curved her course as she backed on one side and stroked on the other, the wind catching her big antenna as she came out from the shelter of the cove, driving her south, counteracting the momentum of her rush north. Isam glanced up from the knighthead where he was working and saw the black rocks rush past close enough he could have held a conversation with them, if they had tongues to speak. That sent a spike of alarm through him, but he was busy, he had no time to worry about whether the ship was going to clear the submerged rocks that extended the line past what he could see—that was the captain's worry.

The main chief bawled, "Loose brayles! Haul the sheet!"

Willing hands cast off the brayles from their belaying pins while others seized the sheet and pulled the clew of the great triangular sail down hard and fast. It plummeted, drenching them with the rain it had kept in its furls, and nearly smacked Isam in the head. Normally hands should ease the brayles to keep the sail from smacking down like a half ton sledgehammer, but they were in a hurry. Nobody complained; if a sailor failed to mind himself and was knocked cold by the weight of the sail, that was a small price to pay for escaping the teeth of the crocodile.

The immense mainsail billowed to port, full of the northwestern wind. The ship plunged ahead, skimming southwest, bucking across the swells.

"Did we make it?" Isam asked. In the dark it was hard to know. The men looked around.

"Boat oars! Set the foresail!" came Rajet's voice from the darkness of the quarterdeck.

"We made it!" Isam exclaimed.

A cheer went up. The men capered across the deck, Isam with them. They had escaped the deathtrap!

Once they were clear of the stony teeth, Rajet set a course due west to carry them as far off the coast of Africa as possible. He wanted a hundred miles of sea room so that he could not be driven onto that dark and dangerous shore again.

CHAPTER 16 : INGLORIOUS HOMECOMING

After breakfast, or what would have been breakfast if they had had anything to eat, Rajet turned the ship south.

"Why?" Isam demanded. "We're this close to the Pinch! We could have made it!"

"Not in this condition we couldn't. We are less than two miles from Tanger. If they heard our guns, and they surely did, they'll send a coastguard to investigate. As long as the wind was roaring out of the west, they couldn't beat around Cape Spartel, but now that the wind has fallen, they will come search for us. They'll find the Spanish wreck, and whether there are survivors or not, they'll know we were there. I'm going to Tanguel to refit and lie low until they give up looking for us."

"I can't go back to Tanguel. Not yet!"

Rajet shrugged. "Too bad. You're going."

"But in my letter to my uncle, I told him I wasn't coming back to Tanguel until I was a rich and famous corsair!" Isam wailed.

Rajet showed his teeth in a humorous smile. "That was the wrong thing to say to your uncle. You shouldn't boast about things you haven't yet done."

Isam cradled his aching nose and sulked. Glumly he watched the sky clear up and the wind moderate. It continued swinging around to the north and they made a good passage. On the third day after he had shaken the dust of Tanguel from his feet, Isam bin Hamet returned. He wasn't a rich and famous corsair, he didn't have any prize money, he hadn't made his reputation, and he hadn't gotten promoted. He was just a youth of nineteen with two black eyes and a busted nose. Although he had done a glorious thing in cutting the Spanish cables, he didn't want to tell the tale. That would require explaining how they had come to be embayed, and that was a tale of woe.

The *Grey Wolf* glided into the harbor in a less glorious condition than she had left. That naturally attracted attention. The harbor officials came aboard and met with Rajet Rais. Everyone was hungry and more than glad when the first order of business was contracting a lighter to come along side and deliver bags of couscous. They were given a late breakfast of couscous boiled with olive oil and nothing else, but it helped. By lunch time, rice and vegetables were coming aboard, and by dinner time, they had mutton. Tough, stringy mutton that needed to be boiled to death before it could be eaten, but at least they were eating.

Fresh water came aboard too, and the mood lightened. Still, it was not a happy crew. Several men slipped ashore and were never seen again.

Isam asked for and received leave to go ashore that evening. He didn't go home. He was ashamed to face his uncle. Instead he walked up to Hosaam's coffee shop, but there were no messages for him. That disgruntled him even further, so he hiked over to the Golden Lamp Inn. He let himself in the side gate, then haunted the backyard and listened to the music and watched thin rays of light escaping from the fretted windows.

At last a maid came out to fetch water from the well, and he stepped forward to accost her. She gave a shriek, dropped her bucket, and Isam held a finger to his lips. "Sh. I won't hurt you. I just want to know if Maureo is still here."

She nodded without speaking.

"And his slave, Gregorio?"

She nodded again and clutched the bucket to her stomach.

"Are they here right now?"

Another nod.

"Send Gregorio to me. Don't let Maureo know."

She nodded once more and started backing away. He faded into the shadows along the back wall once again.

A few minutes later Gregorio's slender form was limned against the lighted doorway. He paused and looked around, but with eyes unaccustomed to the dark, he couldn't see anything. Trembling, he stepped out and shut the door. He wandered through the back yard until Isam stepped forward. Gregorio recognized the stranger immediately and went rigid.

Isam put an arm around him and drew his unwilling steps into the far corner of the yard. The corsair's heart thudded as he remembered how good it had felt to press himself against the body of the other man. How soft his skin and voice were! How firm but yielding his flesh! Isam had been uncertain exactly what he wanted from the slave before, but now he knew. He blocked the smaller man in the corner and pressed close enough to feel the heat of his flesh radiating through the slim space that separated their bodies.

"You didn't leave me a message," he said in a low throaty baritone.

"I'm sorry, effendi. I couldn't do what you asked. Maureo keeps it on his person."

Isam pressed full length against the other man. "I don't accept excuses," he snarled.

"I'm sorry, effendi! Please forgive your humble servant! I couldn't get it! I swear!" The man was shaking, and when Isam bent his face very close to his, he turned it away.

Isam kissed the beardless cheek and trailed his lips to the shell of the ear. His hands pressed against the wall to either side, trapping the youth. Gregorio shut his eyes tightly and cringed. "Mercy, lord. This slave can't do what you ask."

Isam gripped the man's flanks and caressed them eagerly. Again his mouth quested for the slave's, but the youth said bitterly, "Ruin me as you will. I can't do it."

This was not the reunion Isam had planned. He wasn't enjoying it, even though he was trying to. He scowled. "I can take you as I please."

Gregorio heaved a sigh and slumped. "Yes, effendi." His voice was weary with resignation.

Isam was annoyed and baffled, so he kept up the pretense of having a reason for what he did. "Tell me about the woman. Does she send him messages?"

"No, effendi, but he sees her at the well sometimes."

"Does she speak to him?"

"She tries, but her sister drives her away."

"What are his plans?"

Gregorio hesitated.

Isam pressed himself against the smaller man and forced him against the mud bricks of the wall. "Answer me!"

"He plans to carry her off!"

Isam snorted and stepped back one step. "Does she agree?"

"I don't know. I am not close enough to hear what they say."

"Why doesn't he marry her? That would be simple enough. There's no need for all this sneaking. Halim has nineteen daughters. He'd be happy to marry one off."

"He's already married, and still owes his first wife part of her dower. He's in debt and doesn't want to pay another dower."

Isam glared. Gregorio couldn't see his expression in the dark, but he felt the air bristle with the corsair's anger. He held up his hands to ward off a blow, but Isam didn't strike him. "She's a fool if she goes with him."

"I think she's in love with him," Gregorio replied.

"He's a disreputable seducer, that's what he is."

"At least he's seducing her," Gregorio blurted out.

"What do you mean?"

"Some men just take what they want."

Isam was getting grumpier by the minute. His cousin's problem was interfering with his attempt at having a love life and he didn't know how to fix it. The news that Maureo was trying to elope with Rabiyah was something that he should tell his uncle, but he didn't want to see his uncle, and he didn't want to think about Rabiyah, not when the object of his desire was right in front of him. Halim and Rabiyah could wait until morning; the man wasn't carrying her off tonight.

When Isam didn't speak, Gregorio, who felt he had nothing to lose, dared to ask, "Why do you care anyhow? Are you her suitor, too?"

Isam laughed at that, and the noise was a genuinely pleasant sound. "No, I'm her cousin. Have you told Maureo about me?"

Gregorio shook his head.

"All right. I'll tell you then. I'm Isam bin Hamet. Don't tell him about me! I'm trying to watch out for my cousin, that's all."

Gregorio heaved a sigh of relief. "That's all right then."

Rajet had educated Isam about sex, but not love. Although Isam liked having sex with Rajet well enough, it was not Rajet's face that came to him in his dreams. He thought he had learned enough from the older man to move confidently into an affair of his own, but it wasn't working. Fumbling his way forward, he said, "I had another reason for coming."

Gregorio stiffened in alarm. He gave Isam a wary look. "What reason?" he asked suspiciously.

This was not the welcome Isam wanted. "I like you," he replied. He tried smiling winsomely at the youth. That didn't work either.

Gregorio peered at him in consternation. "Like me? I don't understand."

Isam lifted a hand to run callused fingers along his cheek. "You're pretty and soft and I like kissing you."

Gregorio stiffened further. He tried to back up but ran into the wall.

"This isn't how you acted the other night," the corsair complained.

Gregorio started to panic. "I don't know what you mean!"

Isam stepped forward. "You panted when I kissed you."

"I was frightened!" He was panting again. His heart thudded in his chest and the black eyes darted left and right in search of escape.

"I won't hurt you."

"If you do what you threaten, it'll hurt plenty," he said bitterly.

"It doesn't have to. I can show you."

Gregorio threw him a resentful look. "What would you know about it, mighty lord? You've never had Maureo beat you black and blue and rape you."

"He does that?" Isam asked in shock.

"Sometimes." Gregorio hung his head.

Isam cupped his face in his hands. "I would never do that to you."

Gregorio gave him a scornful look. "Forgive me, master, but you said you would last time you were here. Either you lied then, or you're lying now."

Isam dropped his hands as if they'd been stung. "I didn't mean it. I was pressing you to make you talk."

Gregorio wriggled out from between him and the wall and started to walk away.

"Wait!"

Gregorio hesitated, then stopped in his place.

Isam came up next to him. "I'm sorry. I shouldn't have done that."

Gregorio's jaw dropped and hung open. "You don't have to apologize to me. I'm a slave."

"You're a man, too."

"Less than that. I'm a eunuch. I'm nobody you need concern yourself with."

Isam reached out to cup the man's crotch through the loose pantaloons, but he had told the truth. There was a stubby shaft and nothing else. Gregorio's face turned crimson, and the darkness on his cheeks was visible in the light of the crescent moon. He shut his eyes and gritted his teeth in humiliation. Isam removed his hand.

"I'm sorry," Isam said again. He didn't know what else to say.

"It doesn't matter. What's done is done." Gregorio tried to school himself to resignation, but his voice was bitter.

"I still like you."

Gregorio looked at him like he was crazy. "Why?"

Isam spread his hands. "I don't know why. I just do."

"If you like me, why don't you talk to me during the day where I can see your face? Or are you ashamed to be seen in the company of a creature like me?"

Isam's head reared back. His eyes blazed and he almost said something stupid, but bit his tongue. He was in the habit of acting before he thought, but if he had learned one thing from Rajet, it was to think ahead. Still, thinking required an effort he wasn't used to making.

"All right," he said. "I'll come tomorrow morning before I go back to my ship."

"You're a sailor?" Gregorio asked. He knew nothing about the other man.

"A corsair," Isam replied proudly. "With the *Grey Wolf*. Although, you might not want to see me. My face is smashed up. I have a broken nose and two black eyes right now."

"Were you wounded in battle?" Gregorio asked.

"Yes," Isam said. "Sort of. I'll tell you about it tomorrow. If you'll meet me for breakfast at Hosaam's coffee shop."

"Maureo rises late because he stays out all night. I can be there."

Isam's heart lightened. "I'll look forward to it."

Gregorio was suddenly shy. "I have to go. My master will be missing me."

"I'll see you in the morning."

"Yes." Gregorio hurried back into the inn.

Isam let himself out the back gate and whistled a merry tune as he walked through the city. Then he remembered he needed to tell his uncle what Maureo was up to and suddenly stopped whistling.

CHAPTER 17 : HALIM'S WRATH

Isam turned reluctant steps through the streets to Halim's neighborhood. Respectable people were all indoors at this hour; lights glowed in shutters and fretted windows to light his path. He had neither lantern nor linkboy. It didn't matter; he could have found his way in absolute darkness. He knew his neighborhood. Like all boys, he had roamed freely, climbed its few trees, wriggled under fences, and otherwise made himself acquainted with every inch of it. He was now too old for climbing trees, but the neighborhood had changed little since he had shinnied up a palm and had a tin cup chucked at him by an irate maid. Arriving at Halim's doorstep, he tried the front door, but it was locked. He lifted the bronze knocker and let it fall.

Masum opened the peephole, exclaimed, "Isam!" He drew back the bolt and opened the door. Isam stepped into the familiar hallway that he had left a lifetime ago.

"Tell Halim I'm home for the night. I have something important to discuss with him."

Masum bowed, and hurried into the house. Isam let himself into the reception room. He removed his dusty sandals and wool coat, put his scimitar on the two pegs above his usual couch, and sat down to await Halim. He left the door to the entrance way open so that lantern light streamed into the room. The servant had not lighted a lamp for him.

Masum returned and stopped at the entrance to the reception chamber. "Halim will not see you. He says to come back when you're a rich and famous corsair." His posture and voice were both stiff.

Isam jumped to his feet and hurried to the door. "Tell him I'm sorry I said that. Apologize to him for me."

Masum shook his head. "You've hurt his feelings. He's a congenial man, but you've hurt his pride and his heart. You were like a son to him. You left in a very bad way," he chided the wayward youth.

"I have to talk to him. I have something important to tell him!"

"Go away. Wait a few days. Come back when he's had time to get over his anger."

"I don't know if I can! I don't know when the *Grey Wolf* will leave again!"

Masum crossed his arms and looked stubborn. "He doesn't want to see you. Please respect his wishes this time." There was a sarcastic emphasis on the last two words.

"It's about Rabiyah. There's a man named Maureo who's been talking to her."

"The one with the flute?"

"Yes."

"We know about him."

"Oh."

"Do you know she tries to talk to him at the well?"

Masum nodded. "She's not allowed to leave the house anymore."

"Oh."

"He wants her to run away with him."

"We know."

"You know?"

"What do men always want? 'Run away with me. We'll get married. I love you!' And what do young women always say? 'I love you! I don't need a dower, as long as I'm with you, I'm happy!'" He mimicked a male and female voice protesting their love.

"I guess you already know then," Isam said. "I just wanted to warn him about that."

Masum walked past him into the room, brought him his coat and sandals, and stood by as he put them on. Then he went and got the scimitar and brought it to him. Isam thrust it through his sash, checked to make certain the hook had caught, and said, "I'll go back to the ship then."

Masum nodded. "It's better this way. Give him time to get used to it. Better yet, bring some prizes with you! Anyone can forgive success."

He escorted Isam to the front door, drew back the bolt, and heaved the heavy wooden door open. Isam stepped out into the street. This time when he left home, he felt he was losing something, something he didn't want to give up. Yet out there in the world, a very different future beckoned, and it included a comely male slave named Gregorio. Who baffled him. He felt mixed up inside.

Isam turned to the servant and asked, "Masum, do you ever resent becoming a eunuch?"

Masum glared at him. "Only when I think about it."

The servant had always been meek and mild to members of the household, but Isam was no longer a member of the household. The slave's sudden rancor startled Isam.

"I'm sorry if that was a rude thing to ask, but I'm trying to think about the world and understand the people in it better."

"About time. You always did think too much of yourself," Masum replied coolly, shocking him again.

"Do you really think so?"

"If you cared about your uncle and his family, would you have taken the coward's way leaving a note instead of saying good bye to his face?"

Isam's cheeks grew hot. "You'll keep a civil tongue in your head, or I'll beat you!"

"You always did think you were a high and mighty corsair, but you're not." Masum slammed the door and bolted it.

Isam pounded his fist against the door in rage, but nobody answered "Damn you, Masum!" he shouted at the door. "Damn you!" He stomped away from the house and kicked a loose stone all the way to the crossroad.

He didn't return to the ship. He was too sulky, embarrassed, and dispirited. There was one bright spot in his life: breakfast with Gregorio. He dearly wanted to ask advice, but he thought he ought not ask Rajet for advice on courting the slave boy, and he couldn't ask Halim's advice on anything. If the mosque were open at this hour, he might have gone in hopes of finding Abdulhamid, but the wise old man was no doubt safe at home, drinking sherbet, and dandling his grandchildren on his knee.

When he finally arrived back at the ship, Demirkan was sitting and smoking on the main hatch. "Peace be upon you, Isam," the big black man greeted him.

"And also upon you," Isam replied gloomily as he climbed down the cannon to the deck.

"Is something wrong?" Demirkan asked.

Isam hesitated. "I need some advice, but I have no one to ask."

"Smoke?" the man asked, holding out the pipe.

It was a friendly gesture, so Isam sat down next to him, took the pipe, and sucked in a deep breath. He was immediately overcome by a paroxysm of coughing and nearly dropped the clay pipe. Demirkan retrieved his smoking implement before the ensign could accidentally destroy it. He thumped Isam violently on the back. That only made him cough worse. The black man said, "You're supposed to puff, not inhale! Haven't you ever smoked before?"

"I've had a little shisha," Isam coughed. "It was mellow."

Demirkan made him sit down and catch his breath. He puffed calmly on his pipe as he waited for Isam to sort himself out. Isam wiped his eyes with his sleeve, said, "ow" when it hurt, and settled into a grumpy silence.

"What's the matter?"

"I can't tell you."

"Can't or won't?"

"Can't, although I wouldn't, either."

"You've slept with Rajet," Demirkan guessed.

Isam shot him a scandalized look. "How dare you!"

"Because I've slept with him, too." He said it as calmly as if observing what a dark night it was. Only the faintest sliver of moon was showing herself in the heavens. Seeing Isam's scandalized look, he added, "Not recently."

Isam sputtered something unintelligible.

Demirkan grinned around the pipe at him. "So has Haris. We all have. Again, not recently."

Isam was crestfallen. "He's slept with the entire crew?"

"Not all of them. Just the good-looking ones." Demirkan's teeth flashed in a good-natured grin.

"Oh. Does everyone know I've slept with him?"

"Haris knows. Several of the officers too. You're what he likes. Fortunately for the rest of us, you turned out to be useful as well. Speaking of which, how's your nose?" His voice was amiable and demeanor comfortable.

Isam gingerly touched the injured proboscis. "It hurts." He mulled over Demirkan's revelations. "Don't tell anyone, please. I didn't sign on to be his paramour. I want to learn navigation. That's why I'm here."

Demirkan blew smoke through his nostrils as he chuckled. "You'll learn a lot more than that from Rajet. He'll make a man of you—if he doesn't get you killed first. That took stones to cut the Spanish cables. I couldn't have done it. I'd have panicked under all that water and drowned myself."

"I'm a good swimmer," the ensign said proudly, although a little self-conscious about the boast. Yet it was something he had done, not something he intended to do, and so it fell within the advice Rajet had given him. "But it was more than I bargained for all the same." He pointed at his face significantly.

Demirkan thumped him on the back again, threatening to break another piece of his anatomy. "That's a good lad!" he said jovially. "You'll be fine. Don't let Rajet talk you into anything crazier than that, though. His plans don't always work."

"Yes. I know," Isam said with feeling. "Can I ask your advice on something?"

"Sure."

"You won't tell? Especially not Rajet."

Demirkan studied the matter for a while. "It depends on what it is. If it's none of Rajet's business, I won't mention it. But if it has something to do with the ship and crew, I may have to. My duty is to the welfare of the ship."

"It's not the ship. It's personal."

The big agha relaxed. "I promise. What is it?"

"Well, there's this slave boy, see. I like him. A lot."

Demirkan tapped the end of his pipe against his lips. "I see. No, this is definitely something Rajet doesn't need to know about. Go on."

"He belongs to somebody else. I bullied him at first, so he doesn't trust me. I said I was sorry for that; I was trying to impress him with what a mighty corsair I am. This was before I signed with the ship. Do you think I should try to buy him from his master?"

Demirkan grew grave. "I see. You lust for him, but he doesn't return your interest, so you tried to coerce him into having sex with you?"

"Um . . ." Isam wondered how the man drew that picture from the scant information he'd been given. "Not exactly. I was trying to get him to tell me about his master courting my cousin. But now I like him. And it turns out my uncle already knew about Maureo, so there's no reason for me to worry about it anymore."

"Congratulations. You've succeeded in intimidating the man. He won't forgive you for that."

Isam drooped. "How can I show him that things are different now?"

Demirkan peered at him. "Are they? Different?" There was a challenge in his voice.

Isam frowned. "I think so."

"Suppose you had reason to suspect this slave knew something else about his master and your sister. What would you do?"

"Uh, I don't know. Beg him to tell me."

"Do you really want a lover who is willing to betray his master?"

"No . . ." That gave Isam pause. "But he refused to do what I asked, so he won't."

"So if he refuses to tell you, then what will you do?"

"See, if I buy him, Maureo is no longer his master and the problem is solved."

"Not solved. Merely displaced."

"Huh?"

"The problem remains, but now you can ignore it. That's no way to solve a problem."

"What should I do?"

"Find a different slave boy and forget that one."

"That's not the answer I wanted to hear."

"Why did you ask advice if you're only going to do what you want to do anyhow?"

"I was hoping there was a better answer."

"The better answer is not always the easier answer, Isam."

Isam held out his hand for the pipe and Demirkan gave it to him. He puffed gently, handed the pipe back, and blew smoke. "It used to be," he said regretfully.

Demirkan smiled and smoked. "How old are you?"

"Nineteen."

"You're not a child any more. You're becoming a man."

"I am a man!" Isam snapped.

Demirkan said mildly, "Don't look for offense where none was intended."

"Sorry," Isam muttered.

Demirkan smoked in silence for a while, but then offered it to Isam again. The young man smoked a bit and found the harsh weed strangely soothing. He mulled matters over in his mind as he handed the pipe back to Demirkan.

"Thank you for listening to me. I didn't know who I could talk to."

"Any time, Isam. I'm the big bad agha, but only to the enemy."

Isam smiled crookedly. "I was an agha for a little bit, but I resigned it to learn navigation."

They fell into companionable silence after that. The pipe went back and forth between them until the tobacco was all gone. Demirkan yawned and said, "Time for bed. You, too, my bold corsair."

Isam said, "Aw," but he went to his hammock.

CHAPTER 18 : THE RUNAWAY BRIDE

Isam slept poorly that night. A certain dark-eyed slave boy kept invading his dreams. At last he gave up trying to sleep, dressed himself in the dark, and crept ashore. The watch on duty watched him go without a challenge. Isam's sandals slapped the dock as he strode with long strides over the worn grey planks. By dawn he had reached the coffee shop and ensconced himself on one of the wooden benches under the pergola. The muezzin called the prayer, but he remained curled up in the corner of the bench. Eventually the sun rose and the city came to life. Water sellers took their donkeys to the wells to fill their panniers, then went off on their rounds to the private establishments that could afford to have water delivered.

The coffeehouse servant opened the door and swept the dust out of the room, glanced at Isam, said, "Salaam, effendi," and swept out the pergola too. The scant dew swiftly dried. Isam stood up and waited while the servant put cushions on the wooden benches to transform them into comfortable seats. The servant wiped down the tables that bore the marks of beverage rings and daggers. Isam paced impatiently.

"Coffee, effendi?" the servant asked.

"Yes, please. Breakfast too."

"We have fresh bread baking. It will be ready soon."

"That will suit me."

Customers began arriving at the coffee shops. Some were respectable, white-cloaked men with turbans, while others were ragged porters with nothing but their own hair to protect their heads and not even sandals for their feet. Isam ate hot bread and drank sweet black coffee, but there was no sign of Gregorio. He consoled himself that the slave must wait on his master's breakfast before he could escape.

Eventually the breakfast trade petered out. Isam paced again. The sun was warming the mud brick building and chasing away the chill of the spring night. Women walked past with jars balanced on their heads. Porters trotted past with yokes supporting canisters of fermented butter. Still Gregorio didn't come.

Isam walked partway down the street, stumbled over a stone in the road, kicked it with a sandaled toe, yelped, and hopped on one foot. That made him mad, so he kicked it hard, this time taking care to mind his toes and thump it with the bottom of his sandal. The stone loosened, and just as he was about to knock it loose and send it flying, he heard a familiar voice.

"Isam! Praise Allah, I've found you!"

Startled out of his wrath, Isam looked up. "Cousin Samir. What is it?"

The handsome young man in his green coat strode up. "Rabiyah has run off! It's that man Maureo—Halim is sure of it. He's taken her!"

The news startled Isam out of his own doldrum. He pulled himself up to his full height. "What! Taken her!"

Samir bin Hadad took his arm and pulled. "Come with me. Uncle Halim has called his kin together to decide what to do. I went to your ship looking for you, but they said you weren't there. I've been all over trying to find you!"

"Yes, I'm coming!" Isam started forward, then stopped. "I'm in disgrace. I can't go home."

Samir was not as tall as Isam, but he was taller than average, well-built, and athletic. He dragged Isam by the arm and made him walk. "Yes, you can. Halim is cursing himself for driving you off. He thinks you were trying to warn him. Now he's sorry. You must come home and tell us what you know."

Isam didn't know anything, but he was willing to be forgiven all the same. He fell into step beside his cousin. The two of them hurried along together, one green-clad arm hooked into the other blue-clad arm. Samir was a corsair too, and he automatically took Isam's right side so that his sword arm (the right) and Isam's sword arm (the left) would be free. The two of them were as unlike as cousins could be. Although they were both tall and fit, Samir had sandy brown hair, green eyes, and an ivory complexion while Isam was black-haired with coffee-colored eyes and a swarthy complexion. Isam was a hirsute man, as could be told by the hair on his knuckles and toes, but Samir was a smooth-bodied man with hands that he kept soft and neat. He was handsome with a European cast to his features, including a long straight nose and large eyes. Although Isam was considered a good-looking man, Samir was beautiful. He would have outshone his younger cousin even if Isam's black eyes hadn't turned a shade of green that nearly matched Samir's long coat.

"What happened to your face?"

"I got hit by a Spanish anchor cable."

"How did that happen?"

"I cut it."

Samir laughed out loud. The merry sound rolled through the street like the peal of a cymbal. "Thereby hangs a tale, no doubt."

Isam grinned. "There does indeed."

"You must tell it to me, but not yet."

They arrived at Halim's house and were ushered in. Masum had to open the door for them, but he kept a wary lookout in case Isam decided to hold a grudge. Fortunately, the youth had too much on his mind to remember the eunuch. He rushed into the reception room with Samir striding in his wake.

Three middle-aged brothers sat together on the divan at the head of the room: Halim, Bazam, and Hadad. Their sons were also present, but they were not numerous. Their lineage was abundantly gifted with females, but not so many males. A few sons-in-law were present, but not many because few of them considered it their business to worry about their wives' misbehaving cousin.

Isam toed off his sandals and left them at the edge of the rug. Samir had a greater effort to remove his tall black boots, and he was still struggling to get them off when Halim walked up to Isam, grabbed his biceps, and said, "Forgive me. In my wrath I wouldn't listen when you tried to warn me, and now Rabiyah is gone."

Isam accepted the man's embrace, pleased to have a home again, even if he was eager to leave it for adventure. "We can overtake them. He's a Glawa tribesman; he must be going home. We have to catch up to him before he reaches their lands. When did they leave?"

"At dawn. They couldn't get out until the city gates were open. Where have you been? I need you to lead the search party! We are hours behind!"

Isam decided to put his own activities in the best light possible. "I was looking for his servant Gregorio. He had promised to meet me and tell me their plans."

"Did he?"

"No."

"May he burn in Hell and his children too!"

Isam decided Gregorio being a eunuch wasn't relevant. He focussed on more important things. "Can we get horses?"

"Yes. It will cost me. I haven't any money so early in the season, so I'll have to borrow it, but I'll get it." Turning to the room he asked, "Who else will go with Isam?"

Samir bin Hadad raised a well-manicured hand. "I will."

Another cousin, Umar bin Bazam hopped off his divan. "Me too!" Both of the cousins had been enamored of the beautiful Rabiyah.

Halim waited expectantly. Uneasy looks were exchanged around the room. Nobody else volunteered. "Who else will help?" he asked sharply.

"I don't think we need a large party," Samir replied. "My servant is an able man and he comes from that country. He'll be more useful to us than a posse. If we can't overtake them, we'll need to travel inconspicuously through the Glawa country. We can't do that with a band of raiders."

Murmurs of assent greeted this assessment. Bazam, a stout fellow with grizzled streaks in his beard, rose and said, "I'll go about the horses if you'll give me your pledge for the money."

"I will," Halim agreed. "Meanwhile, my servants will prepare food and supplies. Isam, Umar, Samir, go and fetch what you need. Take whatever I have that will help."

The men split up to fulfill their parts, but Samir stepped out with Isam and caught his sleeve. Speaking quietly so no one would overhear, Samir said, "You know she won't be a virgin when we find her."

Isam paused at that. "You can't be sure. They're traveling."

"If you stole a bride, wouldn't you consummate the marriage immediately? Knowing that once the deed is done, her family would demand a dower instead of the bride?"

"I see what you're saying," Isam replied unwillingly.

Samir shook his head. "No, you don't. It will be worse than that. He won't pay a dower. Not for her." He walked away.

"What do you mean?"

Samir turned and walked backwards. "Men don't pay for used goods, Isam." Then he turned around and hurried out of reach.

"Wait!"

Samir stopped. His back was a stiff wall that would not answer his cousin.

"You can't say such things about your cousin!" Isam said indignantly. He overtook the older cousin.

Samir finally looked at him. "Can't I?"

Isam puzzled at him. As those green eyes stared at him, he suddenly understood. "No. You didn't. Not your own cousin!"

Samir shrugged. "I wasn't her first, I'm sure. She asked me to marry her, but I refused. I like to lie with women, and I don't much care if they've laid with other men, but I'm not going to marry a whore. When I have children, I want to know they are my own."

Isam punched him in the nose. Samir was expecting that sort of reaction and jumped back. Isam's knuckles grazed his face, but he spun away.

"Stop and think! If you act like this, everyone will guess! Her only hope is to get married to that fool, Maureo. You must keep her secret as I have."

Isam stopped.

"Think, damn you! You always did go off half-cocked. The huntsman makes his mark when he has patience. If you have a brain in your head, use it!"

Rajet's teaching rose up unbidden. His advice applied equally well to matters ashore as at sea. Isam didn't like yielding to his cousin, but he seemed to know a good deal more about the matter than he did. "What do you suggest we do?"

"We must push hard. When we catch them, insist upon an immediate marriage—on the morrow. That will give us time to prepare her. We will give her a little knife, and she can prick herself so that there is blood on the sheet."

"What sheet? We're camping!"

"We will bring the sheet." Samir cuffed him across the head. "Think! Plan! Prepare!"

Isam rubbed his head. "Ow! Stop hitting me. What if he won't marry her?"

"Umar will, he's that besotted. But he must believe she's a virgin, or he won't do it, so mind your tongue. Now, hurry! We must catch them before he has time to sample the goods and finds them soiled!"

"He has a long head start. I don't think we can catch him that quick."

"Then he'll kill her. His honor will require it. If he won't, then we must. The matter will come out. The family name can't bear the shame of it. She must marry or die."

Isam's heart leaped within his chest. "I have to get leave from my captain."

"Send him a note. Every minute counts."

Chapter 19 : Pursuit of the Moor

"We'll never catch him by nightfall," Umar moaned. They were stopped at a well in the country. Three roads stretched out around them. The road upon which they had just ridden ran to the city, but the one on the right continued to follow the seacoast while the one on the left rose toward the mountains.

Other travelers were at the well. Dusty and hot, they threw back their cloaks and drank from the water amid the rocks while their camels stretched out their long necks and lapped. Most of them wore white or grey or tan to resist the heat of the sun. The cousins dismounted, watered their horses, and slaked their thirst. Then they separated to question the travelers.

Samir walked among them in his green coat. "Pardon me, but I am looking for a Moor on camelback with a woman and a Nazarene slave. Have you seen them?"

The traveler bowed deeply to his green coat and answered in respectful tones, "No, sharif. We just arrived. No one has been here but your esteemed self."

Samir moved among the other travelers, then returned to his cousins to report. "They haven't seen Maureo."

Isam couldn't restrain himself. "You're not a descendant of the Prophet! Why are you wearing green? Those people think you're a sharif!"

"I am a descendant of the most holy messenger, Muhammed," he answered with the complacency of a man sure of his superiority.

"You're my cousin! Our fathers are brothers. We're not descendants of the Prophet!"

Samir had told the lie so many times it came easily to his lips. It required a moment to recollect he was among family members who did not share his story. "Through my mother," he explained.

"Your mother is Italian!"

"Only half Italian. She's the daughter of a true believer who married an Italian woman. They had a daughter, my mother. When my grandmother was ransomed, she carried her infant daughter back to Italy with her."

Isam glared at him. "Do you really expect me to believe such a preposterous tale?"

Samir's green eyes glinted dangerously. "I do," he replied in a silky voice. "Because if you refuse, I shall have to beat you."

Isam's eyes darted up and down his cousin's form. Isam was taller, but not by much. Samir was older and more experienced, but again, not by much. It would be an even match.

Umar interrupted. "Peace be upon you both! What good will it do for you two to beat each other up? Maureo is getting away! We must ride! We have wasted too much time already!"

The taller cousins glanced at Umar. The smaller man glared at them. He was wiry, bearded, hook-nosed and hard-eyed in the white haik and turban. Isam grunted an acknowledgment, but he was still unhappy about Samir.

"You must not question me," Samir said as he gathered his horse's reins. "This green coat means people will answer me when they would not otherwise answer a stranger. Whether you believe it or not, it is in your best interest to act as if you do."

Isam scowled, but he had to admit there was logic in his cousin's words. Samir, the charming one in his green coat, was having better luck with the interviews than Isam with his short jacket and banged up face. Isam looked a ruffian, but Samir looked like a person of consequence. That made Isam take an active dislike to his relative.

"Which road?" asked Umar.

The servant had been moving their saddles and packs to the remounts. He spoke up. "The shore road."

"Why? The high road leads to the mountains and the Glawa territory," Isam said.

The servant replied, "It leads first through the Zayanes' territory, and the Zayanes are no friends of the Glawa. Besides, he will expect pursuers to take the mountain road. If he follows the seacoast further south, he can skirt the Zayanes and deceive his pursuers. Plus, there are towns where he can take shelter and travel comfortably."

The three cousins looked at each other. Each was keenly conscious that a wrong choice now meant they would never catch their man. Samir spoke, "I trust Athar's advice. He's a Glawa; he knows these things."

Isam peered suspiciously at Athar. "But if he's a Glawa, maybe he is deceiving us to help his tribesman."

Umar looked uncertainly between his cousins, then at Athar.

"In that case, maybe I will slip a knife between your ribs tonight," Athar replied calmly. "Either you trust me, or you don't. If you don't trust me, ride for the Zayanes' country yourself."

"I don't think we should split up," Umar said. "If we catch him, it will be the three of us versus him and his servant. We should stick together."

Samir swung onto his horse. "Whatever you decide, do it quickly. Delay is more dangerous than decision. I'm taking the sea road."

Isam chewed his lip. His instinct was to barge ahead by the straightest path, but he was learning that the obvious choice was not always the best choice. Still, he didn't trust Samir or his servant.

"I'll take the sea road," he grumbled. He mounted up.

They reached Dlalha by sunset. The village was composed of a few hundred souls and one caravanserai. The smells of dinner issued from the mud brick houses and dogs barked at them. An elderly man came out to meet them when they pulled up in front of the caravanserai. Seeing Samir's green coat, he bowed deeply.

"Peace be upon you, noble son of the Prophet," he greeted him.

"And also upon you, old man," Samir replied politely, sliding out of the saddle and stretching his back. "We're looking for a man, a woman, and a servant, mounted on camels. Did they pass this way?"

"They did, effendi. They stopped at the caravanserai and took their midday meal and watered their animals, then moved on."

"Noon?" Isam questioned as he let himself down from the saddle. His butt was aching from the unaccustomed riding.

"Early afternoon." The old man shook his head, the hood of the white haik shadowing his face. "May I ask why you seek these people?"

"The woman is our cousin and the Moor has carried her off," Umar replied. He had to give his leg a tug to get it over the saddle he was so stiff.

"Ah. That's too bad. You won't catch them. They were mounted on maherries."

At this news, the cousins grew glum. Maherries were the swift riding camels of the Sahara. They were bred for speed, not cargo.

"Maherries!" Samir moaned.

Isam swore in Turkish.

Umar insisted, "We must keep on. We'll never catch them if we rest!"

The old man nodded. "You'll need food and water. They left by the river road. If they pushed hard, they could make Souk el Arbaa tonight."

"Then we must push harder," Umar said.

They ate standing up. The food was cold and dry, but they were in a hurry. Athar switched the saddles again. They refilled their water skins, then, with a groan, heaved themselves onto their horses. At least the sun was dropping and releasing them from its bronze heat.

Mountains rose to the east and thrust their shoulders against the road. The road itself was bad—if such a collection of ruts and rocks could be named a 'road'. It rose and dipped, twined through a forest of deciduous trees covered in fresh new foliage, and was dim beneath the leaves. The woods were thick, but the cousins came to a bald spot and could look west where the sea had turned to lavender as the last of the light drained from the sky. Darkness closed around them. Atlas of the Greek myths had once stood on those mountains to hold the heavens on his shoulders, and they felt his burden.

After three hours they had not traveled more than seven miles from Dlalha. Dispirited, with darkness glooming their path, they dismounted to walk the horses. The trail was so narrow only a few moonbeams slanted through the foliage.

"I think we should camp," Samir said. "There's no point going on like this. If we lame the horses our cause is lost."

"He is striking out for the Glawa country now," Athar commented. "This is an obscure route. He won't expect us to follow him here. He has probably slowed down."

Isam was happy to be off the horse's back. His nether parts ached in a way they had never ached before. He longed for a hot soak in a tile bath followed by a massage administered by a man with hands strong enough to pull the knots out of his muscles.

Umar dismounted and walked up next to Isam. "Push on," he urged. He was as grimy as the rest of them, but unlike his cousins, he had faith in Rabiyah's fidelity. He had a burning need to rescue her and save her from ignominy. "If we rescue her, she will have to marry one of us."

The taller cousins exchanged glances.

"I don't want to marry her. She's like a sister to me," Isam replied.

Umar brightened to learn Isam would not challenge him for the hand of the runaway bride. He turned to Samir. "You're a handsome man, cousin. You'll have no trouble getting a wife. Let me have Rabiyah," he pleaded.

Samir looked down at the shorter man. His expression was unreadable in the darkness. "Do you truly love her?"

Umar went to his knees and held his hands up to the other man. "May God strike me dead if I am lying! I adore her, but she would never speak to me. If I rescue her, she'll see that I am a fine man and will accept me out of gratitude!"

Isam slapped himself in the face to see Umar's folly. Unfortunately, his nose was still broken. "Ow." He cradled his aching face.

Umar and Samir looked at him.

"My injury hurts," Isam explained. "I want to rest."

Umar jumped up. "We must push on!"

"Good God, you have an iron butt," Isam complained.

"Umar, we'll make better time by daylight when we're rested," Samir replied.

"The moonlight is good. Let's travel while we can. If we get over this ridge tonight, we'll be able to see the lay of the land in the morning. We might spot his smoke when he breaks his fast."

Samir and Isam looked up at the dark bulk of the ridge above them. "There's something in what you say," Samir admitted.

Isam groaned. "An hour. One hour more, then we must rest. We do ourselves no good if we use up our strength the first night."

"All right. We'll eat and water the horses, then push on," Samir decided.

They didn't light a fire even though the chill was clamping down on them. They switched the saddles again, and the horses drank from their cupped hands, then cropped weeds. They gave the animals a little grain.

Suddenly Umar raised his head. "Do you smell that? Woodsmoke!"

The four men stopped in their tracks. Athar twitched his nose. "You're right."

Isam snuffed, but could smell nothing through his injured nose. All day in the saddle had made his face throb mercilessly.

"They can't be far!" Samir exclaimed. The knowledge sparked them with renewed vigor. Leaving the horses and servant behind, the three cousins started forward with Samir in the lead. Umar eagerly hurried after him and Isam brought up the rear.

Suddenly Samir tripped and fell heavily to the ground. The clatter of stones startled birds into flight and their dark shapes erupted through the branches with an alarmed twitter. Before Samir could pick himself up, rocks came tumbling down upon him. Stones bounced over him as he shouted, "Trap!"

CHAPTER 20 : BATTLE FOR THE BRIDE

Umar drew his scimitar and looked around wildly. His eyes darted this way and that, and he swung his scimitar to ward off . . . nothing. No brigands leaped out of the woods at them. The birds settled once again in the branches; insects resumed their shrilling. While Umar stood guard, Isam knelt next to Samir, tossed aside rocks, and asked, "Are you hurt?"

"Not seriously, but damn it, I took a thumping!" Samir sat up and winced. His ear was cut and he was bruised in various places, but he was most annoyed when he discovered the rip in his green coat. "My coat's torn!"

"You're bleeding," Isam said. He pressed the tail of Samir's turban against the wounded ear.

Samir put his hand up to hold it. "Don't get blood on my fancy coat!"

None of them heard the soft steps of the broad-footed camel coming down the trail. Suddenly the maherry burst upon them, and the bright flash of Maureo's scimitar lashed out at Umar. Startled, Umar leaped to the side. Isam jumped to his feet and drew his scimitar. Still on the ground, Samir threw himself aside and gave himself a few new bruises as he rolled over the scattered rocks.

The maherry whirled in place and metal rang on metal as Isam parried the blow the Moor aimed at his head. Umar ran to attack his flank, and Maureo kicked the beast's side and made it dance sideways. Samir had to scramble to avoid being run over. Seated seven feet above the ground on the camel's saddle, Maureo's long blade had the advantage over the shorter scimitars carried by the cousins. Samir and Isam both owned swords suitable for sailors and the confines of a ship. Umar had a longer sword and charged at the interloper. Metal sparked as their blades clanged together.

In the narrow confines of the road, the cousins got in each other's way. Samir opted for the better part of valor and retreated. Athar scrambled out of the way, taking his mount into the brush to escape the melee. Isam was taller than Umar, but that didn't make up for the longer blade used by the Moor. Isam stepped into the woods beside the trail, tripped over a vine, fell, and ripped his pantaloons on thorns. He swore in Turkish, rose, and slogged his way through shrubbery choked with vines to try and flank Maureo. He used his sword as a machete to slash his way through the undergrowth.

Maureo was accustomed to fighting from camelback. He knew the lay of the land and used it to his advantage. He danced the camel sideways along the trail so that his sword arm was always presented to Umar, and he could move fast enough on the trail to prevent Isam from getting around him. The camel's feet were the size of dinner plates and they kept him steady on the uneven footing.

Samir reached down, and picking up stone the size of his fist, hurled it at Maureo. It missed, but Maureo recognized the danger. Missile weapons, even as primitive as stones, could knock him down. He clucked to the camel and whirled away. Man and beast disappeared in the darkness with scarcely a sound; the broad, well-padded feet of the camel were nearly silent even at a gallop. Umar ran after him, but he couldn't keep up with a maherry. The camel was born to run.

"Come back!" Isam shouted, but Umar paid him no attention. Isam ran after him, scimitar in hand.

Umar burst out of the woods and onto the damp ground of a mountain swale. Knee high ferns white with moonlight and dew lay on either side of a stream lazing its way through the hollow to eventually disappear around a bend. Trees were close to the stream except for the small clearing. Maureo's camel splashed across the stream and mounted the hill on the other side. It disappeared in the woods.

Umar turned around and ran back the way he had comes. "Horses! He's getting away!" He nearly collided with Isam.

Isam stepped around him. Holding his scimitar before him like a shield he descended to the stream bed. He found crushed ferns and a stony circle holding embers on the muddy bank that marked the Moor's campsite. They had nearly had him, but the clever creature had given himself warning by setting up the rockfall on his trail.

Samir and Umar came up on horseback, leading a mount for Isam. "Athar is rounding up the rest of the horses. He will catch up to us, " Samir said. He eyed the remains of the campsite. "A good place to rest."

"We can't rest!" Umar said. "We must pursue! We almost had him!"

Isam flung himself into the saddle. "Let's go, but watch out for traps! He's a clever bastard."

Umar took the lead. He kicked his horse to make it run, but it would only trot. He lashed it with his quirt, and the animal leaped and started to canter. Going uphill on the rocky, dark trail, it faltered. Umar lashed it again. Isam followed him, and Samir came after. Their horses were tired, but the camels must be more tired; the Moor didn't have remounts. He was somewhere ahead of them in the darkness.

A musket shot barked and Umar cried out and toppled from his horse. Isam swung his horse to the side, pushed into the foliage, and dismounted. He wormed through the trees and brush until he came up beside Umar. Umar had lain stunned a moment, then crawled into the brush to take shelter behind a tree. Isam knelt beside him.

"Where are you hit?"

"My shoulder," Umar groaned.

Isam could see the white blur of the man's face and haik in the darkness, and a dark stain spreading. He pressed his hand against the wound. "Samir!" he called.

No one answered, but a couple of a minutes later, Samir came wriggling through the brush.

"Umar is hit," Isam told him.

"Damn. How bad is it?"

"Not fatal. His shoulder. He's hurt, but he'll live."

"Get the bastard for me, Isam," Umar pleaded. "I can't fight like this."

Samir took Umar's turban and turned it into a bandage. "He must have a vantage where he can watch the trail. He knows this road." His voice was grim.

"I'll see if I can find him," Isam replied.

He pulled his rifle from the saddle boot, slung the straps of his cartouche and powder horn over his shoulder, and fervently wishing he'd worn something sturdier than sandals, crept into the shrubbery. He pushed through brush, got smacked in the face by a branch, and detoured around brambles which he discovered by blundering into them. He hoped there were no snakes or poisonous insects about. If there were, he couldn't see them in the dark. He navigated by sticking close to the trail where slanting beams of moonlight served as his guide. Easing up close to the trail in the shrubbery, he parted the leaves and peered carefully out. A break opened up the trail about fifty yards ahead. Moonlight gleamed on silvery rocks. That must be Maureo's redoubt.

He measured out a thimbleful of black powder, but otherwise loaded his musket principally by feel. He was a corsair; he was accustomed to doing what needed to be done in the blackness of night. His weapon loaded, he eased himself through the shrubbery with the intention of flanking Maureo's position. He came to a place where the ground was knee deep in sweet-scented mountain flowers. He flitted quickly across them, glad of the easier footing.

The crack of a musket sounded and a ball whizzed through the leaves two feet away. He threw himself flat.

Maureo called out, "You're no woodsman, corsair! I can hear you crashing through the brush. Go back where you came from, or go to Hell."

Isam sulked. He thought he'd been quiet, but Maureo was right. He was out of his element. He crawled on his belly to get behind a tree. "Give us Rabiyah, and we'll let you go!"

He peered around the bole of the tree, but the woods were a maze of moonlight and shadows.

Maureo jeered at him. "Do you think I'd give up the prize after going to so much trouble for it?"

Isam shouted, "Rabiyah! Come out! All will be forgiven! Umar will marry you! He loves you!"

Again the crack of a musket. The ball buried itself in the tree Isam was hiding behind. He had assumed that darkness and woods would conceal him, but now he wasn't so sure. Maureo knew where he was. He was pinned in place.

"Why don't you come out and fight me hand to hand? We'll finish it ourselves, you and me, winner take all," Isam challenged him.

Maureo's laughter drifted down to him. "I have no intention of giving you a free shot. I doubt you could hit the mountain while you were standing on it, but you might get lucky."

"We'll come out together on the count of three! All right?"

After a pause, Maureo replied, "All right."

"One!" Isam shouted.

Being left-handed, he shifted to that side of the tree. Some shrubbery provided a screen to hide behind while letting him look through it. He knelt behind it and put the musket to his shoulder. He scanned the rocks intently. He had good eyes, but he couldn't see any sign of Maureo.

"Two!" He tensed, finger on the trigger, eye sighting along the barrel of the gun.

"Three!"

A muzzle flash lit the rocks in a momentary orange glare. The crack of Maureo's musket rang loud. A ball whizzed through the shrubbery beside him. He fired at the muzzle flash, then darted behind his tree. He reloaded, and was tamping down the ball when a second muzzle flash erupted. This time the ball whizzed through the shrubbery where he had been a moment before. If he had still been there, he would have been hit.

He broke out in a cold sweat when he realized that Maureo knew where he was and could load faster, too. He finished loading, but he didn't dare take another shot. Maureo was too well protected by the rocks. Raising his musket up high, he pointed it in the general direction of the rocks, and fired. He jerked his hand and gun back behind the tree as Maureo fired at his muzzle flash. He leaped up and ran past the shrubs and towards the rocks as fast as he could go. He darted behind another tree and stayed there. He hastily reloaded the musket, then dared to stick his head out for a quick look. He couldn't see anything. There was nothing for him to fire at in the dark. He needed at least one other man to keep Maureo occupied so that he could sight on the muzzle flash or maneuver his position.

He couldn't take Maureo by himself. Even if it were daylight, it wouldn't help. In fact, it would make matters worse. Maureo would be able to see better while staying holed up in his rocks. Isam needed help. He worked his way back to Umar.

"Did you get him?" Umar asked eagerly. Samir had made a sling to cradle his arm against his chest.

"No. He's in some rocks. He's too well fortified. I can't dig him out by myself."

"There's nothing we can do in the dark," Samir said.

"Yes, there is. Listen to me. Umar, can you walk?"

"Yes, I think so."

"All I need from you is to hide behind a tree and fire a musket. Athar can reload for you. You're not trying to hit anything; you're the decoy. He'll fire at your musket flash. Samir and I will be watching. When we see him pop up, we'll shoot him. If we don't get him, we'll keep moving through the woods to a better vantage. After a few minutes, you'll fire again. Once again, we'll aim for him when he returns fire. Eventually, we'll either hit him or reach the rocks where we can fight him."

"I can do that," Umar replied.

Slowly, as quietly as they could, the corsair cousins moved through the woods. Athar helped Umar, then settled down to wait. Isam and Samir conferred, then Samir rested his musket on a tree branch and sighted on the rocks. Isam leaped across the trail and into the woods on the other side, but Maureo didn't fire. Isam congratulated himself for moving too fast for the Moor to track. Samir kept watching the rocks as Isam moved upwards over the rough terrain. The opposite side of the track was rockier with sporadic bare patches. He moved through the shadows, then stopped and took up a position where he could look down at the rocks where Maureo was hiding. He hooted like an owl.

Samir went squirming through the thicker underbrush. Isam winced as he heard it. No wonder Maureo could track them. He kept watch on the rocks and waited for the flash of Maureo's gun. The Moor didn't fire.

An owl hooted on the other side of the trail. A musket shot rang out. Isam kept his eye to his sight, but Maureo did not return fire. Puzzled, he waited and watched. Had Maureo caught onto their scheme? Was he delaying his shot to fool them? Isam waited several more minutes, but Maureo didn't show himself. Isam moved stealthily through the underbrush. He went slow and quiet and made certain of his footing before he put his weight down. He breathed deeply and slowly to keep himself silent. Little by little he edged up higher. He had a clear view of the boulder and the jumble of smaller rocks around it. Vines laced the rocks together. A scar of dark earth showed where the boulder had come tumbling down some time before. He hooted. Once again, Umar's musket barked. Isam could see the flash of orange amid the trees below.

Maureo didn't fire.

Suspicion niggled at Isam. Carefully he moved through the trees to the edge of the scar. Now he could look directly down behind the boulder.

No one was there.

"He's gone!" he shouted into the night. Jumping up, he skidded down the scar of dirt and landed amid the scree. He kicked it and sent pebbles rattling among the underbrush. He swore in Turkish.

Samir clambered up to him. Together the two cousins examined the disturbance of the weeds and leaves. Maureo had been there for sure, but he had outsmarted them and escaped again. A few minutes later, Umar and Athar came up with the horses. Wearily, they mounted up.

CHAPTER 21 : INTO THE CITY

A long hour later they reached Souk al-Arbaa. They pounded on the gate and a guard opened a peephole in the pedestrian door. "Who are you?"

Samir beat the dust off of his green coat, but the color didn't show in the faint light of the aperture. "I'm Samir Sharif Hadad and these are my cousins and servant. We're looking for a man named Maureo. He has kidnapped a woman of our clan. Did they come here? It would have been an hour ago or less."

"A man came with a woman and servant. They said they were ambushed by bandits."

Samir laughed shortly. "He lied. Look at my green coat. Am I a bandit? We are respectable men from Tanguel. The woman is Rabiyah bint Halim. Maybe you've heard of Halim of the Many Daughters?"

"Who?"

"Open up and let us in. We're weary and we want shelter. We're respectable men. If we were bandits, would we pursue him into the town itself? Our mission is righteous. A woman's honor is at stake!"

"Wait." The peephole shut.

A few minutes later the commander of the gate came and looked out the peephole. They had to tell him the story all over again. He wouldn't open the gate. "If your story is true, you can go to the caid in the morning. There's nothing you can do tonight."

"We want shelter. We've ridden hard all the way from Tanguel."

"No."

"You let in Maureo! Let us in, too!"

"They said their lives were in danger. That's the only reason I let them in. If you're what you say you are, camp by the walls and no one will bother you."

"But he'll leave the city in the morning! You're delaying us!"

"It's the caid's business now. We won't allow lawless ruffians to roam about the town at night."

Try although they might, they could not persuade the commander of the gate to let them in. They moved away from the road and made their camp. They didn't bother with tents or a fire. They threw themselves on the ground, rolled up in their cloaks, and slept like dead men. They couldn't have kept watch if they wanted to. They were too tired.

The clatter of farm wagons woke them at dawn. They were cold, stiff, and sore. The call of a muezzin drifted faintly on the air, but Samir and Isam ignored it. Umar, who had a sincere reason to beg God for his favor, washed himself and performed his prayers. Meanwhile, Athar made hot porridge with apple slices. It was the first hot food they'd tasted since leaving Tanguel. They wolfed it down.

A small crowd of wagons, donkeys, and camels laden with firewood or bags of vegetables milled outside the gate as they waited for it to open. The rosy aurora of the eastern dawn pinked the sky. Everything came dimly into view. Forms that had been grey and blurry in the twilight gained form and color. When the morning prayers were over, the gate creaked ponderously and swung open. The cousins quickly packed up and joined the line of vehicles and pedestrians wending into the city.

They found an inn not far inside the gate. It was a simple thing, but it was shelter. Umar was hurting, so they rented a room. He stretched out on the low bed while Samir and Isam squatted beside him.

"I think I had better go to the caid," Samir said. "We don't want to get into trouble with the law. Stay here, Isam. Rest. Don't do anything to annoy the locals."

They nodded agreement. Athar took Samir's green coat to the courtyard to beat the dust out of it. Meanwhile Samir washed up and changed into his other shirt and pantaloons. When Athar returned with his green coat, he wrapped his turban, and looking as respectable as possible under the circumstances, took his leave.

When he was gone, it occurred to Isam that Maureo might have done as they were doing: pausing at the first inn they came to for rest and refreshment. He might even be within the inn itself right now!

"I'll question the servants to see if he was here," Isam told Umar and Athar. He let himself out of the room and made his way downstairs.

The kitchen was pleasantly dim and cool. The ceiling was supported by beams from which depended copper pots and bags of garlic. The copper fireplace hood protruded into the room like the pregnant belly of a fecund woman. Startled, the kitchen maids and cook looked up at his intrusion. Before he could say anything, the cook screamed, "Bandits!"

Tall, dusty, his face still green and streaked with purple from the broken nose, Isam was a disreputable apparition. As he opened his mouth to explain himself, another woman shrieked and a ball of dough came flying at him. He ducked. The cook grabbed the rolling pin and beat him. More dough flew and in spite of his dodges, some of it struck him. It left flour splotches on his navy blue jacket. Knowing that help would come from the inn in response to the women's cries, he darted in the opposite direction and burst out the back door into the alley. He looked swiftly left and right, then ran left, away from the street. Spotting a wooden gate, he leaped up and hauled himself over it to drop into the yard of another building.

The hard packed earth was well trodden by laundrywomen at their tubs. They looked up in surprise. Had he been inclined other than he was, he would have paused to appreciate the sight of wet chemises clinging to the women's bodies, but he was not so inclined. He held a finger to his lips and pleaded with his eyes for silence as the back door of the inn clattered open. Men, both guests and servants, ran left and right along the alley.

One of the women clapped both of her hands to her face to suppress a cry. None of them dared disobey the ferocious-looking stranger. He had a short scimitar thrust into his sash and his beard and clothes were laden with dust from the road. No one doubted they were in the presence of the bandit that gossip had warned them about that very morning.

As the sound of the searchers faded in each direction, Isam was rather embarrassed to find himself in the company of so many indecently clad women. Having grown up in a house full of women, he was keenly aware of the inappropriateness of his intrusion.

"I beg your pardon," he said, touching his turban and bowing left and right. "Please pardon me. A misunderstanding, I assure you. A mistake."

They covered their wet breasts with their arms and stared at him with wide black eyes. He tiptoed through the courtyard and into the building. More women were at work inside where they were pressing cotton and linen clothes with hot irons.

He held his finger to his lips. "Shh. Pardon me. On my way out. Please excuse me."

Bewildered, they watched him go.

Reaching the door, he peered through the fretwork. Not seeing anyone on the street who looked like a searcher, he let himself out. A typical town street, it was so narrow that he could stretch out his arms and almost touch the walls to either side. Shallow steps led up to the left, so he went that way. Attempting to walk nonchalantly along the street, he came to a café. He entered the open door, and with great dignity and a pretense of unconcern, he settled himself in a dark corner of a divan. Several regulars in their long white wool robes and pantaloons were sitting cross-legged on the divan opposite. Smoke from their long pipes wreathed their bearded faces.

"Peace be upon you this fine morning," he said politely.

"Peace be upon you as well," the oldest man replied. He had a grizzled grey beard that hung halfway down his chest. "You're a stranger here."

Isam thought he would do himself a favor and tell his story. "I am. My cousins and I have come in pursuit of a man who carried off a woman of our family."

Three pairs of brown eyes fixed on him with great interest, although their owners continued smoking as if this was a matter of no importance to them.

Isam pressed on. "Have you seen a tall woman dressed in blue in the company of a Moor? She is very beautiful."

The two younger men (who were young only relative to the greybeard, each of them being old enough to be Isam's grandfather) turned their gaze to the old man. He puffed thoughtfully for a while, then removed the clay pipe from his mouth to speak, but before he could, there was a clatter of footsteps outside, and an armed man burst into the café.

"Has anyone seen an armed man go by?"

Skulking wouldn't help, so Isam spoke up. "I did. He almost ran over me. He ran up the steps. A middle-sized fellow with a hooked nose and a long scimitar. He wore a red fez and turban." Those were Maureo's details. "You'd better hurry," he added helpfully.

"Did anyone else see him?"

The greybeards shook their heads.

The soldier ran out and continued up the hill. Isam's coffee arrived. He drank it as placidly as he could manage. He was intensely aware of the old men's eyes resting on him.

"I wonder what that was about," one of the younger old men said.

"I expect the caid's men are looking for the bandit that carried off my cousin," Isam replied.

"Why aren't you looking for him?"

Isam was starting to sweat. "My cousin went up to the palace to ask the caid for help, and now men are searching for the bandit. I had better return to the inn to meet him and see what has happened." He unfolded long legs and walked calmly out of the café.

When Isam had left, he was a topic of conversation. The younger old man on the right asked, "Did you see anyone run past?"

The younger old men on the left replied, "No, I didn't."

"We would have seen a shadow flicker past if he had."

"We certainly would have."

"Maybe he was coming down the steps, but turned around and went back the way he came."

"Why would he do that?"

"Perhaps he saw that tall young man coming up from below and wanted to avoid him."

"If the young man saw him, why didn't he pursue him? If I saw the man that carried off my cousin, I'd go after him, if I was young and had long legs."

"He had very long legs."

"He certainly did. His turban nearly touched the ceiling beams."

"Maybe he was afraid."

The three smoked in silence a while.

"He certainly didn't seem eager to meet up with the man."

"No, he didn't. Sending his cousin to the caid! A red-blooded man would settle an affair of honor himself."

"He must be a coward."

"I thought he had a skulking, untrustworthy look."

The oldest old man finished his pipe and nodded. "Indeed. He obviously comes from the coast. Did you see his short jacket? Positively indecent. His mother is probably an infidel. They have no modesty."

"If I had a son like that, I'd beat him," said the man on his left. There was no heat in his voice. It was merely an observation.

The three greybeards nodded. The matter settled to their satisfaction, they continued as they were. Only the smoke puffing around their heads said they weren't statues.

CHAPTER 22 : FUGITIVES AND RUNAWAYS

Hurrying down the street, Isam paused when he came to a barbershop. He turned in immediately and found a barber at work trimming an old gentleman's beard. He waited patiently in the little room. When the old fellow left, he settled in the seat and said, "A shave, please."

The barber, a fat little man with a congenial smile, wrapped the white cloth around his neck and over his clothes. Then he slathered shaving cream over the short beard and remarked, "You're a stranger here."

"I am," Isam replied. Once again he told the tale of the runaway bride and her bandit lover.

The barber stropped his razor as he listened, then said very seriously, "You won't get any justice from the caid if the man is from around here. Unless you pay very well. If you can pay very well, you will excite his greed, and it's you who will find yourself in jail until he's drained you of every drop of cash your family can raise."

Isam shuddered, and for the first time, worried about Samir. "Samir has a silver tongue. If anyone can manage the matter, he can."

The barber scraped off the beard, and patted Isam's face with a warm towel. "I have a salve for those bruises if you'd like it."

"I would. In fact, if you've got anything that will cover up the bruises, I'd like that too. I look a fright."

"Hmm, hmm. I believe I have something that will answer," the barber replied. He went into another room. He was gone for several minutes, but when he returned, he had a face powder that lightened Isam's complexion. "It won't last. You'll have to reapply it in a few hours, but you look a good deal less green now." He held up a hand mirror.

Isam was pleased to see that the green was hidden under the face powder. A couple of shades paler than his own complexion, it had lightened his face over all. With the loss of the beard he looked quite respectable and not himself at all. "Is there a tailor near by? I have damaged my clothes while traveling."

The barber gave him directions for a shop around the corner. Isam went and bought a robe of tan camel hair. With it covering his blue jacket, he was less conspicuous and decidedly unlike the 'bandit' who had invaded the kitchen and frightened the women. Feeling himself safely disguised, he ambled along the street in the direction of the inn. He walked casually but kept a sharp lookout for soldiers. Reaching the intersection with the inn's street, he looked to the right and saw a party of soldiers loitering in front of the building. He worried about Umar and Athar, but getting himself captured wouldn't help. He did an about face and walked briskly back the way he'd come. He turned down the first side street and found himself in a narrow lane lined by workshops. Open doorways showed men hammering brass or carving leather. He continued walking until he heard footsteps pattering along behind him.

At first he paid no attention to the footsteps. He wasn't the only person in the street, but as he turned into an even narrower street, the footsteps continued behind him and drew nearer. He took another turn and discovered a dead end. Whirling around, his hand went to the hilt of his scimitar. "Who are you?" he demanded.

Startled, the woman stopped in her tracks. She was clad in indigo from head to foot. A veil of faded grey-blue covered her head and hung down to her knees. Netting covered her eyes. She didn't speak.

Isam removed his hand from his sword when he realized it was a woman. "What do you want?" he asked curtly.

The woman looked around the cul de sac, then stepped up closer to him. She lifted up her veil and held it around her head like a hood so that only he could see her face. Not that there was anyone else in the street to observe what she did. Kohl-lined green eyes gazed back at him from a lightly tanned complexion. She had angular features, her nose was a little too large, the lips colorless and thin.

"It's me, Gregorio!" the stranger hissed at him.

Suddenly Isam recognized the man he had only seen at night. "I thought you had black eyes," he said stupidly.

"At night everyone's eyes are black," Gregorio replied, lowering the veil.

"What are you doing here? Where is Maureo? Why the disguise?"

"I'm afraid of Maureo. He beat Rabiyah. We snuck away this morning when he went to the caid. He's going to swear out a warrant against you. He says you're bandits who ambushed him at night."

"Why did he beat Rabiyah?"

Gregorio didn't answer.

"He knows she's not a virgin," Isam guessed.

The veiled head nodded. "He forced her last night. When there was no blood on the sheet, he beat her."

"Where is she?"

"In hiding. I came out in disguise to see if I could find out what's happening. When I saw you in the street, I followed you."

"Take me to her! And by the way, I'm in a bit of trouble myself. I frightened the women at the inn. I didn't mean to, but they screamed and I ran. Now I can't go back because the soldiers are there, but that's where I'm supposed to meet Samir. I've changed my appearance as much as I can, but I'm worried it won't fool them."

"Come with me," Gregorio said. "And by the way, I am now called 'Shirat.' I'm hiding from Maureo." The eunuch led him through the streets until they came to the front door of the laundry.

Isam hung back. "I can't go in there, they'll recognize me!"

The eunuch took his hand and dragged him in. "I'll make it be all right."

Inside, the eunuch spoke to the headwoman, who pulled up her scarf to cover her hair as he spoke. She glanced curiously at Isam but didn't speak to him. She led them both up a narrow flight of stairs into a tiny room. It held a cot and not much more. A single slit window illuminated the room. A female form lay on the bed.

"Rabiyah!" Isam exclaimed. He knelt beside her.

She turned her battered face to him. She was bruised with one eye so swollen she couldn't open it. She groaned. "Isam? Is that you?" She lifted a broken hand. Three of her fingers were splinted and the bandage wrapped around her wrist and forearm. She had tried to defend herself. The rest of her was covered by the blanket.

"It is! You're safe now, Rabiyah. We will take you home. Umar will marry you. He loves you."

"I don't want to marry Umar," she groaned.

"You have to marry somebody. There's no other way. He was very brave. He was shot trying to rescue you. Did Maureo tell you that?"

"He said he shot one of you, but he didn't know which one. I'm glad it wasn't you." Her voice was very low and racked with pain. She gazed at him with her one good eye. "Will you marry me, Isam? Father would like that. You need a wife."

"No!" he exclaimed. "I'm too young to marry."

"Please?" she begged.

"Ask Umar. He'll do it. Look, Rabiyah. Samir told me what he did. Umar doesn't know. Only Samir and I know, and we won't tell."

"He won't want me. Maureo's had me. I was so tired and sore from riding! I only wanted to sleep, but he said we were safe inside the city now, and he wanted me. I said he had to marry me first, but he wouldn't wait. He said he had to make me his so that you would give up and go home. I didn't want to, but he wouldn't leave me alone!"

"That was cruel of him."

"I want to go home!" she wailed.

"You will go home."

"They'll hate me!" She burst out in tears.

"Umar doesn't hate you." Isam dug out a clean handkerchief and gently daubed her tears.

"He will when he knows my shame!"

"We won't tell him. I'll talk to him. If he marries you, you must be grateful to him."

"I don't like him!"

"If he saves you from disgrace, you will have a good reason to like him."

She was silent for a long time. Finally she said, "All right. I'll marry him if he wants me."

"It will be all right," Isam said. He patted her arm awkwardly.

Rabiyah sobbed brokenly and rolled away from him.

Gregorio lifted the veil from his head and hung it around his shoulders like a shawl. "What are we going to do?"

"I have to find Samir and find out what the caid said."

"You can't go out. You'll be recognized."

"Can you go? Disguised as a woman, you can ask the servants at the inn what has happened to Umar."

"I'm afraid to go there!"

Isam stepped up close to the eunuch. "Please?" he asked, invading the slave's personal space. Gregorio backed up until his back hit the wall. Isam gave him his best smile.

Gregorio slumped. "Do you still want me?" He kept his voice very low. His eyes darted past Isam to Rabiyah's back.

Keeping his voice low, Isam replied, "Yes. I'll keep you safe from Maureo. I promise." Exactly how he was going to do that if he and his cousins were considered bandits was a question he would answer later. Right now he was too busy kissing the pretty eunuch.

Gregorio turned his face away. "We are not alone!"

The impetuous corsair recalled himself and drew back. "I think it's best we keep up your disguise. I don't think Samir and Umar need to know who you are right now. I think Umar might thrash you. He wants to thrash somebody, even if he's not fit for it."

Gregorio resigned himself to his fate. "Whatever you say, master, it will be done."

Isam wasn't sure he wanted to be called 'master,' even if he was one. "I'm your lover now. You should called me 'habibi,'" he corrected the slave.

"I can't call you that. Everyone will know."

"True. But in private, you are my darling. My sweetheart. My lover. You can say it then." He kissed the man's neck eagerly.

"As you wish, habibi," Gregorio told his new owner.

Isam's hands roamed over flesh of his new slave. His body was definitely male, but it had a softness that was pleasant to squeeze. He gloated to have possession of something he very much wanted: the body and affections of the slave.

Gregorio twisted away. "I'll go to the inn and find out what's happening." He pulled the faded veil over his head. Thus clad, only his sandal-clad feet and hands (not particularly large for a male) showed. Isam impulsively kissed him through the veil.

Gregorio suffered the kiss, then pushed the amorous corsair away. "I'll go now. Do you have any money? I'll buy us food on the way back."

Isam dug into the pocket in the seam of his pantaloons and pulled out a small leather purse. He opened it and took out several silver coins.

"Food won't cost that much."

"You may need to bribe a guard. If you have any left, buy bread and oil and a cask of water. We may need to hole up here and not go out for a day or two, depending on how hotly they're searching for me. Are the laundrywomen trustworthy?"

"A bit of money for the headwoman will keep things quiet. I gave her everything I had to hide me from Maureo. She's a widow and the sister of the innkeeper, but they don't like each other."

Isam kissed the veil over Gregorio's nose. "May Allah protect you. Go."

Gregorio left.

CHAPTER 23 : PRISONERS OF THE CAID

Both Samir and Umar were in prison. Athar escaped, but the cousin's horses and equipment were seized. All Isam had left were the clothes on his back and the money he was carrying. He had no idea where Athar had gone. Run away to save himself, he supposed. Gregorio tended Rabiyah while Isam paced in the narrow confines of the small room.

Isam said, "I have to go to the prison in disguise and see what I can find out. I can't make a plan without information." He opened up the powder the barber had sold him, but he had no mirror. "Help me with this. Cover up my bruises so they won't recognize me."

Gregorio finished giving Rabiyah water and came over to attend his master. He carefully brushed the cosmetic on, then said, "I can do better than that. Hold still." Taking out some of his own supplies, he lined Isam's eyes with kohl. "You must change the way you walk. Glide along, don't swagger. Be effete. Then they won't see you as a bandit. Don't take your scimitar. If you kill any guards, they'll behead you, so there's no point in having it. If anyone questions you, tell them that you're a servant to a merchant passing through the town. Tell them you want to know if any of the prisoners are for sale because one of your master's porters is sick and he needs a replacement."

"You're clever," Isam said, giving him a grateful look.

Gregorio made him practice a slow, graceful, gliding walk. He taught him to keep his eyes down and to speak humbly. The lessons were hard for Isam. He had always taken it for granted that he could walk where he pleased, say what he pleased, and punch any man in the nose if he didn't like it. He was a free man, a corsair. If he got into an argument, he could defend himself with his fists or his blade. Those were no longer options. The current situation called for guile, not belligerence.

His disguise complete, he let himself into the street. He had to concentrate to keep his gaze lowered and to walk with graceful swaying steps. A long-legged man, he had always walked briskly with strides that ate up the ground. Now he shortened them. He kept his character in mind: he was a servant in no hurry about his master's business. The longer he took, the less work he would do. It was to his benefit to be lackadaisical. He was sweating beneath his clothes, but he kept up the graceful slow walk. It racked his nerves to move so slowly, but eventually he arrived at the prison.

Isam found his way to the prison and was admitted to the commandant's reception room. A pair of divans flanked each other at the opposite end. Tiles in a geometric pattern of terra cotta and green covered the floor, but the walls were whitewashed. Wooden beams supported the ceiling. He advanced and bowed very deeply to the man seated on the far divan. The commandant was a man in his prime, lean, bearded, and wearing indigo pantaloons and shirt. A white turban topped his head. A small scar nicked his cheek beneath his left eye. The skin of his face was tanned and leathered.

Isam bowed deeply with his hand to his forehead. "Peace be upon you, effendi."

"And peace also upon you, stranger. Who are you and what is your business here?"

"I am Moustafa, servant to Abu Rashid, a merchant passing through the city. Are there any slaves for sale here? One of my master's porters is sick and he needs a replacement."

"Yes. We have lots of debtors. Pay what they owe, and you can have them."

"Thank you, effendi. May I see them?"

"Yes. Ugwistan, take him to Lieutenant Afra and let him pick a man. When he's made his choice, bring him back and we'll settle the debt."

Isam and the servant bowed out, both murmuring, "Yes, effendi."

Lieutenant Afra was a black man in a white turban. He and several guards entered the cellblock with Isam. The stench was the first thing Isam noticed. Men had been kept in prison for weeks or months without any way to bathe or change their clothes. The cell smelled like moldy laundry. Listless knots of men sat on the floor with their heads hanging. They were thin and filthy. They turned to look at the intrusion, but nobody spoke. Some gazed at the strangers, hoping against hope that their families had managed to raise the price of their debt to free them, but Isam was a stranger to them and their hopes sank again.

Samir leaped to his feet. Umar remained sitting. He didn't recognize his disguised cousin.

Isam pointed at Samir. "I'll take that one. He looks healthier than the others."

"That one is a bandit, not a debtor," the lieutenant replied.

"My master will know how to tame him. Hobble his feet so he can't run, and I'll buy him."

Catching onto his ploy, Samir pretended he didn't know him. "We are not bandits. We are men from Tanguel, and we have come to Souk al-Arbaa on a mission of honor."

Isam pointed at Umar. "I'll take that one too. He doesn't look as scrawny as the others."

Umar gave him a haggard look. Something about the stranger niggled at his mind and his brow furrowed, but he couldn't figure it out.

The guard replied, "He's wounded and no use to you."

Isam scowled. "He's faking. Anyone can see there's nothing wrong with him. Get up, you. Take off that sling. Nobody believes your sham."

Umar got to his feet and said indignantly, "I am wound—"

Samir's elbow struck him in the ribs. "Shut up. Let me do the talking," he hissed at Umar.

Isam turned his back on him. He told the lieutenant, "These two will do. Hobble them, please."

"I don't think I can give them to you. They haven't been tried yet," the lieutenant replied.

"If they aren't convicts, what are they doing in prison?"

"You'd have to ask the caid," the lieutenant replied.

"I'll ask the commandant. The rest of these men are skinny and they stink. My master needs porters who can carry a heavy load."

The lieutenant, Isam, and the servant went to the commandant, who stroked his beard and considered. "I grant you, they're in better shape than the others. They haven't been in here for months. However, the caid has not yet decided their case. There's a third bandit they're looking for. I really can't let them go before their case has been heard. Pick someone else."

Isam said, "My master said to get a stout fellow, two if I could find good ones. I don't think the others will satisfy him. How much would they cost if the caid agreed to sell them?"

The commandant stroked his beard again. "If the caid says they can be sold, I could let you have the wounded one for twenty-five sequins and the tall one for a hundred sequins."

Isam didn't have that much money. "I will let my master know and see what he decides." He bowed deeply.

The lieutenant walked him out. "You don't want those two. They'll slit your throats in the night. Take a couple of the old debtors. They'll be grateful to leave the prison and will serve you faithfully."

"I suppose that's true, but they don't look like they can carry the load."

"They'll do anything you make them do."

"I will see what my master says." He walked out the gate. He walked too fast and had to remind himself to swish.

Isam was in despair. He only had fifty-five sequins left to buy his cousins, assuming the caid would sell. Even if he sold his sword, he wouldn't have enough money. Suddenly, he had an idea. He marched up to the caid's gate.

"I am Abu Rashid, a merchant passing through the town. I have business with the caid."

He was admitted to the courtyard, led through a cloister, into an antechamber, down a hall, and eventually found himself in the caid's reception room. It was much more splendid than any other reception room he had ever been in. The walls were covered with elaborate tile work in the ever popular blue and white color scheme. It gave the room a cool and restful feeling. Blue and red rugs covered the floor. Red divans topped with sheepskins formed a group on the raised level at the far end. Fretwork sandalwood filled the windows and faintly scented the room. Isam gave his name to the secretary, and joined the men milling about the lower part of the reception chamber. He had to wait a long time.

One by one supplicants were called up. A pair of Jews prostrated themselves before the steps leading to the raised half of the room. They had a dispute about a cow.

After much arguing with each other, the caid interrupted. "Enough. I have made my decision."

The Jews bowed down and waited for his judgment. "I confiscate the cow that is the source of so much trouble to you. I fine you each ten sequins for disturbing the peace of true believers with your petty nuisance. Put them in jail until their debt is paid."

The Jews rose up in horror. "But effendi, we are poor men! The matter of the cow is nothing to a great man like you, but it is a great matter to us! I beg you to reconsider!"

"The bastinado for that one. Fifty strokes. He is insubordinate."

The unfortunate Jews were dragged from the room by soldiers.

Isam had heard that the Jews were exploited by government officials, but he had never paid attention to such tales. With the complacent certainty of a true believer, he had never thought such things would matter to him. Now he was alarmed. If the caid treated men of his own city like that, how would he react to a stranger who had been unjustly accused of banditry?

"Abu Rashid, come forward," the herald called.

At first he didn't react to hearing his alias called.

"Abu Rashid! Come forward! Is he here?"

Isam shook himself and hurried forward. He stopped before the step and bowed deeply with his hand to his forehead. "I am here, noble lord."

The caid was a corpulent man. He was dressed in blue and black with a red turban. A heavy gold chain hung around his neck in support of an amulet case. Rings adorned his hands. He leaned forward to inspect the stranger. "I've never seen you before. Who are you?"

"If it please your lordship, I am Abu Rashid, a merchant from Meknes on my way to Kenitra. One of my porters has fallen ill and I need to replace him. Another one is lame and is slowing us down. I went to your prison to see if there were fellows fit to carry burdens, and I found two, but the commandant says they are bandits who have not yet been tried. I would like to offer you twenty-five sequins for each of them. I'm sure they must be guilty, or you would not have detained them." He bowed deeply again.

"I know the ones. We caught them this morning. I'm happy to sell them to you, but first I must see if the price satisfies the man they have wronged. If he agrees, you will pay him. Send for Maureo."

Isam's heart thudded in his chest. He was certain Maureo would recognize him. He replied, "You are wise, effendi. It is fair that those they have wronged should receive their price. I will go and fetch the money immediately." He rose and started backing away.

The caid's mouth curved faintly in a gesture that could not be called a smile. "Stay. You will need to know the price so you can pay it. I insist."

Isam swallowed hard. "As you wish, effendi." He turned his head toward the door, but the guards crossed their spears over it. He could not leave. His heart sank into his stomach. He was cornered and he knew it.

Two more guards dressed all in white with yellow sashes moved in on him. They seized him by the arms and pulled him aside. They shoved him to his knees, twisted his arms behind his back, shoved a staff through them, and bound them in place. A heavy hand shoved his head down. He gritted his teeth as the fierce binding made his shoulders hurt. Held in that position, he could see nothing but his own knees and the boots of the men around him. He had no doubt that he would shortly join his cousins in prison. Maureo had won.

CHAPTER 24 : JUSTICE FOR THE BRIDE

Maureo arrived in three quarters of an hour. When he was called forward, he bowed deeply. He didn't pay any attention to the other men waiting in the lower part of the room; his eyes were on the caid. He paused before the steps and bowed deeply to the man. "You summoned me, noble lord?"

Smiling at him, the caid said, "A merchant from Meknes has a proposition for you. He wishes to buy the bandits who wronged you. Name your price, and he will pay it."

The guards seized the staff and raised Isam to his feet. They drove him forward and forced him onto his knees at the foot of the steps. Astonished by this turn of events, and more than happy to see the cousins sold into slavery to his own profit, Maureo turned to see who was making the offer. At first he didn't recognize Isam, but then he blinked and exclaimed, "That's him! That's the third bandit!"

The audience rumbled. The caid gloated. He was well-pleased that he had seen through Isam's deceit.

Isam spoke up, "You have been deceived, great caid. That man is the bandit. He has stolen a woman of our clan and made off with her. We are her cousins come to fetch her back."

Maureo scoffed. "He lies. She is my wife. These bandits saw her beauty and tried to steal her to satisfy their lust!"

Isam interrupted. "Summon the woman and let her testify. If she says she is his wife, then he can have her. But if she claims us as cousins, you know we have told the truth and he has lied."

Maureo objected. "My wife is a modest and respectable woman. I will not subject her to the profane gaze of men."

"Because you're afraid of what she'll say!" Isam argued.

"Enough!" the caid bellowed. "Summon the woman."

Maureo began to squirm. His goatee jutted out as he tried to ingratiate himself with the caid. "I beg you to be merciful, noble caid. She is exhausted after our long flight. Let her come tomorrow."

The caid's eyes narrowed. "I said, 'Summon her!' If you don't call her here, I will send guards to fetch her."

"I will go and fetch her myself," Maureo promised.

"You will not. Guards. Fetch the woman. Where is she?"

"At the Mountain Star Inn, near the western gate," Maureo replied.

A guard was dispatched. When he had gone, Isam said, "No, she's not. I've already been there."

Maureo recovered himself. "If she's not, it's because this one carried her off in my absence!"

"How could I do that? I've been here all along!"

"Your henchmen. You've hired footpads and ruffians to help you!"

"Nonsense. How could I do that in the short time I've been in the city? I wouldn't even know where to look. I'm not acquainted with gutter scum like you."

The caid roared, "Silence! Maureo, when was the last time you saw your wife?"

"This morning, just before I left to come here," the Moor promptly replied.

"He lies. He tried to force himself on her last night, but she wouldn't yield, so he beat her. She escaped in the night. I know where she is. I found her. Her loyal servant helped her escape and hid her. When he saw me in the street, he told me, and I have put her in a safe place. She is badly injured."

Maureo sputtered, "He lies! She has no servant! There is only my eunuch, Gregorio!"

Isam spoke hotly. "The eunuch is my property. When I saw Maureo following her, I set him to spy upon him. When this man Maureo persuaded Rabiyah to run away, my servant told me. That is why we were able to come so swiftly and to know which road he took. Rabiyah was foolish to run off with Maureo, but he deceived her. He told her he would marry her once they reached his own people. He said they would have a great feast, attended by all the most notable people in the district, that he would give her sheep and camels, that she would have servants to wait on her, and that she would be held in the highest honor. Poor gullible girl, she believed him. Last night he showed what he really was when he demanded from her what only a wife may give. She refused, so he forced himself on her."

"Balderdash! He lies, he lies! I said no such thing! She is my wife, I swear it! We have been married for three years. I adore her, so I brought her with me when I came to Tanguel on business. This one lusts for her and importuned her in the streets. I blacked both his eyes and drove him off."

Isam sneered. "It wasn't Maureo that struck me in the face. It was a Spanish anchor cable. I cut it and wrecked the Spaniard at Cape Spartel. Ask my cousins how it happened. They can tell you."

The caid watched the two men shouting at each other. He was immensely entertained. "Somebody is a very great liar, but the truth will out. We'll know soon enough. You, what is your true name?" He pointed at Isam.

"I am Isam bin Hamet, an ensign aboard the *Grey Wolf*. My father Hamet Rais was the captain of the *Seahawk* before his death. My uncle is Halim of the Many Daughters and Rabiyah is his daughter."

The caid looked surprised. "I have heard of Halim of the Many Daughters. Allah favors him. They say he is a lucky man that never fails to get his prize."

"Allah has blessed him," Isam replied.

"Do you truly know where this woman is?"

"I do."

"Summon her." He gestured and another soldier came forward.

Isam gave him his instructions. "Tell Gregorio that his master Isam summons him and not to be afraid. Tell him to bring Rabiyah with him." He gave the address and the soldier departed.

The first soldier returned to report. "The woman is not at the inn. The innkeeper says she left in the night. He doesn't know where she is."

Maureo ground his teeth so hard that his beard bristled.

The caid lifted a bushy eyebrow. "Last night? You said you saw her this morning."

"This man has bribed the innkeeper to lie on his behalf!"

"If I believe you, he has been very busy since he arrived in Souk al-Arbaa," the caid replied.

"I didn't have to bribe anyone," Isam replied.

"We'll know soon enough. In the meantime, tell me about the Spanish ship you say you wrecked." The caid interlaced fat fingers and watched Isam with glittering black eyes.

Perhaps he thought to catch the young corsair in a lie, but Isam was on secure ground now. He settled back on his heels and regaled the caid with the story of how the *Grey Wolf* sought refuge in Tanguel and all that came after it. The audience was pleased to hear of Rajet Rais' cleverness in defeating the Spanish frigate, and they looked with approval on the young corsair.

"You can't believe him, effendi! He is a Scheherazade beguiling you with tales to evade your judgment!"

"Scheherazade was an honest woman, and in time, the sultan came to know it. Then he loved her and kept her close to him," the caid observed.

Maureo gnashed his teeth.

A noise announced an arrival in the antechamber. The secretary went to see who it was. Gregorio, dressed in his own clothes, helped support a figure into the room. The faded blue veil covered the brighter blue of Rabiyah's clothes. When she saw Isam bound on his knees, she rushed to him and threw her arms around his neck. "Cousin!" she cried. "What have they done to you?"

"Who are you, woman?" the caid demanded sternly.

She turned to face the caid. "Rabiyah bint Halim of the Many Daughters. Why have you tied up my cousin? He came to rescue me from that lying thief!" She pointed at Maureo with her bandaged hand.

"She could be any slut they hired to lie for them!" Maureo objected.

"Show your face, woman!" the caid thundered.

Gregorio gently lifted the veil from her. The company gasped when it saw her swollen, battered face. Her waves of tangled black hair fell around her shoulders. She covered her face with bandaged hands and sank down. She sobbed into the bandages.

"Who did this to you?" the caid asked in a gentler voice.

Still weeping, Rabiyah pointed a splinted finger at Maureo. "He said he would marry me, but when I went with him, he beat me and raped me!"

"She's a slut! She's no virgin!" Maureo raged. "It's true I promised her marriage, but I thought she was pure!"

"Then you admit it. This woman is not your wife," Isam pointed out.

Maureo realized his error. Before he could equivocate, the caid spoke. "Rabiyah bint Halim, you have done a shameful thing. You have run off with a man who is not your husband. The only honorable solution is marriage. You and Maureo must keep the foolish promise that you made."

Rabiyah burst out in fresh weeping.

"No!" Isam shouted. "Effendi. I have told you the truth. Release me and my cousins. Let us take her home. We will find a husband for her, an honest man."

"No honest man will want her. She has made her bed; now she must lie in it," the caid announced.

Rabiyah wailed and threw herself on the floor. "Mercy! Please, I want to marry my cousin Umar! He asked before, but I was silly and rejected him! I have learned my lesson! Please don't make me marry Maureo! He'll beat me!"

"You deserve it," the caid replied.

Isam spoke up. "Effendi, if Umar wants her, isn't the wish of an honest man more worthy of fulfillment than the lies of a rogue? Won't she be better off with a moral husband, a man who has risked his life and been shot for her? If you give her to Maureo, you're letting him profit from his villainy while poor honest Umar has nothing to show for it but a bullet hole. Is that fair?"

The room murmured. The caid considered it. "Send for Umar. Bring the other one as well."

The room buzzed with conversation. Each new twist and revelation titillated the people. Rarely were audiences in the caid's chamber so entertaining. It was like watching a puppet play, but with flesh and blood actors.

When Umar and Samir arrived, the wounded cousin saw Rabiyah and flung himself on his knees at her side.

"Rabiyah! Thank Allah, we found you!"

She flung her arms around him and wept against his neck. "Umar! Save me!"

He pulled her tight against his chest with his one good arm. "Of course! I've been so worried about you. You have suffered so much! Oh, my foolish girl! Why did you run away?"

Rabiyah cried and cried. "I'm sorry, Umar. I'm so sorry! You were so ordinary and he was so charming! Now I know it's better to have an honest husband than a liar! Please forgive me! I'll be a good wife, I promise! I will be forever grateful and obedient if you will have me! I swear it!"

"Of course I'll marry you!" he exclaimed. "I forgive you everything."

Samir beamed at the two. Having been released by the soldiers, he sidled over to Isam. Out of the corner of his mouth, he said in Turkish, "I told you I could talk him into it," in a low voice.

The caid was well pleased. "Umar bin Bazam, you are a generous and noble soul! What a privilege it is to meet such a fine youth! You shall be married immediately, and I shall give the bride a dower myself. You shall live in comfort for the rest of your lives. Truly Allah is merciful."

Maureo sulked. Isam beamed, then rubbed his arms when they released him and he could stand up and get the kinks out. Samir kept his thoughts to himself. Later, when Rabiyah gave birth to a strapping male infant a month early, they attributed it to the vigor of a healthy father. They were right, although only Isam and Samir knew how right. As for Umar, he was proud to see his virility so handsomely validated.

The caid didn't return their horses. Instead he gave them fine new horses with better saddles, a pair of donkeys with packs full of supplies, costly fabrics, ostrich feathers, and spices. As for Maureo, he was thrown into prison and bastinadoed five hundred strokes on the soles of his feet and kept in prison until his clan paid his ransom. He was lame after that and harbored a hatred for corsairs and everything having to do with the sea. He never went within sight of it again.

Umar adored his wife and was very pleased to be married to such a beautiful woman. Rabiyah was pleased to be married to a man with money, thanks to the caid's largesse. Umar gave his cousins spices and ostrich feathers in gratitude for their help. Samir sold them and split the money with Isam. They could have lived happily ever after, but they were corsairs, and they had hearts as restless as the sea.

CHAPTER 25 : SILVER SADDLES

The cousins and their servants rested in Souk al-Arbaa for several days, then descended to Tanguel by easy stages. Arriving at Dlalha, they found the caravanserai full of dusty, dispirited people. Men, women, children, camels, donkeys, horses, and porters were loaded down with possessions. One camel had packs upon its back, and on top of that, an upside down table, and a pair of stools. Elsewhere, three small children and a cat were riding in panniers on either side of a packhorse. Women with infants on their backs went to the well to draw water. Tents were set up in a line outside the overflowing caravanserai.

Speechless, the cousins surveyed the mass of human beings. Samir called out to a man who carried a spear in his hand and had a blue turban wrapped around his head. "What has happened here?"

"The Spanish are besieging Tanguel. They are bombarding it with shells and doing much damage. These people are fleeing for their lives."

The cousins swung off their horses and had to wait in line to draw water. Hundreds of people were camping at the caravanserai for the night. Once they had slaked their thirst, Isam said, "We should push on. We will arrive in Tanguel tonight if we hurry."

They looked at one another uneasily. "I don't think we should put ourselves into a city under siege," Samir replied.

"Our families will worry about us," Isam replied.

"No, they'll be glad we're not caught in the siege. Besides, you know what we're carrying. We could get robbed by desperate people." Samir lowered his voice for the latter remark.

Isam looked around and saw a couple of young men eyeing their silver inlaid saddles. Keeping his own baritone quiet, he said, "They're noticing our horses and saddles. We'd better move on. If we stay here, we'll be robbed."

"You're right," said Samir. "We'd better throw blankets over them so they're not so obvious on the road."

"I think it's too late," Isam replied. "We must hurry."

Switching the saddles to their remounts, the party moved out at a brisk trot with Samir in the lead and Isam in the rear. They kept Rabiyah, Gregorio, and the remounts in the middle with Umar and Athar riding on the flanks. Once out of sight of Dlalha, they put spurs to their horses and cantered. Rabiyah clung desperately to the pommel, but managed to remain in the saddle. Isam kept checking over his shoulder in case they were followed.

Their way was quickly checked when they ran into a crowd of refugees on foot. A pair of ragged, thin men pulled and pushed a cart by hand. Wooden wheels thumped noisily over the uneven road. Dusty, bowed women trudged with children on their backs. Wary men eyed the cousins and felt for their daggers, just in case. Slowly the crowd moved aside for the mounted travelers. The cousins' party slowed to a trot and passed single file through the narrow space.

Looking back, Isam saw another party of horsemen come out of the trees. He made a shrill whistle between his teeth, then pulled his musket from its boot. Refugees scattered when they saw his weapon. They scrambled over low stone fences and ran through the fields of grain no more than calf high. Some of them dropped their packs so they could run faster.

Isam whirled his horse and put his musket to his left shoulder and sighted. Athar slapped the packhorses with his quirt to make them run. Rabiyah and Gregorio ran with them, but Athar came to Samir's side to help reload. Umar and Samir both paused to load their muskets. They were twenty and thirty yards away from Isam respectively.

Half a dozen men on nags fanned out across the road. Only one of them had a musket. The others drew scimitars. "Throw down your weapons and we'll let you live!" the leader shouted. He was a wiry man with a black curly beard and a red fez.

"No! Go back where you came from, or I'll shoot you!" Isam shouted.

"Even if you're a good shot, you can only kill one of us. As you see, we are six in number. We will cut you down before you can reload."

"I am Isam, son of Hamet Rais, and I am a true son of Tanguel! You are cowards who run away from the Spanish dogs!"

The leader spit on the ground. "What do I care about a stinkhole like Tanguel? The Spanish have done me a favor. Now I can become rich."

"Or dead," Isam replied. He took a careful aim on the leader.

"Shoot him," the bandit told his musketeer. "Charge!" He kicked his horse forward and crouched low over its neck.

The man disappeared from Isam's sight as he hid behind his horse's head, so Isam dropped his aim lower. He pointed directly at the center of the white horse's broad chest and squeezed the trigger. Red blood splattered from the wound and the horse crashed to the ground. The leader summersaulted over the animal's head and rolled across the road. Meanwhile, the brigand musketeer was frantically reloading, but what had become of his shot, Isam didn't know. He didn't care. He drew his sword with his left hand, kicked his heels against the sorrel, and charged the bandits. The wild ululating cry of an Arab warrior burst from his throat. The bark of muskets sounded behind him; Samir and Umar were shooting. He hoped they wouldn't hit him but didn't worry about it. It was up to them to take their aim.

Surprised by the sudden attack, half the bandits turned and fled. The musketeer loaded again, but he couldn't get a good aim at Isam on account of one of his comrades charging forward sword in hand. Umar and Samir plunged off the road, leaped their horses over ditches and fences, and opened up their shooting angles so they could both snipe at the musketeer without hitting Isam. He didn't notice. He was too busy.

The bandit and the corsair flashed past each other with a clang of swords. They whirled around and charged at each other again. The bandit was the better horseman, but the sorrel beneath Isam was the better horse. The gelding knew more about mounted combat than his rider did, and trumpeting, bared his teeth and snapped at the other horse as they came together. The bandit's nag shied away and the rider missed his aim. Isam slashed his arm. Red blood stained the white wool shirt.

Meanwhile, the bandit leader picked himself off the ground and ran towards Isam with his scimitar in his hand. He had a longer sword than the short Moorish blade the corsair carried and it helped. Isam found himself flanked on either side and kicked his mount to spurt between them. He cleared his two opponents and whirled back. The agile horse snorted and reared up, lashing out with his front hooves at the man on foot. The bandit leader scampered away, but the mounted bandit pressed him. Side by side they battled, swords flashing in the sun and ringing as they struck each other. The bandit suddenly kicked Isam's horse in the throat and the animal shied away and neighed unhappily.

Isam couldn't defend himself while grabbing the pommel and trying to stay on his mount. He saw movement from the corner of his eye and threw himself off his horse. He crashed to the ground and lost his sword in the process. The sorrel danced over him but didn't step on him. When the horse cleared him, he found the bandit leaning down to stab him. He rolled away, and learning a dirty trick from the bandit, kicked up into the bandit horse's groin. The bandit's nag squealed in pain and jumped away. The bandit clung to his back and fought to get the horse under control as it bucked. Isam rolled the other direction.

Another musket barked, and the bandit dropped his sword. Red stained his right arm. Looking around swiftly, the wounded man saw that he was alone. His leader was sprawled in the dust. He put heels to horse and sprang away. He had run about ten yards when another musket barked, but the shot missed. Umar swore and reloaded as fast as he could, but Samir got off another shot before he did. He missed too. It took three shots by the cousins, but they finally brought him down.

Surveying the scene, the cousins found two dead bandits and two wounded bandits. They herded the survivors together. Slowly, refugees reappeared from behind stone fences or crawled out of ditches. They spit on the wounded bandits. "Allah will burn your souls!" they told the captives.

"What are we going to do with them?" Isam asked.

Samir dismounted his horse and walked up to the captives. "You attacked us. You tried to kill us. You deserve this," he told the bandit leader. He swung his blade and chopped halfway through his neck. The blade jammed in the spine and he had to put his foot on the dead body to wrench it loose.

The other wounded man saw what had happened, saw the angry faces of the refugees, then jumped to his feet and ran as fast as he could. From somewhere among the refugees, a pistol fired. Red blossomed right in the middle of the fugitive's back. He sprawled in the dust.

They left him lying in the dust. Refugees gathered up the bandit horses and brought them to the cousins. Three of the animals were still alive. The dead white horse lay in the road. "Clear that obstacle," Isam told the refugees. Working together, a team of ten men dragged the animal into the ditch and left it. They brought the saddle to Isam. "I don't want it. Somebody else can have it."

The three horses were nags of no particular merit, but they were horses and therefore booty. They went through the saddle bags but found very little in them and nothing that they wanted. They left the bandits' personal possessions scattered on the road. When it was apparent they didn't want them, refugees darted forward and looted the saddlebags.

Collecting the three new horses, they trotted down the road to catch up to their servants and train of animals. They had no further problems on the road to Tanguel.

CHAPTER 26 : THE SPANISH BOMBARDMENT

The Spanish sent a squadron to punish Tanguel for its impudence in harboring the *Grey Wolf*. Survivors from the wreck at Cape Spartel had told them who was responsible. When they found their missing frigate captive in the Tangueli harbor, they grew even more wroth. Accordingly, they sent their messenger ashore under a white flag of truce, demanded the release of Spanish prisoners and the return of the frigate, and settled in to bombard the city until the rovers gave them what they wanted. The corsairs, equally stubborn, refused.

The Spanish squadron consisted of five warships and an advice boat. The flagship was a frigate of forty-four guns. Too big to get in close, she was moored outside the shoals and lobbed shots at the fortress from long range. Four frigate-rigged xebecs of twenty to twenty-eight guns formed a line about six hundred yards offshore. One was just north of the fortress, one abreast it, one across the harbor entrance, and one just south of it. The smaller xebecs at the southern end of the line were lobbing their shells into the harbor. The trapped vessels had lowered their antennas so they wouldn't show above the spit of land that separated the harbor from the sea, but the Spanish were uncanny good marksman. The corsairs moved the galleys, but pretty soon the Spaniards found them again and the bombardment continued. The defenders had to do something.

Isam was sweating inside his wool coat even though it was a cool spring day. A drizzle of rain annoyed the men, but made the officers happy. If it would continue. Darkness would help their plan. But not yet. First they had to prepare for the attack. Accordingly, he led a party among the dunes to discover the best spot to carry it out. He had no fear of being seen—until a pair of shots rang out. He flung himself into the weeds beside the trail, but it was too late. A ball passed through the top of his fez. One of his men cried out in pain and toppled into the weeds on the other side of the trail. For a moment his boots lay in the path, then drew up into the dubious shelter of the weeds. The other man with him dove into shrubbery a few feet behind him.

Isam swore. "They've got a lookout on the dune ahead!" Now he knew how the Spanish always managed to hit their targets. They had landed a spotter to spy on the harbor and signal the ships. For his plan to work they had to clear the Spaniards from the point and keep them away.

"Malek! Run back and tell Samir we need support! The Spaniards have lookouts with at least two muskets on the dunes!" Assuming they were safe on the inland side of the dunes, none of the corsairs had brought a musket.

"They'll shoot me if I run!"

"We can't stay here!"

"Then we both run in opposite directions."

"I'm not keen to be shot."

"Now you know how I feel."

Isam swore again. "We can't stay here!"

"Why not? Maybe Samir has heard the shots and is coming up."

Another musket rang out and a ball plowed into the earth about a foot in front of Isam. "Because they've found the range and we'll be dead if we stay!"

Malek swore. "All right. I'm going to run to the rear. Don't run into me!"

"What about me?" the wounded man called from the other side. "I can't run; they hit my leg!"

"Play dead. We'll get help," Isam told him.

"Hurry!"

"All right. Ready? On the count of three. One, two, three!"

The two unwounded men leaped up. Isam sprang to the left, then dove behind a driftwood log lying a few feet further along the trail. He had no eyes to spare for Malek, but he heard the man's boots thudding as he ran. Two shots rang out, but no cries answered them. Malek disappeared around a bend in the trail.

"Are you all right?" the wounded man called anxiously.

"I'm fine. Now hush. We don't want them to hear us."

The Spaniards tried a couple of pot shots, but they couldn't get at Isam even though they knew he was hiding behind the log. About fifteen minutes later he heard the thud of feet on the trail. Squirming around to look behind him, he saw Samir at the head of a troop of men. He held up his hand in warning, then gestured up to the top of the next dune. Samir nodded. He gave orders to his men and some slunk around the rear of the dune. After fifteen or twenty minutes, shots rang out on the seaward side of the dune.

"They're getting away!" a voice cried in Arabic.

Isam flung himself to his feet and sprang into the deeper brush on the side of the dune. Nobody shot at him. Running between the two dunes, he looked up, but couldn't see anyone amid the shrubs atop the hill. He plunged into the swale that divided them and ran toward the sound of the shots. Burrs and sticks poked at him, then he burst out on the seaward side.

The Spanish had piled into their boat and were pulling as fast as they could toward the nearest xebec. She ran out a pair of guns and fired at the shore to cover the boat's retreat. Fountains of sand flew up and showered the Moors with debris. They turned and ran back into the dunes.

Two more shots plowed deep into the flanks of the dunes. The shots opened a pair of sandy scars that sent miniature landslides of sand and shrubbery down to the beach. The layer of topsoil on the dunes was very thin and easily torn. The boots and sandals of the retreating corsairs left sandy pockmarks wherever they scrambled. Samir's men peppered the Spanish boat with their muskets, but the Spanish had too great a head start. They wounded a man, but inflicted no other casualties.

Isam scrambled up the dune. At the top he found a small camp where half a dozen men had spied on the harbor and stood watch in case the rovers were smart enough to figure out they were there. A good brass spyglass was left behind. He appropriated it. It hung heavily against his leg in the seam pocket of his pantaloons. A canvas tarpaulin formed a shelter under which were Spanish bedrolls and personal items. There wasn't much: a few shirts, a shaving kit, coarse crockery dishes, pots, and food. They had kept a cold camp; they couldn't run the risk of having a fire.

Bounding down the dune, he ran into Samir.

"There you are! We've driven off the Spanish. Where were you?"

"Searching their camp. I didn't have a musket. We need to occupy this camp to make certain they don't come back. We can't run the risk of them interrupting our plan."

Samir nodded. He gave orders, and his men climbed up the dune to take possession. He surveyed the swale. "I think this might be a good location for our plan."

"I think so too. That inlet dips in part way between the dunes, and the swale is low and muddy. There's water in here at high tide."

Samir nodded. "It will work."

The rovers went to work. With log rollers under the boats and tackle to pull them, men heaved the boats up onto the beach behind the dunes, dragged them through the ravine, and left them between the dunes. They covered them with brush to keep them hidden from Spanish eyes. Boat after boat accumulated in the dunes, and sentries were left to guard them. The rest of them went home to eat, sleep, and prepare.

After dark they assembled again. Rain spit intermittently. It was enough to annoy them, but it also served to cover up the moon. That was the drawback to their plan; they had to carry it out at high tide so the captive frigate with its Muslim crew could get over the sand bar. They needed the vessel's firepower to back up their sortie.

Isam led his boat down to the water. Further along the beach, Samir and his crew wrestled their boat to the water's edge. More boats came out of the dunes and launched into the chilly sea. They waded into the water and tumbled over the gunwales into the boats. Floating freely, they wrapped rags around the thole pins and settled the grommets into place. Isam took his place in the sternsheets and put his hand on the tiller. Speaking softly, he said, "Oars, silent rowing. Make way together."

As quietly as they could, they rowed across the gentle swells. Samir and his boat was to his left and a few yards behind. He looked back in time to see another boat launch and her crew hop silently into her. Boat after boat came out of the dunes and followed him through the water. They spread out in a wide semicircle to make it difficult to aim at them. The smallest xebec was closest to them. She had put out two anchors to hold her in position. It would only take a few minutes to row up on her; they might make it undetected.

They didn't. They had crossed half the gap when suddenly the xebec's bell clattered out the alarm. They kept rowing silently; they didn't want to give away their numbers or position. "Row like your lives depend on it! Faster, damn you, faster!" Isam hissed at them.

The oars leaped with sudden energy as they pulled as hard and fast as they could. All the other boats did the same. The Spanish bowchasers opened fire. Two shots went whizzing harmlessly overhead and into the sea. Isam instinctively ducked at the sight of the fiery tongues as the cannons belched brimstone. The Spanish ran the guns in and reloaded. Isam found himself strangely calm. The plan was in motion. There was no need to worry. All he had to do was what he said he would do.

They arrived under the bows of the Spaniard before she fired again. The figurehead of a bishop in a miter looked down on them in disapproval. If Isam could have read the Nazarene script, he would have known her name to be *San Fermín,* but he couldn't, and he wasted no time wondering about it. The attackers scrambled up the chains and rails, forced their way in through the gun ports, and met stiff resistance. Isam clambered up to the foredeck and battled the sailors he met there. Below him, someone cut the anchor cable and the bow began to drift gently out to sea. She could no longer use her guns against the town.

More boats arrived and swarmed alongside. There was no need for silence any longer. The Sallee rovers swarmed up the sides shrieking their battle cries. The defenders on the foredeck realized they had enemies behind them and whirled around to fight them, or to jump over the side to escape. Isam found himself in control of the bow of the vessel. He let out an ululating cry and brandished his scimitar aloft. "*Allahu Akbar!*"

The corsairs took up the cry. "*Allahu Akbar!*"

The Spanish crew retreated and on the quarterdeck, sailors loaded up the swivels and fired down into the boarders below. The small shot was devastating at short range. Corsairs fell bloody on the deck while others leaped into the shelter of the coach.

Spanish marines took aim at the tallest figure among the attackers. "Get down, rais!" one of his men called urgently. Isam retreated behind the mast.

A rover lay on his belly to present a minimal target for the quarterdeck marines, carefully aimed, and fired. Other boarders lay, knelt, or stood, taking advantage of the cover afforded by the mast, guns, rembate, and belaying furniture. It wasn't much, but it was what they had. Half a dozen more swarmed up the shrouds to the fighting top.

"Hold your fire! Wait for my signal!" Isam barked.

The fire from the quarterdeck became lively now that they were unopposed. A man near Isam gasped and gurgled. He fell on the deck.

"Rovers, on my signal!" He took a breath, then shouted, "Now!"

A volley of musket fire erupted from the bow. A Spanish officer spun around and died. The men who were sheltering in the coach swarmed up the ladders to the quarterdeck the instant they heard the crack of the muskets. The Spanish marines swung their muskets like clubs to knock them down again. The Tangueli musketeers aloft aimed carefully, but had few available shots as the battle turned into a melee.

"Men of Tanguel! Follow me!" Isam jumped out from behind the mast, ducked under the rembate, and charged the length of the main deck. The men from his boat followed him, and other corsairs joined the rush. They threw grenades onto the quarterdeck and explosions split the night with light and noise. A grenade came rolling back, caught against the railing, and blew it to flinders. Peppered with flying splinters, Isam charged up the ladder shouting at the top of his lungs. The rovers roared and surged up after him.

The yellow and gold flag of Spain came down.

Isam grinned as he took possession of his prize. "Send them to the benches, all of them, and quickly!"

The prisoners were made to row with well-armed corsairs standing guard over them. Isam found himself in charge of a twenty gun xebec. His victory had not gone unnoticed. As soon as the red flag of the Sallee Republic rose, a hail of nine pound shot rained down on him from the nearest Spanish vessel.

"Helm, hard to port! Oars, out oars!"

Isam's crew clubbed some captured Spaniards to make them obey. They bent their backs for fear the corsairs would kill them if they didn't. The drum beat set the rhythm and the oars turned white with foam as the blades dipped into the sea in unison. Meanwhile Samir clambered up to the quarterdeck to serve as his lieutenant.

"Make the signal!" Isam shouted.

Samir moved to the swivel guns and commanded the gun crew. They fired one, two, paused, three, four. That was the agreed upon signal. Sallee boats poured out of the harbor mouth and raced for the second xebec. Isam stepped to the rail of the vessel and gazing down, shouted, "Man the larboard guns!"

He had about a hundred men on board. He wished he had double the number. Half his crew was needed to work the boat and half to fire the guns. He wasn't able to maneuver very quickly with only captive Spaniards at the oars, but he didn't need to. All he needed was to keep his broadside to the enemy.

"Double shot, grape and round! Aim for deck level! Wait for my command!"

He looked around frantically. So much to keep track of! The progress of the Salletine boats. The actions of multiple enemies. The shot and powder flowing along his own deck. The movement of his vessel. The nearness of the shore. The shoals. He thought it would tear his brain apart to hold so many things in mind at once. He felt immense pressure. He must see everything. He must make the right decision. He must give the correct command. The success of the mission depended on him. Sweat trickled along his scalp and made his wool collar itch against his skin.

What had Rajet told him? Plan ahead! How could anyone make plans in the midst of chaos like this? Suddenly he understood. If he had planned ahead, he wouldn't have to plan in the midst of chaos. He sucked in a deep breath to steady himself. Right. He had a plan. That plan was to take the second xebec. With that goal in mind, it became much easier to juggle the many strands of combat. He looked down to see his gunners standing and staring up and him. They were ready. They had finished loading while he was in his funk.

The Salletine boats were half way to the second target. The second xebec had let loose her blast and was cranking around on her springs to present her broadside to them. She knew the greatest danger came from being boarded. Well then. He must time his shot to the best advantage of the boarders. He must hold his fire until they were right up close so that his shot could sweep her deck and make the defenders duck down. That would give the attackers a precious moment to get up her side.

Big shot whistled through his rigging. Something cracked and a piece of yardarm dropped down and dangled from its rigging. He had no time and not enough crew to rig a debris netting. "Are you ready, lads?" he roared out.

"READY!" they roared back.

"Aim true! Sweep the infidels from their deck! FIRE!" He brandished his naked sword at the enemy.

The little xebec's broadside thundered out. His heart swelled with elation at the destruction unleashed in response to his command. Yes. This was the man he was meant to be.

Gunsmoke drifted aft and surrounded him. He waved his hand frantically. When he could see, he saw the boarders swarming up the other xebec's side. "Marksmen aloft!" he shouted. He couldn't risk firing his cannons into the other xebec now that the rovers were aboard. It would be up to the sharpshooters to help them out. He should have sent them aloft sooner. Timing! So many things to do.

More cannonballs smashed into his little ship. He felt the shock beneath his feet as the big frigate pounded his exposed stern. It was a very great distance, but she had found the range. He swore in Turkish.

"Oars! Port oars, back oars. Starboard oars, forward!"

Slowly, painfully slowly, the little xebec rotated and brought her broadside around to face the distant frigate. What could his guns do against her? He had nine pounders at long range. There was no point. However, there was something useful he could do.

"Oars, pull together! Helm, half right."

The *San Fermín* pulled ahead and the frigate's balls went skimming a few feet above deck level, clipped the far rail, and plunged into the sea alongside. She came up on the other xebec's quarters.

"Rake her stern!" Isam shouted.

"Rake her stern, aye," Samir replied. "You do realize that when we do that, we'll no longer be hidden behind her, and the next vessel in line will get a free shot at us? We'll get it on the nose."

"Shit."

CHAPTER 27 : SORTIE

"What's the draft of this ship?" Isam asked Samir. His cousin was serving as first lieutenant, second lieutenant, master, mate, and midshipman, all rolled into one.

"I don't know."

"Find out!" Isam snapped.

Samir leaned over the forward rail. "Bo'sun!"

"Bo'sun, aye!" the man sang out from somewhere near the foredeck.

"What's our draft?"

"I don't know!"

"Find out!"

"Aye aye, sir." He dispatched his mate below.

A minute later a teenage boy came running up to the quarterdeck with a message. "The boatswain's mate said to tell you the Spanish say nine feet, sir."

Isam looked up and down his length. "I think they're lying to me. We're ninety feet long. The Spanish don't like a boat as shallow as we do. I think she must have ten feet at least. Damn him for trying to trick me into going aground. Very well. Get the lead out. I need to know how much water I have."

Samir leaned over what remained of the forward railing, and called, "Bo'sun! Get the lead out!"

"Aye aye, sir!" Then the boatswain bawled, "Carpenter's mates into the chains with lead lines!"

Two men scrambled to the foredeck and went below to search for the carpenter's tools. It took them a few minutes to find them. In the meantime, the *San Fermín* was running up to her neighbor's stern.

"Fire into her quarterdeck!" Isam shouted.

Quoins were adjusted. He kept his course steady to assist the gunners' aiming. That also assisted the enemy's aiming. For every action there is an equal and opposite reaction. The little xebec passed fifty yards behind her neighbor. One by one her guns belched smoke and iron in a rolling broadside. Then her bow emerged from behind the screen of their victim, and Isam braced himself for the counterattack.

When it came, the third xebec pummeled the second. He stared in astonishment. Then he realized what she saw. She had seen corsairs swarming aboard the second vessel, and not knowing that the first xebec had been taken, believed she was a friend firing into the corsairs' prize. For a moment he doubted himself; had he made the same mistake? No. The red and gold of Spain still flew from her flagstaff.

"Load! Double shot! Oars, hold water!"

With Isam's Man in the Crescent Moon flag still behind the screen of the second xebec, the captain of the third xebec was not yet aware of his mistake. The oars dragged through the water and Isam's vessel lost way. She drifted slowly in a northeastward direction. He kept his eye on the second victim. "Oars, two strokes!" That eased her ahead a bit. He watched his guns reloading as fast as they could. They weren't fast enough. In a minute the red and white flag of the Sallee rovers would appear and the ruse would be revealed. If he didn't keep moving, he would drift onto the second xebec. "Oars, slow speed, give way together!"

His baritone was loud in the night. Surely the Spanish could hear him shouting Arabic. Why didn't they fire? Then he felt stupid. They needed time to reload, too. He had fired before she did; he would get in his broadside before she did. He watched the rammers pounding home the balls. "Oars, charge!"

"Four fathoms!" came the cry of the leadsman. Good. He had plenty of water.

Meanwhile, the fortress was not slack. She was firing upon the third and fourth xebecs. They were irresistible prizes for the corsairs. They would strip off the square-rig and put on their own lateen rigs, then sell them in a market like Fezakh or Zokhara. They'd bring good money. Isam thrilled to realize he had a prize beneath his feet and could expect a good piece of money for his part. He smiled and quoted the Qu'ran, "It is the enemy who is without issue." Samir grinned at him. Not a pious man, he knew only those verses which promised victory.

The Spanish men at the oars were less than thrilled, and the rovers beat them with their muskets or menaced them with their scimitars. Slowly the *San Fermín* increased her speed, but she couldn't make even half of the nine knots that was the top speed of a rowed warship. Still, the stranger wasn't far. Why wasn't she turning to give him her broadside? Isam glanced at the red and white ensign behind him. It fluttered only slightly in the mild breeze of the slow charge. It had not opened.

"They still don't know," he told Samir. "We're going to surprise them."

The captive xebec crossed the third Spaniard's stern and fired. Their broadside shredded the Spaniard's rear. Her sternchasers roared damage. Not expecting such a close approach by the enemy, she had fired without taking time to adjust her quoins.

"*Allahu Akbar! Allahu Akbar!*" he shouted. His men joined him in a chorus that sounded like it came from Hell itself to Spanish ears. Looking back, he saw a red and white flag hoisted on the stern of the second victim. A man in a turban was limned by the light of the lanthorn. The rovers had finally gotten control of the second xebec! Not only that, he saw the *Grey Wolf* coming out of Tanguel, and behind her, the frigate.

"Double shot! Oars, hold water!" He must be careful not to use up his oarsmen too quickly. The Spanish prisoners were happy to lie on their oars and do nothing.

They were now within traverse of the third xebec's larboard battery. At that short distance, the enemy couldn't miss. Wood splintered with a wild crash and Isam grimaced as he was peppered by debris. Bits of wood impaled his arm. He plucked them out while he swung around and to see everything at once. "Casualty report! Damage report!"

Samir repeated the order. A couple of minutes later the main deck chief passed word. "Two rowers killed, six wounded. One Salletine wounded."

"Throw the dead and wounded Spaniards overboard." He had no surgeon to care for his own wounded, let alone the enemy.

Meanwhile, the lead was still going. "Four and a half fathoms and a white sandy bottom!" The leadsmen would continue until told otherwise. In the shoals around Tanguel, the captain needed to know his depth.

Isam paid no further attention to the Spanish casualties. He had to tend his ship. "Oars, give way together!"

The vessel began to crawl slowly forward, but as he looked, the fourth xebec was turning on her springs to meet the new menace. The *San Fermín*'s identity was perfectly understood now. There was no mistaking her hostility to the Spanish vessels. Shot flew around him from both sides: big round shot from the frigate and smaller round shot from the third xebec.

Samir stepped up. "The damage report has arrived. We have two feet of water in the well, one gun dismounted, and more than a dozen holes betwixt wind and water. The carpenter requests the use of his mates to plug the holes."

"In a minute. We're going to rake her stern again. As soon as we've done that, he can have them." Turning to the tillerman, he said, "Helm hard left."

"Hard left, aye, sir."

The little xebec curved back the way she had come. "Two fathoms, muddy bottom!" the larboard leadsman sang out. If she stuck on the mudbank, the Spaniards would turn her into kindling.

Isam checked the loading of his guns. A piece of round shot whistled past not two feet from his head and took a bite out of the mizzen mast. It creaked ominously. He swore. "We'll need to fish that."

Samir leaned over the railing and shouted the information to the boatswain.

"Fish the mizzen mast, aye," the boatswain replied. No one came. The danger of sinking had the carpenter belowdecks mending holes.

"Three fathoms less a quarter!" chanted the starboard leadsman.

The small xebec was back in the channel. Isam was relieved, but he had no time to think about it. "Larboard guns, wait for my command!"

The third xebec cranked around on her springs to present her broadside, and they received it at nearly pointblank range. Debris scattered across the deck and men shrieked. Blood splattered Samir's green coat. The wounded man fell in convulsions at his feet. He thrashed for about thirty seconds, then lay still.

Isam had no time to worry about such things. "Fire!" he shouted.

Twelve guns belched hellfire and shattered the other vessel. Gaps appeared in her wales and he could see shadows of men silhouetted against the lantern light as she reloaded.

He noticed that his vessel was listing. "Man the pumps!"

"We don't have enough men to man the guns and the pumps," Samir replied.

Isam swore again. "Put some prisoners on them!"

"We're shot to hell. We need to get out of here," Samir said.

Isam scanned the scene. The *Grey Wolf* was engaging the fourth xebec, and galleys were darting out of the harbor mouth to swarm around the Spanish. The big Spanish frigate fired on them one more time, then shifted targets to assault the newcomers. Aboard the *San Fermín,* more bodies were thrown overboard.

"Helm, due south."

"Due south, aye."

The battered xebec crawled southward as her exhausted hands threw themselves on the oars. The Spanish prisoners were happy to row out of the battle; they had suffered more casualties than their captors had. The boatswain ran up the ladder to the quarterdeck to personally report. "Two and a half feet in the well, rais. She's taking on water fast."

Rais! How the word rang in his ears! He loved the sound of it. If he wanted to keep hearing that word applied to himself, he had to keep his first independent command from sinking.

Isam Rais said, "We're out of combat. Take however many prisoners you need to pump. Keep a good guard over them. We don't want to give them a chance to retake the ship."

"Aye aye, rais." The boatswain went below and requisitioned a gang to work the pumps and men to guard them.

"Oars, port oars, back water." He turned her around to present her broadside to an approaching enemy, if any enemy should approach. "Drop anchor, set springs."

When the anchors let go, he let the oars stand down. They were allowed water and rest. The dismal sound of the pumps sucking and clanking seemed loud to him, in spite of being nearly drowned out by the sound of nearby gunnery.

"Casualty report. Prisoner report."

It took a little time to gather it, but at last Samir said, "Four rovers dead, seventeen wounded. We have one hundred and twenty-one surviving prisoners."

"That's not as bad as I feared," the young captain replied.

"What about you? You're a bloody mess from ear to elbow."

"I am?" Isam Rais asked in surprise. He rubbed his left hand along his neck. It came away bloody. "So I am. It's nothing serious. I caught some splinters is all."

"That's good. You look a fright."

"How are you?"

Samir held up his pinky finger. "I think it's broken, but that's the worst of it for me. This isn't my blood. We were lucky."

Isam looked around. The quarterdeck was shot to pieces. The bulwark was holed in five places, the skylight shattered, and the larboard pinrail gone. Brayles hung loose like a slattern's hair, but their opposite numbers were still secure and the sail had not dropped down on top of the new rais and his cousin. On the main deck, things were even worse. Blood stained the planks and pieces of timber and fallen blocks were scattered on deck. The starboard main yardarm was shot away. That left a cascade of canvas trailing down from the fighting top. It was hanging from its buntlines, but its starboard bowline was shot away too, so its marlets and clewlines drooped in ugly bights. Part of the fighting top was missing. The mizzenmast listed further to the starboard with an ominous cracking sound.

"Shit! I think the mizzenmast is coming down!" Isam exclaimed.

They both scampered out of the way. The mizzenmast continued to bow. More wood creaked and squealed, and then, with a sound like a tree falling, toppled over the side. The last piece of timber snapped with a loud report, and the whole thing splashed into the water. The larboard shrouds held, so the heap of debris clung to the starboard quarter. The broken stump of the mizzenmast jutted over their heads.

Isam Rais swore in Turkish. His first command was a wreck.

CHAPTER 28 : SUNK!

The prisoners pumped and pumped, but the water gained on them. The carpenter and his mates scrambled through the hull, but they couldn't reach the holes underwater to fix them. Isam Rais heeled the vessel over to help the carpenter and his men get at the damage, but that revealed a shattered plank along with the holes. Ominous rumblings came from below. The timbers quivered, then all was still. Isam didn't know what the noise was, and it worried him. All he could do was to wait for his crew to report on progress. Or lack thereof.

"I don't think we can save her," Samir opined.

"We have to try," Isam replied.

"I suppose we do." Samir glanced north to where the sound of cannon fire was slackening. "We'll have help soon."

"Fother a sail. Use some of the prisoners to do it," Isam ordered.

"I don't think we have time to thrum it."

"Use a plain canvas. Get something over that hole. Anything to slow the leak."

Samir went below and rounded up a work crew and canvas. Prisoners with lines around their waist walked down the side of the hull slippery with green weeds and arranged the sail. They didn't want to sink, either. As much as they disliked their captors, they liked drowning even less. A Salletine diver shivered in the cold water, then dove down to take the line under the belly of the xebec. The canvas slowed the inrush of water. Unfortunately, the vessel remained listed over and did not want to right.

"Something has shifted," Isam said. "I'm going below."

"Isam, be careful. Don't get caught down there. She's going to sink. We have only slowed her down."

"She's my first command! I have to save her."

"There will be other ships."

"You have the conn. I'm going below."

"Aye. I have the conn." Samir gave his cousin a worried look.

Belowdecks Isam found himself in a wet, slippery, slanted world. Ordering some sailors to open the hatch, he stuck his head into the bilge. He could vaguely make out a jumbled mass of lumpy darkness, and it filled him with dread. "I need a lantern," he told the sailors. One of them went and fetched it. When the light arrived, Isam lowered himself into the ballast and took the lantern. The light showed him water and rock well mixed. He balanced on the jumble of wet stone and looked up at the sailors. "The ballast has shifted."

He didn't need to explain what that meant. They all knew the *San Fermín* was doomed. He handed the lantern up, caught the edge in his hands, and hauled himself out of the bilge. Bracing himself on the sloping deck, he shouted, "All hands on deck!"

The cry was echoed through the confines of the berth deck. "All hands on deck!" The young captain joined the stream of wet, cold, tired men as they climbed the crazy slant of the ladders to the deck. His wet boots left a trail of slime as he skidded into the water way, picked himself up, and hauled himself aft along the rail. The crazy angle of the vessel meant he had to shinny up the ladder to the quarterdeck.

"Ballast has shifted," he informed Samir.

Samir was standing with one leg braced and the other bent on the slanting deck. "She's turning turtle, Isam. We have to abandon ship. There's no time for anything else."

He was right. The slant of the deck was sharper than a few minutes ago when he had left the quarterdeck. Below him the prisoners gathered amidships and looked up at him. Their guards stood in front of them with their guns and scimitars in hand. They were all bracing their legs against the slowly increasing incline.

Isam looked around at his scant quarterdeck crew. "Haul down the colors. Fire a gun to draw attention to our distress. Get out the boats. Any prisoner who wants to swim for it may do so." Two sailors in wet jackets hurried to haul down the red and white flag of the Sallee rovers while Samir repeated his orders to the deck crew.

Isam Rais took out his spyglass and swept it over the battle. The two remaining small vessels were fleeing north with the big frigate in their train to cover their retreat. The captured frigate that the corsairs had intended to match against the Spaniard was wallowing in irons. The Muslim crew aboard her was not used to working such a big and complex square-rigger and had stalled her in the channel. The other rovers didn't wait for her; the smaller, more agile vessels could skim over the shoals and were in pursuit of the prizes.

As he watched the mass of mixed vessels running north, Isam felt his heart sink. What if nobody came to help? He didn't have enough boats to evacuate the vessel, let alone manage the prisoners. A single gun boomed out and a puff of gunsmoke drifted across the tangled wreckage on his deck. Try as he might, he did not discern any reply. He was on his own.

He surveyed his difficulty. "Put the wounded in the first boat. Send an able-bodied man to town to call up the militia to take charge of the prisoners. Do that now."

Samir picked a cockswain and crew, and they went over the side into the first boat. The boatswain rigged a chair to send the disabled men over the side.

"Run a cable to shore, too," Isam Rais ordered.

Samir wanted to know, "What are we going to secure it to? All that scrub is weak and shallow-rooted. It will pull right out of the ground."

Isam Rais replied, "Kedge anchor."

"Ah. Of course."

Able-bodied seamen were dispatched to gather up the kedge and cable. The end was secured to a bitt and a tagline bound to the anchor's shank. The arm tackle hoisted it over the side. The tagline was tossed to the men in the second boat as it rowed up, and they pulled hard to heave the flukes of the anchor away from the exposed side with its canvas bandage. Slowly they eased the heavy weight into the boat. The boat settled a few inches. Untying the tagline, the boatswain called, "Ease away!"

The boat rowed and slowly the cable uncoiled. It stretched long and heavy across the water. The droop sank down below the surface of the waves, but eventually the boat arrived ashore. They heaved the kedge over side. Its stock propped on the wet beach and the fluke dug in.

"That won't hold. We'll have to drag it into the water. It'll find something to catch on." Isam leaned over the remaining piece of forward rail. "Boatswain! Take up slack on that cable! Drag it until it bites and holds! It doesn't matter if it's in the water; they can walk or swim the last few yards."

"Aye aye, rais," the boatswain replied.

The first boat delivered the wounded to shore while the anchor was being rowed ashore.

"You need an officer and crew ashore to keep control of things at that end," Samir pointed out.

Isam Rais sighed. "I suppose I do. Samir, will you go?"

With a sudden smile, Samir replied, "Of course I will!"

Isam's expression turned sour when he realized what his cousin was angling for. "You're going to leave me alone on a sinking ship," he complained.

Samir shrugged. "You're the captain. You're last to leave. Therefore, I must go. Somebody had to keep order on the shore."

Isam sulked, but it was as his cousin said. They were outnumbered by the Spanish two to one. He was now glad all the other ships were running north. If the prisoners thought they had a chance of rescue, they would probably revolt.

"All right. Fire another gun, then take a crew ashore."

Samir crawled down the badly slanted starboard ladder and bellowed, "Bow chasers, fire another signal!"

Hanging onto the rail, he worked his way hand over hand to the cable forward. A line of prisoners waited their turn at the cable. When the boatswain was satisfied the vanished anchor had grabbed something below the surface, he nodded to them. One by one they wrapped their arms and legs around it and shinnied along. Where the cable sagged into the water, they were dunked, but it didn't matter, because it started raining a cold, thick rain. The shore disappeared in the caliginous murk.

Another melancholy gun fired into the night. Isam wrapped an arm around a pinrail and held on. He watched as the number of men aboard slowly dwindled. The damaged xebec listed still further. He managed to keep his feet under him as the quarterdeck rolled. He began to worry about his own safety, but he said nothing. He knew his duty. The captain was last to leave the vessel. He must think. What should he do that he hadn't done? Papers. Yes. He must collect the Spanish captain's papers. There might be something important in them.

He gingerly made his way down the dangerously tilted ladder and crawled through the coach and into the captain's cabin. He ransacked the desk, but didn't find the log or signal book. The captain must have sunk them over the side when he came under attack. Going through the desk, he did find a purse with money in it: lots of silver coins. He stuffed it into his sash.

With a creaking groan, the xebec went over on her beam ends and her yardarms splashed into the water. Rumbles and loud clatters shook the vessel as her contents went crashing to the low side. Isam found himself tumbled in a heap on the larboard wall of the cabin that was now the floor. Furniture came crashing down around him, and he was knocked violently as the sofa, desk and rug swept down on top of him. The desk drawers opened and spilled papers, quills, and an ink bottle on top of him. The lantern swung crazily, but stayed on its hook, canted against the ceiling that had now become the larboard wall. Its wildly swaying light cast writhing shadows in the tilted space.

Water poured in through the broken quarterlight. Isam shoved furniture left and right, then scrambled frantically to the forward bulkhead. His heart hammered in his chest as he splashed through water that was already knee deep and cold as a tomb. His tomb. Looking around desperately, he saw the passageway door had flapped open and hung there. In a panic, he leaped up, caught the hinged side of the door, and hauled himself up and into the passageway. Walking on the side wall that was now the floor, he jumped over doors and scrambled out onto the deck.

The capsize had sent the prisoners rolling and sliding to crash into the larboard bulwark. The bulwark was now underwater, and they were scrambling frantically fore and aft to try and climb up. The rovers were no help to them; they were busy trying to save themselves.

"There's the captain!" somebody shouted.

He waved a hand to show them he was all right. Fear raced hot and desperate through him. When she turned turtle, he would be trapped beneath her. To his left, Spaniards were scrambling forward along the submerged rail to get to the ropes that hung down across the deck and led to the high side. To his right, the starboard guns hung in their tackle like bronze pendulums. He had to get to the high side of the vessel!

Climbing onto the heap of larboard guns, he was able to grab the line that ran between the gun and the ring on the deck. He hauled himself up by his arms, grabbed onto the dangling starboard gun that was still warm after battle, then crawled up the gun carriage. The trunnions and trucks gave him something to grab onto. The line creaked ominously. Still, if it could resist the force of a one ton gun leaping against it in recoil, surely it could support the addition of a man's weight. So he reassured himself, but he didn't quite believe it.

The gun closest to the passageway was housed under the ladder. He climbed up the gun until he got hold of the ladder's side. He pulled himself up by his arms, worked a foot into the rungs, and was able to scramble up onto the gunwale. From there he moved carefully over the slippery hull to the quarterdeck. He stood balancing on the curved hull with one foot in the starboard channel and another on the railing. The shrouds, instead of rising up in the air, were now a tangle of black strands on the larboard side. The main- and foresails and their spars helped arrest her capsize for the time being, but once they were thoroughly waterlogged, the added weight would help drag her down. It was a few moments respite only.

Forward, men on the bow had scrambled onto the side of the hull and clung to her chains and channel. They stood or sat on the head rails and he saw heads bowing as men began to pray. He thought he ought to pray as well, but he was too busy trying to save himself. Time enough to pray when he was safe ashore!

Still, the vessel had not rolled completely over, and he was not trapped beneath her. For that he did manage a swift, "Thank you, Allah." And having learned a lesson, "In the future, assuming I am lucky enough to take another prize, I will secure the captain's papers and search his cabin first!"

"Captain! The anchor's dragging!" the boatswain shouted at him from the bow.

The ship had capsized away from shore and pulled the anchor out of its ground. The ship was now adrift and the anchor wasn't set. She was slowly, very slowly, drifting away from shore. He watched for the muzzle flashes from the fortress for a bearing and saw the angle gradually, almost imperceptibly, widening. The anchor cable was no longer a means of escape.

"How many are with you?" he called to the bow.

The boatswain paused to do a head count. The rain poured down harder. "Eighteen Salletines and twenty-two Spaniards." Neither of them counted the men thrashing in the water. There was nothing they could do to save them. When they went under, they were gone.

"Two more boats will take us off, lads!" he told them cheerfully. "Be of good cheer! We'll soon be safe ashore!" He put a heartiness into his words he didn't feel.

"Aye aye, captain," the boatswain replied. "You heard him, men. It won't be long and we'll be safe ashore with a hot fire and dry clothes!"

Isam was soaked by sea water and shivering with the cold. The rain coming down couldn't make him any wetter than he was, but it prevented him from drying out. He huddled in the channel. The black painted wooden shelf normally held the shrouds away from the hull, but in its current position, served him as a bench to sit on. The vessel bobbed gently on the swells. He held still and tried to gauge them. They seemed a little larger than when he had rowed out to attack the xebec.

"Ahoy the xebec!" a distant voice called out in Arabic. "Where are you?"

The men on the bow began to shout and call in delight. "Over here, over here!"

In a few minutes, a boat appeared under the bow and plucked the corsairs off. It picked up a few Spaniards as well and rowed away. More minutes passed. Isam and the remaining Spanish prisoners waited tensely, each at opposite ends of the vessel.

Another boat rowed up to the bow of the sinking ship. Spaniards scrambled into the boat and thanked their saints to be taken off.

"Where's Isam?" he heard Samir asking. "Isam! Where are you?"

"Over here! I'm on the stern quarter! In the channel!"

They rowed along the keel and came under him. He saw the pale oval of Samir's handsome face looking up and forgave him everything. He caught hold of a brayle, threaded it over the side, and slid down the wet hull and into the boat. Many hands grabbed him and eased him down into the sternsheets next to his cousin.

Relief flooded through him. He was safe! In a paroxysm of relief, he grabbed his cousin by the shoulders and kissed him full on the mouth. "Praise Allah, you came!"

Samir laughed a little. "I said I would."

CHAPTER 29 : THE BOTTOM OF THE SEA IS COLD

Isam was eager to salvage the prize. Lying in only forty feet of water with her spars propped on a mudbank, it would not be difficult to raise her. To be nearer the work, he commandeered the former Spanish dune camp as his base of operations. An assortment of ammunition, food, and camp furniture remained; he supplemented them with more supplies for his own comfort. He had his own tent with Gregorio to attend it. Being a rais now, even if his ship was at the bottom of the sea, he felt entitled to certain creature comforts, the most prized of which was privacy.

Gregorio fitted out his cot with fresh linens and made a pallet for himself on the ground as far away from his master as he could manage. A threadbare Turkish rug lay on the ground to provide a floor for them while a copper Moorish lantern hung from the ridgepole. The Spanish eunuch kept his back turned as the young captain changed into clean drawers and undershirt, then crawled into bed. He lifted the covers and invited Gregorio in.

The eunuch pretended he didn't see. He fussed with his own bedding to make certain it was just right.

"Come sleep with me. The cot is narrow, but I don't mind. You'll have to sleep right next to me. It will keep us both warm." Isam smiled.

It couldn't be avoided. Fully dressed, Gregorio crawled into bed with his master. He settled with his back to him. Isam didn't mind; he liked the feel of Gregorio's warm butt pressed against his groin. He pulled the covers up and hugged him close. He kissed the eunuch's neck.

"What about the salvage?" the servant asked in an attempt to distract the amorous corsair.

His ploy worked. If there was anything Isam liked as much as sex, it was ships. "The salvage hulks will row out tomorrow morning and bring a diving bell with them. I told the salvor he ought not call it a 'bell' because a bell is a Christian thing, but he shrugged and said he learned to dive in Sweden, so he called things by their Swedish names." There was no response from the eunuch. "Are you listening to me?"

"Yes, rais. The salvor is a Swedish renegade, but I don't know what a 'diving bell' is."

Isam used his left hand to sketch a conical shape in the air. "A large wooden bucket turned upside down to trap air and take it to the bottom. A man rides inside so he can work below the surface of the water."

"How could that work? The bucket will fill with water as soon as it goes under."

"It's caulked to be waterproof."

"The bucket has a lid to keep the water out?"

Isam had never seen a diving bell. He was dependent on the Swede's explanation. "I don't know how it works, but I'll find out tomorrow. Marten says it is very safe, but if there is an accident, we can save ourselves by swimming to the surface. I'm a good swimmer, so I'm not worried."

Gregorio was pleased to hear Isam was going down with the diving bell. Anything that would keep him away was a good thing as far as the Spaniard was concerned. "I hope you are successful, rais," he said dutifully.

Rais! Isam's heart leapt at the word. He was enjoying the title while he had it. He snuggled with the servant. "I am glad to hear you call me that," he purred and kissed the man's neck again. "Sadly, the xebec must be sold for prize money. I don't have the funds to buy out the other shares. If I did, I would raise her and keep her." He heaved a sigh. "Some day I'll be a captain in my own right. I'll own my own vessel. I'll be a famous corsair! I know I will! Look at the other corsairs. Do they burn with ambition like I do?"

Gregorio's stomach clenched. "You'll be a menace to the Nazarenes."

"Ha! I will! I'll take many captives and make them row my xebec!"

Gregorio tensed. "Will you make me row, rais?"

Isam kissed and petted him. "Of course not. I love you. Rowing is hard labor. You'd get calluses and the sun would broil you until you were black like an African! I like you as you are."

Gregorio shut his eyes and lay stiffly next to his master.

Isam stroked his arm and kissed his shoulder. "You are not like other slaves, you know."

"Is that so?" Gregorio asked as neutrally as he could manage.

Isam stroked his curls and cooed, "It is so. You rescued Rabiyah. For that we can never repay you."

"I would like a reward for that, master." Gregorio tried very hard to keep his voice flat and not let his anxiety show.

Isam hugged him. "Of course! You deserve a reward! What would you like?"

"I would like my freedom."

A long silence fell. Gregorio braced himself. His request would be refused and he'd be beaten. He was sure of it. What foolish hope had made him say the words? If Isam were inclined to be generous, he would have given him a reward a week ago. Now his young master would watch him like a hawk in case he tried to escape.

Escape he must. When the Spanish shells had burst in Tanguel, they had filled him with hope, not fear. For the first time in his captivity, he had thought he might be rescued. Spanish military success was his only hope. He would not be ransomed; he was too unimportant a person. A eunuch. A man with no family. A slave. If he ever got free, he would go to Madrid in the exact center of the country where it would be impossible for a corsair raid to snatch him up again. He could get a job as a servant somewhere.

Impossible. Why did he torment himself with such dreams?

Meanwhile, Isam was thrown into confusion. Freedom? Why did Gregorio want to be free? "Aren't you happy being my slave?"

"No."

"Why not?"

Gregorio didn't answer. He clenched his hands into two tight fists and tried not to speak. He didn't want to enrage the man. Finally he said, "I want to go home."

Isam was even more startled. "Home?" Home was Tanguel. That's what his gut told him. Gregorio was not from Tanguel. He was a Spanish Christian. "Spain?"

Gregorio nodded without speaking.

"Why in the world would you want to go to Spain? They burn men like us at the stake."

"They burn men like you, rais," Gregorio corrected him. "I would not do this if I were not a slave."

"You like it."

Gregorio's face burned hot. "I don't want to like it. But if I must do it, I don't want to suffer while it happens."

Isam scowled and sat up. "You like kissing me!"

Gregorio slithered out of the bed and dropped onto the rug. He crawled warily away and crouched upon his pallet like a wounded animal driven into a corner. He was very much afraid of the corsair's temper, even if the man had not yet beaten him the way Maureo used to. He was a slave. If he made his master angry, he would be punished. He should not have said anything at all. He had not said anything to Maureo, but then, Maureo had never pretended to love him and had never asked his opinion about anything.

"Beat me if you must, but don't make me pretend to like it. For all of his faults, Maureo never made me pretend it was anything other than rape." He regretted the words as soon as he spoke, but at the same time, his heart burned with bitterness. He couldn't keep silent.

"It isn't rape!" Isam jumped to his feet and his fists curled into balls. He stalked towards Gregorio.

Gregorio's eyes went wide and he held up his hands in fear. "Mercy, master. Please. You're a strong man. I can't resist you. I'm a slave. You don't have to hit me to prove your power. I will do whatever you order me to do! Please don't hurt me!"

Isam lifted his fist, but the anguish in his slave's voice stopped him. Everything Gregorio said was true. He could kill the man if he wanted and no one would gainsay him. He owned the man; he had the right.

It felt entirely wrong. "Have you done all that you have done because you fear me?"

Gregorio trembled before him. "Yes, master." He scooted back, but the tent wall blocked his escape.

"But you helped Rabiyah escape. I wasn't there. Why did you do it?"

"Because I pitied her and feared him. When I saw you, I knew you could help us."

"Don't you like me at all?"

"No, master. But I'm grateful you have been kinder than Maureo."

Isam scowled at him. "I'm not that bad! I never beat you."

"Yes, master." Gregorio gave up the fight.

Isam glared at his slave in frustration. "Then why don't you like me?"

"You don't care about anyone except yourself." Gregorio clapped his hands over his mouth, but it was too late. The words were out.

"That's not true! I helped Rabiyah, didn't I?"

"Yes, master. You did. All credit goes to you." He bowed his head.

"Not just me. Samir and Umar helped too."

Gregorio kept his eyes down.

"And you," Isam conceded. "I'm willing to give you a reward for that. I said so."

"All I want is my freedom. It won't cost you anything! You didn't buy me. You stole me from Maureo."

"You stole yourself from Maureo."

"Then you don't own me at all."

"I have laid claim to you."

"Then you're a thief."

Isam cuffed him across the forehead.

Gregorio fell over. He remained lying on the pallet while his head rang. "I'm sorry, master. I spoke out of turn. I shouldn't have said anything. I should have lied and said I didn't want anything when you offered me a reward. A slave has no right to anything. A slave isn't even human."

"You're a man! You should have something. Even a slave ought to be rewarded when he does his master a favor." Isam's voice was getting louder the more frustrated he became.

Gregorio crawled to him and kissed his bare feet. "You are my master. I will obey."

"Go to bed! I don't want to talk to you. I don't want to look at you!"

The corsair was a looming column in the dimness of the tent. Gregorio couldn't see the Turk's face, but he could hear the resentment in his voice. "Yes, master." He crawled swiftly to his pallet and pulled the covers up over his head so that he disappeared completely.

That wasn't what Isam had meant, but he couldn't blame the slave for taking him literally. He smote his thigh with the palm of his left hand. "You're so stubborn!" He flung himself onto his cot. He stared into the night for a long time.

Gregorio held his breath and listened carefully from under the covers. When Isam settled down, he heaved a sigh of relief. He had escaped the corsair's wrath. He hoped the man would leave him alone for the rest of the night. Softly, so softly that only the Virgin Mary could hear him, he prayed.

CHAPTER 30 : THE DIVING BELL

Two galleys used as salvage hulks rowed into position. One held the diving bell and settled its anchors so that it lay next to the hull of the ship. The other rowed over the mudbank taking soundings. Isam had himself rowed out to the first of the hulks. Coming aboard, he was met with a sight he'd never seen before: a huge lead-coated wooden bell sitting on chocks on the deck. Ropes and leather hoses led up into the rigging. The bell's top was flat and about three feet across with a thick glass window in it. The exit points and attachments for the various lines and hoses were as near to the middle as could be arranged. The bottom of the bell was about five feet across and supported additional lead weights lashed around the rim. While he was gawking at it, a short, wiry, blond man approached him.

"Peace be upon you," the salvage master greeted the corsair.

"And also upon you," Isam replied.

Marten the Swede, for that's who he was, said, "We're in place. We'll drop the bell amidships for our first look, then will survey her fore and aft. Soundings are a quarter shy six fathoms at the deepest. That's deep enough to be awkward, but we shouldn't have any trouble. It's the cold that will limit our work. I plan to do as much as I can from the bell."

Although the sun beat down warm and fair upon the deck, it was still spring and the rivers were carrying icy runoff from the mountains to the sea.

"I suppose there's nothing for me to do but wait and watch," Isam said glumly.

"Unless you know how to dive, I'm afraid that's all you can do."

Isam brightened. "I'm a strong swimmer. I swam underwater with bladders of air to cut a Spanish cable."

Marten stroked his goatee. "How deep have you dived?"

Isam tried to estimate the depth of the murk he'd been in at Cape Spartel. "Five fathoms and a rough sea. I could hardly see to find my way, but I did it. It was cold!"

Marten nodded. "I'll take you down in the bell then. If anything happens, swim for the surface. Follow the line up and they'll fetch you on board. Don't try to help me; I know what I'm doing and you don't. Save yourself so I don't have to worry about you."

Isam's jaw set and his new beard bristled, but Marten cut him off before he could say anything. "Rais, the vessel at the bottom is yours, but the vessels at the top are mine, and although you have hired me, I am the master of my vessels. In all matters pertaining to the salvage, you will follow my orders."

Isam sulked, then said, "Very well. The wreck is my business because she is mine, but once I have told you what I want for her, you may do as you please."

Marten gave him an exasperated look. "Of course, rais. If you don't mind, we shall carry on."

Isam scowled and nodded.

A small, muscular, dark man that looked a mix of Arab and African came over to them. "The bell is ready, rais," he told the salvor in a nasal voice.

Marten explained, "This is Tasegmant, my second in command. He manages the diving bell."

"Are you a Berber?" Isam asked.

"I am," Tasegmant replied.

"He's a damned good diver too," Marten interjected. To the assistant he said, "Isam Rais knows how to dive. He's going down in the bell with me."

Tasegmant gave Isam an appraising look, then gave a significant look to his master, who nodded. Mutely agreeing to put up with the puppy, they went on with their business.

Marten removed his clothes and told Isam, "Strip down to your drawers. Anything else is wasted weight. Bring your knife. If you've got a stout belt, wear it."

Marten himself had on exactly what he advised Isam. Isam stripped down to his drawers and left his folded up clothes on the deck beside Marten's. He had no belt, so he obtained a bit of twine and hung his knife on a cord around his neck. The sun beat down warmly on his naked back and he stretched luxuriously.

Tasegmant ignored them as he went about his duties. The slack was taken up and a team of men hauled the taglines and held the bell in position over the deck by winding them around belaying pins. In this way a small team of men could control the one ton diving bell as it lifted off the deck. The bell rose above the height of the railing and paused. Tasegmant walked around and looked at it critically. The bell was not perfectly level, so he and his assistants shifted the lead weights strapped to the brim of the bell. That done, the assistant salvage master stepped back and squinted. The galley bobbed gently on the sea, and the bell swung ever so slightly as its weight pulled at the lines that held it in position.

"That's well." Satisfied that the bell would descend vertically into the sea, he turned to Marten. "Your chariot awaits."

Marten disappeared inside the bell. Isam ducked and followed him under the edge. Standing up inside, he found a bench spanning the interior. Monkey-agile, Marten was already perched upon it. Isam hopped up beside him. He felt a bit like a canary in a cage. He grabbed handholds inside the bell and braced his bare feet against the walls. Marten balanced perfectly on the bench and held on with one hand. Inside the bell showed its wooden structure with tools of various sorts hung in holders on the wall, including a set of air filled bladders and a weighted belt for a diver. Coils of rope were lashed to the sides. Over their heads, the thick glass in the roof admitted a diffused sunlight. A bight of rope ran through eyebolts to where it could be conveniently reached by the diver. Marten gave it two tugs. The rope ran up inside a leather hose that prevented water from leaking in around it, and protected the rope from chafing. "That is the signal to carry on. Tasegmant is holding the other end in his hand so we can communicate."

"Very clever," Isam said.

The diving bell rose and swung gently. The controlling lines eased it out along the yard until it was clear of the galley's side. The wreck lay directly below them. She was canted over on her side with her spars lying on the mudbank. Even with several fathoms of water between him and the xebec, Isam could see that the mainmast was sprung and had torn out a section of deck amidship. The belaying furniture was a broken tumble of timber and lines.

Marten made a series of tugs upon the line. The yardarm rotated slowly into a new position, then another code caused the bell to maneuver slowly further towards the end of the yard. When they were properly positioned, Marten asked, "Ready?"

Isam gulped. "How do we keep the water out of the bell? Is there a lid?" There was no sign of a lid.

Marten grinned. "No lid. The air itself keeps the water out."

"What do you mean, no lid? There's nothing to keep the water out!"

"Air is not nothing. If it were nothing, it would be a vacuum, and we'd both be dead. But we're not dead because air is something, even if it is invisible to us. The air is an ethereal ocean and we are creatures who live and breathe in it, just like fish live and breathe in the ocean of water. You'll see." So saying, he tugged on the line and the bell began its slow descent.

Isam gripped his handholds and braced his legs. The water rose up to him, then gentle waves splashed against the rim. Gently the bottom of the bell immersed itself in the waves. Both men kept their feet up to keep them dry. After a few slow minutes, the bottom half of the bell was immersed in the water, but the water was not climbing up inside it. Slowly the bell dropped deeper. A greenish hue momentarily dimmed the sunlight coming through the window as a wave lapped over the top, then the green light became permanent as the bell submerged.

Isam gulped hard and felt his ears pop. "Ow!" he exclaimed. He rubbed his ear.

Marten grinned at him. "Yawn, cough, or swallow if your ears bother you. You'll get used to the pressure change. We're barely under water."

About two fathoms down the bell halted. Marten surveyed the interior of the bell, examined his young companion to make certain he was all right, then had a look down at the wreck coming into sharper focus as the water between them reduced, nodded in satisfaction, and tugged on the line. The bell resumed its descent. Marten watched sharply below and kept one hand on the line. When the bell's rim passed the railing, he gave a sharp tug. The bell stopped.

Isam's heart beat faster as he looked down. A section of the damaged deck was directly beneath them. Although the bell's solid sides blocked his lateral view, he could clearly see that the xebec was on her beam ends at a seventy degree angle from the vertical. The shattered deck planks left a gaping hole and the foot of the mast was visible through the breakage. The mast had come unstepped when the spars struck the mudbank and kicked through the planking. Broken pieces of timber and snarled lines fouled the hole. Some of the shrouds had snapped and their tarry black netting hung over it all. The starboard guns hung from their tackle and rested against the crazily slanted deck. One of them dangled in the hole. It twisted slightly in the current and the motion caused the ragged edge of the planking to saw at the frayed line.

"That's going to drop and go right through the hull," Isam said.

"Very soon. All these guns have to come out. They're dangerous. Any of them could let loose."

Marten tugged the line and the bell moved closer to the wreckage. He gave another sharp tug and it stopped. He peered up through the glass. "We must stay clear of the shrouds. It won't do to get our airline fouled. It's hard enough for the bellows to force air this far down." He checked himself one more time. Diving was a dangerous business. "Are you going to help?"

Isam gulped and nodded. "What should I do?"

Marten pointed. "We have to clear those shrouds so we can get at the gun. Our first objective is to cut that line which is tangled around that wreckage, then tie it over there, out of the way. It will take several breaths to get through that line. I'll go first. Mark where I cut it. When I need air, I'll come into the bell and you'll go to the line while I rest and catch my breath. When you need air, you come back into the bell. We go back and forth until the first chore is done. You must plan your work before you go into the water so you know exactly what you're going to do and how you're going to do it. There's no time to dawdle under water. If you are in distress and can't get to the bell, open and close your fist three times and I'll come help you. When I am in the water, you can't take your eyes off me in case something happens. If possible, pull me into the bell and drape me over the bench. Three sharp tugs on the line and they'll haul us up. If there is any question at all, go to the surface. Do you understand?"

Isam made a fist and opened it three times. "That's to get help. Three tugs to haul up the bell."

Marten nodded. "Just so. I'm going in. Keep your eyes on me."

He slipped from the bench into the water without a splash. He breathed deeply, then ducked his head to get himself wet and cold. Taking another great breath, he let go and dropped down to the tangled hole. Moving carefully along lines of the shrouds, he began sawing at one of the thick black ropes. He had picked his target before he even entered the water. In a minute he swam back, stuck his head into the bell and gulped air. "Your turn."

Isam slipped into the cold water. The shock drove the breath from his lungs. He held onto the bench and inhaled noisily. Marten hauled himself onto the bench to wait and watch. Isam ducked his head and the cold made his teeth chatter. He surfaced and wiped water from his face. "By Allah, that's cold!"

"You need your knife out before you dive. You don't have time to fumble around down there."

Isam wiggled the blade out of the wet sheath. Needing both hands to swim, he was at a loss to do with the knife, so put it between his teeth.

"Don't cut yourself."

Isam gave a thumbs up to show he understood. Finally ready to make the plunge, he let go. His own body weight made him drop. He saw the black line passing him and kicked his feet and swam back up to it. He grabbed onto it with his right hand and started cutting with his left. He had barely made any progress when he thought his lungs would burst. Looking up, he saw the dark bulk of the bell a few feet above him. He swam towards it, but it seemed to take forever to claw his way through the cold water. His head burst into the air of the bell and he flailed and grabbed the edge of the bench to keep himself from sinking again. He inhaled mightily.

Marten studied him, decided he was all right, and said, "Move over. I'm going down."

Isam scooted to the side and Marten slipped past him feet first. He was as elegant as an otter as he slipped through the water. He arrived exactly where Isam had been without any wasted moves and sawed at the line. The corsair hung his arm over the bench and caught his breath. Just when he felt strong enough to haul himself onto the bench, Marten surfaced.

"Be careful. The line is going to part. When it does, use this thong to fold it as far out of the way as possible and tie it."

Isam laced the thong around his wrist and fingers, put the knife in his teeth, and let himself drop. He was paying attention, saw the line, and grabbed it. He had a moment of feeling proud of himself for moving smoothly instead of flailing, then the extra strain of his weight on the line caused it to part. He dropped several feet and let go of the shroud in his surprise. Panicking, he swam back up, only to find the freed shroud meandering several feet away in the water. His air was gone already! He was supposed to tie it up, but he didn't have the air. He hesitated for a moment, but there was no way he could complete his task. He swam back to the bell as fast as he could.

Pressure built inside him. He needed to breathe! If he opened his mouth, he would drown. He opened and shut his hand frantically. Instantly Marten dropped into the water, grabbed him by the waistband, and kicking strongly, pulled him into the diving bell. Isam broke the surface inside the bell, grabbed the bench, and held tight. Marten threw an arm over the bench but continued holding Isam's waistband while the younger man gasped for breath.

"Did you inhale any water?" Marten's voice was matter-of-fact.

"No." Isam continued holding onto the bench for dear life. "I feel like my air didn't last at all! Was I down a minute?"

"No, you weren't. You must remain calm no matter what. If you panic, you use up your air in an instant."

Isam nodded. Panic never helped. Boarding a ship or being sunk, keeping his head was the only way to stay alive. "I was surprised. What should I have done instead?"

"You shouldn't have been surprised. I told you the line would part. What was your plan for when that happened?"

Isam looked sheepish. "I didn't have a plan."

Marten gave him a disapproving look. "You're going to go down and complete the task I gave you. What is your plan?"

Isam looked down into the green depths. Then he looked up into the diving bell and eyed the bladders of air. "What if I take one of those with me?" He pointed.

"You can do without. Be chary with your air."

Isam looked down again. "I guess I'm going to point my toes and let myself sink until I can grab onto the shroud. I don't need my knife for this task, so I'm putting it away." He did so. "I'll grab the line and kick my feet to keep from sinking deeper and coil it up and tie it with the thong." He held up the hand to show where the thong was still wrapped.

"Good. I'm going to put a line on you in case I need to haul you in again." Suiting action to words, he took one of the coils from its hook and bound the end around Isam's waist, then ran the other end over a hook in the ceiling. He kept hold of the other end. "Ready?"

Isam took multiple deep breaths and nodded. Marten paid out the line as the younger man dropped into the water. With his eyes wide open, the corsair easily caught the line and coiled it up. His feet moved just enough to keep him from sinking as he tied up the coil with the thong. He swam back into the bell, broke the surface, and grinned at Marten. "That was better!"

Marten almost smiled. "Yes." He untied the line from the young corsair's waist. "My turn."

In twenty minutes they cleared the shrouds and exposed the opening in the deck where the gun dangled. That accomplished, both of them clung to the diving bell's bench and breathed deeply.

"I'm so cold my nose hurts," Isam complained.

Marten looked up at the clock inside the bell. "Twenty minutes. That's enough for us. We'll go up." He hauled himself onto the bench and huddled against the side.

Isam pulled himself up next to the salvor. It was much warmer in the bell than in the water. The air was close and stale. Water dripped from their scanty clothing. "Are you all right?"

Marten cocked a smile at him. "Fine. This is normal for diving. Let me freshen the air." He reached over his head and turned a cock in the ceiling. A massive column of bubbles erupted on the other side of the glass and went boiling up to the surface. Marten closed the cock. The air inside was thinner and cooler. Now Isam could feel the slight brush of air from the hose connected through the roof of the bell. Up above men were working a bellows to force air down to them.

The salvage master reached up and tugged the line. The bell started to rise. Both men put their fingers in their ears in an effort to adjust to the changing pressure. The air flowed more freely through the hose and Isam lifted his face to suck in the fresher air. The thickness of water between them and the surface lessened and the light brightened. The murky green became bright green, then with a splash, the diving bell broke the surface and sunlight streamed through the thick glass. The bell rose up, and with a belching sound, escaped the grip of the sea. They hung in the air as small waves danced below and sent spangles of light up inside the bell. The bell swayed and twisted gently as it was pulled to the side of the vessel. They cleared the railing and the bell came to a halt above the deck.

Tasegmant ducked under the rim. "How are you?" he asked Marten.

"Cold."

More men ducked under the bell. They helped the freezing divers off the bench and out of the bell. They wrapped blankets around them and bundled them into the great cabin where a portable stove was giving off radiant heat. The two huddled over the stove and warm soup was brought to them. Isam didn't bother with the spoon. He lifted the bowl to his face and slurped it down. Marten ate more daintily with his spoon. This was nothing new to him.

"How long will it take to raise her?" the corsair asked as he revived.

"I think we ought to be able to do it in a month, barring bad weather."

Isam nodded. He wondered what he should do. Go to sea with Rajet Rais? Or stay and supervise the salvage? It was obvious that there was a great deal to know and do when it came to salvage, and he knew none of it. Yet he ought to go to sea where he would be useful and could earn some prize money. At the same time, he couldn't let go of his first command. It was his ship. Until it was sold at auction.

He rose and said, "I'm going to consult with the other raises about it. In the meantime, carry on with the guns." He made his exit.

Chapter 31 : Dancing Boys

Isam Rais brooded as he walked through the dunes to town. The rain had left muddy wallows where birds bathed in the puddles. All around him the world was a bright new shade of green, vibrant and full of song. He was the only gloomy thing abroad on a sunny spring day. He kicked a stone with the toe of his boot and watched it bounce and jump over the ruts in the road. When he caught up to it, he kicked it again. The small seaward gate of the town stood open, and he passed between the guards with an absent-minded "Peace be upon you." He didn't hear them when they answered.

Amid the narrow streets of Tanguel, he avoided wagons hauling mud bricks and timber for the repair of buildings damaged in the Spanish bombardment. Donkeys, camels, and porters trudged through the streets laden with burdens. So preoccupied was he that he didn't hear his own name being called. He stopped at an intersection due to a traffic jam and that was when Demirkan caught up with him.

"Isam!" the black man called again.

Finally aware of being hailed, the younger man looked around. Spotting Demirkan, he smiled. "Peace be upon you."

"And also upon you. How is the salvage going?"

"Well, I guess. Marten says it will take a month to raise her."

Demirkan nodded. "That's not bad at all. You're lucky she went down in shallow water."

"I had no idea it would take so long. I don't know if I should stay with the salvage or go to sea with the *Grey Wolf*."

Demirkan's face became carefully neutral. "Are you considering leaving your berth before you've fulfilled your obligation to the ship?"

Isam scowled. "I didn't say that."

"If you stay for the salvage, you must abandon your promise." His deep voice was flat as he stared at the youth.

"I didn't mean it that way," Isam replied.

"How could it mean anything else? Either you return to the ship, or you don't."

"I am thinking about the salvage. That's an important duty, too."

"The salvage will take care of itself. Marten knows his business. The prize agent will have charge of the ship after she's raised. There's nothing more for you to do except wait for your share of the prize money."

Crestfallen, Isam mumbled, "But I like being a rais."

Good humor restored, Demirkan slapped him on the shoulder and laughed. "Then sail with us and learn how to be one."

Isam smiled in spite of himself. "The *Grey Wolf* is a good berth," he agreed.

"Then it's settled. Give your report to Rajet Rais and stop worrying about the salvage. You can't carry the world on your shoulders."

"I know, but there's something on my mind."

Demirkan cocked an eyebrow at him. "Does this have to do with a certain slave boy?"

The younger man flushed in spite of himself. "Yes. Do you think it would be all right if I brought him with me?"

"Sure. We can always use another rower."

"No, not to row. To be my servant. Officers are entitled to servants, right?"

"You're an ensign, and a supernumerary one at that. You'd have to ask Rajet Rais."

"Can I ask you something?"

"Certainly. This sounds like it's going to require coffee. Come with me."

Demirkan led the way through the narrow streets until they came to a large coffeehouse. Infidels went for alcohol, but followers of the Prophet went for coffee. They entered the dim interior and settled cross-legged on a cushioned divan upholstered in brown and blue.

A young man of about sixteen was dancing in the center of the room. A pair of musicians consisting of an oud player and a drummer accompanied him. The dancer was a handsome youth with blond curls that gleamed in the lamplight. He was lithe and graceful as he curved his way through the insinuating steps. His hips gyrated gracefully in a figure eight pattern that made the spangles on the gauzy costume flicker in the light. The waiter delivered their coffee promptly and asked if they wanted anything else, but they didn't.

"What did you want advice about?" Demirkan asked as he picked up his demitasse.

Isam had completely forgotten why they were there. He tried to pull his attention back to his companion. It was hard to remember what had been on his mind. He could still see the dancing boy from the corner of his eye.

Demirkan was amused. He could see the way Isam's brown eyes kept wandering to the side. "Haven't you seen a dancing boy before?"

Isam flushed. "Once or twice," he said off-handedly. Then he admitted, "Never. They don't have dancing boys in the coffee shop

Uncle Halim likes. He says they're pretty to look at, but they exist to separate a fool from his money."

Demirkan laughed. "He's right about that. They are very charming. When they are between dances, they come and sit with the men. They laugh at their jokes and get them to buy more of everything. Some of them are prostitutes, and some are not."

"It's a good idea to have a slave of my own, isn't it? I don't have to worry about the pox or money that way." He looked to the other man for affirmation.

"A good servant makes your life easier, that's true. If there's respect between man and servant, then the employment is good for both. A bad servant—or a bad master—is a special kind of hell. Always be kind to your servants. Then again, don't be too lenient, or they'll become lazy and saucy."

"Do you think I should free Gregorio? I asked him what reward he wanted for helping us to rescue Rabiyah, and that's what he said. I don't want to let him go, but he doesn't like me. I think he would change his mind if he got to know me though."

Demirkan didn't know the whole story of Rabiyah's elopement. "That depends on many things. If you were not enamored of him, would you grant his request?"

Isam tried to imagine Gregorio as a fat old man instead of the green-eyed Spaniard. That put the situation in an entirely different light. "I suppose I don't really own him. Maureo does. But if he's a runaway slave, I can't emancipate him."

"I would write him an emancipation letter anyhow. That will give him some protection."

"I don't want to give him up!"

"Isam, there are thousands of slaves in the world. Why bother with one that doesn't like you? If you push him too hard, he'll slip a knife in your ribs."

Isam's eyes wandered to the dancing boy again. "I suppose that's true, but I want the one I have. I like kissing him."

"Have you ever kissed a boy before?"

"Only Gregorio."

Demirkhan beckoned to the dancing boy. Flashing blue eyes glanced over their table, but the dancer didn't approach. Demirkhan reached into his sash, pulled out his purse, and removed a copper coin. He held it up. Now the blue-eyed boy smiled and his steps glided over to the table. He bent down to take the coin and give Demirkhan a kiss, but the black man pointed at Isam. "It's for him." The blond youth danced over to Isam, cupped his short-bearded chin in his hand, and kissed his cheek softly.

Isam smiled goofily as he felt those lips press against his cheek. He reached up, but the dancing boy swung away and avoided the touch. He backed away from the table, then when he was safely out of reach, shimmied so that the vest over his bare torso shifted left and right to expose the bare skin beneath.

Demirkan sipped his coffee in amusement as the boy teased the ensign. When the boy turned away to vamp the next table, Isam's eyes followed. Demirkhan rapped his knuckles on the table pointedly. "Your Uncle Halim gave you good advice about dancing boys."

Isam startled. Abashed to have been caught staring, he leaned forward to pick up his coffee cup and drink deeply. Still, his eyes followed the youth gliding bare foot around the tables. "Don't you like looking at him?"

"I do. I enjoy beautiful things. But I also keep my head. If you allow your dick to lead you, you will wind up in all kinds of trouble. Dancing boys will give you the pox, or lead you into a dark alley to be robbed, or a jealous patron will beat you up to keep you away from his favorite. Know the risk before making a decision and make certain you decide with your brain, not your balls."

"I like sex. Isn't there any way to get laid that isn't complicated?"

"In my experience, no. However, there are ways to minimize the danger. Putting your dick between his thighs instead of into his butt is a lot less likely to get you clapped up. It also means you can't be whipped if you're caught at it because you haven't committed sodomy."

"I don't care about the law. I want a lover. It's my business and no one else's."

"You're young. Eventually, you'll get your dick under control. It's part of growing up. In the meantime, perhaps we can do something to help you out.

"How?"

Demirkhan leaned over to speak quietly in his ear. "Forget the dancing boy. How about our waiter? Do you find him attractive?"

Isam transferred his attention to the man who was serving another table. He looked to be in his early thirties. He was Moorish and European by the looks of him, with an aquiline nose and blue eyes. His hair was wavy brown and fell down to his shoulders. He wore a red fez at a jaunty angle. He was smooth-shaven and had once been handsome. Now half a dozen pockmarks scarred his face. He wore a white shirt with long sleeves, dark blue pantaloons, and a red satin sash around his waist.

"He's nice looking aside from the pockmarks," Isam agreed.

"Not too old?"

Isam gave him a scandalized look as he realized what Demirkhan was up to. "Are you suggesting I should proposition the waiter?"

Demirkhan laughed. "I was going to, since you're new at this. I think he's a former dancing boy. Look at how gracefully he moves. He's too old and scarred to be a dancer anymore. But waiters will sometimes accept customers the dancing boys turn down. They don't make outrageous demands for presents, either."

Yesterday Isam had felt like the sultan of the world. He had his own ship, albeit a wreck. Now he felt like a young and gawky boy. "Don't patronize me. I can find my own way in the world. Besides, if he was a dancing boy, he could be disease-ridden."

"I don't think he is. He looks clean." He took a pair of copper coins from his purse and catching the waiter's eye, held them up. That was too much money for a couple of cups of coffee.

The waiter came gliding over. "How may I help you gentlemen?" he purred.

Demirkhan asked, "Do you have a private room?"

The waiter glanced at the proffered coins. "I do. Would you both like to use it?"

Isam reddened and stared at Demirkhan.

Demirkhan noticed the waiter hadn't taken the money yet, so he added two more coins to his palm. "Yes."

The waiter smiled and took the coins. They left their coffee cups on the table and followed him upstairs. The waiter's room proved to be a very small one in an out of the way corner.

Since Demirkhan was paying, the waiter stepped up to him with a smile and said, "You're a big strong man."

Demirkhan took his hand, kissed it, and said, "My friend here needs to be educated in the ways of the world. He'd like to see you undressed."

Isam's face turned scarlet and he gave Demirkhan a reproachful look, but he was also curious. Feeling like he ought to have something to say about the proceedings, he choked out, "Were you a dancing boy?"

For answer, the waiter stepped into the center of the small room, raised one hand elegantly above his head while the other stroked down his side, and turned with slow rocking steps. "Yes," he replied, looking over his shoulder at the youth. He swayed his hips through a figure-eight move. Isam was tongue-tied. Demirkhan just smiled.

Seeing that it was up to him to educate the young man, the waiter slowly undressed as he danced. Isam started grinning as he felt his blood rising. He'd never seen a striptease before, and it affected him strongly.

Demirkhan sidled up to him and whispered in his ear. "Don't lose yourself. He's seducing you. Take the opportunity to look him over for any signs of disease or uncleanness. You can enjoy looking at him while still looking out for yourself."

It dampened Isam's ardor to receive such a reminder, but he looked the waiter up and down carefully. He whispered back, "I don't see anything."

"I don't either. I think he's safe," Demirkhan replied. "The coffee shop is a good one; they wouldn't let him work there if he was diseased." They kept their voices low so the dancing waiter couldn't hear them.

Once he was naked, the waiter crawled onto the bed. He propped himself on his elbow and beckoned to Isam. The young man rubbed his short beard and hesitated.

"Do you think I should?" he asked Demirkhan.

The black agha laughed. "I'm paying for it. What do you think? It will take your mind off somebody else."

Gregorio! The Spanish slave had never moved like this. He'd never smiled and beckoned and spread his legs and— Isam gulped. He handed his scimitar to Demirkhan for safekeeping and undressed. He was nervous as he climbed on the bed with the waiter. It was as nerve-wracking as captaining a ship. He had to think, plan, and make decisions. What were the risks? What was his plan? He didn't have a plan. He cursed himself. Here he was in the middle of a situation and he hadn't stopped to think about it before he got there.

He had let his story tumble out in a jumble of lust and frustration, and now, although he liked and trusted Demirkhan, the man had put him in an awkward situation. He had to figure out what to do while his dick was hard and, apparently of its own free will, rubbing up against the waiter's butt. He gave a groan. He wouldn't be able to think straight until he had eliminated the distraction between his legs. His decision made, he carried on.

CHAPTER 32 : A SLEEVE STAINED CRIMSON

The Spanish envoy arrived under a flag of truce. The wreck of the *San Juan de Sahagún*, the capture and sinking of the *San Fermín*, the capture of her sister xebec, the *Santa Eulalia de Mérida,* and the humiliation that started it all, the capture of the *Santa María de Cervellon*, had forced the Spanish governor in Tanger to resort to diplomacy. The Tangueli rovers in their small galleys had never been such a menace before. Previously their prey had been small merchantmen and fishboats; now they had dismembered the Spanish patrol based in Tanger. The Spanish knew the identity of the guilty party, too: a xebec with a grey wolf as her figurehead.

Isam had been given considerable latitude to supervise the raising of the *San Fermín*, but he was required to report for muster every morning and carry out whatever duties Rajet Rais had for him. Sometimes that involved helping with the repair and resupply of the *Grey Wolf*, at other times, a lesson in navigation, and sometimes, when Rajet was randy, more intimate duties. On this particular occasion, it had to do with the Spanish envoy.

"The Spanish want to inspect the prisoners," Rajet Rais informed the younger man as they walked along the quay. Rajet wore his best boots that had a thick sole and heel high enough to lift him up so he didn't appear quite so short next to the massive Demirkhan and the lofty Isam. "If you want to be an officer, you'll need to learn how to negotiate ransoms. You'll come with me and watch."

Isam was dowdy compared to the other men; the ensign's best blue and grey striped pantaloons had been new a few months before but were already worn. His boots were new, but his sword was secondhand. He was as presentable as he could manage. "Doesn't the **bey** do that?"

"He does. However, although the Bey of Tanguel is subject to the Dey in Zokhara and therefore obliged to look out for my welfare, I don't expect him to be as zealous on my behalf as I am. Therefore, as the victor, I insist on being present. My victory cost the bey very little, and I want to make certain he doesn't undervalue it. Let it be a lesson to you: always tend your own business and don't depend on strangers if you can avoid it."

"Don't you trust the bey?" Isam asked.

Rajet Rais looked at him askance. "Did you trust the caid? The caid is subject to the bey, but it didn't do you any good. You're lucky it turned out so well."

It was true, but it bothered Isam to think the world was so untrustworthy. "We are all brothers in Islam and corsairs of the Sallee Republic. Doesn't that count for something?"

"It puts us on the same side in the war, but it doesn't mean we should trust each other. Do you trust your brother?"

Isam immediately thought of Samir, the fake sharif. He tugged his short beard. "I don't have a brother, but I have cousins. Some I trust and some I don't."

Rajet punched his shoulder lightly. "You must learn to understand men. They are what they are, and you can't change them. You'll find rogues on the carpet as well as in the gutter. Use that to your advantage."

"I suppose so."

Isam fell into a brown study. Gregorio was the subject of his ruminations. After a bit, he asked, "But surely if you are a good master to your men, you can win them over, in spite of their reservations?"

"Yes, that's true, but it takes time. You have to reward them for their merits but curb their flaws. That's hard to do when they come for the booty and little else. "

"But, religion," Isam protested.

Rajet rolled an eye at him. "Do you go to sea for the love of Allah or for the love of loot?"

He had him there. "Allah approves what we do," Isam said meekly.

Rajet laughed. "You'll quote the Qu'ran to serve your purposes, I see. Be honest, Isam. Why do you go to sea?"

"Because I want to be a rich and famous corsair. I want everyone to know my name and tell stories of my daring. I want to be rich and have a big house to live in. I like the sea. I like the sun and the waves and the wind. I'm never seasick, and I like it when the ship leaps over the waves like a living thing."

"You have a touch of the poet in you, too, I see. Those are all good reasons to go to sea. Never let anyone tell you otherwise."

Rajet and his party turned a corner into a street leading away from the waterfront. A robed and hooded figure that had been following in their wake hurried past their turn. Going to the next street over, the figure also turned away from the waterfront. Hasty steps carried the stranger through the narrow streets as to weave between donkeys and porters. Getting ahead of Rajet's party, the hooded figure took a cross street and rejoined the street along which the rovers were leisurely strolling. The avenue leading up to the bey's palace was wide enough that two wagons could have passed each other with room for pedestrians on either side.

Rajet and Isam paid no attention to the people in the street. One more man in a plain white haik was not worth noticing. The figure stopped under an awning at the front of a shop and pretended to peruse the notice chalked on the slate. When Rajet was thirty feet away, a slim hand raised a pistol, braced it with both hands, and squeezed the trigger.

The bark of the pistol was loud in the confines of the street. Isam's head whipped around, but Demirkhan was already leaping into action. As Isam drew his sword, Demirkhan drew his knife and threw it. The assassin whirled and leaped down the side street, but the knife struck the left arm and clattered to the pavement.

Rajet gasped in shock and staggered. He pressed a hand to his left breast. Blood welled around his fingers. "Get him! Avenge me!"

Isam hesitated when he saw Rajet was wounded, but one of the marines pulled off his turban to make a bandage and pressed it against the captain's wound.

Demirkhan ran down the side street. Isam tore after him. "Where is he?" he shouted.

Demirkhan didn't answer. The big man could move fast, but not as fast as the long-legged youth. When he paused to scoop up his dagger, Isam caught up to him and they both went careening around a corner after the assassin. The figure had a head start and a good pair of legs; it glanced briefly behind, saw them in pursuit, and dodged around another corner. People looked up in surprise.

"Assassin!" Demirkan bellowed in his bass voice.

Isam reached the corner first and swerved into the alley. Clotheslines criss-crossed the path right at head height for the two big men, but the assassin was short enough to run under the lines. Demirkhan and Isam dodged sheets and shirts, but they lost sight of the assassin. They passed a side street with a swift glance, but didn't see the haik-clad figure. Then they were free of the laundry and came up short.

"Where is he?" Isam asked.

They looked around, but the alley was empty. The weathered wood of shut rear doors were blanks, anyone of which might hide an assassin. Isam ran up to the nearest door and tried it. It opened, and the startled servant woman in the kitchen looked up.

"Did a man in a haik run through here?" he demanded.

She shook her head. Isam shut the door and withdrew. He ran to the next door and repeated the exercise.

"Isam, stop. We've lost him somewhere in the laundry. If he did go in a door, it's back there, not up here."

Isam whirled back the way they had come. He swatted aside sheets and opened the first door he came to. The kitchen was empty. He debated with himself whether he should invade the house to search, but common sense told him that even if the assassin had run through this house, he was out the front door and losing himself in the crowded street. He shut the door. He caught sight of a woman in white moving along the alley ahead of them. "Hey!" he called to her. "Have you seen a man in a white haik?"

The woman turned and looked over her shoulder at him, then shook her head without speaking. She continued on her way.

Demirkhan ducked under a clothesline. "We've done what we can, Isam. He got away. Let's go back to Rajet. He's probably still alive." He forced himself to sound cheerful.

Preoccupied with dark and dangerous thoughts, Isam walked smack into a clothesline that slapped him across the nose. "Ow," he said. He ducked under.

Demirkhan turned around to look at him, then smiled in amusement. "Watch your head." He waited for the tall youth to catch up with him. Isam ducked under another clothesline. The woman ahead of them turned down a side street.

Suddenly Isam's head jerked up and he stared, but she was gone. "Her sleeve has a red stain on the left sleeve!"

"What?" It took Demirkhan a moment to catch the implication.

"Blood!" Isam said.

"The assassin was a woman!" Demirkhan exclaimed.

How simple it had been for her to hide her veil under a long haik, then tossing it off, appear like an ordinary Muslim woman dressed in a white tunic and pantaloons. It was the perfect disguise. Neither of them had guessed the pistol-wielding assailant to be female.

They ran. Isam threw out a hand to grab the corner of the building to help him make the turn into the side street, but Demirkhan bounced off the opposite wall. They were just in time to see the woman turn right onto the next street over. Hearing the clatter of boots behind her, she glanced back, saw them in pursuit, and took off running. Dressed like a proper Muslim woman in pantaloons, she was able to run faster than any European woman could have. She was light on her feet and darted through narrow spaces in the traffic. Startled men turned around to see her flitting past, then two large men charging full tilt in pursuit.

"Stop her!" Isam shouted.

Demirkhan shouted, "Thief! Stop that thief!" He was pretty sure shouting 'Stop that murderess!' would only confuse people.

Startled people in the street turned and looked to see who was shouting, while others looked to see who was the thief. Demirkhan bowled over anyone in his way and Isam came leaping along behind him. The assassin sprinted away. She jumped over a leg put out to trip her and dodged a large hand that tried to seize her. She reached the quay, leaped into the water, and swam.

Demirkhan and Isam skidded to a stop at the edge of the quay. "Boat," Demirkhan said. He hurried along the quay looking for one.

"Hold my sword and boots. I'm going in," Isam said. He toed off his boots, dropped his sword, pulled off his turban, shucked his jacket, and jumped feet first into the water.

She had disappeared around the far side of the *Grey Wolf*. He swam past the stern with its open gun ports beneath the lazyboard, but she was gone. Sailors looked over the side in surprise."

"A woman! Where is she?" he demanded.

"She dove under water," the watch replied.

Under water. She could be anywhere. He searched the waters of the bay; she had to come up for air. He treaded water as he caught his breath, but there was no sign of her. She must have dived under the ship. That meant she was somewhere under the wharf. Clever. The ships would hide her as she made her way through the shadowy world of pilings and still water.

"I'm going under the wharf! Tell Demirkhan that's where she must be!" Gulping in air, he dove.

He had done this before. He'd swum under water to wreck the *San Juan*, and he'd dived the wreck of the *San Fermín*. This was close and shallow with the moored vessels floating sedately at their moorings. He swam under the keel of the vessel and came up next to a piling. He shook his head to get the water out of his eyes. He saw a moving figure much further down the wharf. He swam after her, but his way was complicated by the slanting beams that braced the pilings. She had already figured out the most efficient way to traverse the obstacle course and had a good head start. As he watched, she dove under and swam through the triangular space between the beams. He did the same. Long arms carried him to the next beam in a few strokes and he dove through that triangle too. He came up for air and saw her feet just break the surface as she dove ahead of him. He dove again.

He swam as fast as he could through two braces, came up, and saw her surface. She glanced back, saw him, and dove again. They both swam hard, but the longer arms and legs of the young rover gave him an advantage. He was gaining on her. Again they broke the surface, but she didn't waste time looking back. She dove and he dove. He swam through three braces before coming up for air. When he did, he saw her reach the side of a ship and crawl up the accommodation ladder. It was dangerous to come between a ship and her dock, but the water was still and Isam was in pursuit; she raced up the battens and threw herself over the rail and onto the deck.

Isam dove and swam through three more braces. This time when he came up, a Spanish marine was staring down the barrel of his musket. As soon as Isam's head broke the surface, he jerked the gun to take aim at the rover, and fired.

The ball grazed the top of Isam's head and blood ran down into his eyes. He gasped for breath, dove, and turned back the way he had come. He heard shouts and a clatter distorted by the water. He came up behind a piling for shelter. The top of his head blazed with pain; it felt as if he had been stung by a line of bees across the top of his head.

Spanish marines scampered down the accommodation ladder and climbed into the braces beneath the wharf. He heard them talking urgently to one another. He couldn't understand Spanish, but he could guess the nature of their conversation. He took a deep breath, dove, and heard the report of a musket reverberating under the wharf. He dove under the nearest ship and came up on the other side. He looked around wildly, but there were no searchers on this side. The crews were all looking over the dock side trying to figure out what was going on. He swam past the vessel's stern, looked up, and saw the ornate scrollwork that identified the captured *Santa Eulalia*. He treaded water while he caught his breath, then swam to the accommodation ladder and crawled on deck.

The prize crew looked around in surprise. Fortunately, they recognized him and came to his aid.

CHAPTER 33 : THE STILT WALKERS

The Spanish envoy was evicted from Tanguel without negotiation. Rajet was laid up for a week to recuperate, but he survived. Much to Gregorio's annoyance, Isam had a lot of free time as a result. He was able to spend a lot of his time supervising the salvage of the wreck and living in the camp in the dunes. Although it was cold at night, he preferred to be the master of his own camp than an orphan sleeping on his uncle's divan. He could have been warmer, but Gregorio remained as stiff as ever.

A diversion came in the form of French entertainers on stilts three feet tall. The men wore long sheepskin vests over top of their red and blue costumes and some of them carried musical instruments. The women wore immensely long blue skirts with hoops sewed into the bottom to make them swing like bells. They carried tambourines to jingle and thump in time to the lively French folk songs. Children as young as five walked on short stilts that raised them a foot above the ground.

While the men played their instruments, the women danced on their stilts as easily as if they had been barefoot upon a grassy meadow. Their bell-like skirts swayed and swung, but although mischievous boys tried to peek under them, all they could see were the red and white candy-stripe painted sticks that held the women up. Without breaking step, the women kicked them with their stilts and made them hop and squirm. This amused the crowd as much as the dancing did.

After the women, the men performed feats of acrobatics. One of the men bent completely backwards, put his hands on the ground, lifted his legs and did a handstand, then pulled himself upright again. Delighted, Isam threw a handful of copper coins onto the ground. They glittered and bounced on the cobblestones, but the stilt walkers bent down and picked the coins up with easy grace. Their ability to twist, bend, and balance was amazing to behold. One of the Frenchmen shook out a jump rope and leaped nimbly over it on every turn. The gathering crowd applauded. The corsairs had prize money to spend and they showered it on the entertainers. They especially liked it when pretty young Frenchwomen bent low and their bosoms bulged as if they would pop right out of their bodices.

The children and a youth walked around with their hats in their hands to solicit more coins. The youth was a black-haired and handsome fellow with flashing blue eyes. He was a couple of years younger than Isam and the body under the long sheepskin was lean and fit. All of the entertainers were lithe and muscular, but Isam took a particular liking to him. Since he was only wearing a pair of foot-high stilts, he was close enough to Isam's height for the corsair to be able to speak to him, and he did.

"Who are these entertainers? I have never seen or heard of them. Where do they come from?" He asked it in Arabic because he didn't know any European languages.

The youth bowed and touched his brow. Speaking in accented Arabic, he replied, "France. We were shepherds in the Landes region, but we were so poor that we improved our fortunes by taking to the road as entertainers. We have come over to the Sallee Republic in hopes that an act like ours has never been seen before. Please be generous!" He shook the shapeless red cap and gave Isam an ingratiating smile.

Isam tossed more coins into the hat and smiled back at him.

The youth inveigled him, "Come tonight! We are camping in a field outside the River Gate and we will show you marvels!"

The message delivered, the stilt walkers gathered up the last coins and paraded away. Isam hurried back to his camp to tell his slave about it.

"You can come with me! You will enjoy it," He told Gregorio. If Gregorio enjoyed himself, he might be amenable to his master's desires.

"Stilt walkers?" Gregorio asked. "I know how to walk on stilts."

This news astounded Isam. "You do? How?"

"We used them to walk through wet fields when I was a child. The river would flood and make a mess, so we got up on stilts and waded through it."

"Show me!"

Gregorio had to make the stilts, but that wasn't difficult. They had an axe and saw for cutting firewood, so pretty soon they had cut some saplings and trimmed them into shape. Gregorio made a pair for each of them. They had tall uprights to hold onto but the footrest was only about eight inches above the ground. Gregorio wobbled at first, but quickly remembered how to walk with them. Once he was used to them again, he cut down his sticks and strapped them to his lower legs. He couldn't do any of the tricks the entertainers had done, but it didn't matter. He could walk on them easily enough.

Nothing would do but for Isam to have his stilts cut down and strapped to his legs. Being a sailor, he was nimble and accustomed to balancing on a height, so he soon mastered the art of walking and even dared to run a little. He laughed and caught Gregorio's hands. "Let's dance!"

He tried to imitate the French dance the stilt walkers had done, but he didn't know it. His dance consisted of galumphing about and laughing. Gregorio smiled and pirouetted as he showed off his superior stilt skills. Isam gazed at him with adoring eyes and caught his hands. He tried to pull him close for a kiss, but Gregorio chose to misinterpret the gesture.

"You dance like this," he said. Not that he knew the particular dance the entertainers had done, but he was determined to keep Isam at arm's length. He took Isam's hands and swung them sideways and stepped to the side, then the other direction. Isam stumbled after him and had to grab onto Gregorio's shoulder for support, then tottered the other way. He got his stilts crossed and crashed to the ground.

The sailors at the camp laughed, then one of them dug a wooden flute out of his kit and began to play a tune. Isam scrambled onto his hands and knees, then stumbled to his feet and swayed. He couldn't stand still. He had to constantly take small steps to keep his balance. Gregorio could balance on his stilts as steadily as if he were on his own two feet. When Isam once again approached him, the slave started dancing in time to the wooden flute and whirled away.

The thwarting of his wishes only inflamed Isam the more. He grinned as he watched the teasing, twisting form stepping lightly over the sandy ground. He felt very warm inside and his face was flushed. He tottered over to intercept Gregorio, but the slave danced away. Isam ran a few steps on the stilts to pursue him, but once again Gregorio escaped him. Being more sure-footed on the stilts than the novice, he was able to keep out of the corsair's reach. Isam's shins began to hurt. He wasn't used to stilt walking and it was making his legs ache. He had to constantly flex his legs to keep his balance and that was wearing him out. He plopped down onto the ground and stretched out one leg and folded the other up so that he could rub his shin.

"Come help me, my legs are sore!"

That was a direct order. Gregorio didn't dare disobey it, but he approached warily. He knelt and bent before the corsair and avoided his eyes. "Do you have any liniment?" he asked.

"No." Isam was nineteen. Liniment was for old people.

Gregorio untied the strap from Isam's leg. He left the other stilt in place on purpose. If he had to run, Isam would find it hard to catch him with one stilt on and one stilt off. That Gregorio was thinking such things never crossed Isam's mind. He reached out and cupped

Gregorio's chin in his hand and leaned towards him. Gregorio suffered Isam's kiss without a reaction.

Isam coaxed him. "Kiss me back. I like the way you kiss."

"I need to make dinner, master," Gregorio replied and withdrew. He was suddenly very busy fetching wood to build the fire and water to boil the couscous.

Isam had to take the other stilt off before he could rise and approach. Gregorio was still wearing his stilts and that made him as tall as the Turk. It startled both of them to be able to meet one another's gaze on the level. Isam rarely ever met a man as tall as himself, and Gregorio had never been a tall man in his life. They blinked at one another.

"You're tall!" Isam said. It was what people always said to him when they realized just how tall he was.

"I like being tall," Gregorio replied. "No wonder you think you can do whatever you want!" Then he gave Isam an alarmed look for fear he would take offense.

Isam grinned at him. "Yes. A tall man is a powerful man. Other men look up to him. They have to!"

"But only if he deserves it. If he doesn't, then he's nothing but a midget on stilts." There was a touch of asperity in Gregorio's voice.

"I do deserve it! I captured the *San Fermín.*"

"Which is a wreck on the bottom of the sea," Gregorio replied.

"I'm a rais now!"

"You're a rais when you can keep your ship on the right side of the water."

Isam glowered at him. "It was bad luck. The fortunes of war."

"You never believe anything you don't want to believe," Gregorio replied bitterly.

Isam put his hands on his hips. "Like what? I know what's what."

Gregorio gave him a dark and contemptuous look. "You don't believe that I hate you."

"You don't hate me," Isam said automatically.

Gregorio threw up his hands. "I have to make dinner." He stalked away on his stilts.

"You're just saying that to needle me!" Isam shot back.

"Yes, master. Whatever you say." Gregorio didn't even look at him as he slammed the kettle onto the fire and sent a small inferno of sparks flying into the air.

Isam swiftly stomped on the sparks that settled on the grass, then jumped because he was bare foot. "Ow!"

Gregorio poured water into the kettle with a scowl on his face.

Isam rubbed his burned foot against the other one. The burn was tiny, but it annoyed him greatly. He picked up his boots and stalked down to the water to wash his feet. They both maintained a stony silence through dinner.

CHAPTER 34 : SPANISH PERFIDY

At dusk Isam, Gregorio, and the sailors from camp joined the throng of people looking for the promised entertainment. They knew they were close when they spotted a man in a costume on stilts. He called out in French that meant nothing to them, but they understood his pointing arm well enough. Walking down a lane, they came to a pasture and where tents had been set up. Local peddlers sold oranges, mint water, almonds, candy, and other treats.

Isam didn't realize at first that Gregorio was missing. He thought they had lost each other in the crowd. He scanned the people casually, but when he didn't find Gregorio, he began to worry.

"Where is Gregorio?" he asked his men.

They looked around, but nobody knew. They'd all been enthralled by the fair-like atmosphere.

"Look for him. We'll meet by that striped tent in half an hour."

They scattered and searched, but nobody found Gregorio. Slowly it sank in on Isam: Gregorio was gone. At first he didn't understand. Why would he go? Then he knew: Gregorio hated him. All this time, he had thought Gregorio's complaints were unimportant, yet Gregorio had been telling him the truth. His face burned. He wondered if the sailors had been laughing at him behind his back because he was too stupid to see what was right in front of him. His pride was young and tender and he couldn't stand being laughed it. It was bad enough that Gregorio didn't like him when he liked Gregorio so very much. His humiliation was like a boarding pike to the stomach.

Gregorio was running away. The Spanish slave could walk on stilts; he could join the troupe and escape disguised as one of them. If the troupe would have him. They were all Nazarenes. Of course they would. Somewhere amid the costumes and props was the slave he desperately desired. He had to find him.

Scowling, he stuck his head in the first tent he came to. "Where's Gregorio?" he demanded in Arabic.

The tent housed a male fortune teller and his Moorish customer. Playing cards were laid out on a tablecloth covered in mystical signs. The two men looked up in surprise, but neither of them was Gregorio.

Isam pulled his head out and went to the next tent. Again he stuck his head in without preamble. Men were half dressed as they sat on boxes and helped each other strap on their stilts.

"Where's Gregorio?" he demanded. They didn't understand Arabic, and he didn't understand French. He tossed costumes this way and that while the men watched warily, but Gregorio wasn't in there.

Stalking to the next tent, he once again burst in unannounced. "Where's—"

A woman screamed and hit him in the face with her stilt.

He staggered back. Half dressed women were sitting in their petticoats with their skirts hiked above their knees so they could strap on the stilts. They were wearing white chemises and striped stockings and were entirely indecent. Face turning red, he jumped back outside.

"Sorry! I'm looking for someone!"

The tent flap was jerked closed with a stream of feminine French invective.

His intrusion had not gone unnoticed. A bantam cock of a Frenchman charged at him. What the man shouted at him, he didn't understand, but he could guess well enough. *Pervert. Peeper.* He fled. Fortunately, the Frenchman was content to drive him off and didn't pursue him. Perhaps it was because the Turk was twice his size, or perhaps it was because in any argument between a true believer and an infidel, the law would back the follower of the Prophet. Either way, Isam escaped unscathed except for his pride.

His impetuosity checked for the moment, he skulked away, but once he was certain he wasn't being followed, he slipped behind the tents. Continuing his search with a measure of discretion this time, he discovered caravans with canvas covers. Light shone from the window of one. Not wishing to draw attention to himself, he slipped into the shadows on the far side.

Inside, the occupants were speaking Spanish. He didn't know the language, but he recognized the feminine lightness of Gregorio's voice. The slave was trying to persuade someone of something. To help him escape, no doubt. Another voice had the lisping tenor of a young Castilian; he objected to whatever Gregorio was saying. A third man with a deeper voice spoke with the well-educated and patronizing tone of a Spanish gentleman.

Why were a pair of Spanish gentlemen traveling with a troupe of French stilt walkers?

Spies. He knew it for a certainty. Combat, assassination, and diplomacy had failed, so the Spanish were resorting to guile.

The three voices became more cooperative as an understanding was reached. The door opened and Isam swiftly threw himself under the wagon. He saw a pair of feet wearing Gregorio's slipper-shoes descend the short ladder and walk away. The other men continued talking in Spanish, then they also left the wagon. When they disappeared, he crawled out from under the wagon.

Isam hurried to the rendezvous beside the white and red striped tent. None of his men had had any luck, but he didn't tell them what he'd found. He was trying to decide what to do with his information. Obviously, the authorities needed to know that a pair of Spanish spies had come to Tanguel, but he was worried about what would happen to Gregorio. He assumed that if the slave were apprehended, he'd be tortured to make him talk. He had never concerned himself with the morality of torture before, but now that he thought about it being inflicted on someone he liked, it seemed a bad idea. He cursed himself for falling for a infidel and cursed Gregorio for running away.

He was stewing over it when one of his men said, "There he is!"

Isam turned around as Gregorio walked up to him with a shy smile. The slave extended a small parcel wrapped in wax paper. "I bought you some Turkish delight, master."

Isam was astonished. He was certain his slave had run off with a pair of Spanish spies, yet here he was, delivering candy to him. Maybe they weren't spies after all.

"I hope you like rosewater," Gregorio was saying.

"Yes, I like *lokum*," he replied, using the Turkish word for the sweet. He unwrapped the waxed paper to reveal half a dozen pink rectangles dusted with powdered sugar. He popped one into his mouth and offered a piece to Gregorio.

"Thank you, master." Gregorio picked one out of the paper and ate it.

Isam handed the rest of the treats to the sailors, then he put his arm around Gregorio's waist. "I missed you. You shouldn't wander off!"

Gregorio stiffened, then yielded to the embrace. "I wanted to thank you for bringing me to the show, so I brought you a sweet. I'm looking forward to the performance."

The stiffness told Isam that Gregorio's feelings hadn't changed. The candy didn't taste so sweet anymore. He kept his arm firmly around the slave as anger built inside him.

"I am too." He kissed his slave possessively on the cheek.

Gregorio endured it, but whispered, "Master, we are in public!"

"I don't care. I can do as I please with my slave." Suppressed anger made his voice harsh.

Gregorio squirmed around to face Isam—not that he wanted to look at him—but because he wanted to hide his face from the stilt walkers. "You're attracting attention! We should go home."

"We just got here. I plan to enjoy myself."

"Then let's go off by ourselves." Gregorio had a good idea what might happen, but if it must happen, he didn't want his potential rescuers to know about it. They wouldn't take him if they knew what he was.

"You never asked to be alone with me before." Isam's mood was sour.

"I'm sorry I left without asking. I wanted to surprise you with a treat."

Again the cajoling voice Isam had heard so often, but now he understood what it meant. Gregorio was trying to manipulate him. The young corsair thought he was going to burst a blood vessel he was so vexed. Instead he picked the slave up, threw him over his shoulder, and carried him into darkness. Gregorio clutched at his back but didn't struggle. Isam found a path and walked until he came to a stream. He stepped from rock to rock to cross it, then hiked up the bank on the other side. He kept walking. Finally, when he had walked all his anger out, he put the slave on his feet. The trail widened into a small clearing in the middle of a small stand of woods. Gregorio eyed him warily and backed away.

Isam sighed. "I know there are two Spanish spies in this troupe. You're going to run away with them, aren't you?"

Gregorio went rigid. "I didn't know they were spies. I asked them to help me escape. You will beat me, I know. But they wouldn't take me. They have something else to do and they don't want to attract attention by helping a fugitive slave."

"Spying."

"If you say so, master. I didn't ask." His voice was worried.

Isam saw him cringe. "I'm not going to beat you."

After a pause, Gregorio said, "You're not? Even though I was trying to run away?"

"I don't want to hurt you. I was so angry I almost did, but I don't want to be ruled by my passions. I want to rule myself, even if you do provoke me."

"If you free me, your problem will be gone."

"If I release you, are you going to help the spies?"

After a moment, Gregorio said, "Yes, but if you don't turn me loose, I will help them just to spite you."

"Do you hate me that much?"

"You and everyone here. I hate the Sallee Republic. I hate the town of Tanguel. I hate the pirates that prey on my country. I hate being a slave. I hate Maureo and all his kin. I hate being raped and beaten. I hate being fondled in public and shamed before righteous men. I hate being ruined. I want to go home, but I can't go back to my own people. I will have to go somewhere nobody knows me so I can bury my past. Most of all I hate knowing that I'll die in this damned country where my carcass will be treated like any other piece of livestock."

"If you will point out the spies to me and help me catch them, I will set you free."

Gregorio gave him a look of contempt. "You already made me betray myself. Now you want me to betray my country, too, but you don't keep your word. You offer this, you offer that, but you don't mean it. You'll say anything to get your way."

Isam grabbed him by the ears and shook him. "You're stubborn and foolish! You're better off with me. What will you be in Spain? Someone's servant, the same as here. He'll beat you because you're stubborn and disobedient. Will you like it better because it's a Spanish stick? I've been kind to you, but you're saucy and disobedient. You take advantage of my good nature!"

"If you had a good nature, you wouldn't be a thief and a rapist."

Isam slapped him so hard blood trickled from his lip.

Gregorio tasted it; it had the iron flavor of defeat. He had nothing left to lose. "I bet you feel very manly right now, slapping a helpless slave."

Isam raised his hand to strike again, but struggled for control. "Manliness has nothing to do with it!"

"It certainly doesn't. Real men have honor." Gregorio was going to be beaten; he knew it. He couldn't help himself. Sometimes the words came to his lips before his teeth could restrain them.

"I have honor!" Isam objected.

"You have pride. It's not the same thing."

He saw it then. Proud, young, headstrong, ambitious, brave, all these things, yes. But honorable? Uncle Halim was honorable, and he was nothing like his uncle. Samir was not honorable; he had tricked Umar into marrying the dishonored Rabiyah. Isam and Rabiyah had both lied to get her married to Umar. He had done it to save her, but was it right? Umar was the decent one of the three. There was no deceit in him. They'd taken advantage of him. Samir pretended to be a descendant of the Prophet, and Rabiyah pretended to be an outraged virgin. Who was he pretending to be?

A captain. A mighty corsair.

"Don't boast about things you haven't done," was Demirkhan's advice. That advice had a corollary: do what you say you do. He understood it now. He hadn't given Gregorio the promised reward, even though he deserved it. He had lied when convenient, deceived Umar, and taken advantage of Gregorio.

If he was confident in what he was doing, why should he lie about it? Umar might have married Rabiyah anyhow if he'd known the truth. He was that besotted with her. Maybe he wouldn't have, but that would have been Rabiyah's shame to bear. So complicated! He didn't want Rabiyah to suffer more than she had. She'd been beaten and raped. Wasn't that punish enough for her folly? Lying to save her was justified, wasn't it?

He discovered his upraised hand was still hanging in the air. He lowered it. "I'm not going to beat you."

Gregorio bent and groped the dirt in search of a stone. When he found one, he threw it at Isam. The rock clipped his master's shoulder and bounced away into the darkness.

"Ingrate," Isam said in exasperation.

"You're the ingrate. I was the one that rescued Rabiyah. If I hadn't spoken to you in the street, you never would have found her."

Isam wanted to argue with him, but what Gregorio said was true and he knew it. Why did it rankle to admit it? "You're right," he finally said.

Gregorio bent down and hunted for another stone. In exasperation Isam pounced on him and wrestled his arm behind his back. "Stop that!"

"I hate you!" Gregorio replied as he twisted his arm in a violent attempt to free it.

Isam wouldn't let go. "I'm willing to give you whatever reward you want short of freedom, but you have to help me catch the spies."

"Then it's not a reward, is it? It's a bribe." Gregorio sneered. He hung helplessly with his toes supporting his weight as he tried to ease the pain in his shoulder.

"If I do you a favor, you should do me a favor," Isam wheedled.

"You're not doing me any favors! You're keeping me captive and tormenting me!" Again he twisted and tried to escape the hard hands holding him.

"I can't let you go."

Gregorio stopped struggling and hung limply. "Yes, master. I know," he replied wearily.

Isam let him down. He smoothed the slave's shirt awkwardly. "Let's watch the show. We should be friends," he cajoled.

"As you wish, master."

CHAPTER 35 : IN THROUGH THE HAWSE-HOLE

The next day Gregorio woke before his master. Isam, having stayed up much later than he was accustomed, was sound asleep on his cot. His mind made up, Gregorio stealthily went through his master's duffel bag, found his purse, and tucked the leather bag with its silver coins into his own sash. He pulled his haik over his head and settled it around the body. The falls of wool concealed the bulge in his sash. Putting his sandals on, he slipped out into the misty morning. To the lone sailor on watch he said, "I have errands to do for Isam Rais. I won't be back in time to make breakfast."

The man made a face at the prospect of making his own breakfast, but didn't doubt the slave. Gregorio walked briskly to town with his heart clattering against his ribs. Nobody gainsaid him. He bought himself a breakfast with his master's money, and when the secondhand shops opened, bought clothes. He carried the bundles out to River Gate and found the stilt walkers' camp.

"I have done what you ask. My master will be angry when he realizes I've stolen his money. I can't go back."

The older of the two Spaniards said, "We need a boat that can pass muster as a bumboat. A boat selling vegetables or watermelons or some such thing." He was a man in his mid-twenties, lean and with lively brown eyes.

Gregorio gave him a dismayed look. "A boat! How am I to get a boat?"

"Rent it, buy it, borrow it. As long as you come by it honestly. We don't want the owner to have reason to come after us."

Gregorio wrung his hands. "Why do you need a boat?"

"You don't need to know. I promise you, if you do it, it will resound to your credit and Spain will be grateful."

Gregorio's anguish grew. "You're going to do something dangerous! They'll bastinade me until I'm crippled!"

"If you do it, we'll take you with us when we leave. You'll be a hero when you return home."

Home. The word undid Gregorio's fears. "All right, I'll do it. Maybe I can rent a boat."

"Meet us at the public dock at ten of the clock. The password will be '*Ave Maria*.' The countersign will be '*Deo bonum est*.'"

Gregorio was no scholar. They made him repeat the Latin until he had it memorized. That done, he headed back to town. He had difficulty finding a boat to rent. Not that there was a shortage of boats, but there was a shortage of owners who could be found. Abled-bodied men were heading to work on the various construction and repair jobs necessitated by the bombardment. Eventually he was able to rent a boat for the day. He then went to the market and bought several baskets of vegetables. Isam's money was disappearing fast, so he carried them on his back to the boat. By the time ten o'clock arrived, he was tired, but he had a boat that looked the part of a vegetable seller.

Two men with the hoods of their haiks up to protect their heads from the chilly breeze approached. Gregorio saw them from the corner of his eyes and started up in fear. Then he thought they must see him as the merchant he was pretending to be, so he asked timidly, "Would you like to buy some yams?" His voice didn't carry, so he cleared it and spoke up louder. "Would you like to buy some yams, effendi?"

The two men stopped on the quay above him. They each held the hand of a little girl no more than five years old. She was a dark-eyed child dressed in the Moorish way in a tan wool tunic over matching pantaloons. A little white haik completed her outfit. The sharpness of her features said she wasn't a Moor, but she was as tan as they were. With so many people of different races in the city, she passed as one of many half-caste children.

"*Ave Maria*," said the taller man.

"*Deo bonum est*," Gregorio replied with feeling.

The disguised Spaniards handed the little girl into the boat, then climbed nimbly down into it. They took up the oars and rowed. They stopped first at a galley tied up next along the quay, but didn't sell any vegetables. Gregorio kept his hood up and his hand on the tiller. He was not a sailor, but he soon learned to steer the boat well enough.

Stilt walkers came traipsing along the waterfront with their tambourines and drums. They paused in front of the galley and did their tricks. The handful of sailors on board all went to the landward rail to watch them and toss copper coins at them. The stilt walkers knelt gracefully down from their tall stilts and scooped up the coins, then moved along the quay.

"Pass the next boat. Bring us under the bow of the frigate. If anyone notices us, offer to sell them what's in the basket," the older Spaniard instructed.

They glided silently past the second galley and slipped under the frigate's bow. Something Arabic had been painted over her name, but her figurehead could not be entirely obscured. Beneath the brown paint that obliterated the infidel image, seven male faces, one above another, could be seen. The top head was largest and wore the pointed hat that was a bishop's miter. Thus the captive frigate had been rendered fit for the true believers' service.

She was tied up with her larboard along the quay. No one noticed them. Like all the other boats, the watch was busy gawking at the stilt walkers. Looking around carefully, the Spaniards shipped oars, then grabbed onto the dolphin-striker and pulled in close. The ship's bulk hid them from those on board. Above their heads damage from the fight could be seen: the hawse-hole was broken open above the bolster. It was a raw wound in the red paint.

The taller Spaniard spoke to the little girl, "You know what to do. Do it quietly and you shall have a lollipop." He had to speak French to her, she knew no other language.

She brightened at the promised lollipop and stood up. The Spaniard hoisted her up and she squirmed and wriggled through the hawsehole. Her haik snagged on the broken edge of the hole and he unsnagged her and gave her bottom a push. She was through.

"Row along the side slowly," the Spaniard told his companion.

The youth put his oars out and gave a gentle stroke. Gregorio guided the boat along the side. Two decks of gun ports loomed over their head. Each gun port was a square port in the dark red side of the frigate. A sturdy line ran from the middle of the gun port lid up to a hole in the strake above it, and inside. After a small eternity, one of those lines went slack and hung in a bight.

"Keep us steady!" the Spanish leader hissed. He grabbed the rope and lifted it. The heavy gun port lid lifted half way, and he held it up with his hands. "Now!"

The youth slithered in. He squirmed under the muzzle of the gun, then rose up, hauled the end of the line and pulled the gun port lid all the way open. The little girl crawled out and the Spaniard put her down in the boat. Then he crawled in through the gun port, and turning to give Gregorio orders, whispered, "Wait here."

Gregorio nodded with wide eyes. What they were going to do aboard the frigate he couldn't guess. If he had, he would have fled. As it was, he looked around fearfully. Still, his disguise was good. He was a man with a child and baskets full of vegetables. He looked up, prepared to sing out, "Yam! Buy my yams!" if a watchful face appeared over the side, but it never did. The rattle of tambourine and ruffle of drums echoed off the faces of the buildings as the stilt walkers did their stunts to distract the sailors aboard the vessel.

Gregorio kept hold of the gun lid's rope to prevent the boat from drifting away. Pretty soon his shoulder ached, so he switched arms. The little girl hunched her shoulders and hugged her knees. She spoke to him in French, but he didn't understand. She grew restless, so he picked up one of the carrots and offered it to her. She took it, and starting at the pointy end, began to munch it. He was hungry himself, so he ate a carrot too.

Suddenly the gun lid beneath his hand rose. He let go and the boat drifted away. He grabbed for an oar and splashed as he paddled like a Red Indian to bring it back under the port. The older man slithered out and into the boat hissing, "Sh! Not so much noise!" Gregorio laid the oar over the thwarts and grabbed the edge of the gun port. The young Spaniard slithered out and dropped into the boat. Gregorio let go and sat down and the lid thumped into place.

"Row back! Go up the river! Quickly!"

The two men put their backs to it. Gregorio bent the tiller and the little boat curved away and headed back the way she had come. As they passed the galley, one of the stilt walking children who was the lookout waved to them, then ran to give the message. The stilt walkers grabbed the last of the coins on the pavement, then walked away with long strides and left the frigate behind.

The French girl pouted and said, "I want my lollipop!" in her native tongue, but the men were too busy rowing.

"Easy," the Spanish man said. "We're far enough away. We don't want to attract attention to ourselves." They turned up the river and rowed under the arch of the Roman bridge.

About ten minutes after they had quitted the frigate, a tremendous roar burst the hum of the town's noise. The little girl shrieked and clapped her hands over her ears, but the Spaniards kept rowing. Gregorio was so startled he let go of the tiller. He jerked his head around and saw a rain of debris falling on the waterfront. A cloud of brown smoke rose in an acrid column and drifted over the town. The clatter of wooden debris rattled down on the shops and ships around the frigate's berth.

The two Spaniards grinned in delight. Facing the rear as they rowed, they had seen it all. "Praise God! Our mission is successful! The damned pirates shall not turn our own guns against us!"

The waterfront was in chaos. The vessels moored to either side of the destroyed frigate were damaged, and so were the storefronts facing the explosion. A number of people on shore were injured too. Most of them were sailors or chandlers or otherwise employed in supporting the corsairs, so the Spaniards didn't lament their fate one bit.

CHAPTER 36 : THE THUNDEROUS ROAR

Isam leaped out of bed and swiveled his head in frantic search before he was even awake. The thunderous roar receded, leaving the tent sitting placidly in its wake. Pushing outside dressed in nothing but his drawers and shirt, he found his sailors had run down to the shore. He joined them to gawk across the harbor at the destruction. He was oblivious to the cold mud oozing between his toes.

"What happened?" he asked.

"The frigate blew up," one of the sailors replied.

His stomach tightened. He had a horrible feeling he knew something about that. "Gregorio!" he called, but the man didn't answer. "Gregorio?"

"He went to town on errands for you, rais," one of the sailors helpfully replied.

"No." The unease in his belly reached up and gripped his heart. He ran back up the weedy dune to his tent. He paused to wipe the mud off his feet, then shoved dirty feet into yesterday's socks. Donning the same clothes he'd worn yesterday, he thrust his scimitar into his sash and hurried to town.

In the twenty or so minutes it took him to hike around the harbor and reach the scene of the crime, several thoughts went through his mind, not the least of which was his own culpability for failing to report what he knew about the Spanish spies. He cursed himself for trusting Gregorio and sleeping late. He supposed he ought to be glad he hadn't received a shiv in the ribs, but that was scant consolation. The worry that loomed in his mind was the knowledge that if anyone found out he had been dilatory with important intelligence, the bastinado was the least punishment he could expect. That sealed his lips. What they didn't know wouldn't hurt him. He had to find Gregorio.

He hastened out the River Gate and found the stilt walkers' camp. All was calm as the entertainers were preparing their midday meal over a cookfire. The women were soberly dressed in plain blue skirts and bodices that had been neatly patched. They kept their heads and bosoms covered when they weren't performing. Children were playing a ball game. They ran after the ball, tossed it, caught it, and chased after it as easily on stilts as if they had been afoot.

"I'm looking for Gregorio," he told the nearest woman.

She shook her head uncomprehendingly.

He looked in all their faces, but they were all French. No green-eyed Spaniard among them. He went and looked through their tents, but he didn't find the eunuch. One of the men came over and glared at him and spoke a few words of bad Arabic to him. "Stop! Go away!"

Isam turned and snarled, "Gregorio! Where is Gregorio?"

The man didn't know or wouldn't tell. "No Gregorio. France!"

Isam went between the tents, mounted the back step to the nearest wagon, and yanked open the door. An older woman in her chemise turned around, saw the bearded face and fez, screamed, and hit him with a cast iron frying pan. He tumbled backwards out of the wagon and fell in a heap. Black stars swirled before his eyes as he lay blinking up at the sky. The man who spoke bad Arabic ran at him with a drawn knife. Isam rolled over and staggered to his feet. He glared fiercely at the man, and it must have worked, because the man suddenly sheathed the knife and took off running.

"*Les Sarrasins!*" the Frenchman shouted in warning.

Baffled, Isam swayed as he watched him run. The pounding in his aching head sounded like the thunder of hoofbeats. He turned around to retrace his steps, only to discover a troop of mounted soldiers with spears and turbans sweeping down on the stilt walkers' camp. A shiny spearpoint thrust at him and he jumped back.

He shouted in Arabic, "I'm Muslim!"

The soldier was mounted on a white horse and wore flowing white robes. He snarled, "On your knees! Put your hands up!"

Isam dropped to his knees, raised his hands, and said, "I'm Isam bin Hamet. Halim Many Daughters is my uncle!"

"I don't care," the soldier replied. He dismounted and removed Isam's sword and dagger, then tied his hands behind his back. With the butt of his spear, he shoved Isam toward the other captives.

Turning to another soldier, he tried again, "I'm a Muslim!"

"Then you're a traitor who connives with thieves and spies."

"No! I'm looking for my runaway servant! I thought he might hide with the foreigners to try and escape!"

The soldier replied, "Liar." He shoved Isam into the huddle with the terrified French.

Women and children cried. All of them, even the littlest children, had their hands bound. They were all driven before the spears of the true believers. They trudged to town in a dispirited clump. The soldiers smacked them with the butt of their spears to make them keep moving when their feet dragged. Isam was struck a painful blow on the shoulder.

Eventually they arrived at the bey's palace. They were herded through the tiled halls. Isam had never been in the governor's palace before. He gawked as much as the French at the brilliant zellige that formed intricate repeating geometric patterns all over the walls, floors, and ceilings. Columns and arches of white marble contrasted with the predominant blue-green, tan, and white of the tiles. It was like walking through a jeweled hall. For a moment he forgot that he was a bound captive. When they came into a courtyard planted with mint and other herbs around a central fountain, he thought he had reached Paradise.

The bey was reclining upon a divan placed in a bed of mint in the full sunshine. Two slaves, one black and one white, wafted peacock feather fans over him. The mint crushed beneath the divan wafted a divine scent around his reclining form. He was an older man with pure white hair and the fleshy, bulbous nose of a man who had lived in comfort to a great age. He was a stout, dignified, and beady-eyed old man sumptuously dressed in blue brocade. Two younger men who resembled him in facial features stood to either side of him.

The French and Isam were forced to their knees on the pavement by the fountain. The bey bestirred himself to sit up and have a look at the captives. His lips turned down and the lines running from the corners of his nose to the corners of his mouth were deep and made him look displeased in the extreme.

The captain of the guard stepped forward, and bowing deeply from the waist, said, "These are the foreigners we suspect sabotaged the frigate. We found a traitor among them." He pointed at Isam.

"I'm a Muslim! I was looking for my runaway slave! I don't know anything about these people! I'm not with them!"

"Yet you are with them," the bey replied.

"I thought my servant might have run away to them in hopes of escaping. I told the soldiers that, but they wouldn't listen to me. May it please your excellency, I'm Isam bin Hamet Rais Fawad, the nephew of Halim Rais Fawad of the Many Daughters. I'm a loyal son of Tanguel. I captured the *San Fermín* in battle! Before that, I cut the Spanish anchor cable at Cape Spartel to wreck them! If I had done all that, would I collude with infidels? I'm a corsair! Allah rewards me with prize money for waging holy war." He beseeched the governor with his eyes.

"I've heard of Halim of the Many Daughters. They say Allah favors him. If that's true, you were extremely unlucky just now." He rubbed his chin and stared at Isam.

Isam tried to look innocent. "You can summon my sailors and ask them. They told me Gregorio went on errands for me, but I hadn't sent him on any errands. I suspect he's trying to escape. He's been a quarrelsome slave."

"Summon the sailors. In the meantime, put him to the bastinado and see if he changes his story. Consider your words carefully, young man. We're going to interrogate everyone around you. Tell the truth and help us apprehend the saboteurs. I'm sure your friends know something about it." He waved a be-ringed hand at the French.

The French, who couldn't understand the Arabic discussion, looked hopefully back and forth between Isam and the bey, but at Isam's look of alarm, they began to wail piteously. In French peppered with a few words of Arabic, they tried to plead their case.

The soldiers grabbed Isam and threw him on his back. They grabbed his feet and lifted them up. His boots were pulled off and the bare soles exposed. They tied his ankles together, and with a soldier holding a rope on either side, kept them suspended in the air. Meanwhile, the executioner stepped up with his cane.

"Repent and tell the truth!" he urged Isam. The first blow came whistling down on the soles of his feet.

Isam howled. "It'struemyservantranawayandIwaslookingforhim!"

An interpreter had to be found to question the French. With blow after blow slashing Isam's feet, they were falling all over themselves to avow their innocence.

"We don't know this man, your excellency! He came to our tents twice, once this morning, and once last night, looking for someone named Gregorio, but we don't know anyone named Gregorio! We are French, everyone of us! We are poor shepherds who became entertainers!"

Isam gritted his teeth against the pain. Some men were crippled for life by the bastinado. The thought appalled him, but he was even more appalled by what they would do to him if he confessed knowing about the existence of a pair of Spanish spies he'd neglected to report. Sweat poured off his body and soaked his clothes as the agonizing assault went on.

"Please! My uncle is a righteous man! Call him! Call my cousin Samir! Call my cousin Umar! Call my sailors! Call Rajet Rais! They will bear witness for me!"

By the time fifty blows had landed, his feet were cut and bloody. His shoulders and back ached from having his hands bound under him. He was gasping for breath.

"Rajet Rais is here," the doorkeeper announced.

Rajet was a small man, but he strode into the courtyard with the confidence of a man of large ability. Glancing at the captive ensign, he gave him the briefest of sympathetic looks, then turned his attention to the bey, bowed deeply with his hand pressed to his forehead, and waited to be called upon.

"Rajet Rais. This man claims you will vouch for him." The bey gestured a gold and diamond laden hand in Isam's direction. The soldiers were still holding his battered feet up and the executioner stood by with the bloody cane.

"This is Isam bin Hamet, my ensign. He's a strong and brave corsair who has fought and defeated the Spanish at Cape Spartel, and here at Tanguel. He captured the *San Fermín* and is supervising the salvage. He's a true brother in Islam. Whatever he's done to arouse your ire must be a mistake."

"He was caught with these infidels. They blew up the frigate."

Rajet Rais turned a scornful eye upon the huddle of French acrobats. "He may have been in their vicinity, but he was not 'with' this rabble," he replied. "We all went and watched their show. It means nothing."

"What is his servant's name?"

"Gregorio," Rajet replied promptly.

"Is he a good servant?"

"I've never met the man, but he helped to rescue Rabiyah bint Halim when she was carried off."

"That's the woman that married . . . I can't remember his name, but someone told me about it," the bey remarked.

"Umar bin Bazam," Isam spoke up helpfully. "Umar, our cousin Samir, me, and our servants hunted down Maureo, who had made off with her against her will." Rabiyah had turned on Maureo to save her own hide; Isam felt no compunction about doing the same.

"Make him sit up and tell the story," the bey said.

Isam was put right side up by the soldiers, but he still had his hands bound behind his back. He groaned and gritted his teeth. His legs stretched out before him—his feet hurt too much to try and fold them into a cross-legged position. No other relief was given to him while he told the story. Rajet followed it up by telling about his heroics at Cape Spartel and Tanguel.

The whole court was delighted and entertained with the tales. The bey mulled them over. "You have a very staunch defender in your captain, and I concede, it seems unlikely that you would blow up your captain's prize since doing so would cost you your prize money. The Spanish would have had to pay you a great deal to make it worth your while. Captain of the Guards! How much money did he have on him?"

"Not a penny, your excellency. In addition, while you have been interviewing him, my men have arrested his sailors and searched his camp. There was no money or anything valuable there, either."

Isam had been angry when he discovered Gregorio had stolen his purse full of Spanish silver, but now he was grateful. "I'm waiting for my prize money, sir."

"Bring the sailors."

The four men were thrust onto their knees and bowed their faces down to the pavement and stayed there.

"Rise. Who is this man?" the bey demanded, pointing a finger at Isam.

"Isam Rais," they replied.

The bey questioned them, but they told the same story that Rajet and Isam had already told. They also confirmed the story of the runaway slave and added the opinion that they thought he'd been talking to the stilt walkers at the show.

The bey's eyes bored into Isam. "He was talking to the stilt walkers?"

Isam was sweating again. "As I said, your excellency, I thought he was asking them to help him run away. I beat him and lectured him about his good fortune to be my servant, and he cried and swore he would be a good and obedient slave."

"And you believed him?"

Isam looked chagrined. He mumbled, "He promised to behave himself."

"Isam Rais is only nineteen years old, your excellency," Rajet Rais put in. "He's at the age where lessons are learned the hard way. We were all like that."

The governor snorted, then said, "Bastinade the little girl. Beat her until somebody tells me about Gregorio."

When the child was seized and put upon her back with her skirts falling immodestly around her hips, her mother shrieked and lunged to try and protect her. When the translator had finished explaining to them, the leader of the stilt walkers broke down and told the story.

"We were arrested by the Spanish in Tanger and they made us take two Spaniards with us to spy on Tanguel. They kept our *grand-mère* and some girls as hostages. We had no choice! We didn't know what they were going to do! We thought they were just going to spy and return to Tanger! They told us to perform on the quay but they didn't tell us why! Please, your excellency. Have mercy. We are innocent pawns who have been tricked and forced. We are poor people trying to make a living as entertainers. We came to the Sallee Republic in hopes of amusing you and nothing more! We are the victims of the Spanish as much as you are!"

"You admit conniving with the Spanish. Very well. Enslave them all."

The stilt walkers wept. Isam's feet were a blaze of pain and theirs weren't, so he couldn't feel sorry for them, even though they were caught in the middle through no fault of their own.

"You can release Isam Rais," the governor said. "As for you, young man. Let this be a lesson to you. You must keep control of your slaves. Put heavy chains on them so they can't run and beat them regularly so they respect you."

The guards untied his wrists at last. He was so stiff he could hardly move his arms. "I won't forget it, excellency." He never would. Still, although he was wary of the governor, there was something that needed to be settled. Speaking as politely as he could, he asked, "May I have my sailors back?"

The bey gestured and they were also released. Isam refused the support of his sailors and limped out of the palace on his own aching feet. By the time he reached Halim's house, his boots were full of blood.

CHAPTER 37 : OUED MHARHAR

The bey's men didn't find the Spanish fugitives in spite of a reward of a hundred sequins being offered for them. Feeling his guilt intensely, Isam called for his cousins Umar and Samir. They gathered at the side of the divan where he lay with bandaged feet in his uncle's house. His scimitar lay propped on the usual pegs above his boyhood bed, and he himself was clad only in his drawers and shirt. The room was warm enough even though a light sprinkle of spring rain cooled the day to a misty grey.

Samir perched on the arm of the divan. "What makes you think you can find them when the bey failed? He has troops looking for them."

"I don't know if I can, but I want to try. I think they are disguised as women. Remember what Gregorio did when he helped Rabiyah escape? The soldiers won't be looking for women."

Umar nodded uncertainly. "I was going to ask you to sell him to me and make him Rabiyah's slave, but now I'm glad I didn't. I would hate to have my money run off like that."

Isam hadn't paid a single sequin for the slave, so it wasn't his money running off that concerned him.

Samir stroked his beard thoughtfully. "I think you might be right. There is only one road north, but we can't be sure they took it. They may have hidden a boat somewhere along the coast."

"The stilt walkers said nothing about a boat. It could be so, but it's still worth the effort to try the road," Isam replied.

"It could be a wild goose chase," Samir replied.

"We've lost our share of the frigate prize money. If we could capture them, the hundred sequins divided among us would go a long way towards replacing it."

That caught Umar's attention. "I want to catch the spies who destroyed our prize money. I'll kill them with my own sword!" He put his hand upon the hilt of his scimitar that peeked out from beneath his white haik.

Samir mused, "It wouldn't take more than a couple of days to ride the road and see what can be found. If we find them, the reward will be ample."

"I don't care about the reward! I want to recapture Gregorio," Isam replied.

Samir gave him a skeptical look. "How are your feet? Can you even ride?"

"I don't need feet to sit a saddle."

"That's true. All right then, I'll go along on this adventure with you."

Isam's bandaged feet wouldn't fit into his boots, so he wrapped them with canvas strips from knee to toe like a tribesman of the interior. It hurt to put his feet in the stirrups, so he rode without them by gripping the sorrel gelding with his knees. That stuck him to the saddle well enough, but having his feet dangling down meant that they swelled and ached even with no pressure on them. He had second thoughts then, but it was too late. All he could do was grit his teeth and lead on. The pain was a fitting penance for his guilt. By the time he reached Gregorio—if he found him at all—he would be in no mood for mercy. Would he kill him? After what the slave had done, he surely must.

The cousins, along with Samir's servant Athar and a string of remounts, rode north along a hard-packed dirt road with ditches on either side. Weeds choked the ditches, but beyond the ditches were fields of wheat, sugar cane, and cotton, or pastures with fluffy white lambs gamboling. As they departed the vicinity of Tanguel, fields became sporadic and pastures more common, broken up by woods and salt marshes. Then the wilderness took over, interrupted by occasional patches of cultivation surrounding villages.

They rode all through the day. They ignored the traffic traveling towards Tanguel and hurried to overtake small parties on the road, but didn't find their quarry. They made inquiries in the villages they passed through, but with no luck. After about twenty miles, there was no traffic at all. At twenty-five miles, they passed a caravan of ten camels heading north. At thirty miles they stopped and took their midday meal.

Isam ate, then gingerly unwrapped his feet. He washed the bloody soles with water from his water skin. Samir sat crossed legged on the weedy grass while Umar stretched out, threw his arm over his eyes, and took a brief nap. His fine white haik and pantaloons were covered in dun-colored dust. Samir's green coat was likewise besmirched. They had traveled a long way and had nothing to show for it but the dust on their clothes.

Samir asked, "How far north do you intend to go before you decide we haven't found them?"

"All the way to Tanger if I have to."

Samir grunted. "If they're walking, they can't have made more than forty miles, assuming they walked all night. If they're riding, they already reached Tanger."

Umar said nothing. Never the brightest lamp in the chandelier, he was content to let his smarter cousins do the thinking. A little silence fell. Isam's feet hurt very much and he wanted an excuse to go home, but going home would hurt just as much as going forward, so he said, "To the gates of Tanger, then. If we don't overtake them by nightfall, then there is nothing to do but camp and head home in the morning."

Samir grunted. "All right then. It was a fool's errand, but I had nothing better to do."

Isam wrapped his feet up, sighed, and said, "Let's mount up."

He walked gingerly to his animal, then putting his hands on the saddle, vaulted up without using the stirrups. Athar handed the reins up to him. The corsair gritted his teeth, then tapped the horse's flank with his quirt. Samir and Umar swung easily onto their mounts and followed him. Athar gathered up the string of remounts and followed in their wake.

In another ten miles they reached the Oued Mharhar. The river was broad and brown. It curved back and forth across low marshlands and was joined by a second, smaller river as snaky as the Mharhar. For almost a mile the road followed a low ridge between the tributary and a bend of the Mharhar. Tidal mudflats and marshes lay on either side, but along the ridge, trees covered most of the eastern side of the road and sometimes the western. The sea was a few hundred yards to the west, and the land between that and the slow curve of the river was a brilliant green salt marsh full of ducks. They rode from shadow into sunlight and back again several times before they reached the crossing.

The ferry boat was pulled up on the other side. Samir shouted and waved his hand, and a couple of figures dressed in white bestirred themselves. Slowly the sweeps worked and the flat-bottomed boat glided over the turgid waters to receive them. They paid, and binding cloths over the horses' eyes, walked them onto the vessel. Isam limped aboard and settled on one of the benches that lined the sides. He held the reins to two horses. The animals snorted and twitched their ears uneasily, but with the blindfolds in place, they couldn't see the flimsy railing nor the water beyond it. He petted their noses and crooned soothing words of Arabic to them. They continued swishing their tails uneasily but stood still.

A boy of about fourteen had the tiller. Navigating across the river was easy enough, so Isam didn't worry about distracting him and asked, "Has anyone passed over heading north recently, a party of three men, or two men and a woman?"

The boy's brown eyes flicked over to Isam as he shook his head. "A man and his family crossed about an hour ago, but that was all." The boy continued watching the far shore. The tail of his turban fluttered about his shoulder, and he wore an embroidered red vest over top of his white shirt and pantaloons. It was a very nice piece of work and much better than the worn and dusty garments of the two men who pulled the oars. The ferry moved slowly across the expanse of water. Isam thought the boy would be quite handsome when he grew up. All of nineteen himself, he felt quite lordly and mature compared to the young ferryman.

"Did your mother make your vest?" Isam was man enough to buy his own clothes with the money he earned.

"Yes, she did. She's good with a needle." The youth was unaware that he'd lost a comparison in his passenger's mind.

Picking on a fourteen year old was poor sport, so Isam lifted his legs up and stretched them along the bench. The throbbing in his feet eased and he sighed in relief. Something niggling at the back of his brain finally came to the surface. "A family? How many?"

"A young man, his mother, his wife, and his daughter," the boy replied.

"Was the wife wearing a blue veil?"

"Yes, both of the women were veiled. I thought he must be a rich man to have such refined women. My mother wears a hijab, but she doesn't have a chador."

"Did he speak with an accent? What language did he address you in?"

"Arabic. He spoke it very well. No accent."

Blue was a popular color. It didn't prove anything. And a child! What sort of fugitives would burden themselves with a child? It couldn't be them. Isam leaned against the railing and watched the wake streaming behind them. He was grateful to be off his feet and out of the saddle for as long as the ferry ride lasted. Samir was right; they had come on a fool's errand. Still, the effort was easing his conscience. If he reached the hills above Tanger without finding Gregorio, he could go home knowing that he'd tried his best to make amends, but Allah did not permit it.

"How far to Tanger?" he asked.

"Ten more miles." He pointed to the low mountain looming ahead of them. "That's Cape Spartel. Once you go around it, you'll see Tanger lying before you. Don't go there; it's Spanish. If you do go, take the right fork and pass the mountain to the east. The left fork dead ends at the Caves of Hercules where they cut millstones."

"I'm not going all the way to Tanger, but thank you for the warning. Say, did you see or hear anything about a battle between a Spanish frigate and a Sallee rover at Cape Spartel?"

"We did! It was great news! The corsair drove the Spaniard onto the rocks and it broke up! Many men died, but another Spanish ship saved a few survivors. They were very angry about it. We saw a Spanish fleet sail south, then come back north. The Tanguelis beat them!"

Isam grinned at the enthusiasm in the youth's voice. "I was the man that cut the Spanish anchor cable so they wrecked."

The young tillerman gave him a dubious look. "If you say so, effendi."

"You don't believe me?"

"It is very rocky at Cape Spartel and there was a storm. The Spaniards were driven on the rocks."

"So they were. But they had anchored outside the rocks. I swam underwater and cut the cable."

The youth remained skeptical. "In a storm? There are rough currents around the Cape, or so my uncle tells me."

"It was difficult," Isam conceded.

"Ha. I bet it was!"

Samir came back and asked with a smirk, "Are you reveling in your glory?"

Isam scowled at him. "I did a noteworthy thing. I have a right to be proud of it."

"He's only a ferryman and too busy working to sleep with you."

Isam colored and scowled, "I don't want to sleep with him!"

Samir laughed. "Are you ashamed of being a boy lover?"

"I'm not a boy lover!" He gritted his teeth and glared at him. "I prefer men."

The youth at the tiller thought Samir was merely teasing him and grinned at him. Isam glared back at him. Then the tillerman (tillerboy?) had to pay attention to his business because the ferry was approaching the northern shore. The boat slid into shallow water and the older men left the sweeps and ran out the gangplank. The cousins led the horses into fetlock deep water and up onto solid ground. A limping Isam followed and mounted up from the gangplank since he had no boots. As soon as they were off the boat, the three ferrymen gathered together to gossip about their most recent passengers.

As they made their way ashore, Isam hissed at Samir, "Why did you have to say that?"

"If you're ashamed, you ought not do it. If you do it, you ought not be ashamed," Samir replied as he mounted up.

"And what if I gossip about the women you ravish?"

"You know what happens to women when their reputations are ruined, so you ought not do it for their sake. As for you, you're a man and can defend yourself."

"Maybe I should punch you in the nose."

Samir laughed. "Maybe you should. But come on. Are you going to go around Cape Spartel? There are bound to be Spanish patrols. We are risking our lives for little reason at this point."

"A little further. Tanger is ten miles away. I'll decide what next when we get to the foot of the mountain."

The cousins rode on.

Chapter 38 : Spanish Death

They overtook the family as the sun sank in the west and lit up the flanks of Cape Spartel like a lamp. The green foliage of spring was luminous in the slanting light, and the sea itself turned to gold. The travelers cast long shadows to their right that fell on the last pasture before the mountain became too rough for human use. Isam was debating how much further on they should travel when suddenly his eyes came to rest on the blue veil.

He knew that veil. He knew it very well. The faded grey-blue color, the raveled bit of hem, the faded streak on the left shoulder . . . "It's them!" he called to his cousins. He kicked his horse's flanks with his bandaged heels and the horse sprang forward.

Up ahead, the little party turned around at the sound of hoofbeats. Seeing the cousins charging them, they threw off their disguises. The two Spanish spies had been heavily veiled while Gregorio, who spoke perfect Arabic, had posed as the male head of household. Gregorio spoke to the little girl and she scrambled through the coarse weeds lining the road and ran across the pasture for an outcropping of rocks. As the two Spaniards drew their weapons, he retreated into the weeds to get out of their way. Not a warrior, he had no weapon.

Isam drew his scimitar but being a left-handed swordsman proved a disadvantage when his foes were gathered to the right. He flashed past them without engaging and wheeled around to approach them with his left side leading. Umar, being right-handed, suffered no such handicap and charged straight at them. The older Spaniard parried his slash with his sword. The younger Spaniard, a youth of no more than seventeen, was armed only with a dirk. Isam recognized the youth who had passed the hat in Tanguel. It galled him that he had given money to a Spanish spy and ogled him. The young Spaniard darted at Umar, but Umar kicked his horse away. The shortest cousin looked around for Samir, but he wasn't there.

The Spanish swordsman drove at him while shouting something in Spanish to his companion. The youth once again darted to Umar's side and tried to attack. Umar liked glory, but not when he was outnumbered two to one. "Help!" he called in Arabic. His horse danced away from the attack.

Isam struck at the Spanish swordsman. The man whirled to meet him and sword clashed on sword. The two exchanged a series of thrusts and ripostes, but the advantage of height enabled Isam to force the swordsman along the verge of the roadway. That man had played the part of the young couple's mother in tan pantaloons and tunic thereby escaping detection by the soldiers. He had kept his sword hidden under the voluminous veil and was now using it to good effect.

Meanwhile, Umar attacked the dirk-wielding youth. The boy was dressed in Gregorio's old blue disguise. His beard had not yet come in and he was slim and had not yet obtained his full growth; he was at a gross disadvantage. Umar was only a few years older, but the advantage of sword reach and horse kept the youth dodging and twisting like an acrobat. He was already panting for breath and knew he wouldn't be able to keep it up for long; he took a desperate chance and lunged in under Umar's guard.

The scimitar slashed down and caught the Spanish youth at the junction of his neck and shoulder. His dirk hand lost all its strength and the blade fell from it without scratching Umar. He stumbled, his gaze went dark, and he fell. Blood dyed his tunic crimson. He lay glassy-eyed amid the weeds at the edge of the road. His chest fell in shallow susurrations and his left hand feebly lifted, but he was mortally wounded and would not rise again.

At that moment, the Spanish swordsman made his own lunge. Distracted by Umar's triumph, Isam parried an instant too late and felt the cold steel penetrate the flesh under his arm, ride along his ribs, and tear out his jacket. Blood spilled and he clapped his sword arm against the wound to stop the bleeding. He couldn't fight like that and his eyes went wide with alarm. Seeing his advantage, the Spaniard poised to take advantage, but Samir's voice interrupted.

"Throw down your sword, or the girl dies."

Samir held the small child in the saddle in front of him. One green-clad arm wrapped around her middle while his other hand held the scimitar to her throat. The grim expression rendered his face ugly and no one had any doubt that he would do it. The Spanish sword clattered to the ground.

Isam switched his scimitar to his right hand and rested it on the pommel in front of him. He clamped his arm against his wound, but he could feel the blood trickling down inside his shirt to soak his sash and then the top of his pantaloons. The excitement of battle had momentarily blotted awareness of his body from his mind, but as the action came to an end, ordinary awareness returned to him. He felt the pain in his feet and an ache in his head. He gritted his teeth and leaned on the pommel.

The Spanish swordsman and Gregorio raised their hands and stood together on the side of the road. The dying youth panted for breath and groaned. Samir guided his horse through the weeds and joined them in looking down at the stricken youth.

It was Samir who asked, "Are you going to let him bleed out or administer the mercy blow?"

"I'll kill him," Umar replied.

He dismounted and stood over the mortally wounded youth with his bloody scimitar in his hand. Fear turned the youth white, but the ugly wound was deep enough to show the broken collarbone. Blood pulsed out in time to his heartbeat and stained the ground in a growing puddle.

Umar knelt and wiped his bloody blade on the leg of the youth's pantaloons. He sheathed it, then drew his dagger. It was one thing to kill a man in battle, but another to dispatch a helpless victim. He wasn't sure he had the stomach for it, yet clearly, it was more humane to finish the dying boy than to let him suffer.

"I've never delivered a mercy killing before. How do I do it?" He looked to Samir for guidance.

The Spanish swordsman spoke Arabic very well, although with an accent, growled, "For God's sake, don't botch it!"

When Umar gave him an uncertain look, the Spaniard lowered his hands, stepped forward, knelt by the youth, and said, "I'll do it."

Umar let him take the dagger from his hands.

The Spaniard rested his left hand on the younger man's chest and said gently, "Rubio, you are dying. I am sorry, my friend. I led you into this and I have not brought you safely out. All I can do is ease your suffering. Know that you are going to a better place. You will join the angels in Heaven and they will sing your praises. You are a gallant youth. You will suffer no more but will enjoy everlasting peace. All those you love will meet you there." Tears welled up in his eyes as he said it. He rubbed them away with his dusty sleeve.

Rubio nodded slightly. He could scarcely move his head because of his injury, and when he did move, a fresh gout of blood erupted from the wound. He was very pale and his eyes were glazed. The tension went out of his body as he resigned himself to his fate.

The older man put the point against his stomach just under the ribs and angled it upward. The youth's eyes sprang open in alarm, then his pale lips began to murmur the Ave Maria. The soft Latin was barely audible. More tears streamed down the older man's face as he waited. When the prayer came to an end, he thrust the blade deep into the yielding body.

The youth's back arched and his eyes flew open as the blade penetrated his heart. His feet kicked and his hands fluttered. For a few long seconds he struggled. Then the blade withdrew and a rush of blood flooded from the wound. He fell limp and lay still and staring. His chest no longer moved. His companion reached out, closed his eyes, and kissed his lips in farewell.

The rovers didn't interfere. The only sound was the crying of the little girl. She was frightened by the blade at her throat and terrified by seeing a grown up she trusted kill another she liked. She didn't understand any of it. Her sobs were the only human sound. The sea soughed in answer as if it too felt her grief. Samir didn't comfort her; he kept the sword at her throat. He was watching the man with Umar's dagger in his hand. He didn't trust him not to try and kill Umar.

Isam sheathed his scimitar awkwardly. His blood was continuing to flow and he felt lightheaded. He was afraid he was going to faint. He pressed both hands as hard as he could against his wound, but the bleeding didn't stop.

Umar felt bad that he had not known how to give the death blow, so he was grateful to the Spaniard for doing it humanely. Staring at the beardless face, he thought it sad such a young man had to die, but he'd gone to war at the same age, so he resigned himself to the death. That reminded him that the Spaniard still had his dagger, and he turned to him.

The Spaniard didn't give it to him. Instead, deciding to cheat the Salletines of the opportunity to torture him, he thrust the blade up under his own breastbone and into his heart. He remained kneeling while the severed organ struggled to beat, then toppled over. His breath stopped and his eyes closed. He was dead by his own hand.

"No!" Umar cried out, but it was too late.

Isam swore in Turkish. "I wanted him alive!"

"I'm sorry, Isam. He did it before I could even move!"

Samir tapped his horse with his heels and shifted his scimitar to point at Gregorio. The frightened slave put his hands up again and said, "Kill me quickly. If you won't let me go, then for the love of Allah, be merciful and put an end to me!"

Samir swung the girl down to the ground by her arm. She collapsed in the weeds and continued crying. That adults might choose to fight and die or even take their own lives seemed fair to Isam; they reaped what they sowed. That such little girl should be played as a pawn in a bloody game bothered him immensely. He didn't like his cousin very much in that moment. He spoke up.

"Don't, Samir. He's my slave. I'll decide what to do with him. Tie him up and help me before I faint. My head is spinning."

Umar jumped up and looked at his cousin in alarm, said, "You'd better get down before you fall down."

"Help me." Isam loosed the grip his legs had on the horse and half slid, half fell off. Umar caught him, but blood spurted in response to the movement. He said, "Shit," and passed out.

CHAPTER 39 : BACKWARD FACING VANTAGE

Isam woke on the ground amid the weeds. He was lying on his back and staring hazily up at the bright blue sky. For a moment he didn't remember where he was or what had happened, but as he stirred, Umar said, "You're awake! Good. I'm glad."

"Water," Isam croaked.

Umar brought a skin to him, helped him sit up, and braced his back to support him. Isam uncorked the water skin and drank deeply. Sitting up made him dizzy, so he fumbled the cork back into the skin and lay down again.

A few feet away Gregorio sat with his hands tied behind his back and his feet hobbled by a short piece of rope. He sat with his ankles crossed and his legs bent in the butterfly shape. His head hung upon his shoulders and the expression on his face was despair. Isam stared at him. Gregorio's green eyes met his briefly, then flicked away. Neither spoke.

Umar was oblivious. He said, "Samir and Athar have loaded up the bodies and are taking them to Tanguel to claim the reward. We will share it equally."

That was a goodly sum of money for their troubles. It cheered Isam and he didn't mind the slash to his ribs so much anymore, but he resented his battered feet even more. Now that he had succeeded in capturing the spies, he felt virtuous.

"I told the bey I wasn't complicit with them! Now he'll know he wronged me."

Still his conscience panged him. None of this would have been necessary if he hadn't been besotted with a Spanish slave. At the malevolent look he gave Gregorio, the slave scooted around so that his back was to them. If Isam was going to kill him, he didn't want to see it coming.

"Can you ride? If we go now, we can make the ferry by dark, I think. I don't want to spend the night so close to Cape Spartel. What if we meet a Spanish patrol?"

Isam groaned. He had no desire to get up, but he knew he must. "Yes. I won't like it, but I'll do it. If we can get to the other side of the Oued Mharhar, we should be safe. We can ask the ferrymen if the Spanish patrols ever come so far. I wish I'd asked them on the way north."

Umar started up, then asked, "What are we going to do about the slave?"

"Put him on a horse facing backwards and tie his feet under its belly."

"Right."

Having made up his mind that he must move, Isam sat up carefully. He surveyed his surroundings, and noticed something missing. "Where is the little girl?"

Gregorio replied, "Samir has taken her."

"What is he going to do with her?"

"I think he's going to give her to the bey."

That bothered Isam. Surely such a small child should be immune to prosecution, but small as she was and through no choice of her own, she had traveled with spies. That made her guilty in the eyes of the law. He thought hard thoughts about grown men using a child to help their disguise, but the deed was done.

Samir had taken five horses and left them with three. Umar tightened the cinches and checked the bridles, then brought them over. He looked around worriedly, but they were alone as the sun slowly sank towards the horizon. It was growing chilly and he pulled the hood of his haik up over his head. Gregorio wished he could do the same, but he was too dispirited to ask his captors for anything. Umar boosted him into the saddle and he slumped as his feet were tied. He made no protest and did nothing to help or hinder his captors.

Next Umar helped Isam to his feet. The taller corsair felt a trickle of blood under his bandage and had to pause to catch his breath. "I'm dizzy," he told Umar.

"You lost a lot of blood. Your clothes are soaked with it. I was afraid you were going to die."

"I'm not dead yet," Isam replied, trying to cheer them both up. He contemplated the horse. In his current condition, it seemed impossibly high. "Help me."

Umar put an arm around his waist to steady him and the wounded man shuffled over to the animal. He winced at the pain in his feet; they were badly swollen after a day of activity when he should have been resting. He lifted up his foot but couldn't get it in the stirrup. Umar bent over, made a stirrup of his hands, and when Isam stepped into it, tossed him into the saddle. Isam landed with a thud and a groan. He gripped the pommel while the world rotated around him. Slowly the horizon settled back into its usual position. Once he was sure he wouldn't fall out of the saddle, he straightened up cautiously. Umar handed him the reins with a worried look.

"We must get across the river. I can do that. It's not far." Isam said.

At the very least, if he was going to faint, he wanted to do it further away from Cape Spartel. That caused him to reflect on how he had come to be in such a condition. He deeply regretted not giving Gregorio his freedom when he asked for it. Now that his own survival was at stake, he could see very clearly the errors that had led him to his predicament. He had thought that if only he were stubborn enough, he could force the world to conform to his wishes. It hadn't. On the contrary, acting as if his wishes had the power to change the world had given him the very opposite of what he wanted.

"If I had freed you when you asked, would you have helped the spies blow up the frigate?"

Gregorio lifted his head slightly. "If you had freed me, I would have walked to Tanger and never met them."

"I wish I'd freed you."

Gregorio straightened up. A desperate light lit his eyes. "You can still free me."

"Not anymore. You helped the enemies of my country harm us. Now I must turn you over to the authorities. Samir and Athar will tell the bey that we caught you. If I release you, he'll have my head instead. It's too late now to do what I should have done then."

Gregorio slumped again. "Yes, master," he replied wearily.

Isam was finally starting to recognize that fatalistic subservience. "Do you think I was cruel to you?"

"No, master."

"You do though."

"I have not said so, master."

"You're saying what you think I want to hear!"

"What else should a slave say? Should I contradict you and quarrel with you? You would beat me and be right to do it."

"If I had the strength to do it, I'd beat you now. You're a vexing creature!"

Gregorio said nothing more. There was nothing to gain by provoking the one who held his fate in his dismal hands. He gazed longingly at the bulk of the mountain rendered bronze by the glare of the descending sun. On the other side of the mountain was Spanish-held Tanger. He had very nearly made it. The closeness made him bitter. Still, he didn't regret the attempt; he was resigned to losing his life. He expected it would be a particularly horrible death, given that he was the only adult to be brought back alive. He thought the little girl would probably suffer the same fate, although if she were lucky, she would merely be sold into slavery. As for the Spanish spies, he didn't regret their fates; they had dragged him into their plot and paid the price.

Umar swung up into his own saddle. Keeping an eye on Gregorio and Isam (although for different reasons), he urged, "Let's go."

Isam nodded and gave his horse a weak kick. The animal ignored him in favor of nosing among the weeds for something tasty to eat. Isam kicked him harder. Reluctantly the gelding began to move. Umar caught up the reins of Gregorio's animal and led him along. Facing backwards, the captive had to suffer the ignominy of watching Cape Spartel receding into the distance.

Twilight was gathering as they finally arrived at the ferry. Tendrils of mist were rising from the warmer water into the cool air. Fortunately the boat was on their side of the river. The ferrymen were huddled in their haiks with the hoods up, but they rose when they saw the trio approach.

"The man in green said you'd be coming. He paid your fare and told us to wait for you," one of them called out to them. The gangway was already in place.

Umar dismounted, then untied Gregorio's feet and marched him onto the ferry. "Keep an eye on this one while I fetch the horses and my cousin. He's wounded."

Isam was pretty sure he'd fall if he tried to dismount by himself, so he waited for his cousin's return. Umar reached up for him, and he half-slid, half-toppled into his cousin's arms. Suddenly Umar froze.

"What is it?" Isam asked.

"Hoofbeats." Umar turned to look behind them, then suddenly grabbed Isam's arm, pulled it over his shoulder, and urged, "Hurry! The Spanish are coming!"

Isam looked over his shoulder and saw a party of five horsemen rushing along the road. At this distance he couldn't make out the color of their clothes, but they wore tricorne hats and that told him all he needed to know. Lethargy was suddenly replaced by a frantic energy. "Help me get on board!"

Gregorio had been standing blankly aboard the ferry, but when the ferrymen startled into alertness, he looked back at the shore. Umar and Isam were splashing through the shallows in a rush for the boat. Although he couldn't see or hear the riders beyond the brow of the bank, he could guess what had caused the cousins to panic. His feet were unbound, and he used them.

"Gang way!" he shouted and charged down the gangplank.

Umar and Isam had just arrived at the bottom of the plank, but not wanting to be run over, Umar swerved aside.

"No!" Isam cried. "Stop him! Don't let him get away!" Unfortunately, he wasn't strong enough to do anything about it. He flung out his arm, but Gregorio barreled through it without slowing down. Isam yelped as the impact knocked him aside and set his wound on fire.

Umar dragged him up the gangplank as fast as he could. "Cast off! The Spanish are coming!" he shouted.

As soon as the two rovers were aboard, the ferrymen tossed the gangway into the shallows and started rowing. They could hear the approaching hoofbeats now, even though the Spaniards were still out of sight beyond the crest of the bank. A ferry was never a fast boat, but Isam had a profound desire to fly. Pulling himself together, he went to the tiller and said, "Help row. I'll steer. I'm a sailor, I can do this." And calling to his cousin, "Umar! Help row! Two men on each oar!"

Umar would rather do something—anything—that sit and stare in sick fascination as the Spanish appeared at the top of the hill, so he hastily joined the rower on the larboard side. The young tillerman hesitated, but the sight of the grey Spanish coats and their white horses put a sudden energy into his movements. He leaped to join the older man at the other oar.

Isam sat down on the deck and wrapped an arm around the tiller. Partly he wasn't sure he could stand all the way across the river, but mostly he wanted to make as small a target as possible. He began singing a rowing chantey in a creaky baritone. He had to gasp for breath, but he kept the tune. The oars stroked in time to it and the vessel picked up speed. They were moving twice as fast as they usually did, which wasn't fast at all. If a child could have walked on water, she could have outrun it.

Gregorio arrived at the top of the long sloping bank about the same time the Spaniards did. He was too far away for them to hear anything he said, but they could guess well enough as the cavalrymen gathered around him. The Spaniards listened as he quickly told his story, then not bothering to untie him, puts spurs to horse and swept down the long slope in pursuit of the fugitive ferry.

"They're coming! Row faster!" Isam cried.

The oarsmen groaned and tried harder, but there was little gain for their effort. The sight of the Spanish cavalry inspired them to make their best efforts, but the ferry was designed to be a stable vessel, not a fast one. They reached the middle of the river at the same time as the Spanish splashed into the shallows. The squadron's officer rose in his stirrups and shouted in bad Arabic at them, "Stop, or we'll shoot!"

Isam ducked his head and tried to fold his lanky frame into the smallest possible area while still keeping his eye on the far shore.

The Spanish pulled their muskets from their saddle boots, uncapped their powder horns, and measured the grains of black powder with their thimbles. The oarsmen could see very plainly what they were about and strove to widen the distance. They were red in the face and gasping from the exertion.

Once more the Spanish officer shouted at them. "Surrender, or die!"

"Allah defend us!" one man gasped out. That was all the prayer they had breath for.

The crackle of muskets sent balls buzzing at them. One plunked into the stern of the vessel two feet from where Isam was sitting. Another whizzed past his head. A third splashed into the water. Where the other shot went he didn't know.

"Reload!" The officer's command carried across the water. They didn't need to know Spanish to guess what he was telling his troops.

"We're getting close! More than half way there!" Isam encouraged them. They brightened and rowed with renewed determination.

A second volley erupted. Isam cringed, but with the greater distance, the balls missed their marks. He saw a splash a few yards beside them but not the rest. He scanned the rowers, but they were all flexing their backs and throwing their weight onto the oars. No one was hurt.

"We're almost out of range! It will take a lucky shot to hit us now!"

Once again the Spaniards reloaded. As they did so, the ferry slid to a stop on the muddy bank. The oarsmen leaped up and jumped off the front of the vessel to splash through the shallow water, Umar included.

Isam slumped at the tiller and called, "Hey! What about me?" but his voice was too weak to carry.

CHAPTER 40 : LULLABY OF THE WORLD

The ferrymen had done their job by delivering the cousins to the southern shore and felt no further obligation. They ran for the woods. Knowing the local territory as they did, they were determined to disappear in case the Spanish decided to swim their horses across the river. The Mharhar was five hundred feet wide but slow and shallow. If the Spanish were determined, they could do it.

Left alone at the top of the riverbank, Umar realized Isam was missing. Horrified, he saw his cousin lying in the bottom of the ferry. In an agony of indecision, he wondered if Isam had been shot. If so, there was no point going back for a dead man. But he might have passed out and still be alive. The rim of the sun slipped behind the horizon. The grey Spanish uniforms were impossible to pick out in the grey twilight, but the muzzle flashes of their muskets told him where they were. He decided it was better to be a moving target than a stationary one and ran back down the bank to the ferry boat. He clambered aboard crying, "Isam! Isam! Are you alive?"

Isam rolled onto his right side and said, "Yes. Get me out of here. I can't stand."

Umar knelt, pulled Isam's arm over his shoulder, and grabbing him by the waistband, heaved his cousin to his feet. He dragged him off the boat and up the riverbank. The Spanish could see them moving and kept firing. A ball plunked into the dirt ten yards from Umar, but that was the closest shot. Nonetheless, every crack of the muskets made him jump and inspired Isam to do his best to keep up.

As they staggered over the top, Isam said, "Umar, I can't breathe. I need to rest."

"Keep going! As long as they can see us, they will shoot and they might get lucky!" Umar kept moving.

Isam tried to keep up, but his long legs were getting tangled under him. His vision was growing black. "Ummmaaar, Iii—"

Isam fainted. His full weight came on Umar's shoulders. The shorter cousin went to his knees and let Isam lie on his stomach on the dirt road. He checked his pulse and found it weak and rapid. He rolled the bigger man over and watched the rising and falling of his chest. Glancing back, the crest of the bank was between him and the Spaniards; they were out of the line of fire.

Umar shook his cousin. "We must get up, Isam. What if they swim their horses over? Please wake up, Isam!"

There was no response from the unconscious corsair. Umar began to panic. "Don't die, Isam! You're the clever one! What will I do without you? I can't go home alone!" He slapped his cousin's face.

Isam's eyelids flickered open. He stared up at the lavender sky with glassy eyes. He didn't answer his cousin.

"Isam, please. We must hide. What if the Spanish come?"

Isam's eyes shut again.

"Don't die! Allah, help him! Don't let him die!"

Getting up, he grabbed his cousin's jacket by the shoulders and dragged him into the weeds along the east side of the road.

Isam groaned, "Put me down."

Umar dragged him deeper into the scrub. It was the best he could do to hide them from the road in case the Spanish came. There he uncapped his water skin and lifted the wounded man's head.

Isam drank thirstily. "Where are we?"

"A few yards from the river bank. I don't know what the Spanish are doing."

"Are we alone?"

"Yes, the ferrymen ran away."

"I don't blame them. We're nothing but trouble."

"Don't say that. We've got to do something."

"I'm bleeding again."

Without their horses they had no supplies. They had some water in their skins, but nothing else. No blankets, no food, and no mounts.

Isam said, "Help me sit up."

Umar did that. Isam buried his face in his knees and tried not to pass out again. He inhaled deeply. When he was able to lift his face, he looked around. "Let's try to get to those woods."

Umar supported him and they trudged through the weeds. It wasn't far, but they had to stop every couple of minutes for Isam to catch his breath. Umar kept looking around, but there was no sign of the Spaniards. He started to hope they would not pursue. That didn't lessen the need for shelter though. Eventually they made it into the woods. They blundered through underbrush and tripped over roots. They stepped on sticks and rustled through leaves.

Isam fell. "No farther. I can't do it."

Umar sat next to his cousin in the dark. One spot was as good as another he supposed. Slowly his eyes adjusted, and he could make out the vague shape of shrubbery and the blackness of tree boles. Feeling around, he discovered tall ferns, so he pulled them up and buried Isam in them to keep him as warm as could be managed. After heaping greenery onto his cousin, he wiggled under them and pressed himself against him. The ferns were not the most convenient cover, but they helped. He spooned against Isam and said, "We must stick together so we don't freeze."

"Yes," Isam replied in a slurred voice.

"Don't die in the night. I don't want to wake up next to a dead man!"

Isam almost smiled. "I don't want to wake up dead. You must keep me awake to make sure of it."

"I will."

A little silence fell. After a bit, Isam said. "Umar."

"Yes?"

"I like you better than Samir."

"Nobody ever said that before. It's always, 'Why can't you be clever like Samir? What were you thinking, you idiot? Why did you do that? Where is your common sense? Umar, just stop!'"

Isam smiled faintly at that. "Yes, it's true. You are stupid, but I have discovered that as useful as brains are, what a man does with them matters more. Samir has left us to fend for ourselves while he goes off to claim the reward."

"He'll share it with us."

"Yes, he will. He's not a complete rogue," Isam conceded. "If he doesn't share, then you must promise to help me beat him when I'm able."

"Sure. If he doesn't share, he'll deserve it."

A silence fell. Umar couldn't hear Isam breathing, so he slipped his arm around him and tried to feel his heart beating.

"Ow. Please don't do that, it makes my side hurt."

"Sorry. Are you still bleeding?"

"I think so. It feels warm, so I must be."

Umar sat up carefully so as to not disturb the fern cover. Working by feel in the dark, he slit the edge of his tunic, put the dagger away, and ripped a strip from the bottom of it. He folded it up and stuffed it under the existing bandage.

"Tighten the bandage," Isam whispered.

Umar carefully felt along the strip of cotton until he found the knot. He undid it, tightened it, and asked, "How's that?"

"Tighter."

Umar tightened again. "Now?"

"Good."

Umar tied it and settled down next to him. Another silence fell. Umar was too worried to sleep. "Are you awake?"

"Huh?"

"Isam, don't sleep. I know you're tired, but I'm afraid you won't wake up."

"Talk to me."

Umar racked his brain for a topic of conversation. "Is it true you like to sleep with boys?"

The question irked Isam awake. "No, I don't. I like men."

"Huh?"

"I'm not like other men. I can't help it. It's just the way I am."

"Do you mean grown men? With beards?" Umar didn't understand, so he was asking questions.

Isam had a sudden memory of Rajet Rais' furry chest. He missed him very much at that moment. He wished he'd stayed with him instead of mooning over the smooth-skinned eunuch. "Yes."

Umar puzzled over it. "I can understand going with a boy if there's no other choice, but Samir says you don't like girls at all. He says you slept with Gregorio. Is that true?"

"Samir talks too much. Yes, it's true."

"I suppose a eunuch's all right. They aren't hairy like men."

"Do I ask you if Rabiyah's hairy?" Isam asked petulantly.

"She's a woman. She's not hairy," Umar replied, missing the point.

"The point is, I don't ask nosy questions about your wife. I don't decide if she's attractive enough for you to fuck. Who you fuck is your business. Who I fuck is mine."

"Don't talk about my wife that way."

"Then don't talk about my lovers that way."

"You were in love with Gregorio?" Now Umar was truly shocked.

"Umar, just stop."

It wasn't the first time in his life Umar had been told to shut up. He resented it, but he always lost the argument when he complained about it, so he didn't answer. He did twist under the ferns so that his back was to his cousin. He fired off one final shot. "Don't die. If you die, I'll hit you."

Isam groaned. "Fine. Hit me when I'm dead. I'll come back and haunt you for being stupid and cruel."

"I didn't mean it."

Isam said wearily, "Umar, go to sleep."

The frogs in the river sang their evening songs. Owls flitted among the boles and small creatures scurried through the underbrush. Slowly the lullaby of the world soothed the cousins to sleep.

CHAPTER 41 : BLINDFOLDED HORSES

Isam, being unconscious, had forgotten the blindfolded horses left on the ferry. Umar, being worried about Isam, had simply forgotten them. Having been blindfolded to prevent them panicking at the sight of moving water all around them, the horses were in no position to take care of themselves. They trembled as the boat shifted slightly in response to their movement. They were accustomed to ground that might contain a hole or vine to trip them up, but it held still. This footing seemed solid, but it rocked as they paced the narrow confines of the boat, and that unnatural situation made them swish their tails and twitch their ears.

The crack of muskets disturbed them even more. One of them whinnied in alarm, but no human came in response. After a bit the shots died away and they settled unhappily. Again they whickered, but no human voice soothed them or removed the blindfolds. They were hungry and thirsty too. They could smell water all around them and found it by reaching their noses cautiously over the side. They accidentally dunked their muzzles, then drank eagerly. Thirst satisfied, they were now hungry and wanted to eat their fill of oats. They were tired and footsore and wanted to lie down in green grass. They wanted to roll in mud to soothe the itching under their saddles, and they wanted reassuring hands to take the saddles and bridles away and brush them until they were free of burrs. Again they tossed their heads and called.

Still no human came. They knocked their hooves against the planks and whinnied more plaintively. They swished their tails and shook their heads, but the blindfolds remained securely fastened under their bridle straps. Darkness grew and what little light had seeped under the cloths disappeared entirely. The chill of night settled on them and the dried sweat crusted and clung. They bumped into one another as they explored the confines of the wobbly stall in which they had been left and nipped one another in annoyance.

A faint splash perked their ears. They turned to face it, but they couldn't see anything beyond the blindfolds. Darkness pricked their senses and made them keener to compensate for the loss of sight. The sloshing sound continued and it grew closer. The low voices of humans clucked and urged their companions on.

Equine nostrils quivered: they could smell horses and men, but they were strangers. They wanted their own humans, but their growling bellies were pleased to meet any humans. They whickered and again knocked their hooves impatiently against the deck.

The Spaniards swam their horses across the river under cover of darkness. They came ashore beside the ferry boat and used it as cover, but no alarm was sounded and no musket fired. The Salletines had abandoned their horses. They wouldn't get far on foot. Unfortunately, the Spaniards wouldn't be able to track them very well in the dark, either, and might stumble into an ambush. Yet one of the corsairs had fallen and been retrieved; they couldn't have gone far with a wounded man. They were sure that when the corsairs had rested and treated their companion's injuries, they would come for their horses. And so, to keep the animals settled, they gave some of their own oats and tore up grass and brought it for them, but they left them blindfolded in the boat. The corsairs must find the scene the way they had left it.

The horses munched eagerly. They were annoyed by the blindfolds, but their bellies no longer tormented them. After that they dozed in the upright position. Meanwhile, the Spaniards retreated behind a curve in the river, piled up driftwood for protection, and posted a watch. They loaded all their muskets and kept them covered to keep the dew off them. Whenever the corsairs returned for their horses, they would be ready. They were particularly keen to kill or capture the tall one. Gregorio had told them the part he'd played in the various disasters that had befallen their squadron.

"The grey wolf Rajet is training his cub to hunt, and we don't want that," the officer remarked to his men. "Don't sleep. The one who can still walk might have gone for help."

Minutes, then hours slipped past. In spite of the order, they did sleep. The officer gave up trying to keep them awake and set watches. Gregorio was extremely tired after his day's travel and racked with nerves. He wished the Spaniards would go back to Tanger, but the wishes of one escaped slave didn't weigh very heavily with them. They wanted revenge, bloody red revenge steaming in the chill night air. He had no blanket, but a couple of the soldiers felt sorry for him and let him sleep between them. As long as he didn't move, he was warm enough, but if he rolled over, he bumped into one or the other and displaced the blankets. Finally he did sleep.

The next morning the ferrymen came to the boat as usual. They were surprised to find the blindfolded horses standing in the boat, and unhappy when they discovered that the horses had done what horses do, and now the boat needed mucking out. They couldn't get the horses off the ferry without a gangplank, so they had to row to the north shore and find their gangplank. It had been carried upstream by the rising tide and left on a mudbank. They were filthy to the knees by the time they got it back. The ferrymen rowed back, took the horses off, removed their blindfolds, and debated what to do with them. They finally decided to take them to their village and hold them. If the corsairs didn't claim them, they would sell them. They were unaware of the Spaniards watching from their hiding place.

Elsewhere, Umar woke. He was groggy and cold, but when he remembered the previous day's events, he shook Isam frantically. "Wake up! Wake up, oh please Allah, don't let him be dead!"

Isam's eyes flickered open and he groaned.

"Praise Allah, you're alive!" Umar hugged his prostrate cousin.

"Ow. Stop squashing me! I can't breathe!"

Umar knelt beside him and was so relieved he felt giddy. "We need food and water." He found his water skin amid the ferns, took a mouthful, then carefully lifted Isam's head and gave him a drink.

Isam drank thirstily. He wanted more, but Umar said, "We must make the water last until we reach the village. All the water here is brackish."

Isam tried to roll over, but he was so stiff and tired he could barely manage it. Umar's stomach growled. "Are you hungry? I'll try to catch a duck."

"No. Let's go to the village. Where are the horses? Help me ride. We can rest and drink and eat at the village."

"Horses? Uh, I think we left them on the boat."

Isam groaned. "Didn't you bring them?"

"The Spanish were shooting at us. I barely managed to fetch you. I left the horses." He sounded apologetic.

With a sigh, Isam realized he was going to have to get up and be useful, like it or not. "Help me up."

Umar caught his hand and pulled him to a sitting position. That was all Isam could manage. He put his head on his knees and wrapped his arms around his legs. He breathed deeply while he tried not to faint.

"I'll go see if they're still there." Umar got to his feet.

"No, wait. Be careful. Look around. Go through the woods to the river and stay hidden while you reconnoiter. A Spanish patrol might come."

"All right then."

Umar walked quietly through the woods. As soon as he was out of earshot, Isam regretted his leaving. He was badly wounded and couldn't fend for himself. He didn't think he could even get to his feet without help. He rolled onto his hands and knees, and dragging the water skin, crawled toward the misty light at the edge of the woods. He managed to crawl about thirty feet before he had to flop down and rest.

Minutes ticked by, then Umar returned. Sticks cracked and leaves rustled. He was trying to be quiet, but he was no woodsman. He found the bed of ferns, but no cousin. He called softly, "Isam! Where are you?"

"Over here."

Umar followed the faint voice and found Isam at the edge of the woods. "Don't go out there! The Spanish are hiding in the riverbank! I came out right above them, but I don't think they saw me."

"Do they have our horses?"

"No, the ferrymen have them."

"What are they doing with them?"

"Walking them south along the road."

"We need the horses! But I don't want the Spanish to hear us." This conundrum was too much for Isam's weary brain to solve. Loss of blood made it hard for him to think.

Umar suggested, "Maybe I should go and ask them to give our horses back?"

"Yes. Don't let the Spaniards see you."

Umar chewed over that problem for a while. "There's a hollow a little way south of here. I'll go through the woods and meet them there."

"All right." Isam was worried that this was not a sound plan, but he had nothing to offer in its place. "Go with Allah, Umar. I hope he keeps you safe."

Umar smiled and kissed his cousin's cheek affectionately. "He'll watch over both of us. We're true believers." Certain that it was so, he moved off.

Minutes ticked by. Isam couldn't tell how long he had laid there, or if he had fallen asleep or swooned. One moment was identical to the next. His heart thudded numbly in his chest. If anything happened to Umar, it would be his fault. Then he would be stranded all alone on a dangerous frontier. That he might not survive was a very real possibility. He thought it was easier to face death in battle. There he had work to keep him busy. It was up to Allah to decide if he lived or died. Now there was no imminent prospect of death, but he was in danger all the same. Worse, he was unfit to meet the challenges that were certain to arise. He bitterly regretted not giving Gregorio his freedom. He had been Maureo's slave, not his, and he had escaped Maureo through his own wits, only to fall into Isam's clutches.

"I did not treat you fairly, and I am sorry for it," Isam told the shrubbery.

The sound of a pistol cocking ended his reverie. Rolling onto his back, he stared up at the grey uniforms of Spaniards as they surrounded him. He was unfit to run, resist, or even bargain. It was over. The Spanish would have their revenge.

CHAPTER 42 : RESCUE

All Isam could do was to lie there dumbly in the weeds as the Spanish encircled him like dangerous ghosts. His body was weak and drained of vitality. He felt supremely helpless. Unable to even sit up, he had no power to resist them. He looked up at them and felt no fear, only a slow, sad resignation. He had struggled and lost. He had always known he would die a corsair like his father before him, and although he was unhappy to die so soon, there was nothing he could do about it. Allah had decided.

He said nothing to his captors. They addressed him in Spanish, but he didn't understand. Gregorio had to translate. The freed man avoided looking at Isam. Isam looked at Gregorio once, then turned his face away. He knew it was his own fault that he had come to be in this position. So many mistakes he had made along the way, and unwilling to admit his errors and correct himself, he had bungled even worse. He had piled error upon error and was about to pay for his mistakes with his life. He didn't like it, but there was no point lying to himself about it. The Spaniards were merely implements of Allah's unerring justice.

The Spanish knew nothing about his fatalistic philosophy. On the contrary, philosophy was far from their minds. They grinned down at him with the feral grins of predators. Their officer was a lean young man of about thirty. His skin was so fine and pale the blue of his capillaries showed through, illustrating why the Spanish aristocrats were known as 'bluebloods.' Unlike his soldiers, he wore a broad brimmed hat to keep the sun off his face. He couldn't tan; he could only burn. His paleness made him seem a fey creature that belonged to the grey-green woods and not the world of men.

"So this is the famous Sallee rover, Isam the Swimmer." He spoke with a sneer.

That didn't sound very awe-inspiring, even if Isam had distinguished himself as a swimmer more than once. Annoyance made him speak, "I'm Isam, son of Hamet Rais."

"Never heard of him," scoffed the pale man.

That rankled too, but there was nothing he could say that was worth spending his breath on. As short as their conversation had been, he was nearly out of air.

"Get up, you." The officer kicked his boot.

"I can't. I'm wounded."

The officer spoke to his men, and two of them handed their muskets to other soldiers, then seized him by the arms and heaved him to his feet. He rose up, but blackness rushed in from the sides of his vision and his legs buckled. He collapsed in a swoon. The soldiers couldn't hold him and he slid to the ground. They let him lie while the officer peeled back his eyelids and peered.

Isam blinked. He couldn't focus his vision. He was in danger. He wasn't sure why, but he was pretty sure he had a reason to think so. Somewhere nearby was an explanation, but his brain couldn't find it.

Gregorio knelt beside him. "Isam, are you awake? Isam Rais!"

"We should kill him right now," one of the soldiers said.

"I want to take him to Tanger and burn him at the stake as an example to all the heretics. The Governor needs a salve for his wounded pride. This one's not Rajet, but he's one of his lieutenants. He captured the *San Fermín* and wrecked the *San Juan*. I want to watch him burn."

Gregorio shook him. "Isam, wake up!"

The corsair's eyes rolled in their orbits. He must be dreaming. Gregorio had run away. He couldn't be here beside him.

"Take him with us," the officer ordered.

The soldiers improvised a stretcher by using a soldier's coat. Isam's head and legs hung down, but they were able to cart him out of the woods that way. They were walking north to the river when they heard the rumble of hoofbeats and looked south. There, cresting the hill behind them, was a sheik in full regalia mounted on a white horse. He was followed by a dozen mounted men. When they saw the Spanish carrying off the Prophet's martyr, they let out an ululating battle cry that shrilled through the air like the cries of demons loosed from hell.

The soldiers dropped Isam and took flight. They ran for the river as fast as they could go. Shots rang out, but the Spanish dove below the crest of the bank and scrambled for the ferryboat. They were shoving off as the riders came over the bank and charged pell mell down the slope. Scimitars flashed and muskets cracked.

White garbed tribesmen urged their horses into the shallows. Hoofs threw up great arching sprays of water that shimmered in the dawn light. The Spaniards shoved off frantically and put the oars out, then used them to beat at the horsemen like giant flies. The nimble horses danced away. Scimitars flashed in retaliation, and steel rang on steel as some of the soldiers protected their comrades at the oars. The ferrymen were nowhere to be found; they had hung back after meeting the riders. A pistol shot rang out as the Spanish officer fired, but he missed his target. The sheik slashed the arm of a rower who screamed and let go.

One of the horsemen seized the ferry's mooring line and tied it to his saddle. His horse, up to its belly in the water, planted its feet and braced against the pull of the boat. A soldier ran forward with a knife to cut the line, but a tribesman cut him dead.

Not bothering to reload, the Spanish officer seized an oar and used the long wooden weapon to outreach the blade of a scimitar and knock a rider off his horse. The man couldn't swim and foundered—until he discovered the water was shallow enough for him to stand up. He slogged back onto his horse and resumed the fight.

Umar didn't follow the fighters into the river. Instead he reined up and ran to his cousin. He threw himself on his knees next to him.

"Isam! Isam, are you alive! Cousin! Speak to me!" He cradled Isam's head in his hands.

Isam gave a groan. "Umar? Where are the Spanish? I thought I was dead!"

"They ran! They saw us coming, and they ran, the cowardly dogs!" His voice was jubilant.

Isam had been vaguely aware of the horses that swept past on either side of him. "Who came?" he asked faintly.

"Khalid Sheik. He's the local chieftain. Samir went to his house this morning and told him about us. I met them coming up when I went to fetch our horses. Samir warned him about the Spanish. They came prepared."

Isam was relieved to hear it. "Praise Allah for our deliverance!"

The sounds of battle ceased. A few minutes later Khalid Sheik came over the riverbank with his bloody sword in his hand. Being a tribesman, he never walked when he could ride, so he trotted his horse over to the fallen corsair.

"Is he alive?" he asked Umar. He wiped his blade with a cloth and sheathed it.

"Yes, yes, he is! Thanks to you. The Spanish were going to kill him." Umar put his hand to his forehead and bowed deeply to the man.

The sheik spit on the ground. He wore a white turban and long flowing robes with black boots and black trappings for his horse. "Cowards. All infidels are cowards."

"He's very weak, sheik. Is there a doctor near by?"

"No doctor, but a wagon is coming. You will both stay at my house until he recovers."

"Gregorio," Isam said. "My slave was with the Spanish. He translated for me. Where is he?"

Khalid's eyes narrowed and his lips thinned. "In Hell, where he belongs. Samir told me what he did."

Isam lay stupidly trying to take in the news. "He's dead?"

"They all are."

Isam was quiet for a long time. "I didn't wish him dead."

The sheik snorted. "Better that he is. Allah will judge him." He rose in his stirrups, put his fingers in his mouth, and whistled shrilly. His men came from the river and formed up. They had taken Spanish muskets as souvenirs.

Isam owed his life and freedom to the sheik. He struggled to tell the man something that would make it worth his while. "They had horses. Somewhere there are horses."

Khalid bent down to hear what he was saying. "Horses. Yes, very good loot. We will find the horses." He turned to face his men. "Tarik, take four men and find the Spanish horses. Ali, go tell the wagon its safe to come up."

The men separated to perform their duties. Umar gave Isam water from his skin. Isam wetted his mouth, then strove to speak. "Bury Gregorio decently. Don't treat him like an animal. He was a man. He did me a good service, and if I had rewarded him fairly, he wouldn't have run away."

"He's an infidel and deserves to be eaten by carrion," Khalid replied.

Isam grew stubborn. "Umar, cousin. Do this for me. Make certain Gregorio is buried decently. If not for me, then for Rabiyah's sake."

Umar wanted to be stubborn, but he sighed. "Very well. Since you invoke my wife's name, yes. I will do it."

Khalid didn't know the story, but it seemed important to the two of them, so he said, "Very well. Abdul, go to the village. Get some peasants to bury these infidels in the marsh. They'll foul the ford if they're left."

"Thank you, effendi," Isam said. He raised a feeble hand in salute.

Umar said, "Now you need to rest. I'll ride in the wagon with you."

"I want to see the body buried."

Umar, who had some idea of what the slave had meant to Isam, even if he didn't understand it, said, "No, you need rest. You can go to the grave when you're better."

Meanwhile, Tarik and his party had found the Spanish horses. They were pleased with the loot; to a tribesman a horse was even better than gold. Meanwhile, the wagon rattled up and they lifted Isam gently into the back. Umar climbed up next to him. Isam closed his eyes. He was very tired and very sorry. Tears leaked from his eyes. The wagon started up and rattled as it rolled over the rough road. Isam brooded all the way to the sheik's house.

CHAPTER 43 : ABSOLUTION

After a week of comfortable care in the sheik's house, Isam was well enough to ride a few miles. Umar and some of the sheik's men escorted him to the river. Umar led them along a deer trail. Speckled ducks were startled by their intrusion and rose in a great cloud that blotted out the sun. The graves weren't far. A series of low mounds on a hummock marked where the Spanish were buried. One in particular was marked with a stone at each end.

Isam didn't dismount. He was supremely weary. He just sat and looked. He had imagined this last conversation in his head many times, but now that he was here, there was nothing to say. Nothing could be said; it was too late. Gregorio was dead.

He looked for a rock to place on the grave, but the marsh was made of mud and weeds. Sea lavender was blooming with its branches of purple blooms, so he reached out and snapped off a stem. He slid out of the saddle, walked up to the grave, and laid the bloom on the mound.

"I'm sorry." That's all he said. His boots slowly sank into the soft earth as he contemplated the mound. The horses nickered and lifted their hooves periodically to free them from the creeping ooze. Finally he remounted. Getting back into the saddle took all his strength. He turned his horse around and so did his companions. They slogged back through the wet land and up the slope to the road.

"I don't ever want to be sorry for something I did or didn't do ever again," he told Umar.

"It wasn't your fault," Umar said sympathetically.

Isam couldn't take comfort in that because Umar didn't know everything he knew. "Umar, do you think you should tell someone something if no good can come of it? If someone is happy not knowing, should you leave them be?"

Umar thought it over. "If it affects them, then they have a right to know."

"But what if it changes nothing?"

"If it's important, you should still tell them."

Isam thought it over. "I have something to tell you then. But not here. Come with me." He pulled ahead of the others, and turning in the saddle, raised his hand to keep them back. "I want to talk to Umar alone."

Umar was getting worried. "About what?"

"Rabiyah wasn't a virgin."

"I know that, but it wasn't her fault that Maureo raped her."

"No, before that. He beat her because she wasn't a virgin when he had her."

Umar's head snapped around and he stared at Isam. "What are you saying?"

"That's why she ran off with Maureo. To save her reputation."

Umar was stunned. "But who?"

"Will it do any good if I tell you?"

Umar was in a torment. "You have to tell me now!"

"It will cause trouble."

"You've already caused trouble by even saying it!"

"Are you angry with Rabiyah now that you know?"

Umar brooded. "I knew she wasn't a virgin when I married her. How many men has she had? Will I be a laughingstock?"

"I only know about one." That was true. Samir had hinted there were others, but Isam didn't actually know anything about them. The Qu'ran forbid gossip and said that a man ought not say anything against a woman's virtue unless he could prove it. He was glad of the Qu'ran's guidance in that moment. Had it been left up to him, he would have bungled it.

Umar's face hardened. "Who was the man who ruined her but was too cowardly to make things right?"

"Samir."

Umar nearly fell off his horse. "Damn him! You have to help me beat him up."

"All right. I will." The prospect cheered him up.

Umar brooded a while longer. "He took advantage of her, then he abandoned her. That's why she went off with Maureo. It all makes sense now."

Isam was pretty sure that Rabiyah had been Samir's willing partner, but still, he had used her and discarded her. Umar's interpretation covered the basic facts pretty well. Everything else was a difference of opinion, and there was no point arguing it. He nodded.

Umar rubbed his face and sighed heavily. "I knew she'd never marry me if she had her choice. She's too beautiful for me."

Isam stopped his horse and turned to face him. "She is not. You are too good for her. She did wrong and you are generous to forgive her. You have been kind and brave and loyal and trustworthy. I think she's starting to realize that matters more than looks or honeyed words. Be kind to her, and she will learn to love you. I am sure of it."

Umar brightened. "Do you think so?"

"If you treat her as well as you have treated me, she would be hard-hearted not to." He extended his hand.

Umar clasped it wrist to wrist with their beating pulses pressed together. "I never thought I should be better than I was. It's all I can do to be what I am."

Isam smiled. "You're a good man, Umar. I'm glad you're my cousin."

Umar smiled back. "I'm glad you're still alive. I was worried about you."

"All right then. I'm well enough to ride, so lets ask Khalid Sheik for supplies so we can go back to Tanguel. My ship is waiting. Rajet will have recovered. He will sail without me if I take too long."

"You'll be a famous corsair some day! When they're talking in the coffee shops, I'll say, 'That's my cousin! We rode together and fought side by side.'"

Isam smiled. "Indeed we have." He kicked his boots against the horse's flanks and the two trotted down the road.

Much later when they were safely home in Tanguel, the two cousins confronted Samir. In the argument that ensued, Isam punched Samir. Samir punched him back and broke his nose for the third time. That time when it healed, a slight hump remained. Thereafter whenever Isam looked in the mirror, he was obliged to acknowledge that as good as it had felt to thump his roguish cousin, the results weren't worth it. Some lessons leave scars.

Sometimes, especially on spring days when the land breeze carried the scent of sea lavender to him, he felt his scars very keenly. On those days, he wrapped himself in the comforting constraints of seamanship. He had a lot of sex partners and even sex friends, but no lovers. He was a man sufficient to himself. Give him a fast ship and he was happy. When he fell in love at last, it was in a most unexpected way.

But that's another story.

Publications by Keibooks

M. Kei's Novels
in print and ebook

Pirates of the Narrow Seas 1 : The Sallee Rovers
Pirates of the Narrow Seas 2 : Men of Honor
Pirates of the Narrow Seas 3 : Iron Men
Pirates of the Narrow Seas 4 : Heart of Oak

Fire Dragon

Coming Next Year!

The Sea Leopard: A Pirates of the Narrow Seas Adventure

Poetry Anthologies

Fire Pearls : Short Masterpieces of the Human Heart (Vols. 1 & 2)
Take Five : Best Contemporary Tanka (Vol.4)
Catzilla! Tanka, Kyoka, and Gyogoshi about Cats

M. Kei's Poetry Collections

Slow Motion : The Log of a Chesapeake Bay Skipjack
Heron Sea : Short Poems of the Chesapeake Bay

www.ingramcontent.com/pod-product-compliance
Lightning Source LLC
Chambersburg PA
CBHW072233170626
46813CB00003B/1208